# A LARK'S CONCEIT

## VERITY LARK MYSTERIES
### BOOK III

## LYNN MESSINA

potatoworks press • greenwich village

Title Production by The Book Whisperer

Never miss a new release! Join Lynn's mailing list.

To Ann-Marie Walsh, for making these covers match the vibrant
burst of color I see when I close my eyes and picture Verity

# Prologue

*Tuesday, June 16*
*1:59 p.m.*

As Gertrude, Dowager Duchess of Kesgrave, nurtured an abiding dislike of being told what to do, it was especially vexing that she suffered from so many ailments requiring medical attention. Physicians, with their forceps and their tinctures and their condescending attitudes toward the helpless patients under their care, which Hubble described as his "bedside manner" with pompous self-regard, delighted in providing comprehensive instructions that entailed slavish compliance.

A sample: Take your saline draught every morning at nine with half a spoon of honey and two grains of salt, then proceed to the garden to travel the perimeter eight times before returning to your bedchamber for a bowl of barley gruel and thirty minutes of rest followed by a lukewarm bath with three drops of balsam oil.

She would not mind smelling like a fir tree if she could identify a benefit to the practice, but after a decade of elaborate remedies and charlatan doctors, she knew one thing for certain: The more precise the prescription, the more incompetent the prescriber. Despite years of cures, the joints in her fingers grew ever more defiant of her command.

Her infernal pinkie—refusing to bend!

And her knees, so swollen and achy.

Enjoying an invigorating stroll around the garden was easy enough for Hubble, with his spry limbs, barely into their fifth decade, but some mornings the stairs to the ground floor presented an almost insurmountable challenge. On those days she chose to forgo the pleasure of a walk.

And the draught.

And also the gruel.

If creeping down the steps required more internal fortitude than she could muster, she adamantly refused to strain her meager resources on stomaching that thin concoction, with its strangely bitter aftertaste.

She would have berries and cream, thank you very much!

Naturally, the commands were not limited to her health.

Society had its own compendium of rigid codes to be followed, the enforcement of which was left largely to a gaggle of biddies who resented any attempt to flout their authority. Miss Hyde-Clare's flagrant disregard of the rules was a particular outrage, for they could not fathom how she had managed to come from seemingly nowhere to nab the Marriage Mart's greatest prize. Somehow the girl had contrived to enjoy six seasons without earning their notice, let alone their imprimatur. It was almost as though she were a specter made suddenly visible by the Duke of Kesgrave's attention, and her ability to cloak her presence to escape their censure struck the biddies as a personal affront. They called on the dowager to voice her disapproval of the match in the strongest possible terms. Even if Miss Hyde-Clare had not tricked them with her phantom ways, she was too old and plain for the illustrious Matlock line. To allow a dowdy nonentity to rise to ducal heights would be an insult to every miss who sparkled with youth and beauty. Even the previous duke, a provocateur who delighted in scandalizing the *ton,* abided by the stricture for physical perfection. Having the vulgarity to marry his mistress, he nevertheless selected one of the most ravishing creatures to ever adorn London. La Reina might have been depravity incarnate with her lack of conscience or kindness, but she at least had the good manners to decorate any room she entered.

In that regard, the spinsterish Miss Hyde-Clare made them all look a little worn around the edges.

Gertrude, whose familiarity with her daughter-in-law's personality ensured that she cared nothing about her appearance, thought the beau monde's response to her grandson's betrothal was a little immoderate. To be sure, nobody wanted to welcome an ape-leader into the family, and a diamond of the first water such as Miss Petworth or Lady Victoria would have lent an appealing graciousness to the drawing room at Kesgrave House. Be that as it may, the girl was presentable enough despite her age, and she had a remarkable ability to form judgments using logic and reason, a trait that was frequently in short supply among famous Incomparables.

If Miss Hyde-Clare was not a credit to the Matlock name, she was neither a disgrace, and Gertrude could not conceive of any argument she could make against the girl that would not give grave offense to the duke.

Having no desire to alienate the affections of her grandson, she was even less interested in falling in line with the biddies' dictates. Although she had originally planned to greet Miss Hyde-Clare coolly, their insistence that she reject her outright prompted the adoption of the opposite strategy.

Her intentions, good or ill, ceased to matter, however, the moment she beheld Miss Hyde-Clare in her drawing room at

Clarges Street, her shoulders tight and unbending, her gaze sharp and unflinching.

The poor girl was terrified and determined not to show it.

It was, Gertrude divined in that moment, the way Miss Hyde-Clare went through life, tensed and ready for the inevitable blow.

What a wretched way to live, she had thought, examining the girl for some sign of the harridan who had shouted at Damien in that very room a few weeks before and noticing a smattering of freckles that danced across her nose.

It was charming.

Commenting on the freckles, Gertrude had the ineffable pleasure of watching Miss Hyde-Clare emerge from her cocoon, her pose loosening, her features softening as she looked at the dowager with relief and kindness.

And there she was: the combative harpy who refused to cower in the face of the duke's disapproval.

It was then that Gertrude decided her grandson had made an excellent match, for what she had said to Beatrice about Damien was true: If left to his own devices, he would grow into a tyrant. All Matlock men did eventually. With so much power at their disposal, it was simply easier to run roughshod over all opposition than try to overcome it with reason or yield to another's preference. She had seen it with her husband and sons.

Damien had always been different, which she attributed to the horrors of his childhood. Although the cruelties of a murderous uncle would make any child anxious or brittle or cynical or cruel, either in succession or all at once, it seemed to have the opposite effect on her grandson, giving him an inexplicable empathy. Despite the many ways she had failed him, he had never treated her with anything but thoughtful consideration.

Until eleven days ago, when he had shown up on her

doorstep unannounced late in the evening demanding she tell him everything she knew about the child.

His color high, his eyes a little wild, he pressed her for information, expecting her to have it all at her fingertips despite the decades that had passed.

She would never demean herself by asking for latitude based on her age, but in this case, she did indeed require a few minutes to gather her thoughts, to understand what precisely the topic of conversation was and what he wanted to hear.

It did not help her frame of mind that he had sounded so much like his father.

That snap of impatience.

Gertrude knew it well.

It had been years since she had heard it, but it tore through her heart like a bullet, shredding it.

She had been especially nonplussed because she had assumed he had called to apologize for telling the heartless Lady Abercrombie the wonderful news before her. Only a few hours ago she had called on Beatrice, who had been certain the duke would want to make amends as soon as possible.

But he kept asking about Verity Lark.

Verity Lark, he barked in his father's snapping baritone.

She knew nothing about a Verity Lark.

The name was alien to her.

But the child—his mother's child, a brown-haired thing called Mary Price—well, yes, Gertrude knew considerably more about her, for she had discovered the sordid story years before when she still had hopes of routing that vile woman her son was determined to marry.

Although it dredged up horrible memories, she told him everything that pertained to the child, leaving nothing out. All that she could recall in the moment, the information did little to improve his temper. If anything, it made his fury worse, and taken aback by its intensity, she had summoned Sutton to bring a tisane of soothing chamomile petals and passionflower, and even contemplated sending for one of Hubble's calming elixirs.

Neither option was necessary.

Damien settled himself, seeming to stuff the anger into his pocket like a handkerchief, and coolly bid her good night.

He even apologized for disturbing her evening!

The civility in his tone was quite the most cutting thing she had ever heard.

A full week later, he sent a note expressing regret for how he had handled the affair. He should not have called on her in such a mood, but having made that ill-considered decision, he should have been more cognizant of the constraints of her upbringing. She was as much a product of her time as he was of his.

It was a brutal letter, so kind and condescending in its understanding of her limitations, and if its punctilious tone seemed to mark a new phase in their relationship, she was nevertheless grateful for it because it meant they would continue to have a relationship.

The Matlock men were so good at severing ties.

Even so, Gertrude had no intention of leaving matters where they stood, for she was the victim of a grave injustice. She had not abandoned the child to the machinations of fate when her usefulness to her was at an end. Although she owed the child nothing, she was aware of her duty as a Christian woman and had made arrangements to ensure the child had the best care possible in the reduced circumstance in which she was placed by her indifferent mother.

Obviously, the Duchess of Kesgrave was not going to remove the girl from the asylum and give her to one of the peasant families on the Matlock estates. That sort of interference into the child's life was intolerable, unnecessary, and messy. But she was not entirely insensible to the problem and had arranged for her solicitors to provide the headmistress with a modest annuity to ensure the child had basic amenities.

If she could not purchase kindness, then she could at least buy a modicum of comfort.

The allowance was more than anyone else would do, she was sure of it, for the child had no claim to her generosity. It was not her responsibility to see to its welfare when its own mother could not be bothered.

Or its father.

My goodness, yes, the father, she thought, shivering slightly as she pictured the rakehell who was the girl's father. Although La Reina herself had abstained from informing him of the happy event, Gertrude was convinced he knew all about the child and chose not to exert his influence out of laziness or indifference.

His apathy was the best thing for the child, as Brownie was not fit to be a father. The three sons he had had a hand in raising had all turned out deplorably. To a man, they were hateful, dull-witted, and depraved, which was a description that could be applied to the dowager's own progeny, a fact she readily admitted. The difference, she believed, was that she had raised immoral human beings quite by accident. Her road to hell had been paved with good intentions while Brownie carefully laid each stone. He had done everything possible to create mirror images of himself, and now that he had accomplished his goal, he appeared to loathe the product, as if disgusted by how easily his own children had allowed themselves to be molded.

A worthy son would have thwarted his authority to become a decent man.

As Gertrude had acted out of her own sense of morality, not obligation, it doubly annoyed her to learn the child had

had a wretched time of it despite her contributions. That the outcome had not been altered by her munificence offended her viscerally, for she had lowered herself to care about something that was well beneath her—a harlot's daughter, for God's sake. When she succumbed to that sort of sentimentality, the very least fate could do was bend itself accordingly.

Determined to find out what had gone awry before deigning to offer a defense to her grandson, she had charged her solicitor with interrogating the headmistress with whom she had struck the original bargain. The answer was as unsatisfactory as it was predictable: The woman—a pinch-faced harridan named Agnes Katherine Wraithe—kept the money for herself and then treated the girl with excessive hostility for having the presumption of possessing grandiose connections. Spivey reported that the headmistress felt no remorse at all and cackled evilly as he tried to articulate at length the depth of her grace's displeasure.

Miss Wraithe, it turned out, was not a very charitable person.

Rather, she was terrible, wholly without conscience, and Spivey had some choice words for his predecessor, who had decided the headmistress was worthy of her grace's trust. It was not the first tangle of his he had been forced to unwind.

It did not matter, however, who was at fault. The mistake had been made in Gertrude's name, and she would not shirk her responsibility. Despite her benevolence, she had enhardened the child's life and intended to make a clean breast of it. She would explain what had happened, apologize, and offer restitution. Intimately acquainted with La Reina's avaricious little soul, she knew the child would accept whatever amount was offered without complaint and had arrived at a sum that was fair but not extravagant. Now, as then, she sought to provide basic amenities.

Too much would spoil the child.

Having conducted all previous business regarding the child through an emissary, she climbed into her carriage now to call on her personally. She wanted to be able to relay the details of the conversation to Damien before putting the matter behind them once and for all. His level of interest in the child continued to baffle her, but she did not have to understand something to respect it, especially when he had made his disapproval plain. He had never presented the cold edge of his anger to her before, and although his flash of temper had been short-lived, he had adopted a chilly politeness in his dealings with her. It was the same frigid courtesy with which she herself had treated his mother, and she could not bear the thought of his holding her in so much contempt.

She refused to accept it.

As the carriage turned onto Bethel Street, she contemplated the visit and realized it would have to be of some length. It would never do to enter the house, offer an apology, and fling money at the child. The niceties would have to be observed, and if that meant having tea with La Reina's by-blow, then she would have tea with La Reina's by-blow. She would talk about the weather and inquire about her health and compliment her on the elegance of her drawing room regardless of how garishly it was decorated.

Noblesse oblige was easy if tiresome.

Inevitably, the child would be overwhelmed by her consequence and be barely able to eke out replies to her queries. The dowager would no doubt be required to conduct the exchange entirely on her own, asking *and* answering the questions.

It had happened before.

Mrs. Whitley, for example, who had visited her theater box to wrangle an invitation to Gertrude's garden party and then fell silent after making her bid. The silly woman had no other conversation prepared, not even thoughts about the performances, which were excellent, or the play, which was not, and lacked the good sense to make a timely departure. She had hovered and hovered, compelling the duchess to compliment *herself* on the lovely lace trimming her gown, which had been imported from France only days before war was declared. It was *indeed* quite precious.

Already annoyed by the errand, she found herself further irritated by this prospect and was frowning by the time the carriage arrived at number twenty-six. The structure was tidier than she had expected, with a brick facade and a pair of white columns that had recently been painted. The windows would benefit from a vigorous scrubbing, for she could see dirt streak even from several yards away, and the paving stones looked slightly rutted. Although it was not her duty to point out these oversights, she would kindly mention them. It was mortifying to be caught with imperfections.

The carriage had just stopped when the front door to the home opened, and the dowager got her first glimpse of the child. She knew it was the former Mary Price because she looked like her mother, so much so Gertrude felt her heart trip in her chest. After all these years, she was staring once again at that detestable chin, all pointy and narrow and cruel. And those cheekbones—as sharp as knives. The child had her mother's chestnut hair, although she wore it unfashionably short under an atrocious mobcap, and she was tall. Towering in the entrance, she appeared to be slim, but it was impossible to tell with the pelisse she wore, its wool far too warm for June.

Well, at least she is modest, Gertrude thought, noting how well the garment obscured her figure. Everything the child's mother had worn had been vibrant and plunging, its sumptuous fabric cut in scandalously tempting ways, and oftentimes the dowager had been embarrassed to look at her.

Determined to catch the child before she left on her

errand, the dowager did not wait for her driver's assistance and disembarked from the carriage on her own with only minor difficulty. Gripping her cane tightly, she took a cautious step forward as Miss Lark turned left, her pace labored and slow as she contended with a rather pronounced limp.

Gertrude wondered if she had recently suffered an injury, for Damien had mentioned nothing about a limp. Perhaps it had something to do with the unruly dog tugging on the lead. It certainly seemed to be in charge. The enthusiasms of a pet were all well and good, but it fell to the owner to keep them in line, which the child appeared incapable of doing.

The dowager was just about to call out to demand Miss Lark forestall her venture when a figure dressed in a long brown coat and wide-brimmed hat lunged forward, seemingly out of nowhere, and grabbed Miss Lark from behind, one hand wrapping around her neck while the other slammed into her back.

Furious at the audacity of the modern criminal—not to have the decency to creep in dark shadows—Gertrude lifted her cane and marched forward several steps to whack the assailant on the head. Her left knee throbbed as she put all her weight on it at once, and struggling to swallow the yelp of pain that rose to her lips, she said with tart displeasure, "You have caused me no end of trouble, child!"

# Chapter One

*Monday, June 8*
*4:39 p.m.*

The only person who did not understand that Lord Colson Hardwicke was courting Verity Lark was Verity Lark. She knew something was afoot, to be sure, for she was not a ninny. A man did not spend hours asking gently probing questions over tea or present a gold-topped walking stick with which its recipient may pretend to be an experienced physician without making evident his interest.

What she could not fathom was the purpose of his gifts and attention, for he had been decidedly opaque about what he hoped to achieve or what it would cost her in return.

Delphine believed with every fiber of her being that Hardwicke was one slightly breathless cup of bohea away from proposing marriage. It was due to this conviction that she frequently excused herself from the parlor when he visited, claiming to have forgotten one of her knitting needles upstairs or needing to give the servants an important instruction regarding dinner or the cistern. She always returned within five minutes, for no amount of trust in their caller could overcome the fact that he was a man. Although acting as chaperone did not number among her responsibilities at Bethel Street, she considered it at once an obligation and a joy.

Freddie also insisted an offer was imminent, for he had seen the glint of respect in Hardwicke's eyes and swore he would never demean her with an insult.

Verity, noting it as well, did not doubt the depth of his admiration. She surprised and challenged him in ways he never anticipated from a woman—or perhaps anyone—and he found the pull of that irresistible. He desired to spend more time with her being surprised and challenged. He had stated that quite plainly.

Even so, he had been less clear in his intentions, and given the great disparity in their situations, she could only assume he would propose an arrangement outside the bounds of traditional matrimony. Even if she were not the baseborn daughter of the most famous courtesan of the late eighteenth century, she was still a rumormonger and a sensationalist with a vast repertoire of personae to be adopted at various times to achieve assorted aims. And Hardwicke was still the second son of the Marquess of Ware whose reprehensible reputation was naught but a fiction conceived to allow him to perform a heroic service for his country. If he were actually a ne'er-do-well, then Verity might have been able to imagine an alternative future, but he did not live amid the muck like her. He merely pretended to get his hands dirty.

It was an insurmountable obstacle, and Hardwicke was too clever to believe he could link his illustrious name with her sullied one.

He did not, she was certain, have in mind an arrangement as sordid as the one offered by the cit who had rescued

Lorraine Price from the tedium of her father's cobbler shop. He would not treat her as a fleeting convenience.

Hardwicke would cherish her.

For as long as the fascination held, he would honor her with fidelity and affection. He would be sweet and considerate and thoughtful and dear. Keenly aware of the gulf between them, he would make no attempt to change her or mold her into his image of a proper lady. He would merely try to live alongside her for a little while and then move on. He would be gentle about it, hoping only to bruise her heart, not break it.

It held some appeal.

Having never met anyone who could outwit her once, let alone repeatedly, Verity felt the same tug of fascination. There was something oddly pleasurable about spending time with a man whom she considered her equal, and if he was not quite as devious as one could wish, moving openly through the world as only himself, he was still impressively sly.

Allowing herself to plunge into that wily cunning, into all that alarming shrewdness, would be so easy and satisfying. She was so close to the edge.

But Verity Lark would never jump.

Despite Delphine's conception of her as a reckless creature who spared no thought of consequences or bodily harm, she was in fact quite deliberate in her actions. She saw life as a series of riddles and equations and held tightly to the answer even when she appeared to be flailing erratically.

At heart, Hardwicke's attraction was that he defied calculation. All the motives she ascribed to him, all the goals she attributed to him, turned out to be wrong, and she did not know what to do with the sense of uncertainty she felt in his presence.

It was thrilling and terrifying.

And yet she would not refuse his proposition because he

unsettled and confused her. Her reasons were mundane and conventional, and for all her outlandish behavior, she was simply not audacious enough to trust her happiness to any man. Her mother had tucked herself under the thumb of men for the whole of her career, and although it appeared to have worked out beautifully for her, the wealth and status she had attained seemed to provide her with little comfort. By all accounts, La Reina had been miserable—cruel and biting, yes, but also deeply unhappy.

At four and thirty, Verity had arranged her affairs nicely. Having neither sought nor imagined the satisfaction that could come from writing for a newspaper, she was grateful to Freddie for suggesting it and to Delphine for supporting it. The amiability of her present situation—warm home, full larder, loyal friends—had been inconceivable to the hungry girl shivering in her bed in the frigid night air surrounded by whimpers of despair. Even her encounter with the Duke of Kesgrave was a source of pleasure. Discovering the depth of his decency firsthand filled her with an unexpected peace.

Yes, by and large, Verity was content.

And then Hardwicke introduced her to his brother.

*Monday, June 8*
*6:12 p.m.*

Verity assumed it was a mistake. They were in Hyde Park, after all, during the Fashionable Hour on a mild day, and carriages passed in every direction. Inevitably, an awkward meeting would ensue, and Hardwicke, recognizing the difficulty of the situation, was far too nimble to worsen it by scurrying away. He would hold his ground, exchange a few pleasantries, and then proceed as if nothing untoward had happened. If a presentation could not be avoided, he would make it with a minimum of fuss, drawing no undue attention to its inappropriate nature before continuing onward.

Verity, extending her hand graciously to the Earl of Gold-hawk, waited for a desultory reply and a prompt dismissal.

She received neither.

Rather than move them along as quickly as possible, Hardwicke lingered in conversation with his brother, inquiring after the health of his nieces, a pair of precocious four-year-olds who delighted in throwing themselves into any mess they could find. Of late, it had been the linen pile in the scullery, and as Hardwicke called the girls hardened scamps, Verity marveled at how grossly she had misunderstood the relationship. If Mr. Twaddle-Thum had bothered to look at the brother as anything other than a foil—the Gold Son to highlight the dross of the Coal Son—he would have noticed the vein of friendship between the supposedly estranged siblings.

Most likely, yes, but the focus had never been on the earl. Verity had reported only on the incensed patriarch's dissatisfaction with his wastrel son, and relations between the two men had been frigid for years. Any wary French spy who doubted the rupture would have his suspicions quickly allayed.

Goldhawk complimented Verity on her bonnet, which was a slightly more lavish affair than she customarily sported, possessing a second ostrich feather. Delphine had pressed it on her as Hardwicke arrived, and not wanting to quarrel, she had submitted without protest. Now she felt quite foolish in the confection, as if she had gilded herself in anticipation of their meeting, and she reviewed her repertoire for a character who would feel comfortable meeting an earl in an elaborate chapeau.

Mrs. Delacour, she thought. The wealthy widow would do

well, although it felt odd to adopt the woman's airy confidence without also wearing her cheerful robe à l'anglaise and pannier.

Nevertheless, she trilled lightly and praised his lordship on his ready command of his mount, a large but seemingly gentle black beast. Then she asked if he had been to the theater yet to see Kean in *Bertram,* and she could only imagine how ridiculous she must appear to Hardwicke, offering bon mots with breathless excitement. He drew no attention to the strangeness as his brother bid her good day and left to greet Brownell, who had hailed him from across the path.

He made no comment about any of it—the introduction to his brother, her odd descent into character—and regaled her with the Society of Yarwellian Philosophers' latest attempt to earn his forgiveness. Having trussed him up like a Christmas goose for roasting in the erroneous belief he was a government spy, the founders had been mortified to learn the informer was a member they had never suspected. Determined to make restitution, they had proposed half a dozen correctives in the four days since the event, all of which Hardwicke had stoutly refused. He could not conceive of anything more horrifying than a newspaper advertisement praising his decency or a room named in his honor.

"A room?" Verity asked, tilting her head to the side as she tried to decipher what precisely that meant. "As in the front parlor in Mr. Anderson's home? He will henceforth show his guests to the Colson Hardwicke Memorial Parlor?"

"Commemorative," he corrected as he maneuvered the pair of bays around a gig that stopped suddenly in the path. "And it would be at the society's headquarters, the room with the printing press."

She laughed. Despite her nerves and preoccupation, she laughed without restraint as she pictured the grim basement where Hardwicke had been held captive. "The cellar? *That* is what they want to name in your honor? Will they hang a plaque?"

"With my family crest, the date of my confinement, and a few words proclaiming the service I performed in thwarting the real villain," he said soberly, but his eyes—a confounding teal—sparkled with mirth. "Anderson proposed an unveiling ceremony. It would be an intimate gathering with just the original thirteen founders and anyone I cared to invite. I have been assured it will be brief, as they still had much work to do to bring the Burnley Blanketeers to fruition, but there would be speeches. Both Lemon and Oxenford would like to say a few words."

"I must attend!" Verity said ardently, already sifting through the various disguises she could assume to gain entry.

He reminded her that he had declined the offer.

"Then you must tell them you have changed your mind at once," she exhorted. "Robert Lark will write about the momentous occasion for the *London Daily Gazette*. I know! We shall make it the first act in the larger project of rehabilitating Lord Colson. We can arrange other events showcasing your heroism. By the time we are done, Parliament will have named a bridge in your honor. Which do you prefer: Kew bridge or Richmond?"

He looked at her sidelong, his expression at once amused and horrified. "The son of a marquess aligning with reformers who seek to dilute the power of the aristocracy by increasing their own influence is hardly the ingratiating position Robert Lark thinks it is. Perhaps he does not understand the workings of society as well as he believes."

"Society—bah!" Verity said with a dismissive wave. "Robert Lark would never limit himself to such a narrow slice of the populace. He will make you a hero of the people. And Twaddle will help. He tore you down and can build you up."

Fervently, Hardwicke said no.

But Verity was tickled by the prospect and proposed several possible stories the infamous gossip could write to increase his popularity, starting with a fawning account of his work for the Alien Office during the war. "It could be a weekly series. Freddie says the advertisers adore when Twaddle centers his column on a principal character. It provides a sense of continuity for the readers."

"And I adore having every embittered supporter of Napoleon within a hundred miles of London decide to take their revenge by running me through with a blade," he replied mildly. "After the machinations of the hapless Yarwellians it will be a nice change of pace to be threatened by adversaries who know what they are doing."

Although she could not decide if he was exaggerating the threat for comic effect, she understood the gravity of the situation. It was not merely that he had undermined the French war effort with his lies and deceptions; it was also that he had accomplished the feat while preening like a drunken buffoon. It pinched more to realize you had been gulled by a facile ploy. She knew this from painful personal experience, as she had been Hardwicke's first dupe.

Curious as to the extent of the problem, she asked how many resentful Frenchmen remained in the country. "A few, several dozen, hundreds?"

Again, he regarded her with humor as he said, "Why do I feel as though Robert Lark has already begun to compose an article on the subject?"

"Because you are unduly suspicious," she replied tartly, although in truth she had no sooner issued the retort than her mind began to whirl with possibilities. Perhaps there was a significant contingent of Bonaparte faithful in London who continued to scheme on behalf of the moribund empire.

Given the thorough trouncing their leader had suffered at Waterloo, she did not imagine they could do much damage.

"*Duly* suspicious," Hardwicke amended with pointed emphasis as they passed through the park gate onto the street. "Every doubt I harbor, I come by honestly."

"Well, you *would* think so, wouldn't you," she murmured.

Hardwicke, allowing this provoking comment to pass unchallenged, invited her to call on Gunter's the next day.

Verity frowned.

As much as she loved orange flower ices—and they were among her chief delights—she could not bear the thought of yet another outing with Hardwicke. A visit to the tea shop would be the fourth excursion in as many days, and although she found spending time with him highly enjoyable, she hated not knowing precisely where she stood. If he intended to offer her a carte blanche, then she wished that he would simply do it already and cease with the trappings of courtship. Every gallantry he extended made the situation worse, and she cringed imagining Delphine's excitement when she learned of her meeting with Lord Goldhawk.

Except Delphine would not be excited.

She would be smug, which was a thousand times worse.

Even now, Verity could picture the gleam of triumph in her friend's eye and knew better than to try to persuade her. It would be a waste of time.

Indeed, it was all a waste of time—the outings, the conversations, the endless fretting over his intentions—and she wondered if that was not Hardwicke's purpose all along. Her stubborn competence had irritated him from the very beginning, and there was no better way to undermine her proficiency than to distract her with trifles. There she was, after all, driving in his curricle when she should have been in her study writing an article about the new penitentiary in

Millbank or sifting through notes from the spies she employed to stay apprised of the beau monde.

Twaddle was already behind for the week, finding it curiously difficult to uncover tales that were even half as interesting as Her Outrageousness's antics. She had, according to a recent report from Mags, induced her husband to purchase a steam carriage concern. Not content with identifying the man who had murdered the inventor of the *Bright Benny* engine, the irksome duchess had decided to acquire the contraption itself. Its patents were now in her possession as well as various metal components and the contents of a charred foundry in Bloomsbury.

Verity's half-brother, the Duke of Kesgrave, was now in trade.

It amused her to no end to think of him sullying the ancient family name with ash and soot, and if she could not picture him slipping off his elegant topcoat to tighten a bolt, she could easily envision him reviewing schematic drawings alongside his solicitor. Lacking formal training in the workings of mechanical devices, he nevertheless possessed a keen intellect and a calm temperament. What he did not comprehend at a glance, he would quickly figure out from the context provided.

Verity, who counted these traits among her most valued attributes, could only assume the qualities had been inherited from La Reina.

It was a disquieting thought.

Having failed to anticipate meeting her brother, let alone thwarting a massacre with his assistance, she had never considered the possibility of their having readily identifiable commonalities that could be traced back to their mother. Verity wanted her resemblance to La Reina to begin and end with her angular features, and the notion that she might take after the woman in other respects unnerved her greatly. It was especially worrying in light of the attraction she felt to Hardwicke, which seemed to deepen the more time she spent in his company. While his behavior remained above reproach, her own conduct continued to spiral downward until she had to physically restrain herself from touching him. His imitation of the home secretary demanding the right to manipulate reality and the army to achieve the suspension of the writ of habeas corpus that he ardently sought was so accurate and monstrous, she chortled and reached out her hand to squeeze his arm.

She stopped herself.

Clumsily, she tugged at the edge of her sleeve as if to smooth an impertinent wrinkle, a hint of pink warming her cheeks as she contemplated the embarrassment of actually making contact.

As though chortling were not humiliating enough!

With these thoughts in mind, she knew she should refuse the visit to Gunter's.

She did not truly believe, of course, that he was conspiring in some devious way to undermine her abilities. The theory was absurd, and yet its very absurdity illustrated the problem, for she *was* distracted and not thinking clearly. Whatever he intended by bestowing his attention on her, the result was a diminished version of herself. Where she had always been decisive, now she was hesitant—wringing her hands over an invitation to a tea shop.

It was deplorable!

Obviously, she must decline. It did not matter how many family members he introduced to her, either on purpose or because it could not be avoided, allowing the courtship to continue was irresponsible. If the impulse to touch him signified anything, it was that she should remove herself from his presence at once.

Verity Lark did not indulge in foolish behavior.

And yet somehow she heard herself accept.

❦

*Thursday, June 11*
*2:04 a.m.*

Having snapped at every member of the household and an unfortunate butcher who had the poor judgment to step outside his store just as she was passing the door, Verity could not decide to whom she should apologize first.

Well, obviously, she could start by removing Mr. Conway from the list, as the shopkeeper's mood had been just as savage as hers and he had responded to her terse criticism with a string of invectives. If anything, she had brightened his day by providing him with a suitable target on which to vent his spleen.

Delphine, however, had received Verity's biting reply with meek acceptance, tilting her eyes downward and apologizing for asking if she had heard from Hardwicke. Lucy had not even posed a question. She had merely laid the tea tray two inches to the left of where Verity thought it should be. For that very huge infraction, the maid was exhorted to learn what the edge of a table looked like so as to avoid putting items near it in the future.

And Cook—having the temerity to serve lemon ices for dessert! She had noticed her employer's dejected air in recent days and had thought to cheer her up with one of Verity's favorite treats.

A reasonable proposition, yes, and yet Verity snarled about wanton extravagances as she thwacked her hand against the table and then marched from the room. She had even slammed the door behind her like a petulant child.

It was not her finest moment.

Alas, she'd had very few fine moments in the three days since Hardwicke had canceled their outing to Gunter's with a tersely worded message stating he could not keep the engagement.

A second missive had arrived that morning, as abrupt as the first and even more vague as it alluded to a change in his circumstance that prevented further contact. It was not difficult to figure out what had spurred the reversal. Lord Goldhawk had made his displeasure known, either on behalf of himself or his family. She imagined it had been an awkward conversation, embarrassing for both parties, and attributed the curtness of his missives to the fresh sting of mortification. No grown man relished being put back in line by an elder brother, and Hardwicke was more accustomed to freedom than most. Adopting the role of debauched scoundrel, he had inevitably assumed some of his character's louche habits and had forgotten the constraints of his position. In light of the recent development, Verity allowed Delphine and Freddie's understanding of the situation might not have been as wide of the mark as she had believed. Perhaps he had had a more outré scheme in mind wherein he called her Mrs. Lark, provided her with a house in Edgware Road, and introduced her to society. Not unheard of, the arrangement had worked nicely for the Honorable Charles Francis Greville and Emma Hart—for a while, that was. Then Greville decided to marry an eighteen-year-old heiress to refill his coffers and pawned his mistress off onto his brother.

It made no difference now what Hardwicke had actually had in mind, and the fact that Verity could not stop herself from thinking about it only darkened her disposition. It was not like her to waste time on irrelevancies, and determined to overcome the sentimental feebleness—she could think of no other way to describe it—she had thrown the note into the rubbish bin and sat down at her desk to return to work. As she was behind on several articles, there was plenty to keep her occupied, and just the day before, Freddie had sent a gentle but slightly pressing missive asking when he should expect Robert Lark's account of the benighted prison, whose inferior construction required three of its towers to be torn down.

Twaddle was also delinquent. The story he owed Freddie for Friday's edition was just a handful of notes about Mrs. Fawcett's renewed efforts to nab a principality for her daughter. Leaky Fawcett, as she was known to the Twaddleship for her fondness for bringing young misses to tears, had been trying for weeks to secure an invitation to Mrs. Markham's salon. Rebuffed by the hostess, she had resorted to openly offering a reward of ten pounds to anyone who would consent to bring her as their guest. So far there had been no takers.

A renowned London hostess bribing her way into an exclusive society event was perfect fodder for Twaddle, and yet Verity had no sooner begun to chronicle Mrs. Fawcett's efforts when reports arrived of Her Outrageousness's latest exploit to thwart the enterprise. Over the weekend, the duchess had been spotted in the company of Penelope Taylor, and there had been several sightings. Mags observed them in the former's carriage, driving past Trafalgar Square, and Clancy saw them call on the Earl of Audenshaw together.

It was a remarkable development, for Mrs. Taylor was a courtesan of some renown who counted many distinguished nobles among her stable of current and former lovers.

The most prominent among the fabled assortment?

Kesgrave.

It was years ago now. The duke had been little more than a pup, enjoying London for the first time at the grand old age of nineteen.

Or perhaps he had been twenty.

Regardless, he arrived in the capital with a fat wallet and a confident swagger and leveled his interest with singular focus on the most sought-after courtesan of the season. By all accounts, he had won her handily, making a very generous offer and remaining satisfied with the arrangement for almost a year.

Verity, noting the tiresome predictability of young rich men, had not even bothered to roll her eyes in disgust, for it was precisely what she had expected of him. He was a product of his upbringing in every disappointing way, an opinion she would hold for well over a decade. Even his highly unusual choice for a bride could not overcome her conviction that he was more or less a dull, conventional lord.

His few bright spots, a willingness to follow his wife on absurd murder investigations being the chief among them, only served to heighten his dullness.

And then she met him.

Verity would never forget that moment: her rambling nonsensically about unfolding tragedies while wearing a footman's garb and his calm reply: Very well, then, let us take my gig.

Also observed in the company of Mrs. Taylor—Kesgrave himself.

That was right, yes: Her Outrageousness had spent two days racketing around London with her husband's former mistress *and* her husband. Obviously, they were not paying social calls on the various men in the courtesan's life but rather trying to identify who among them had murdered her dear friend. As the woman had been stabbed in Mrs. Taylor's home, the latter had been the principal suspect and would have hanged for the crime had the duchess not intervened.

None of the reports Verity had received explained how exactly Her Outrageousness contrived to prove Mrs. Taylor's innocence, and the lack of specificity caused her almost physical pain. There was a story here, wild and wonderful, and where previously she would have donned epaulettes and a mustache to Twaddle out the truth, she could do naught now but put the notes in a drawer and return her attention to the Leaky Fawcett.

It made her surly.

Complying with her resolve never to write about the Duchess of Kesgrave was the correct thing to do, but it blackened her already dark mood. The snapping began and the impatient replies, culminating with the slammed door, and now she was lying in bed replaying moments from the past few days as she had been doing for the last several hours. Her thoughts leaped from one thing to the other, from Hardwicke's defection to Delphine's dejection to Her Outrageousness's shocking behavior, seemingly designed with the express purpose of taunting Verity Lark out of her high-minded ideals. She recalled the duke's impenetrable calm and Hardwicke's imitation of Sidmouth and Freddie brushing her shoulder with a look of concern and the butcher's shouted insults following after her in Cranley Street.

It was all a mad jumble, cacophonous and loud, and as hard as she tried, she could not quiet her mind. It continued to race with discordant thoughts, creaking and groaning like a floor with boards that were worn from use.

Oh, but no, she thought, a quiver of alarm traveling up her spine as she realized the sound was not in her head. It was an actual floorboard.

Someone was in the room.

# Chapter Two

❧

L ying on her back, Verity resisted the urge to swivel her head toward the door. Instead, she opened her eyes slowly and reviewed the protocol she had established for an uninvited guest in her bedchamber in the middle of the night. The first imperative was to confirm that the intruder was neither Delphine nor one of the servants. Although it was too dark to make a conclusive determination, she could reasonably assume that none of them would have cause to skulk furtively in her bedchamber. If they needed to fetch something from her room or wake her up, they would carry a candle and announce their presence.

The next item on the list was to secure a weapon, and she slid her arm along the smooth linen of the sheet until she located the tipstaff she kept tucked between the mattress and the headboard. She had realized the utility of placing a small club within reach after rescuing Mrs. Norton from a knife-wielding killer who had struck while the society hostess was abed. The silly peahen had managed to convince—via the most heavy-handed way possible, it must be noted—a nefarious contingent of conspirators that she was Mr. Twaddle-Thum.

It had been a revelatory moment for Verity, who, in the guise of the *London Morning Gazette*'s celebrated gossip, reported on such notably weighty society matters as who slighted whom at Almack's on Wednesday night. It had never occurred to her that someone would wish to murder her in her sleep in retribution for these triflings. Even as she acknowledged the possibility, she still believed it was unlikely. Nevertheless, she had responded sensibly to the minor threat and purchased the tipstaff a few days later, placing it within easy reach. She had felt more than a little foolish about taking the precaution and was deeply grateful to Lucy for lacking either the curiosity or the impertinence to ask why her employer had hidden a menacing-looking stick behind her pillow.

Verity tightened her fingers around the thin metal end and drew the tipstaff toward her.

It felt reassuringly solid in her grasp.

Very good, she thought.

Now step three: gather information.

To leap into action when she did not yet know with what she was actually contending would be the height of recklessness. Furthermore, her greatest advantage in a situation like this was the element of surprise, which she would need if she had any hope of apprehending her attacker. Allowing him to escape would expose her, as well as Delphine and the staff, to future incidents. She had to know what he wanted to ensure he would not try to get it again.

Lying still, however, was difficult, for she felt quite vulnerable, like a duck sitting in an open marsh to the delight of its hunter, and she tilted her head ever so slowly to the right, toward the entrance, to see if she could make out the figure in the gloom. All she saw was the outline of the open door, which she had closed upon retiring to her chamber. It was a faint shadow in the thin light.

He was already inside the room, then.

Tempted to turn her head in the opposite direction to examine the other side of the room, she forced herself to remain still. Too much movement in the bed might rouse his suspicions, and she needed to retain the upper hand.

In the silence, Verity waited to hear something that would reveal more information about his location: another creak, the rustle of the curtains, a smothered expletive. The fact that the floor did not squeak again made her think he was quite close to the bed now, for the boards on the far side of the room were in better condition than those nearest the door due to less wear.

The attack could come any moment now, she thought, her entire body tensing in expectation as her heart began to pound. Despite the anticipatory dread, she continued to assess the situation and noted the floor had groaned only a few times. That indicated that it was just the one intruder. An associate, if he had one, was either lurking in the hallway or waiting outside. Given the nature of the undertaking—the stealthy approach in the middle of the night, the victim's age and gender—she decided he had most likely entered the house alone.

He had little expectation of encountering resistance.

That was also to her advantage.

The big question, of course, was what weapon he carried, and it was difficult to plan a defense when she did not know if she was to confront a gun or a knife or bludgeon or simply the meaty hands of a well-muscled behemoth.

She did not think it was a gun.

If the situations were reversed, she would avoid using her

pistol because the discharge would make a loud boom and wake up the entire household. Then she would be compelled to beat a hasty retreat through unfamiliar corridors in the dark while evading other occupants. Tripping and falling down the stairs was not an insignificant threat under those circumstances. She would also have to get very close to her victim to ensure an accurate shot, which posed its own risks.

Although those hazards applied to a knife as well, a blade had several advantages over a firearm, the most significant of which was that it did not require gunpowder. Having missed his target on his first thrust of the blade, an assailant could immediately make another attempt and another, stabbing with random and vicious intent without having to pause to reload. A dagger was also silent, which allowed—

Air swirled above her!

The hair on the back of Verity's neck stood up as she realized he was there, right there, just inches from her nose, dislodging the air with his movements. And then suddenly it was his breath, hot on her cheek as his fingers wrapped around her chin, his grasp oddly gentle as he pulled her jaw down to open her mouth.

What the—

Verity did not even allow herself the time to feel befuddled or shocked. Opening her eyes again, she shifted her weight, raised the tipstaff, and bashed him on the head with as much force as she could muster from her supine position. She felt more than saw the effects of the blow—the rush of air as he gasped in surprise, the loosening of his hand before it fell away—and thumped him again.

He dropped on top of her, leaden and heavy with insentience.

She pushed him to the side, twisting out from beneath him, and lit a candle to take stock of the situation. There was some blood seeping out of a wound on his skull, not a lot, not enough to worry her that she had done grievous harm, but she checked his pulse regardless to confirm his heart was beating regularly. She listened, too, to his breathing, and noted it sounded normal as well. He mewled, indicating that he would not be unconscious for long, and although she considered running to her dressing table to fetch twine, she stayed where she was, next to the bed, trying to make sense of the situation.

Prepared to be shot or stabbed or bludgeoned or strangled in her own bed, she could not get over the strangeness of being ... what? ... poisoned.

Had that been the intruder's plan?

Pour hemlock down her throat while she was sleeping and then run out of the room while she gagged in confusion and quickly succumbed to its toxic effects?

That had to be the explanation.

Otherwise, why open her mouth?

If he wanted to suffocate her, then he could have used one of the pillows in the room. There were several on the bed with her and one on the chair next to the fireplace. A cushion was far more effectual than a handkerchief for stopping up her airway, and when slaughtering a slumbering victim, one wanted to be as efficient as possible.

Poison was the only logical conclusion, and she ran her hand over the blanket as the intruder whimpered again. She found the wet spot immediately and followed it to the edge of the bed, where a small bottle lay amid the folds of the blanket. Raising it to her nostrils, she detected hints of clove and cinnamon and, almost certain she recognized it, had the tiniest taste to confirm.

Laudanum!

Just as she suspected!

But that did not make sense.

Why give a sleeping woman a sleeping draught?

33

To ensure she did not wake up, she thought, and wondered if the assailant intended to abduct her. It was a reasonable conclusion and yet a confounding notion. Neither Robert nor Twaddle had done anything to warrant such a vehement response.

At least she did not think so.

The truth was, seeking to identify a single action was a waste of time, for she had learned from the escapade with Altick and Mrs. Norton that she could not control the way her name and reputation were manipulated by others. She did not *have* to do anything to elicit a murder attempt.

Requiring significantly more information than was currently available to her, she decided her best chance of learning more was to allow the intruder to underestimate her. The fact that he thought a gambit as facile as administering a drug to her while she slept had a chance of prospering indicated that he did not consider her a legitimate challenge.

He had expected to saunter into her bedchamber and swiftly saunter out again.

To help him continue in his mistaken belief, she grabbed the floral vase on the nightstand and hurled it to the floor. He groaned as it shattered, and she cried for help. Blinking his eyes, he stared at her with blank incomprehension in the dim light of the candle, and, clasping her hands together, she eked out tears of shuddering terror. She called out again as the attacker swiveled his head left and right, struggling to understand what had transpired.

"You monster!" Verity shrieked.

Still dazed, he nevertheless understood enough to spring into action, darting toward the edge of the bed to jump to his feet. But Verity was faster and tugged the blanket, which caused him to lose his balance and he topped back onto the mattress. She threw the blanket over him like bundling a small child in a cloak, all the while yelling for help at the top of her lungs, her tone trembling in fear. She was tying the sheet around his torso to secure his arms to his sides when Delphine came bounding into her room, a frenzied look in her eye.

"Good God, Verity, what is going on?" she asked, running to the bed, incapable of comprehending what was happening, although it was the sound emanating from her friend that confused her more than the squirming lump on the bed.

It sounded like panic.

Verity never panicked.

And she did not look scared now, only sullen and annoyed.

"Thank heavens!" Verity said breathlessly as Delphine stared at her. "I have captured a villain who was here to ravish me in my sleep. Quickly fetch my hair ribbons so that I may tie him up before he can escape. Hurry!"

Smothering a dozen questions, Delphine dashed to the dressing table just as Lucy rushed into the room followed several paces behind by Cook, who was panting heavily. The maid reared back when a dark head emerged from beneath the blanket, but Cook shook her head and scurried over to help Verity restrain the intruder. She seized his legs as they kicked at the blanket, and when they did not cease their wild flailing, she threw herself onto the limbs. The prisoner wailed furiously, twisting his torso to dislodge her, which failed to achieve the desired result. Cook did not budge.

"Here!" Delphine said, all but throwing the assortment of silk ribbons at her friend.

Verity tied the ribbons around the man's wrists, and although her movements were deft and assured, she maintained a fluttery, overwhelmed affect, like an angler shocked to discover a trout at the end of his fishing line. The display was for the benefit of her assailant, which she felt certain Delphine must know, but she winked at her friend just in case. Then she applied herself to securing his ankles, which was much easier because Cook's weight held his legs in place. As she tightened the ribbon, he began to spew curses and Lucy stuffed satin gloves into his mouth with an apology to Verity for using a freshly laundered pair.

"They were the most convenient and I did not want to waste time looking for dirty ones," the maid added with an abashed grimace.

The prisoner, issuing guttural noises that conveyed nothing save his dissatisfaction with his current situation, glared first at Verity, who made a great show of shrinking back in terror. Now that the room was well illuminated, she could see her assailant clearly. Dressed simply in unadorned black, he was taller and bulkier than she had originally thought, with wide shoulders and a thick neck. If he had taken a more straightforward tack, seeking to overpower her with his mass, she might have had a harder time repelling him with her club. It was a surprising choice for him, for he was young, possibly only twenty-five or so, and should know to exploit the advantages of brute force while they were still available to him.

Delphine, out of patience with Verity's dramatics, pulled her aside and softly begged her to explain. "Who is he? What does he want?"

Replying in a whisper, Verity swore she had no idea. "Truly! I am as puzzled as you. Perhaps it has something to do with Twaddle-Sham or with Grimston or even an article Robert published recently. Maybe Fitch has another confederate or Miss Copley has an irate lover or the Yarwellian Society somehow figured out that it was I who wrote about their unholy deal with Blasingame? It is impossible to say! All I know is that I was lying in bed trying to sleep when suddenly I heard the floorboards creak. I realized it was an intruder, so I lay very still and waited for him to make his intentions known. Then when he was close enough to strike,

I bashed him on the head with my tipstaff. He collapsed at once."

Delphine regarded her friend with alarmed surprise. "Your what?"

"My tipstaff," Verity said matter-of-factly. "It is a small club."

"Thank you, yes, I am familiar with the implement," Delphine said with an air of forbearance. "I simply do not recall your having one."

"It is a recent acquisition," Verity replied. "I purchased it after the unpleasantness with Mrs. Norton, as it made me newly aware of my vulnerability to middle-of-the-night incursions, a precaution that now seems quite justified. You might consider getting one yourself, my dear, for they are handy little clubs that slip neatly behind your mattress. I hope you would never have cause to use it, but I believe it is better to be safe than sorry."

Delphine, sighing deeply at this communication, said, "I suppose I should just be grateful you do not keep a flintlock under your pillow."

Well, naturally, she did not, for only the veriest greenhorn would do something so foolhardy as to sleep on top of a loaded firearm! But rather than respond to the insulting comment, Verity explained that after knocking the intruder out with the tipstaff, she had taken pains to make it appear as though she had used a vase. "I wanted it to look as if it were merely a stroke of luck or a fortunate accident on my part. Posing as vaguely incompetent is part of my plan."

Nothing struck fear into Delphine's heart as much as these words. Even the prospect of a burly villain attacking her in her own bed paled in comparison. "You have a plan?"

"I have a plan," Verity confirmed with a firm nod.

Of course she did, Delphine thought. Her friend was

nothing if not strategic. "May we discuss the plan or are you set on it?"

Verity laughed lightly as though it were a frivolous query. "Naturally, we shall refine it together. I would do nothing without first gaining your and Freddie's opinion. As soon as it is light enough, we shall send Lucy to fetch Freddie. If these intrigues continue, then I shall have to consider hiring a footman in earnest. I cannot have Lucy running around London at all hours of the night."

Although the moment did not strike Delphine as particularly opportune for a discussion about staffing decisions, she had been lobbying for just such an addition for several months and agreed that it would make things easier all around to count a footman among the servants. Then she returned to the matter at hand and asked about Hardwicke.

Taken aback by the question, Verity rushed to assure her friend that the disgraced second son of the Marquess of Ware had nothing to do with the break-in. "I am sure of it. If Hardwicke wanted to abduct me, then I would be in whatever dank dungeon he wanted to confine me in right now. He would never do something so amateurish as creak a floorboard!"

Delphine, provoked by Verity's deliberate obtuseness, offered a snapping reply louder than she had intended, then lowered her voice before continuing. "I was asking if you intended to seek his opinion as well, as gaining information from a late-night intruder would almost certainly fall under his area of expertise. I think he would bring a valuable—" But she broke off suddenly, her eyes flying wide as she stared at her friend aghast. "Wait a moment. What do you mean *abduct*? You said ravish. Earlier, when I ran into the room, you said ravish."

"Well, yes, because it does not serve my purpose for him to know that I know what he intended, does it?" Verity observed logically. "If I want him to believe I am a silly female, then I must act like a silly female and to assume any man who enters my bedchamber under the cover of darkness must have evil designs on my body. But he brought a bottle of laudanum and intended to drug me—in anticipation, I believe, of carrying my unconscious form out of the house. He is certainly large enough to bear my weight, and I suspect he has a confederate waiting in the street, although I have not had an opportunity to check yet. But now that he is tied to the chair, we will be able to gather that information and gain a more complete understanding by the time Freddie arrives in a few hours. Now I should warn you, my dear, that I am about to break out into hysterics and nothing you do or say will calm me. I shall be beyond comforting. I advise you to make sure the knots around our guest's wrists and ankles are very tight indeed before you lock him in this room and post Cook as watch."

As sensible as it was, neither servant found the plan satisfactory, as Cook did not think it was wise to allow Lucy to make breakfast, as her eggs were always either runny or burned, and Lucy worried that Cook was too slow to give chase should the prisoner manage to escape. In the end, they swapped assignments and lamented the lack of a footman to perform guard keeping duties.

*Thursday, June 11*
*6:04 a.m.*

Although deeply troubled by the events that had transpired in the early morning hours at twenty-six Bethel Street and profoundly grateful its occupants had managed to escape without injury, Freddie remained unduly focused on the vase.

"It just seems to me that if the intruder was already unconscious and you had the presence of mind to conceive and implement a plan, then it would have required only a minor alteration for you to fetch something else to break for dramatic effect. There are several bottles on your dressing table that would have done very nicely," he said irritably.

Verity, sipping tea that had grown cold while she had napped in the parlor waiting for Freddie to arrive, asserted for a second time that she had shattered the vase to maintain the appearance of hen-wittedness. "I *caterwauled* for dramatic effect."

Delphine affirmed the accuracy of the statement by noting the effect the display had had on the servants, who had never seen their employer descend into a fit of tears before, let alone enact a Cheltenham tragedy with three distinct acts. "Cook was alarmed and insisted on making a calming tisane of rosehip and chamomile, and Lucy was bewildered because only last week Verity had brushed off a knife wound in her shoulder."

Although diverted by the image his friend painted, Freddie refused to be distracted from his point and emphasized again the availability of other options, such as the porcelain jewelry box on the cabinet. "I simply do not understand why you had to destroy *that* vase. It was valuable."

Stung by the criticism, Verity assured him with some asperity that she held the vase in very high esteem, for it numbered among her most treasured belongings. "That is why I kept it beside my bed—so it would be one of the first things I saw each morning when I opened my eyes. I intend to buy another just like it as soon as this business with the late-night intruder is resolved."

Alas, this plan did little to appease Freddie, who noted that there were no other vases like it, as it was from the workshop of a potter who had died several years ago. "His work is highly sought after now and impossible to find."

Naturally, these dire predictions did not daunt Verity, who employed a network of informants across London. She had little doubt that one of them would not only locate another vase within the week but also secure it at an agreeable price. "Regardless, you must know that I would never destroy a beloved possession without good cause. I did only what was necessary, and I am surprised, Freddie, that you are not chomping at the bit to discover *why* it was necessary. I expected you to march into the parlor demanding to hear every detail about my encounter with our uninvited guest."

Freddie, owning himself quite anxious indeed to know everything, added that he was merely making idle conversation while they waited for Hardwicke to appear.

Verity's heartbeat ticked up at the mention of the notorious wastrel, but she kept her expression bland as she said, "I did not send for Hardwicke."

Astonished, Freddie exclaimed, "And why the devil not? He was an agent for the English government for years! Investigating an abduction attempt is his bailiwick, and I am convinced he would have much to contribute to the conversation."

Smoothly, Verity agreed that Hardwicke's familiarity in this area might be helpful. "However, he made it clear that he has no desire to continue our association, and I would never be so discourteous as to pester him with my intrigues when he made his lack of interest known."

Delphine, sitting next to her on the settee, her own weariness apparent in the dark shadows under her warm blue eyes, marshalled enough vigor to huff peevishly. "He begged off *one* time."

Aware of her friend's judgment, Verity kept her tone light and calm as she informed her of a second note referencing a change in circumstance that rendered future contact unlikely. "I think it is fairly clear what he means, as the first missive came only hours after we encountered Goldhawk in Hyde Park. One does not have to be a skilled deductress like the Duchess of Kesgrave to figure out that he severed the connection after his lordship aired his disapproval of me."

Prepared to counter each of her friend's arguments, Delphine stiffened her shoulders in surprise as she raised her chin to look Verity in the eyes. "He introduced you to his brother?"

"He did, yes," Verity replied with cool indifference, which required little effort now that she had had several days to grow accustomed to the development. "And I did not pass muster, which is not astonishing. Perhaps if Hardwicke had actually been disowned by his family as reported by Twaddle, then the earl would have no expectations for him. But he clearly believes Lord Colson can do better than a baseborn mongrel with ink-stained fingers."

Delphine swore it was not true, for she could not believe a man of Hardwicke's character, which she deemed excellent, would abide by any opinion but his own. "Nevertheless, if what you say is true, then he will waste a good deal of his time looking for a phantom, for there is none better than you. Now, regarding our uninvited guest, I understand your plan is to have Freddie question him while you sit nearby wringing your hands in fear and apprehension?"

"Correct," Verity said, grateful to Delphine for not pressing the issue or dismissing her concerns. Defending one's feelings was always a demoralizing exercise. "Having Freddie conduct the interview will provide us with an opportunity to learn vital information without revealing ourselves as competent females, provided he is willing."

He agreed without hesitation, as an extremely valuable vase had been destroyed in service of her ineptitude and he could not allow that singular act of vandalism to be in vain. Verity launched into a full accounting of events, which Freddie listened to quietly, wincing slightly when she mentioned the tipstaff tucked behind her mattress. He started to call the measure excessive before he remembered the circumstance and leaned back in his chair without finishing the sentence. The only time he spoke again was when she raised her theory regarding the laudanum, for he did not think it necessarily meant he intended to carry her away. A man bent on ravishing a woman might want to ensure her insentience before attempting the abuse.

Delphine cried out in protest, unable to believe any man could be so repugnant, forcing Freddie to assure her of the human male's capacity for repellant behavior. To prove his point, he began to list examples as reported in recent issues of the *London Daily Gazette,* and Verity was relieved when Lucy interrupted his recitation to place a fresh pot of tea on the table.

*Thursday, June 11*
*6:38 a.m.*

Assuring his captors in the strongest possible terms that he would not speak a single word, the intruder then proceeded to devote almost ten minutes to the insufficient conditions of his detainment. As a prisoner, he possessed certain rights, among them freedom of movement and sustenance. His limbs had been bound for four hours, which was two more than what was generally deemed acceptable by field generals, and he had yet to be provided with a meal. He did not expect coquilles Saint-Jacques, but a slice of toasted bread with a modest slab of butter would not be an outrageous concession.

Furthermore, he had been left to suffer the discomfort of thirst, for he had not been given wine or brandy or even a bracing port, which was unsuitable for that hour of the morning, but a beggar could not be a chooser.

And speaking of the hour!

Could something not be done about the wretched clock that chimed every thirty minutes? Its heavy bong pounded right through him.

Although Verity assumed that Freddie also caught the slip, for the intruder had dipped into flawless French when describing his meal of choice, she did not draw attention to it. Instead, she shrunk further into the depths of the armchair, as though intimidated by his litany of complaints. In truth, she found his sense of entitlement fascinating and appreciated it on a tactical level. A cornered animal pounced.

Freddie, recognizing the strategic value of appearing to cede ground, apologized for the harsh treatment and explained that Miss Lark and her companion were too overcome with fear to respond appropriately to the crisis. "They are not thinking clearly, which is why I am here," he said before asking Delphine to please fetch their guest a glass of wine, naming a vintage that was of excellent quality. If Delphine thought the request was strange, she did not reveal it as she left the room to comply.

The captive thanked Freddie for intervening on his behalf, then reiterated his determination to remain silent. "There is nothing you can say that will induce me to speak. I shall take my secrets to the grave! That said, please do me the courtesy of loosening the ribbons around my wrists. My fingers are growing numb."

"If you tell me why you are here, I will remove all the restraints and allow you to leave through the front door," Freddie replied graciously.

"Never!" the prisoner cried.

"All right," Freddie said, leaning against the wall with an air of indifference, a pose he held for the ten minutes it took for Delphine to return with the wine. He accepted the tray from her and placed it on the clothespress while she returned to her seat next to Verity. Then he filled the glass with a generous portion of the deep burgundy liquid and held it out to the prisoner, whose cheeks darkened when he realized he would have to drink from another man's hand.

"This is barbaric!" he exclaimed. "You must untie me."

"All right," Freddie said again with that same lack of concern. The captive was sitting near the dressing table, his ankles bound to each other and the legs of the chair. Removing the cord from around his wrists would provide him with an advantage but not enough of one to escape under the watchful gaze of three attendants.

His hands free, the intruder rubbed his wrists with pointed aggression in a bid, Verity supposed, to make her feel bad about tying the ribbons too tightly.

Naturally, it did not work.

Once he felt he had successfully conveyed his point, he took the glass and sipped from it tentatively before realizing its contents met his standards. Then he drank deeply, finishing the libation in a few gulps. Freddie said nothing, content to examine the tips of his fingernails, his insouciance indicating that he had in fact noted the intruder's impeccable pronunciation. He knew the Frenchman would not be able to resist a superior wine.

Indeed, he requested replenishment and Freddie duly complied.

After the prisoner drained the second serving, he rubbed his wrists again and smiled. "Well done! I did not expect you to keep an exceptional wine cellar."

You, Verity noted, not Robert.

Did that mean the intruder knew Mr. Lark did not exist?

Ah, but then he added, "I suppose it is not surprising, given his history."

Whose history, she wondered.

Did he mean Robert's?

The reporter had written dozens of dispatches about England's enemy during the war, most of which examined the progress of the French troops and the condition of the army, although one series did address the smuggling problem. It had begun as a gossip item about Lord Warton buying inferior lace for his mistress and ended as a three-part investigation into a cadre of second sons who sneaked French brandy into the country under the guise of being itinerant weavers.

Was that why the intruder wanted to kidnap Verity—to use her to draw Robert out into the open? If he had kept watch over the house in hopes of spotting the reporter, then he would have almost certainly grown frustrated with his lack of success. Rather than realize Robert Lark did not exist, he would logically assume the journalist was away from home and might conclude that Verity represented an easily exploitable vulnerability.

A fond brother would readily exchange his life for his sweet, innocent sister's.

But what had Robert done to cause such an extreme reaction?

The smuggling articles were years ago, and their focus had been almost exclusively on the quartet of wealthy scions who lead the operation. Robert's reports made no mention of the French participants involved, for he had not taken time to discover their identities, and it seemed inconceivable to Verity that any injured party would wait a full year after the end of the war to exact their revenge. The affront, if there was one, had to be from the more recent past, and she tried to remember the last article Robert had written about France.

It had had something to do with St. Helena, did it not?

A satirical piece about Napoleon issuing commands over his tiny dominion? Conquering the Prosperous Bay Plain and laying waste to the Gates of Chaos?

She had written that, yes, but as Twaddle.

Robert's recent stories about France had been only sober-minded reports of the country's struggle to regain its footing following the harsh penalties imposed by the Treaty of Paris.

Nothing in those articles could have given offense.

And yet something obviously had, and Verity was eager to discover her friends' thoughts on the subject. Delphine, in her role as editress, was particularly adept at noting passages where Verity's tone is needlessly severe or reproving. Perhaps someone had managed to get their hands on an early draft of one of Robert's stories, and their outrage stemmed from an unpublished portrayal.

It seemed unlikely to her, but she could not dismiss any possibility.

While Verity tried to figure out the source of the resentment against her alter ego, Freddie raised the bottle questioningly and their guest accepted a third glass.

He refused the fourth, however, on the grounds that he was too clever to fall for such a blatant ploy. "You think to ply me with wine to loosen my tongue, so I will tell you our scheme. But I am not a lightweight to blather like an idiot after a few sips! No amount of excellent Burgundy will induce me to talk. I will say nothing more! All your efforts are wasted, for we will get him in the end. Then you shall see!"

But of course he did say more, for the infernal clock chimed seven at that precise moment, forcing him to complain about its unsettling clang and tolling his fifth hour without a meal—an appalling record, he said, rubbing his wrists with meaningful emphasis. And the condition of his ankles was no better, scraped raw by the unbearably tight silk.

It was unacceptable!

"And you may assume subjecting me to this abuse will compel me to reveal our secret plan, but I am like the Sphinx, silent and mysterious," he announced self-righteously. "You will learn nothing!"

In fact, Verity had already learned pertinent data: Her would-be kidnapper was French, the attempt was part of a larger scheme, and he was working with at least one other person. As abducting an Englishwoman from the comfort of her own bedchamber was a perilous mission, fraught with danger and grave consequences, she decided her prisoner was not the architect of the scheme.

He was a minion.

A minion with a highly developed sense of entitlement.

It indicated, she thought, an elevated position in life or a certain amount of comfort, and she wondered how he had drawn the assignment given his obvious inadequacies.

Had he volunteered out of a misplaced confidence in his own abilities?

Or had he been enlisted?

Regardless, the mission had failed to achieve its objective, and the leader of the plot would inevitably make a second attempt, either with the same recruit or another one. If he had any intelligence at all, he would send someone who knew to incapacitate his target before trying to drug her. Reaching for the laudanum before retraining her arms was the mistake of a novice.

Even the Turnip could do better.

Freddie, smiling with a hint of menace, said he was confident their guest would change his mind after a few days of bread and water. "And the clock. Although I hope for your sake you grow accustomed to its peal."

"But he cannot stay *here*," Verity objected with a shrill titter of alarm. "In my bedchamber!"

Patently, he could not, and none of the rooms on the upper floors were suitable for a prisoner. And it would never do to displace one of the servants. Freddie proposed the cellar, which was a reasonable solution if a little damp and chilly. Delphine noted that the seating accommodations were lacking, as the options were either the dirt floor or an assortment of rough-hewn chests. Verity acknowledged the point and said they could carry down a bergère from the parlor, but Freddie objected on the grounds that a cushion would undermine their objective, which was to encourage disclosures through physical discomfort. Bearing this in mind, Delphine suggested the chair from the stillroom. Verity, however, thought its smooth finish and molded frame made it slightly too hospitable, and after several minutes of discussion, they settled on the chair at the north end of the kitchen table. It was old, coarse, rickety, and jagged.

Any captive with a modicum of sense and ingenuity would be able to free himself from it within a matter of minutes, which, of course, was precisely their intention.

# Chapter Three

Although Verity realized that most people had not spent a significant portion of their childhoods tying themselves to various pieces of furniture to figure out the most effective way to free themselves, she still expected her would-be abductor to show a little bit of initiative. The situation had been arranged in every possible way to make his escape as achievable as possible. The spindle to which his legs were secured was worn as thin as paper in some spots, and the splintered arm was rife with pointed shards. To escape, all he had to do was rub the ribbon binding his wrists against the spiky fragments until it was frayed enough to snap in half, then smash the spindle before untying his ankles.

It was easy but not too easy.

Verity did not want to raise his suspicions by "accidentally" tying the ribbons around his wrists too loosely, especially after securing them so well previously. She wanted him to feel challenged and as though he had won his freedom through his own ingenuity.

But it had been more than an hour and he had made no attempt to free himself.

"Perhaps he is not uncomfortable enough," Verity said as she strode impatiently across the room to the windows, then promptly turned and marched in the opposite direction. "We should release vermin. I could catch some rats in the square."

Scowling at the truly repugnant suggestion, Delphine begged her to sit down and read the newspaper. "An hour is not that long a period of time in the scheme of things. I suspect he is still getting his bearings. Not everyone delights in leaping blindly like you."

Verity ignored the insult, for she recognized she was being deliberately provoked, and proposed they serve him gruel. "It would be more horrifying than rodents for a man accustomed to scallops in sage sauce."

"He is probably just tired," Delphine replied sensibly. "After all, it was a long night for him, and planning a kidnapping is most likely an exhausting endeavor. Who knows the last time he got a good night's sleep. I'm sure he will try to escape after a brief rest."

But it sounded like madness to Verity, failing to seize an opportunity the moment it presented itself. When the conditions to escape were favorable, you escaped.

That was it, the whole story.

Nothing else was acceptable.

"If that is the case, then he is not worried enough about his future," Verity said with a thoughtful press of her lips. "We should unsettle him further."

"Yes, do fetch your tipstaff and wave it at him threateningly," Delphine replied. "I am sure that will do the trick nicely."

Verity smiled faintly. "I had thought to threaten him with

the magistrate at Bow Street, as the conditions of his jail are far less pleasant than our cellar. But if you think intimidating him with violence would bear greater results, then by all means let's do that."

"I was being facetious," Delphine said.

Verity assured her she was as well. "I just think we should do something. What if he never escapes and we are forced to feed him several times a day for weeks? Cook herself will run him through with kitchen shears if he offers endless critiques of her food."

Her friend swore they *were* doing something: waiting.

It was, Verity thought with amusement, the ideal Delphine answer, for only she could come up with a way to categorize the absence of activity as an activity.

And, to be fair, her friend was knitting, so she was in actuality using her time well as opposed to Verity, who was pacing the floor with growing impatience.

No more.

Spinning on her heels, she crossed the room to the corridor, strode down the hallway, and positioned herself outside the cellar door, which she opened a crack. Then, speaking at a slightly higher volume than usual, she called for Lucy and Cook to hurry up. She wanted to get to the fishmonger before all the mackerel were gone, adding that Delphine was upstairs in her room napping and would not even notice that they had left her alone with the prisoner.

Surely, *that* will move him along, she thought, gently closing the door.

*Thursday, June 11*
*9:02 a.m.*

He led her to the French embassy.

Verity, dressed in the inconspicuous brown of an office clerk, watched with interest as her late-night visitor approached the tall, square building in Hertford Street, its brick arched windows high and elegant. A trio of six-panel doors at the entrance indicated that the single edifice had once been three separate residences. Even as he drew closer, she expected him to walk past it, unable to conceive of his going from incarceration in a basement to his place of business without first stopping at his home to change clothes or brush his hair.

Nevertheless, he tugged the door open with a sense of urgency she could attribute to only one of two things: either a desire to reveal the failure of his mission to the man who had assigned it to him or a desperate need to arrive at his place of business before his employer noticed his absence.

Both options could come with penalties harsh enough to justify his haste.

Intrigued, Verity entered the building a few paces behind him, her steps cautious as she considered what she would say if a porter tried to impede her progress. Distracted by a newspaper, he presented no problem, and Verity trotted after her captive as he raced through the hallway, its walls decorated with elegant sconces and lush tapestries depicting unicorns and apple trees. In his haste, he jostled passersby in the narrow corridor and all but skidded around the corner to mount a staircase. He took two steps at a time until he reached the second-floor landing. There, he paused for several moments to regain his breath, his shoulders heaving with effort, before continuing at a more sedate pace. Halfway down the hallway, he stopped in front of a pristine mahogany door with eight smooth panels and, grasping the handle with his left hand, closed his eyes briefly. He murmured something softly to himself—a few bolstering words, Verity assumed—and curved his lips into a broad, determined smile. Then he opened the door and entered the room with a sense of purpose.

Verity, glimpsing a swath of midnight blue against wood planks as the door swung shut, glanced around for something she could use to gain entry to the space. As there was not an identifying marker outside the office, she had no idea what would greet her—one occupant or a dozen—and required a pretext to justify her presence.

Alas, the contents of the hallway were sparse, with only an aspidistra in the corner, next to a trio of windows. Striding toward it to contemplate its usefulness, she observed that it was twice potted. The brass jardiniere festooned with wreaths concealed another, unadorned container. Far from ideal, it nevertheless presented a solution, and Verity wiped smudges of dirt on her cheeks and hands to give herself a janitorial air. Then she removed the plant from its ornate receptable and lifted the empty pot. It was heavier than she had expected, which made it somewhat unwieldly as a rubbish bin, but her grip on it was firm.

It would do well enough.

Boldly, Verity opened the door through which the intruder had passed and called out in the French she had first taught herself to openly ridicule the Wraithe, whose dull mind could barely master the intricacies of the English language, let alone a foreign one. She ignored the surprised looks of the room's occupants, of which there were only two: her burly would-be abductor and an older man at least two decades his senior, if the gray hair at his temples and the delicate wrinkles around his eyes were reliable indicators. Elegantly dressed in periwinkle silk breeches and an embroidered tailcoat, he blended nicely with his surroundings, the vibrancy of his clothes complementing the dark colors of the room, which was quite spacious.

Striding forward despite the glares of surprise, Verity apologized for taking so long to fulfill his request for a new rubbish bin. "It is only my third day, and I am still learning my way around the building. I hope you will forgive me. Now where should I place it? Over here by the desk?"

Her would-be abductor gasped at the audacity of the janitor as the other man—his superior or coconspirator or both—scowled angrily and swore he had made so such appeal. "As you can see, I already have a rubbish bin. Furthermore, intruding like this is unacceptable. You will knock before entering my office and will do so after six like the rest of the cleaning staff. Now leave!"

Verity, her head bowed in shame, apologized profusely for the transgression and said again that it was her first week of work and she was still getting her bearings. Frantically, she begged him not to mention it to her employer, for she needed the job if she was to have any hope of feeding her four children. "I will do better in the future, I promise! Here, let me empty your bin," she exclaimed, darting to the far side of the desk to grab the wastepaper basket, which was partially filled. She dumped its contents into the brass planter. "Is there anything else I can do? Dust your bookshelves? Sweep your floor? Scrub your windows? Polish your shoes? Anything at all! Let me be of service to you please!"

Unmoved, the man pointed to the door and barked, "Go!"

But he did not reclaim his rubbish.

Clutching her prize, Verity scooted around the desk to get a fleeting look at its orderly stack of papers and hurried to the door. Leaving the room in a rush, she closed the door with a firm snap and then immediately opened it a tiny crack to listen. Hoping to discover something helpful, she heard only grumbles about the inferior quality of the maintenance staff before she had to step away to avoid being caught with her ear pressed against the door.

No matter!

She had about a dozen papers to examine, and after returning the aspidistra to the brass pot, she left the building to inspect her bounty.

❦

*Thursday, June 11*
*9:33 a.m.*

Although a key tenet of Twaddling was "always trust the rubbish," in practice Verity found the refuse heap to be an unreliable source of information. Sometimes it held precisely what she was looking for, such as Peltington's confession that he had abandoned his wife's beloved cat in an alley far from their home because the wretched feline had bitten him on the toe, but more often it was a haphazard pile of seemingly unrelated fragments requiring some form of divination to understand their meaning.

In that way it frequently resembled the strange science of reading tea leaves.

The refuse she had recently collected fell somewhere between tasseomancy and full admission of guilt. Helpfully, it contained his name and position at the embassy: Guillaume Beaufoy, envoy extraordinary to the Court of St. James's. Both were announced in the opening sentence of a speech he was writing on the renewed spirit of Franco-English coopera-tion, which he would deliver to the esteemed members of the Tip-Tapp Club, a sober-minded organization devoted to the furtherance of amity in politics which counted so many members of Parliament among its associates that it had been dubbed Little Parliament by Twaddle.

To describe the activity as *writing*, however, was to be a little overly optimistic.

In truth, the diplomat was struggling to string two words together in a coherent fashion and had tossed away more than a dozen attempts at a first paragraph. Despite his intention to be conciliatory, he seemed incapable of expressing eagerness for a new comity between the countries without allowing bitterness over reparations and occupation to seep into his remarks. The discarded efforts were rife with sarcasm and acerbity, which were the wrong tone for a peacetime address.

In addition to the speech, the rubbish included a note from Beaufoy's wife reminding him to buy a present for their son's fourth birthday and suggesting several promising ideas, such as a toy drum and a kite, as well as a missive from the ambassador himself, Emmanuel Honoré-Gabriel de Chastre, Comte de Morny, reminding his deputy to write more detailed accounts of his weekly activities so his excellency could report their accomplishments to the foreign affairs office with appropriate specificity. Beaufoy was also exhorted to present issues that arose among the staff in a more positive light. There was nothing to be gained by making people feel awful about their shortcomings.

Diplomacy, his excellency urged.

Amused, Verity slipped the discarded drafts into her pocket and returned to the embassy to find out more about her would-be abductor and the man to whom he had reported.

*Thursday, June 11*
*11:01 a.m.*


Among the five French characters Verity frequently assumed, each of whose accents represented specific regional differences, Monsieur Henriot was the most useful because he had a complaint about everything. Rising in the morning, he could grumble for twenty minutes about the chirp of English morning birds—the wren was too loud, the chaffinch was too rattly, the song thrush was too melodic—and stepping outside for his morning constitutional, he could take issue with the very ground itself, for even the dirt was less palatable on this side of the channel. In Paris, he would not mind getting a clump of soil on his shoe, for it brushed off easily. But in London, it clung!

Monsieur Henriot, irate over the price his butcher was charging for an inferior joint of beef—all gristle! all fat!—registered his dissatisfaction with the porter, who reluctantly pulled his attention away from the newspaper to regard her with an impatient frown as Verity demanded to present the problem to the ambassador himself.

Gasping at the audacity, the porter replied with asperity and contempt, "His excellency does not handle disputes with local shopkeepers!"

Well, naturally, he did not, no, as the Comte de Morny was a famous statesman known for his skillful handling of political affairs, ruthlessly squashing the Orléans insurrection as head of Napoleon's Ministry of Police, then leading the provisional government after the emperor was disposed. His instinct for survival was well honed, and every step he took to advance his own agenda was hailed as a brilliant strategical decision, even when he left his royal posting to support the Hundred Days. Somehow his ruthless self-interest made him more attractive to the Bourbon king, who rewarded him with an ambassadorship.

Whether Mr. Henriot was familiar with the famous dignitary's history was uncertain, but he nevertheless found it extremely upsetting that the man tasked with overseeing the care of ordinary Frenchmen far from home could be so indifferent to their suffering. Indignant, he announced that he would speak to the ambassador's second in command, which was, she knew, the envoy extraordinary. "I will accept his deputy in his stead," he said graciously, as if making a grand concession.

The porter, shaking his head, clarified that nobody among the French mission to the Court of St. James's involved themselves in disagreements with merchants.

Appalled by this communication, Monsieur Henriot endeavored to understand how there could be an entire building full of men who served the interests of the French people in England and not a single one who cared about the quality of meat sold to its citizenry. Raising her arm, she pointed to a man walking briskly along the corridor with a distracted air. "What about him?"

"Monsieur Jette?" the porter asked with surprise. "He is a clerk who copies notices."

"All right, then," Verity replied impatiently, lifting her finger again, this time gesturing to her failed abductor, who was striding toward the staircase. It had taken more than an hour for her to spot him again, but she had finally seen him exit the building to buy cherries from the vendor across the road. "What about that man? Why can't he reprimand the butcher for selling substandard meat? He looks like he appreciates the value of a good roast."

"Monsieur Dupont is too busy!" the porter said, dismayed by the suggestion. "He is Monsieur Beaufoy's secretary and attends to weighty affairs of state."

"Well, he should attend to *this* weighty affair because the state of butchery in London is untenable," Verity cried angrily.

Poor Monsieur Henriot, perpetually outraged.

It had to be exhausting!

"You said he works on the second floor?" she added.

"The third," the porter corrected, adding that it was a small office directly above the envoy extraordinary's. "But that is no concern of yours!"

"Very well, then, I won't seek Monsieur Dupont's help," Verity said in resignation before singling out yet another passerby and noting that he did not appear very busy.

The porter escorted her to the door and advised her to buy her joints of beef elsewhere if the problem persisted.

*Thursday, June 11*
*3:22 p.m.*

Having scrubbed the dirt off her cheeks to assume the role of Monsieur Henriot, Verity promptly reapplied it when she realized impersonating a janitor was the easiest way to move around the building without drawing too much attention to herself. By claiming it was her first week of employment, she was able to ask surprisingly impertinent questions without giving offense. Consequently, she had gathered a fair amount of information in a short amount of time and knew the embassy employed approximately fifty people on four floors, the majority of whom were clerks who performed consular duties.

She had also discovered pertinent details about her would-be captor, whose name was Auguste Dupont. He was thirty years old and married to an amiable woman four years his junior called Lucie-Anne. He had been at the embassy for fourteen months, starting as a clerk and earning a promotion three months later to Beaufoy's secretary. Previously, he had worked at the Ministry of Police, compiling dossiers on suspected royalist plotters, an undertaking at which he reportedly excelled. Morny, who had run the ministry for much of Dupont's tenure, had recruited him to the embassy, and his patronage was believed to be the reason Dupont had been promoted before other, longer-serving clerks. Despite this injustice, he was well liked by his colleagues, who swore they would miss him when he returned to Paris in July to take up his new post at the Ministry of Foreign Affairs.

That he was leaving so soon after his promotion was unusual. By all accounts, he worked well with his superior, who entrusted him with a growing list of responsibilities, and speculation was rife that his excellency was sending him to the capital to spy on the Minister of Foreign Affairs himself.

The Comte de Morny's ambitions had yet to be satisfied.

Considering these reports, Verity found it surprising that Dupont had failed so spectacularly as a kidnapper. Given his particular set of skills, he should have learned the truth about Robert Lark, who had not been constructed to withstand the protracted scrutiny of an experienced spy. That neither Dupont nor his associates had taken the time to examine the occupants of twenty-six Bethel Street closely suggested they were compelled by some outside force to move swiftly. Their speed had translated into recklessness, which could have harsh repercussions for Dupont, for the English government would not take kindly to his trying to abduct one of its citizens. The penalties would be severe, and although he would bear the brunt, his wife would not be immune to the consequences.

Had he considered Mrs. Dupont's well-being in his actions?

Presumably, no, which was not shocking, for men were notoriously selfish, craving one thing only until it was in their grasp and then almost immediately desiring something else. They were supported in this endeavor by an ability to render their own needs noble—a sleight of hand summed up best by Richard Lovelace's disingenuous feint in the poem "To Lucasta, Going to the Wars": I could not love thee (Dear) so much, Lov'd I not Honour more.

'Twas all nonsense, Verity thought.

Men always did what they wanted and then cast about for the high-minded ideal that justified it. Even Freddie resorted to the tactic from time to time. He had realized that the musings of an adept gossip would benefit the *London Daily Gazette* before deciding the column would vastly improve Verity's situation as well.

The other possibility was that Dupont's wife endorsed his actions or had a hand in concocting the abduction scheme. Verity harbored no illusions about the so-called gentler sex.

To gain insight into his motivations, she grasped the handle on Dupont's office door and slipped inside the room while the secretary was meeting with Beaufoy. The envoy extraordinary was in charge of planning a reception to welcome the newly arrived ambassador from Spain and introduce him and his wife to London society, to be hosted at the comte's Grosvenor Square address. A lavish affair, it required weeks of preparation as well as a tremendous amount of coordination with various merchants, and although the party was a mere eleven days away, his excellency continued to change his mind about the menu.

Just that morning he had decided the offerings must include pigeon rôti, even though he had disdained the very suggestion two weeks earlier.

Truly, it had been remarkably easy to discover pertinent details about the embassy's staff, Verity thought, contemplating the office, which was small, as the porter had noted, but not tiny. Pressed against one wall was a writing table with scattered sheets of paper and a copy of a French newspaper that was three days old. There was a cabinet opposite, and in between the two pieces of furniture was a set of windows, which were open to allow in the fresh June air.

Verity began with the papers on the table, scanning the first lines swiftly because she knew Dupont would return shortly. He had met with his superior several times during the day, darting down to the second floor to confer on one matter or another, and each of the encounters had been brief.

Finding nothing on the table save sundry embassy documents and notes about sundry embassy documents, she shifted her attention to the cabinet and rifled through the shelves. Buried under a stack of law books, she found an old copy of the *London Morning Gazette*.

"Aha," she murmured as she noted the date. The issue was from the month before and contained Robert Lark's profile of a rising Whig politician as well as one of Twaddle's homages to Her Outrageousness's resourcefulness. Although it was not a particularly noteworthy edition, it was the first and only link she had found connecting the secretary to herself.

If there was one piece of evidence, there was likely more.

Alas, now was not the time to look for it. She had already been in the office for a full ten minutes, and Dupont could return at any moment.

Nevertheless, she filed it away as significant as she efficiently returned everything to the cabinet, confirmed the office was precisely as she had found it, and slipped silently out of the room.

*Thursday, June 11*
*6:12 p.m.*

As Verity had assumed Dupont was as fatigued as she after a sleepless night and a full day of working, she was surprised when he walked to the Speckled Pig, which was twenty minutes away in Petty France. The tavern was crowded, and entering a few paces behind him, she watched as he strode to the counter to secure a glass of dark-colored ale after a brief conversation with the barkeep. Then he carried his drink to a table occupied by a trio of men who greeted him enthusiastically and shifted their seats to make space for him to sit down. There was a fifth drink on the table, indicating that one of their number was currently absent, and Verity swept her eyes around the room to see if she could identify the missing compatriot. Nobody stood out.

She did, however, notice an empty chair two tables away from the group and sat down to listen to as much of their conversation as possible. It was difficult because Dupont and his friends spoke in lightning-fast French and she could hear only a few words at a time over the din. Every so often, the men raised their voices, lifted their glasses high into the air, and cried, "Vive L'Empereur!"

Verity, understanding that much at least, marveled at Dupont's audacity.

As a member of the embassy, he owed his pledge of loyalty to the Bourbon king, for that was who employed him, and she wondered if his plan to abduct her had something to do with a scheme to restore Napoleon to power.

On the face of it, the notion was absurd, for there could be no way of linking Verity Lark to the disposed leader on St. Helena, and yet she knew political currents were strange and winding.

Perhaps there was some way to connect them.

Twaddle *had* been unsparing in his treatment of the emperor's subjects, creating a long-running series of satirical portraits of his supporters based on widely acknowledged French tropes. Written in the style of René Antoine Ferchault de Réaumur's impeccable guide to insects, the compendium described the appearance, customs, and habitat of all known species of Bonapartisans.

Although the taxonomy was not her most subtle work, Verity had made a point of avoiding overly broad caricatures. Nowhere among the collection, for example, was an entry for *Franco froggus*. (There *was* a listing for *Franco smugglerus*, but one could eschew only so many generalizations before a project became untenable.)

During the war—and particularly the Hundred Days, when Twaddle published satires weekly—the *London Daily Gazette* received a steady stream of irate letters railing against Mr. Twaddle-Thum's abuse. Some French readers demanded he cease his ridicule at once, while others called for his head. Although it had been almost a year since the paper had printed a parody (*Franco humiliatus:* short stature, compulsion to subjugate, remote volcanic tropical islands), Verity could imagine the bitterness over the portraits festering among a coterie of angry Frenchmen. Residing in London, they were made to feel the weight of their country's defeat daily. Resentful and seething with the futility that made Beaufoy's speech on cooperation so difficult to write, they might have turned their ire on the scurrilous gossip who derided them at every turn and knew the first step in enacting their revenge was discovering his identity.

To that end, the friends could have researched the various reporters who worked at the *London Daily Gazette* alongside Twaddle and decided Robert Lark would be the easiest to manipulate on the grounds that he had an unmarried sister of a certain age who would readily succumb to brute force.

Taking the decidedly frail Miss Lark hostage, Dupont and his fellow schemers could then persuade Robert to reveal the identity of the notorious prattle in exchange for her life.

As far as connections went, it was indeed strange and winding, but Verity could not dismiss any possibility and decided to get closer to the group. She could not assess their devotion to Boney from two tables away.

First, however, she needed a better disguise.

Stepping outside, Verity examined the passersby and took note of several men whose coats would suit her nicely, but she was not looking for a good fit. Rather, she wanted a garment that was a little too wide for her narrow shoulders and frayed around the edges to give her a slightly threadbare look, as though she had recently endured a difficult time.

It was a privilege to suffer for L'Empereur.

As her own coat was in pristine condition, she had no trouble trading it for a dark blue frock with a tear in its left lapel. It was not ideal because the rent was clearly the product of a mishap rather than years of use. It was, however, the best she could do in the circumstance, and the hat she had managed to snag—a classic bicorn—was perfect. She placed it on her head in the side-to-side style favored by Napoleon and marched back into the tavern with an air of triumph. Then, in French that was flawless if a little slower than the average native speaker, she announced that the next round of drinks was on her.

"I am celebrating a most exciting development and invite you all to join me," she continued as several voices cried out in appreciation. She sauntered to the counter, laid down a handful of coins, and ordered an ale before continuing. "I have just today received news from a compatriot who has pierced the seemingly impenetrable wall Johnny Bull has dared to construct around our beloved leader. How did he accomplish this impossible feat? By tenacity and deceit! He conspired to join an East India ship that was to lay off the coast of St. Helena and leaped into the sea at daybreak. Then he swam to shore, climbed over the rocks, evaded the dull-witted guards who were supposed to keep watch, and visited with L'Empereur's servants. He had brandy with Marchand himself! L'Empereur's valet! He passed on important messages regarding our countrymen's readiness to rise up again, and you may be sure, my friends, that this is the beginning of the new revolution. Soon, the next hundred days will be upon us and the next hundred and the next hundred and the next hundred without end. We shall be victorious!"

A rousing cheer greeted this information, and Verity was pleased to see Dupont add his voice to the lively ovation. Grasping her tankard, she approached the table, asked the men what they were drinking, and called to the barmaid to bring her compatriots glasses of ale at once. "They must not want for anything on such an auspicious day as this!"

Dupont, hailing her generosity, slid closer to the man next to him and invited her to join them. "You must sit down and tell us more about your remarkable friend."

Verity eagerly complied with the demand, placing her ale on the table as she lowered to a chair. "Arnaud is an ordinary Frenchman, no more or no less. He is only responding to the call to restore liberty, equality, and fraternity to our country, as I am certain you yourselves would do."

This statement was enthusiastically affirmed by the men at the table, who exclaimed, "Here, here," as they held their glasses aloft. Then they all drank deeply.

Capitalizing on their interest, Verity relayed several extravagant details about the audacious Léon Arnaud, who would happily undergo the torments of hell for the opportunity to spit in Wellington's eye. She invented an underground organization of which Arnaud was a founder and lavished praise on its members, who were all fierce and brave and ready to give everything to the movement.

"We are so close to triumph, my friends," she added, taking a deep sip of her own brew and sighing with intense satisfaction as she pressed her back against the wall. "We are so close I can almost taste it. Now tell me about yourselves. What brings you fine fellows to the heart of the lion's den?"

As expected, they were all émigrés working in London for various concerns—a footwear manufactory, a hotel, an apothecary—and although they expressed ardent support of L'Empereur and claimed to desire his return, none jumped at the opportunity to further the cause. Indeed, when asked explicitly to lend their help, they all refused.

"We feel the humiliation of being a conquered people strongly," explained Henri Blanchet, who sold medicines from a shop in St. Pancras. Like the others at the table, he was about two decades older than Dupont, with a liberal peppering of gray hair. "We feel it every day, and if Napoleon were to return to Paris tomorrow, I would cheer as loudly as anyone and run home. But I have also grown weary of war. I fought at Leipzig and watched my brother die from a bullet to his stomach. I am content to shoulder the humiliation and have roast beef with potatoes on Sunday for supper."

Verity, loudly proclaiming her horror at this shocking capitulation to ease and comfort, looked around the table in disgust and noted the other men wore the same expression of defiant shame.

Except Dupont.

His thoughts were harder to discern, and she could not decide if it was because he did not share his friends' perspective or was unabashed by it. If it was the former, then perhaps his attempt to kidnap her really was in service to the restoration of the ousted leader in some strange and roundabout way.

"What about you?" she said, addressing him directly. "You are young and strong! You must care more about glory than comfort!"

Dupont, who had so much to say while tied to the vanity chair in her bedchamber, only murmured that he valued glory and comfort in equal measure.

Uncertain of what to make of this reply, Verity said, "How very *uncomfortable* for you."

A ghost of a smile appeared on Dupont's lips as he agreed. Then he asked her to tell them more about her plan to free Napoleon, and she spent the next twenty minutes recounting an outlandish scheme involving three warships, two battalions, and one dinghy manned by an angler who was especially skilled at catching tarpon.

When she was finished, they offered elaborate toasts to the wild plot but remained adamantly opposed to joining her cabal. Wishing them well, she returned her tankard to the table with a jovial thump and said, "If you fine fellows are not game for anything tougher than boiled mutton, then I must be off to find heartier recruits. Have a lovely evening, my friends, and enjoy your creature ... uh ... comforts."

Exhausted from the effort of speaking a foreign tongue, Verity stumbled over the end of her sentence, unsure if the phrase translated into French in any meaningful way. It might sound like nonsense.

Well, there was nothing she could do about it now, she thought as she rose to her feet, tipped her hat at the men, and strode to the counter to settle the bill with the barmaid. Then she left the tavern.

But she was not done, not quite yet, and she positioned herself in the alleyway across the road to wait yet again for Dupont to emerge so she could follow him home. It was another hour before he finally did, and as she traced his steps, she wondered if her exhausted mind would be able to recall the directions—a left on Cowgate, a right on Gherkin, a right on Pleasance, a left on Frederick—well enough to find the residence again in the morning.

※

*Thursday, June 11*
*9:01 p.m.*

Although Delphine wanted to chastise Verity for failing to send word of her progress during the more than fourteen hours she was away from Bethel Street, she could not bring herself to issue the harsh condemnation when she saw her friend's pale features.

The poor darling was weary to the bone.

"Poor darling?" Freddie echoed with puzzled surprise. "You have spent the past hour and a half cursing her utter lack of consideration and vowing to ring a peal over her head, and then the moment she saunters into the house you moue sympathetically? It is highly disappointing, Delph. I know you have more backbone than that!"

"But look at her!" Delphine replied insistently. "She has dark circles under her eyes. When was the last time you saw her with dark circles under her eyes?"

"Two weeks ago Saturday," he said without hesitation. "When she interviewed the croupier at Watier's."

Delphine scoffed. "That was the product of rouge and powder applied for effect. These marks are natural."

Although Freddie allowed the distinction was fair, he nevertheless thought his friend was doing it a bit brown. "You can scold Verity for her negligence while restraining the worst of your temper out of respect for her fatigue. I have seen you do it plenty of times. Indeed, just six days ago in this very room you made your disapproval known."

70

"Oh, but on that occasion, she was only sliced in the shoulder," Delphine explained, noting that Verity routinely endured scrapes and jabs while Twaddling. "I have never seen her so worn to the nub that her skin looks as though it is bruised. The poor darling."

Verity, whose silence on the subject was the true indicator of her weariness, stopped on the threshold of the parlor and asked if Delphine was redecorating. "Or am I in fact so tired my brain has managed to conjure a bed in the middle of the room?"

Soothingly, Delphine assured her the cot was real. "Freddie insists on sleeping here until we know the full extent of the plot against you. I offered him Robert's room, but he wants to remain close to the front door, as that is how the intruder gained entry last night."

Amused, Verity darted a faint smile at her friends. "Is that really necessary?"

Delphine admitted that the precaution had struck her as a trifle excessive when Freddie proposed it, but now she believed it was a vital measure. "For you are obviously too exhausted to defend yourself as you did last night. You would sleep through any number of late-night visitors."

Although offended by this assessment, which was wildly inaccurate, Verity did not have the heart to refute it. Drumming up an argument felt like an inadequate use of her diminished vivacity when all she desired was something to eat and a few hours of sleep.

"You see!" Delphine cried with a speaking look at Freddie. "The poor darling is so exhausted she cannot bestir herself to object. We shall serve her a light meal and tuck her into bed and resume this discussion tomorrow—say, at eight o'clock over shirred eggs?"

It was noteworthy, Freddie agreed, how their friend meekly accepted the insult without a single word of protest, for usually she issued dozens. "Perhaps you are right to hold off on taking Verity to task for her thoughtless treatment. But it *has* been fourteen hours since she left in pursuit of the intruder and since she is not dead in a ditch or at the bottom of the Thames, as you feared, she must have discovered something about him. I think it is reasonable that we learn what it is before morning. I must own myself impatient to know more."

Verity perked up at the mention of her would-be kidnapper, for she was eager to share what she knew and get their opinion as to what business a secretary from the French embassy could have with her or Robert or Twaddle. To that end, she stepped lightly around the encampment in the middle of the floor, requested a meal fit for a battalion of infantrymen—or, barring that, a joint of beef with perhaps a whole loaf of bread—sat down on the settee, and relayed her findings. Although Freddie jolted several times in his seat, pressing his back against the chair and grasping its arms as if physically restraining himself, he allowed her to speak without interrupting. Delphine was likewise respectful, only interjecting once to grumble over the patent absurdity of a sailor having tea with Napoleon's valet.

"I do wish you would rein in your penchant for lavish invention," she said stridently. "An outlandish cawker like that will get you killed."

"On the contrary, it is what keeps me alive," Verity countered as she buttered another piece of bread. "A disguise is only as convincing as its vaguest detail. The secret to a credible character is in the particulars—the more precise, the better."

"Yes, darling, I am familiar with your theory on creating believable personae," Delphine replied with a weary sigh. "You need not lecture us like schoolchildren."

Verity was not persuaded, for the comment had revealed a

fundamental lack of comprehension of her craft, but she refrained from pressing the point. Instead, she returned to her narrative, citing Dupont's inconclusive response to Léon Arnaud's scheme, before breaking off to yawn widely.

Noting the smudges beneath Verity's eyes had grown even darker, Delphine said they would continue the discussion in the morning after they had all gotten a good night's sleep. Although Freddie appeared ready to argue, he merely professed himself grateful for the opportunity to ponder the information and rearranged the linens on his cot.

Twenty minutes later, Verity climbed into bed and promptly fell asleep.

# Chapter Four

I f the sight of her dear friend dressed for Twaddling in the tailored green wool of Jeremiah Stubbs, formerly of the 95th Rifles, unnerved Delphine, it paled in comparison to seeing her sport her own clothes for Verifying. At least the sharpshooter appeared prepared to defend himself against all comers.

Drawing her brows into a frown as she looked up from her plate of kippers, Verity said, "I thought we all agreed to eschew the new usage."

Mildly, Delphine swore she could recall no such compact.

"Neither can I," replied Freddie, whose normally kempt appearance was disheveled after passing the night on the army cot. As he spoke, he arched upward and pressed his fist against the left side of his neck as if to smooth a crick. "Personally, I find it quite handy, and although I do not share Delphine's innate apprehension in seeing you dressed as a version of yourself, I do feel some concern about the wisdom of that choice right now unless you are hoping to goad them into making a second attempt to abduct you."

Although Verity dismissed this suggestion as something she would never be so foolish to consider, the truth was she had briefly weighed the benefits of such a scheme and decided they did not offset the risks—yet. That determination could change depending on how the situation developed. "But I am not dressed as myself or a version of myself. See, I am wearing a necklace with a little bumblebee on it," she explained, holding up the small gold pendant for their inspection. "Obviously, I am a French widow whose allegiance lies with our exiled leader. Vive L'Empereur and all that."

While Delphine muttered that it was not obvious at all, Freddie nodded with approval, noting that an interview with Dupont's wife was the next logical step for discovering his loyalties, which was vital to figuring out his interest in Verity. "Although we cannot be certain he meant to attack Verity," he added with a frown. "All we know is that he stole into the house and tried to attack someone. The target might not have been a particular woman but merely the first one he encountered. If we are correct in the assumption that the intruder had surveilled the house before entering, then he knew Robert was not at home, so there was no risk of stumbling upon him by mistake."

Naturally, Verity had put herself at the center of the intrigue. It had been her room that the invader had entered, after all, and her person whom he had attempted to drug. Furthermore, she was the one who Twaddled and Larked and Veritied. (No, she thought firmly, we are not allowing the verb form to stand.) Delphine gardened and planned menus, and occasionally warred with squirrels. If a rodent with a bushy tail and a fondness for seedlings had sneaked into her room, then she would have immediately reconsidered her place in the drama.

But Freddie's point was well taken. Knowing nothing about the intricacies of the plot against them, they could not draw any meaningful conclusions about its objectives. Delphine could very well be in danger. Unsettled by the possibility, Verity tossed her serviette onto the table as she rose to her feet to gather more information. "I must go. Dupont arrived at the embassy several minutes before nine yesterday, which means he will soon leave his home. I want to arrive before he does and then settle on the best way to approach his wife."

Delphine, who had calmly accepted the notion that she might be subject to an abduction attempt or worse, startled at her friend's announcement. "You cannot go yet. We have an appointment to discuss your appalling lack of consideration yesterday at eight o'clock. If you check your diary, you will see that it is clearly marked. Here, have more eggs," she said, reaching for the platter to serve her friend another spoonful. "You have barely eaten anything."

Amused, Verity replied that she did not keep a diary and as such could not be bound by its contents.

"Oh, but you do," Delphine insisted, fetching the book from the sideboard and placing it on the table.

"Just because you wrote my name on the inside cover does not mean it belongs to me," Verity said. "You are the one who records appointments in it, not me. Nevertheless, I hear your complaint and promise not to disappear again for fourteen hours. I will either return before then or send a note."

Far from satisfied with this response, Delphine rushed to add that thirteen hours was likewise unacceptable, and Verity, looking briefly heavenward as if seeking patience, asked Freddie to distribute notes on Twaddle's behalf to his network. "I have left them on the sideboard next to Delphine's daybook. I am hoping to gather information about

Dupont's friends. They seem benign and uninterested in plotting, but of course we must confirm that."

Freddie agreed at once.

Verity, rising to her feet, thanked him and confirmed that he would keep an eye on Delphine.

"An eye on *me?*" the other woman repeated with astonishment. "You must be joking."

"The villain or villains—there could be several or a whole cabal for all we know—might change tactics and try to snatch you in the middle of the day," Verity explained.

"That is utter nonsense," Delphine growled scornfully.

Her hazel eyes wide with innocence, Verity said, "Do not scowl at me. It is Freddie's theory."

Obligingly, Delphine turned her disdainful glare on the newspaper editor and accused him of being overly dramatic in proposing her as an alternative target. Freddie conceded the likeliness but insisted there was no harm in taking measures to ensure her well-being. "To that end, you will spend the day in the *Gazette*'s offices, where I can make sure you are safe."

Bristling at the information, which was presented as a fait accompli rather than one possible solution to the problem, Delphine said, "And I suppose I shall proof some articles while I am there."

"Not if you do not want to," Freddie said stiffly. "I am your friend, not a taskmaster. But should you choose to put your time to good use, I would support you in that decision."

Delphine thanked him for his generosity as Verity slipped from the room.

*Friday, June 12*
*10:41 a.m.*

Verity waited until Mrs. Dupont had returned her change purse to her pocket before inhaling sharply, grasping her neck, and crying out that her pendant was gone. A mere foot away from the woman, who was holding a lovely bouquet of pink roses, she spun in a circle, seemingly too agitated to halt her movements and properly assess the situation. Muttering with increasing ferocity, she said, "My necklace! My necklace!"

Having adopted a female character who looked vaguely like Verity Lark, she nevertheless raised her voice an octave to give it a pitch that sounded more convincingly French. Lowering her arms, she swung them at her sides, as if trying to grasp something in the air, and wailed, "My necklace! My necklace!"

"Here, mademoiselle, please do calm down," a voice said kindly.

Verity's head was tilted down, toward the cobbles beneath her feet, but she glimpsed the green stems of Mrs. Dupont's flowers out of the corner of her eye, which indicated she had drawn the attention of her target.

Perfect.

Heaving her shoulders, Verity whimpered, shook her head, and mumbled in disjointed sentences to convey her inability to quell the frenzy of panic that roiled her.

"Hush now," Mrs. Dupont continued in the same gentle tone. "Hush. I am sure it is not as bad as all that. We shall find your necklace. Here, tell me what it looks like, and I will help you search."

But Verity, too upset to speak coherently, rambled about beloved insects and muddy boots and calloused fingers and leaping pigs.

Mrs. Dupont, bewildered by the last phrase, ceased her soothing coos to repeat the last two words in heavily accented English. "Leaping pigs, mademoiselle? I do not know what you mean by 'leaping pigs,' but if you would just calm down, I am sure it will all make sense."

Verity burbled an incomprehensible reply.

"Excuse me, mademoiselle?" Mrs. Dupont said politely. "I do not understand."

"It is madame," Verity explained, visibly struggling to compose herself so that she could respond intelligibly. Indulging a bout of hysterics would accomplish nothing. "It is madam, not mademoiselle. Madame Garnier. I am a married woman. Or I was before my husband was killed in battle. Now I am just an inconsolable widow with only a few mementos to remember him by."

"Leipzig," Mrs. Dupont said with a gleam of understanding as she deciphered the meaning *of leaping pigs*. "Your husband died in the Battle of Leipzig."

"He was killed in the Battle of Leipzig alongside so many of his brave countrymen. A bullet to his stomach, I am told," Verity added sadly, summoning tears that glistened on her lashes. "And now I have lost the last thing he ever gave me: a pendant of a bumblebee."

"The emblem of the emperor," Mrs. Dupont murmured.

Despite Madame's efforts to hold her emotions in check, the disconsolate widow was no match for the sadness that overwhelmed her and tears began gently to fall. "The emblem of our leader. Lucas sold his smithy tools to buy it because I think he knew in his heart he would not come back. And now it is gone!"

"Hush," Mrs. Dupont said sternly, refusing to lose heart. "We will find it, I am sure. Here, let us retrace your steps. From which direction did you come?"

But she had no sooner posed the question than a glint of

gold in the sunlight caught her eye and she bent down to examine its source. Shaking her head in wonder, she picked up the charm and held it aloft from its black silk ribbon. "This is it, isn't it, Madame Garnier? This is your lost pendant. What a marvelous coincidence."

Naturally, it was no such thing, not at all, for Verity had dropped it only a few inches from the woman's feet while she was distracted with her purchase.

"It is quite lovely," Mrs. Dupont said softly as she pressed the necklace into Verity's palm. "There, now you can keep it safe."

Beside herself with relief, scarcely able to speak for the gratitude that lodged in her throat, Verity threw her arms around Mrs. Dupont. She thanked her repeatedly before perceiving the impropriety of the display and releasing her abruptly. She took a step back and apologized for her exuberance. "You must think I am a madwoman for attacking a stranger in the market. It is only that I am so grateful for your kindness. I have been in this country for two years and have experienced so little kindness. It is so hard for me to be away from everything that is familiar. I had expected England to feel like home by now, but it still feels like a foreign land."

Ending her speech with a dejected sigh, Verity peered at the other woman through her lashes to see how these words were received. Mrs. Dupont's features were drawn in a sympathetic frown, but she neither nodded nor concurred with the sentiment.

Verity found that revealing.

"But listen to me, going on about my troubles, when you are clearly thriving here," she said with a self-recriminating shake of her head. "You are blooming!"

Graciously, Mrs. Dupont urged her never to apologize for her feelings. "At least not to me, for I know we are all formed by our varying experiences. You have suffered a great tragedy and that must color every moment of your existence. I have been lucky. I thought I would hate London, but it has been pleasant. My husband has a good position that allows us to live in a comfortable home. We even have a maid-of-all-work who helps me prepare meals and keep the rooms tidy. And I have made some English friends. I am surprised to say I will miss it when we leave."

"You are leaving!" Verity exclaimed with feigned wonder. "Are you returning to France?"

"In July," Mrs. Dupont replied.

Unable to detect either resentment or pleasure at the prospect, Verity said, "Won't you be sad to leave your house and your friends?"

Mrs. Dupont, folding her hands across her belly, admitted with a heavy exhalation that she was in fact sad to go. "But I am also excited to return home. I miss my family. It is time, I think. And my husband must go where his superior has determined he will be most useful."

It was, Verity decided, an interesting way to describe the change, and she wondered if his colleagues' speculation that he was returning to France to spy on the comte's behalf might be accurate.

Adopting an air of fascination, she asked where her husband was employed, and discovering he was a secretary at the embassy, she asked what he would do back in France if the mission was in London.

"He will work at the Ministry of Foreign Affairs," Mrs. Dupont replied.

"In Paris," Verity said, owning herself quite jealous of the other woman's good fortune. Clutching the bumblebee pendant tightly in her right fist, she added sorrowfully that she sometimes could not help hating the English for what they did to her dear husband. "To live among them feels like a betrayal of Lucas, and I wish there was something I could do to avenge his death in some tiny way."

Having made this shocking confession, Verity paused to allow Mrs. Dupont to say something equally revealing. It was the briefest interval, a hairsbreadth and no more, but it was all she needed to realize no reciprocal admission would follow. Almost a decade of Twaddling had honed her ability to read people's expressions, and she could see nothing but pity on the other woman's face. If she was part of a secret cabal to weaken England from within, then she was too experienced to reveal her involvement, and while Verity allowed it was possible, she knew it was unlikely. In her opinion, Mrs. Dupont was precisely what she appeared to be: a contented wife enjoying her husband's success. She did not even seem particularly concerned that he had spent Wednesday night away from home.

Verity's assessment could be wrong, for she knew better than to believe herself infallible, but if that was the case, then she would have to discover it in another way. She had learned all she could from Dupont's wife, and thanking the woman again for finding her most precious pendant, bid her goodbye.

*Friday, June 12*
*1:23 p.m.*

As a matter of course, John Pennie did not write about foreigners. A reporter for *The Times* as devised by Verity, he reserved his bold quill and dizzying verbiage for heroes of local vintage, men who proposed audacious legislation or enacted sweeping changes. He had one goal and one goal only —to edify his readers with interviews with fascinating men whose breadth of accomplishment awed him—and it did not take a swellhead to realize that description could never apply to a Frenchman.

Being fascinating was a distinctly English trait.

And yet sometimes he found himself at the mercy of his editor, who did not share his refined ideas about the qualities that comprised an appropriate subject. On those occasions— infrequent, yes, but still too many for his comfort—he was obliged to cast about for any fact, snippet, or tidbit that would raise the subject to his level.

It was not easy, especially now that he had been tasked with interviewing the envoy extraordinary of the French embassy.

Extraordinary—ha!

Pennie would reserve the right to confer laudatory adjectives for himself, thank you very much, and he certainly would not concede the validity of one as a job title.

Beaufoy might as well call himself envoy amazingly exceptional for all the meaning it had.

Despite his churlishness, Pennie owed his readers riveting journalism regardless of the mundanity of the subject and, reviewing Beaufoy's portfolio, he focused on the only thing he could identify that made him the least bit interesting: his forthcoming speech on the renewed spirit of cooperation between the two countries.

Verity, sporting the bright blue silk waistcoat the fictional reporter favored, spied the same porter as yesterday and greeted him enthusiastically in English, for the esteemed reporter from the *Times* had never lowered himself to learn French. It might be de rigueur among the nobility, but he knew it for the heathen tongue it was. "My name is John Pennie—that is Pennie with an *ie*, not a *y,* so as not to be confused with the pence—and I am here to interview Guillaume Beaufoy. You may announce me."

Baffled, he stared at her.

"I said, my good man, that you may announce me," Verity repeated pompously, withdrawing a calling card from her pocket and holding it out to the porter. "He is not expecting me, but I am confident he will make time once he knows that John Pennie is here to profile him for an article in England's premier newspaper."

The porter stared hesitantly at the engraved slip, causing Verity to wonder if Pennie would be forced to employ the *petit peu* French he had, in fact, lowered himself to learn at school—his marks, alas, depended on it. First, however, he would make the same statement louder in case volume was the issue, but as she opened her mouth to reiterate the comment, a voice over her shoulder asked to see the card.

Spinning on her heels as the porter stiffened, Verity turned to find herself face-to-face with the French ambassador himself. He was an imposing figure, with a narrow face, well-kempt white hair, and light gray eyes that managed to look flinty and amiable at the same time. His elaborate cravat was expertly tied, his velvet tailcoat was a deep puce, and his black pumps bore a one-inch heel, which added to his impressiveness, although, to be sure, Emmanuel Honoré-Gabriel de Chastre, Comte de Morny, required no such augmentations. He was famous for his deft political machinations, nimbly straddling the line between revolutionary and royalist without giving grave offense to either. The political winds shifted and so did Morny, and if he had renewed his pledge to serve the emperor upon his return from Elba like so many others, he was the only one shrewd enough to avoid putting it in writing. He was nowhere to be found among the many signatories to the *acte additionnel*.

Bowing respectfully, Verity handed the ambassador the card with a flourish and introduced herself as *The Times'* very own John Pennie—*ie,* not *y!*—and explained that she was there to write a profile about Mr. Beaufoy for the newspaper.

Before she could cite his forthcoming speech to the Tip-Tapp Club as the reason for her interest, his excellency told her she would not have to waste time interviewing his underlings to gather information about him.

"You may start and finish with the source," he added graciously. "Come, let us adjourn to my office, where we may be comfortable. We shall have tea with Macarons de Nancy, for I just received a box from the minister of foreign affairs."

Verity did not want to come.

Well, she did, yes, because he was the famous Comte de Morny, and interviewing him was a coup for her in any incarnation. Freddie's jaw would drop to the floor if Robert Lark submitted a profile chock-full of firsthand quotations.

And Twaddle.

What that rapacious prattle could not do with twenty minutes alone with the great man in his office! Already he had two items, the first extolling the delicious lavishness of Macarons de Nancy. The Twaddleship adored stories about sweet indulgences and would thrill to the description of the extravagant French pastry. The second would marvel at the ambassador's eagerness to be interviewed.

A man of his accomplishments accosting reporters in the hallway!

The story almost wrote itself.

Verity was not there to gather gossip or shock Freddie, but extricating herself from the ambassador's grasp without creating a fuss was impossible. Her only option was to sit down with him, ask a few questions, nibble on one or two biscuits, and allow him to hold forth on the topics dear to his heart. She could not imagine it would take very long. He was, after all, the most important Frenchman in England, and as she contemplated that fact, she realized the encounter with him would redound to her benefit. His excellency's willingness to be interviewed by John Pennie added to the reporter's consequence, and Beaufoy could hardly refuse the very thing to which his superior had consented.

Entering the ambassador's office, she noted it was a sumptuous space, capacious and comfortable, with rich, maroon-painted walls and expertly molded floral plasterwork. Along the far wall, beneath a brooding portrait of a Dutch burgher in a broad-brimmed black hat, was a sideboard with an elaborate tea set and crystal decanters filled with wine-dark liquids. To its left was an amiable seating area flanked by tall vases of colorful flowers, and at the comte's direction, she sat down on a light blue bergère. She withdrew her notebook to record the ambassador's responses as he held out a plate of the promised macarons.

"You must try these," he said temptingly. "They are delicious."

Verity duly complied, selecting one of the cream-colored biscuits and taking a bite. It was perfection: the light, crispy outside and the soft, pliable center. She leaned back in the chair as she thanked him for graciously agreeing to satisfy the curiosity of *The Times* readers. Then she asked what aspect of his position he found the most satisfying.

It was a simple question designed to elicit a straightforward answer, and he would respond with something about the pleasure of being in service to his country. She would ask about his tailor and what he thought of London, he would give further cursory replies, and she would bid him adieu before she swallowed a third macaron. (Well, maybe a fourth. The delicate flavor was exquisite.) Then she would dash up to the second floor to ask Beaufoy about his favorite aspects of the job and slyly maneuver the conversation toward his feelings about Napoleon, his loyalties to his country, and the nighttime activities of his secretary.

Verity's calculations proved inaccurate, however, for she was well onto her fifth Macaron de Nancy by the time Morny even acknowledged a query had been posed. First, he had to give her a complete catalogue of his education, starting with the tutor his father had hired who spoke to him only in Latin, despite his four-year-old pupil's little understanding of the classic language. Then he had to relate a little something of his family's history, for he would be nothing without the influence of his grandfathers, both of whom instilled in him the importance of service to others over himself. Next, a brief recitation of his history was necessary, as his career could only be understood on a continuum, with one achievement leading to the next.

It was all of a piece!

Eventually, he turned his attention to the question at hand and dutifully explained how intensely gratifying it was for him to support the efforts of his king. The restoration of the monarchy was a singular event that gave him pleasure after the rapaciousness of the republic and he lauded his king's many stellar qualities.

It was not a particularly concise answer, but it addressed the question, and Verity, anticipating the end of the interview, closed her notebook.

Alas, bolstering the Bourbons was only one of a dozen or so aspects of his position he found highly rewarding.

"And then there is *this,*" he said, gesturing grandly toward their affable tête-à-tête around the low table topped with its plate of sweets in what was satisfaction number six. "Despite its complexities, diplomacy is at its heart the simple matter of two people talking to each other and finding out what the other wants. What you want from me now is an informative exchange with details that will entertain and inform your readers. What I want from you is the opportunity to explain myself to the best of my ability and the fair presentation of my ideas to your readers. Peace between nations is really just a conversation like this one replicated several thousand times, and I find it intensely rewarding to be able to lead those conversations, especially in a convivial atmosphere with a spot of tea. Tea! Yes, of course! I promised you tea."

Summoning a clerk, the comte begged Monsieur Varon to bring a pot at once and apologized to Mr. Pennie for the egregious oversight. "I can readily imagine the disgust with which your readers would perceive me when they read you were fed macarons without tea."

Varon returned shortly with the tea, and removing the plate of biscuits to make room for the tray, he placed it on the table next to Morny. His excellency, dismissing the clerk, insisted on doing the honors himself, and as he poured the brew into a pair of elegant cups with a primrose motif, he inhaled appreciatively. "This particular variety has an aromatic delicateness that can only be found in tea that comes from the Shantung province in China. It was given to me by the governor of the region, and now I have the pleasure of sharing it with you. That is another rare privilege afforded by my role."

The ambassador expounded for several minutes on the importance of cultural exchanges while Verity sipped the tea, whose light smoky taste varied little from the bohea she routinely enjoyed. Although she did not doubt its origins, she rather suspected the Twaddleship would soon be treated to a meditation on the irksome pretension of aggressive specificity, in which the one square foot of land that received the precise amount of rainfall to produce the optimal sweetness of the burgundy grape was extolled.

Or, better yet, a satirical column in which Mr. Twaddle-Thum identified the origin of each implement he used to produce the sentences: The quill his fingers clutched hailed from the second shelf of the narrow cabinet in the back corner of Arbuthnot's Stationery on Gutfeld Road.

Entertained by these musings, Verity waited for her host to run himself dry.

"If I can impart one thing to your readers it is this: I care," he said, pressing the palms of his hands together and holding them to his lips to present a picture of intense consideration. "I care about the future of our countries. I care about peace and prosperity for all mankind. I care about the divisions that divide us. I am not an egoistic functionary seeking to affirm my own glory or secure my legacy. I care about *them*."

"The readers of *The Times* will be glad to hear it," Verity said confidently before asking if he thought everyone in the embassy shared his point of view. Then she mentioned Mr. Beaufoy, for example, seemingly at random. "Do you think he holds this as his central mission as well?"

Drawing his elegant brows together, as if considering the query deeply, he had to confess that he did not believe so. Then he rushed to add that he did not say that to be critical. "It is merely that we are formed by our experiences, and our experiences are so different. Mine are manifold," he said, which Verity thought was a nicely understated way to describe his history of switching sides depending on the direction of the conflict. "I have had the advantage of discovering the error of my ways and adjusting my path accordingly, whereas Monsieur Beaufoy's perspective has remained constant. His path had only ever been straight, and in the course of following it, he has held on to old wounds, literally, in that his knee was badly injured during the war and now gives way from time to time, but also figuratively in his perception of the world. It is rigid, which, to be sure, makes him an excellent administrator, and I am grateful for his expertise and attention to detail. The reception he is planning for Spanish ambassador on my behalf will be an exquisite affair, with capons cooked to perfection and roses the exact shade as the gown of the new arrival's wife. The embassy would not function nearly so well without his steady hand. But he lacks flexibility, a quality that makes me empathetic and understanding of my fellow man, arguably more important traits in a diplomat."

Sensing from this reply that all questions asked about Beaufoy would be answered in units of Morny, Verity rose to her feet and thanked the ambassador for being so generous with his time and attention. "I am certain my readers will be as impressed as I am."

The comte demurred, insisting that Monsieur Pennie was the generous one, allowing him to ramble on about himself as if he were somehow inherently interesting.

As this was patently true, Verity replied, "Yes."

His excellency laughed, appreciating the humor, which he assumed to be ironical, and asked a porter to show her out. Although she insisted the courtesy was unnecessary, Morny countered that it was in truth a precaution, as the building was a patched together assortment of rooms and corridors and he could not allow a reporter to get lost.

Submitting to the escort, she thanked the diplomat again for his time and followed the porter out of the office and down the stairs. As they turned right on the ground floor and proceeded along the corridor to the entry hall, she contemplated her next move. Obviously, she was not going to shuffle quietly home and try again tomorrow. Learning more about Dupont and discovering if Beaufoy was involved remained her singular goal for the day, and the only question was whether she would reenter the building in Pennie's bright blue waistcoat or alter her disguise. The garment had been cleverly tailored to her specifications, allowing it to be worn with the lining on the outside. Effortlessly, it went from eye-catching flourish to sober vestment.

The answer depended on which identity was most likely

to get the information she needed. A reporter was ideal because he could ask questions without having to step gingerly around the subject, but the more productive interviews were preceded by an introduction. Although John Pennie would never scruple to march back into a building out of which he had just been ejected, the act of finding someone to make the presentation would require Verity to speak to several people, which would increase the risk of drawing undue attention. Morny clearly did not appreciate an underling gaining the notice of a reporter.

What about a shop assistant, then, Verity wondered. It was an excellent ruse for gaining entry to an establishment, but its utility was limited. Archie Jones, who had delivered packages on both banks of the Thames for more than half a decade, rarely managed to get responses to his gently probing queries because nobody wanted to linger in conversation with a delivery boy.

In contrast, people enjoyed talking to the Turnip because his bungling incompetence made them feel reassuringly superior. But for the Turnip to work, Verity would need an excuse for him to approach Beaufoy. What business could Joseph Pope have with the envoy extraordinary of the French embassy and how could he make a mull of it?

Verity considered this problem as the porter opened the door and escorted her outside, bidding her a curt good day—in French, which caused the resolutely English John Pennie to scowl at the brazen display of disrespect. Perhaps the Turnip had a letter for Beaufoy from a minister in the Foreign Office and he dropped it in a puddle of mud, rendering it virtually illegible.

The ploy might admit her to Beaufoy's office, but would it gain her an audience with him?

Most likely not, she thought, strolling around the building to the side, which drew less traffic than the adjacent thor oughfare. She noted there were fewer passersby as well, as she tilted her neck sharply to look up at the building. The second floor was not so very high, the stones were set back in the masonry enough to allow her to get a proper grip, and several of the windows were open. It would not be impossible to scale. All it would require was careful planning and dexterity.

"Now you *are* Veritying," she muttered, annoyed at herself for entertaining such a dangerous idea when there was a perfectly good working staircase inside—three, in fact. Delphine would have her head if she knew what her friend was thinking and rightly so. It was not as though swooping in through the window would solve anything. She was not struggling with how to gain access to Beaufoy but with how to gain access to Beaufoy in a way that allowed her to conduct a meaningful exchange. To figure out the best approach, she needed to learn more about him, information she could get by following him when he left the embassy.

It would not be long now, she decided, recalling that he had finished his work a little after five the day before. It was almost three-thirty now. She would find a spot across the street with a clear view of the front door and perhaps locate the cherry vendor. She was beginning to feel a bit peckish. As delightful as the macarons were, they were an inadequate nuncheon.

Satisfied with this plan, Verity cast a lingering look at the windows on the upper floor and stared with befuddlement as a body hurled toward her.

# Chapter Five

*3:16 p.m.*

The ground smacked her.

Seeming to rise up, it crashed into Verity's shoulder, knocking the air out of her lungs with so much force she couldn't inhale.

And the heavy mass on top of her.

A body, yes, but not *the* body.

That body had landed with a sickening thud.

And it was several feet away—three, maybe four.

She had been pushed clear of its path, shoved forward, then jerked sideward, her body careening to the left as she collided with the pavement.

And then all was still.

The world fell silent and nothing moved, not even the particles of dust kicked up by the violent fall, and Verity felt suffused by peace.

And then the inhale.

The spiky gust of air wrenched deep into her lungs as the

heavy mass began to swear with primal ferocity. The invectives intensified as the weight rolled off her, the hands that inspected her body for injury—shoulder, head, hip—surprisingly gentle.

But Verity, with no time to spare, not for any of it, jumped to her feet, wobbling slightly as her head felt suddenly light and unsustainable. She took a deep breath to counter it and felt pins in her chest.

"For God's sake, Verity, sit down!" Hardwicke spat impatiently, his hands darting out to steady her.

Yes, yes, Hardwicke.

Of course Hardwicke.

Like the proverbial bad penny.

Would she never escape him?

Her own anger rose sharply as she tugged free of his grasp and looked around for her hat, finding it badly crushed only a few inches from the gruesome corpse of Dupont.

Bloody Dupont.

The site of his broken body—the shattered skull, the vapid expression—caused her stomach to roil and she turned away without allowing herself to notice any of the details.

Rage, she thought.

Fury was the antidote to the horror, and picking up her hat, she tossed it onto her head and stalked toward the entrance. Hardwicke reached for her arm, attempting to stop her, and she yanked it away.

"Stop following me," she seethed.

His strange teal eyes flashed with fury, but his voice was calm as he ordered her to leave. "You must go before anyone sees you. I will take care of this. Please go now."

That was a futile hope, for a crowd had already begun to gather. A man could not drop from the sky without attracting interest, and heads peered down at them from the many windows that overlooked the scene.

She ignored his appeal and sped toward the entrance, Hardwicke's curses growing faint as she turned the corner. Taking advantage of the chaos, she slipped into the building as curious bystanders darted outside to get a closer look at the grisly tragedy and mounted the staircase. As she climbed the steps, she swept dirt from her clothes to neaten her appearance as much as possible before arriving at the top floor. Most of the grime came off with a light brushing, but there was nothing she could do about the tear in the shoulder.

In a long and illustrious career, it was the first time John Pennie looked anything but pristine.

So be it.

Breathing heavily from the exertion of the climb, Verity took the last several stairs two at a time despite the prickly ache in her chest. She turned right at the landing and ran down the hallway to Dupont's office, which was stuffed with people, maybe a dozen or more, all speaking at once in a chaotic jumble about Dupont's great leap, incapable of comprehending why he had done it. Beaufoy was there, trying to restore order, his face so pale his skin resembled parchment. Beside him was the clerk who had delivered the tea tray to Morny's office. He alone was abiding by Beaufoy's plea for dignity, perhaps because he was the only one who could hear him. The envoy extraordinary, making little effort to raise his voice above the clamor, told everyone to leave the room in an orderly fashion.

"This is horribly unbecoming," he insisted, hands tightly clasped before him in helpless agitation. "We shall depart in an orderly fashion and allow Monsieur Dupont his ... his ... privacy. It is rude to ... to ... gawk as though he were an unusually large pheasant at the hunt. Come away from the window. Please, I beg of you."

His appeals continued to be unheeded, and even the

clerk, unable to withstand his curiosity indefinitely, crept to the window to peer out over the shoulders of his colleagues.

Impatient with the unruly muddle, Verity wet her lips and tucked a few fingers into her mouth to produce the sort of piercing whistle that instantly silenced a room. It required three toots, but slowly she garnered everyone's attention. Then she made an introduction, briskly explaining her work for *The Times* as one of its premier reporters and distinguishing herself from the pence coin. Given the urgency of the situation, Pennie overcame his prejudice against foreign languages and conducted the conversation in heavily accented French.

"Anyone who doubts the legitimacy of my credentials may consult Mr. Varon, whom I had the pleasure of meeting scarcely a half hour ago," she said, gesturing to the clerk, whose forehead was now pressed against the window as he stared down at the pavement. He had finally managed to get an unimpeded view of Dupont's corpse. "Mr. Varon will confirm that I am a journalist for the newspaper and that I interviewed Emmanuel Honoré-Gabriel de Chastre, Comte de Morny, earlier this afternoon."

As the clerk was distracted by the sight below, Verity had to repeat his name two more times to gain his attention, and when he turned around, he startled to find himself the center of attention.

"Mr. Varon, please assure these men that I am who I say I am," she instructed.

The clerk, displaying no hesitation or reluctance, duly complied with her request.

She thanked him brusquely, lamented the unfortunate situation, and promised the men that each and every one of them would have an opportunity to speak to her. "We will proceed in an orderly fashion. Please remain where you are and patiently await your turn."

Beaufoy, his brows drawn tightly, appeared befuddled by her assumption of command, which was, Verity felt, the correct response to her high-handedness. "I do not think speaking to a reporter is appropriate at this time, Monsieur Pennie. I think it would be best if you leave and come back ... er, never."

Verity pressed her lips together thoughtfully and marveled at his desire for secrecy. "I wonder if it is because you have something to hide?"

Although Beaufoy's eyes flashed in anger at the accusation, he kept his tone cool when he replied. "Your presence here is unseemly. Please leave."

Happy to bow to his wishes, she paused to verify the spelling of his name. "It is b-e-a-f-o-y? I want to make sure I correctly identify the member of the French envoy to the court of St. James when I report to *The Times*' vast readership that the English are not welcome in this building despite it being on English soil in England."

"You left out the *u*," Varon offered helpfully. "It is b-e-a-u ... "

The clerk trailed off at the diplomat's furious growl.

Verity, pretending to make the correction in her notebook, praised Beaufoy for his ethical stance, which his excellency was sure to admire as well. "And it is unlikely that a little scandal will undermine the embassy's standing in London or lead to discord between our countries. I'm sure the English people will understand your need to keep secrets from them and definitely will not complain to the prince regent, who will not then find himself wondering what dire information his friend Louis XVIII is withholding from him. That won't happen at all," she said soothingly.

Beaufoy stared at her impassively, seemingly unconcerned by the prospect of causing an international incident. Then his courage flagged, and anxiety swept across his features. "Very well, you may stay. But *I* am in charge. I will choose the order in which you speak to the staff. Monsieur Varon, you will go first."

Although the clerk frowned at being singled out, he stepped forward without complaint and apologized for having nothing useful to say. "I did not see anything. After carrying in the tea, per his excellency's request, I returned upstairs, where Monsieur Beaufoy sought my assistance in retrieving a ledger from the storeroom. I had no idea something had happened until I heard the excited chatter in the hallway. Then several people told me at once. They rushed here, and I followed them. The room was already crowded when we arrived, and Monsieur Beaufoy was trying to establish order."

Verity asked him to identify the people whom he had followed.

Interjecting before the clerk could respond, Beaufoy wondered if these sorts of questions were really necessary. "I cannot understand how this information is edifying for your readers."

"That is because you are not English," Verity explained with withering condescension. "If you will recall, *we* are a nation of shopkeepers."

Although the relevance of this statement was not immediately apparent, Beaufoy refrained from further comment, clearly reluctant to quibble over the disposed leader's famous observation.

Varon, who was also puzzled by her query, nevertheless answered. "Monsieurs Capdeville and Navarro. There were others, but I can't recall them specifically."

Ascertaining that the room with the ledger was in the corridor on the other side of the building, she marked the clerk as unlikely to be the murderer. She gave the same designation to Capdeville and Navarro. Then she asked about the ledger, a detail that struck her as odd. "You said you were on the third floor to get a ledger for Mr. Beaufoy from the storeroom."

The clerk confirmed that was correct. "He is in charge of a reception his excellency is hosting and required a figure from an old ledger to help figure out how much to spend on pigeons. I was fetching it for him when I heard lots of noise in the hallway and came out to see what had happened."

"For Mr. Beaufoy?" she asked, pursing her lips in confusion. "According to your own report, he was in this room by the time you arrived even though his office is one flight down *and* he sent you to the third floor to fetch something for him."

Beaufoy, taken aback to find himself the subject of the sinister implication, professed amazement at the mundane interests of the English reading public. Nevertheless, he explained that he had ventured up to the third floor to see what was taking Monsieur Varon so long. "I had just arrived on the landing when I heard the commotion and followed the furor to Monsieur Dupont's office, where I found several people looking out the window with vulgar curiosity. I asked them at once to step back."

Wincing, the clerk stammered that he had been unable to find the ledger. "Someone"—here he glanced pointedly at a blond-haired man in a light blue coat—"placed it on the wrong shelf."

The accused, identifying himself as Monsieur Perreault, demanded that the record be corrected for the English people. "I have not touched the ledger in question," he insisted, drawing close enough to Verity that she could detect a hint of brandy on his breath. Then he added angrily that he had not visited the storage room in almost a week. "I have not even walked by it!"

Taking stock of his pugnacity, she wondered if the secretary had been killed in a drunken brawl and asked Perrault when he had arrived to the room. He identified the people who were there before him: Ricard, Farrow, Beaufoy, Gardin, Clément, Ardisson.

That made Perrault seventh, she thought, identifying Ricard from among the crowd. An older man with thick eyebrows who worked in the office next door to the right, he said he looked out the window the moment he heard the scream. "I thought it was an unfamiliar bird. I drew closer to the window to see if I could spot it and saw Auguste lying there. I could not understand it. It made no sense. So I ran to his office to ... to ... prove to myself it wasn't true, I suppose. I collided with Matthias as soon as I darted into the hallway. I was too frantic to explain. And I almost could not open the door to Auguste's office because my hands were shaking so badly. Then we were inside and I ran to the window, which is when Matthias understood. He screamed."

From the throng gathered in the room, Verity identified Matthias Farrow, a clerk with auburn curls, who acknowledged that he had indeed cried out with surprise. "I had no idea what had gotten Michel so upset and never in a million years imagined it was our friend's death."

"That was the scream I heard," Beaufoy murmured.

"We were still staring down at the pavement when Gardin and Ardisson came into the room to look out the window as well. Then Monsieur Beaufoy was behind us and urged us all to step away from the window," Ricard added quietly. "He said there was nothing to be gained from our looking at the terrible spectacle. He tried very hard, but people kept coming."

Verity, recording this information, noted that Farrow was the only person Ricard had spotted in the hallway. That made him a suspect in Dupont's murder.

That the victim had been ruthlessly killed, she did not doubt. He had fallen backward out the window, and no man who plucked up the courage to hurl himself three stories to the ground would bother mustering the extra nerve required to make the plunge backward. Furthermore, Dupont had been embroiled in a nefarious plot to take a middle-aged spinster captive—a task that had been assigned to him, and he somehow managed to bungle. Either something else had gone awry with the scheme or someone had found his inability to carry off the simple abduction problematic.

Was it Beaufoy?

As the person to whom Dupont had reported following his release from the cellar, he remained Verity's best suspect. But he was fifth to arrive, and Ricard had not seen him in the hallway,

Could he have hidden somewhere in the office?

She rather thought not, as the space was small and there were few places to hide. The only option was behind the door, which swung into the room. Beaufoy, with his narrow frame, could press his body against the wall to make himself all but disappear. In their distraction over Dupont's fall, the inhabitants would have been unlikely to notice him there. Then all he would have to do is slip out while the other occupants were staring down at the pavement and chastise them for their morbid curiosities. The same possibility applied to other men in the room, she thought, noting that among the first seven to arrive, all but Gardin had slim builds.

Returning to Beaufoy, she thought it was remarkably convenient that he just happened to have a legitimate reason for being on the third floor at the exact moment Dupont plummeted to his death.

Had he arranged his excuse in advance by moving the book to the wrong section himself?

Verity allowed it was possible, but it also struck her as an incredibly risky way to commit a murder if one had the luxury of planning it in advance. A variety of things could have gone awry, and it was better to avoid them altogether by killing one's victim under the cover of night or in a crowded market. If Beaufoy had time to prepare, then he would have known the ideal opportunity was when Dupont was walking home after a few glasses of ale at the Speckled Pig.

Contemplating the envoy's excuse for being on the third floor, she asked Farrow why he had been in the hallway, and he said that he had been returning from the privy. It was more vague than Beaufoy's reason and just as inconclusive. If Farrow was the culprit, then he was also likely involved in the abduction scheme.

Or were the two events unrelated?

Verity decided not to consider that possibility, at least not yet. First, she had to eliminate the obvious, and the obvious was that the plot to kidnap Verity and the kidnapper's murder were parts of a whole.

Thanking Farrow for the information, she interviewed arrivals three and four: Gardin and Ardisson. Inconsolably shaken by Dupont's death, the latter was unable to provide useful information and contented himself with agreeing to everything Monsieur Gardin said. Accordingly, neither noted anything suspicious before or after the incident and ran to Dupont's office to ogle the scene along with their colleagues, a development that perturbed Ardisson even more because it seemed so ghoulish of him. He looked then out the window, and Verity's gaze following his, noted that Hardwicke was gone.

Of course he was.

Gathered around the corpse now were the dozens of onlookers who had been drawn to the scene by morbid curiosity, and Verity spotted the comte at the center, directing the porters to hold back the huddled mass. Presumably, someone had sent for a Runner, and the ambassador was waiting until he arrived.

As if aware he was being studied, Morny suddenly looked up, and although Verity knew he could not make her out clearly from the distance—for all of John Pennie's peacocking tendencies, he did not look all that different from a clerk or a secretary—she felt as though he recognized her. The sense was heightened by the fact that the ambassador squeezed his way through the phalanx of bystanders to walk toward the building.

*Time to go.*

Stepping away from the open window, she returned her notebook to her pocket and announced she had all the material she needed to write a heartfelt story about the horrible tragedy that had befallen them all. Then she thanked the men for their help, offered her condolences on their loss, called them a credit to their country, and slipped from the room.

*Friday, June 12*
*3:35 p.m.*

Having shied away from the bloody remains of Mr. Smith in the ramshackle rooming house near Saffron Hill only the week before, Verity was determined to get as close to Dupont as possible. If she was going to be compelled by some impish force to solve murder mysteries—and, truly, she wished the universe would return to strewing Her Outrageousness's path with corpses rather than her own—then she would have to figure out how to overcome her squeamishness. There was information to be gleaned from the dead body, which she had realized too late last time, and by refusing to examine the cadaver she was in effect choosing ignorance.

The prospect of willfully not knowing something was anathema to her.

Even so, drawing closer to this particular carcass presented a new challenge as the throng of spectators did not yield to her gentle pushes and prods. In the dozen minutes Dupont had been sprawled on the pavement, the crowd had thickened to include passersby as well as regulars from the neighborhood. The cherry vendor elbowed Verity in the kidney as she tried to squeeze past him.

Suddenly, her arm was yanked in the opposite direction.

With a furious scowl, she turned to deliver a scathing set-down and encountered the angry teal gaze of Colson Hardwicke. He jerked his head to the side, indicating she should follow him, and although her instinct was to argue against the presumption of his issuing silent commands and expecting her to follow, she realized it was not the most constructive use of her time. Undoubtedly, he had already discovered all there was to know from Dupont's fractured body, and despite her efforts, she had made little progress in drawing closer.

Her frown no less fierce, she extricated herself from the horde, stepping on the cherry vendor's foot—an accident, to be sure—as she struggled to slip by him.

There, she thought, huffing indignantly when she was finally free.

"This way," he said with confident authority, as though leading an expedition through a dense thicket of vegetation in a foreign land.

They were in Mayfair!

She could navigate to the corner with the same ease and certainty as he.

Nevertheless, she did not protest.

Having been summarily discarded by him following the disapproval of his brother, she was inclined to quarrel over every syllable he uttered, but she knew a display of querulousness would be fatal. Petulance could be attributed only to resentment, and she would feel resentment only if she begrudged his treatment.

And she could begrudge only something that mattered.

Verity smoothed her features as they approached Down Street and proposed they take a turn around the block so that they could share information—and by "share," of course, she meant that he would tell her what he had found out while she deftly evaded to reciprocate.

Hardwicke agreed to the exchange but suggested they conduct it in a hack, as it would afford them more privacy.

Although it was on the tip of her tongue to refuse, for she was not ready to leave the vicinity of the embassy just yet, she recalled her determination not to quibble over minor points and acquiesced. She even added, "Yes, thank you."

It was the most agreeable Verity Lark had ever been out of character!

Ah, but this was a character too, she thought: a variation on the standard Verity Lark who presumed to feel nothing when her emotions were in fact an unsettling swirl of excitement, confusion, and dread. She could not fathom how he had suddenly appeared, like a fairy in a children's story, swooping to save her from danger at the last possible moment.

Well, it was not the *last* possible moment.

More than a few had remained, and Verity had had all the time she needed to remove herself from the path of the falling secretary, which she would have done with all due dexterity and haste. She was not a deer to startle into stillness in a forest.

Nevertheless, the way he had materialized seemingly out of thin air was breathtaking, and her heart jolted at the sight of him, even then, with Dupont's shattered body lying on the pavement next to them.

Except, no, it was *especially* then.

There was something uniquely comforting in Hardwicke's ability to appear the moment she encountered a corpse, and the two had become inexorably entwined. It was a macabre association, and yet it struck her as the opposite of macabre.

Hardwicke, readily securing a hack, opened the door and held out his hand to help her climb into the carriage. Given her masculine garb, it was an odd courtesy that would attract undue attention, and his failure to notice the blunder indicated he was not as unruffled as his composed demeanor would suggest.

Verity neither refused the gallantry nor acknowledged it, and boarded the vehicle without incident. Settling on the bench, she held herself stiffly as he sat down across from her. As she was tempted to look out the window to avoid the intimacy of the confined space, she met his gaze forthrightly and waited.

Presumably, he would explain, as he was the one who had arranged the meeting. She had been content to shoulder her way through the mass of bystanders to make her own inspection of Mr. Dupont.

And yet he did not speak, at least not for several disconcerting seconds as the horses pulled into the road and the carriage began to sway. They had just rounded a sharp corner, Verity clutching the edge of the seat to steady herself, when he said, "What in the devil are you doing here?"

Was there an edge of anger in his voice?

Oh, yes, most definitely, despite the calm curiosity with which the question was posed. Hardwicke was furious, and although Verity could not be certain of its source, she assumed it was because he thought she had recklessly thrown herself headlong into danger. It was a mark of how little he understood her that he believed she did anything without planning and care.

Hurt by the implication—well, no, Verity Lark, version 2,

was not hurt by anything—she smiled faintly and volunteered that John Pennie, a somewhat pompous reporter for *The Times,* had been at the embassy conducting interviews with various members of the staff. What she did not offer freely was the substance of those conversations or the events that had piqued the journalist's interest.

Hardwicke, not requiring these supplementary details, or even, it appeared, the particulars he expressly sought, continued as if she had not spoken. "I know you think you are invincible, but you are as human as the next person. You must allow me to handle this. I cannot have your life in danger in this way. It is intolerable to me."

Verity, shoulders already rigid, tightened them further at this inconceivable display of arrogance.

Intolerable to him!

To be certain, she took no small exception to it herself.

And his seeming omniscience—that was exceedingly odious as well. In the wild fortuitousness, Verity saw Delphine's steady hand. She assumed that her friend, worried about Verity's welfare *and* determined to promote the match, had seized the opportunity to put them in each other's company.

Keeping the bland smile firmly in place as she restrained her annoyance at these unsubtle manipulations, she firmly declined his offer. "You may bestow your overbearing assistance on another female, as I do not require it. I am perfectly capable of resolving the current situation on my own, and as it is a private matter that concerns only myself, I trust you will do me the courtesy of respecting my wishes."

His eyes flashed dangerously as he leaned forward and said with quiet menace, "How dare you call it a private matter that concerns only yourself!"

Taken aback by his fury, she wondered if Delphine had been forced to exaggerate the danger to herself and Freddie to engage Hardwicke's interest. Unwilling to enter into an argument about which she did not know all the facts, she said, "Regardless, you may be confident I have the problem well in hand. No one will come to harm."

Far from being appeased by her assurances, he was further incensed. "Even if I did not hold you in the highest esteem possible, I would be obligated to protect you from the dangers to which I exposed you—"

"*You* exposed me!" she repeated scornfully. "I can be attacked by any number of intruders in my own bedchamber without it having anything to do with you! Your conceit is stunning!"

"—and for you to turn around and call it a private matter when the attempts were made on my life. *My* life, Verity, not yours!" he said with scathing indignation. "I know you are so damned convinced of your own—"

He broke off abruptly, his brows drawn in astonishment. "In your bedchamber?"

Verity was just as shocked. "What do you mean 'attempts on your life'? For the love of God, Hardwicke, just how many people are trying to kill you?"

But he did not respond to her query.

Rather, he reached across the aisle, clasped her hands in his, clutching them tightly, and shook his head as if to clear it of unwelcome thoughts. "Tell me everything."

Verity did not know what to do with the stab of pleasure, the frisson of delight she felt dart through her at the warmth of his skin, which lived side by side with the inexplicable stab of fear she felt at the mention of attempts—plural!—on his life. Somehow the notion of someone trying to kill him existed outside the realm of possibility, and her first thought was that he was too wily.

Colson Hardwicke was simply too cunning to be murdered.

An accident or illness, sure, for nobody was immune to the vicissitudes of fate.

But homicide?

No, she thought.

And yet the prospect agitated her.

She was calmed, however, by the touch of his hand, and disliking both sensations, she pressed her back against the cushion in a futile bid to increase the distance between them.

It did nothing, of course, for the carriage was small and confining.

Crisply, she replied to his query, asserting that there was nothing she could tell him that Delphine had not already explained. "Whereas I am all at sea. Please tell me what you mean by 'attempts on your life.' I assume they are recent?"

As if sensing her retreat, Hardwicke slid slightly forward so that their knees touched. "I have had no contact with Miss Drayton."

Verity was so surprised by this information that she leaned closer. "But I do not understand. How are you here?"

"Ah, but how are *you* here?" he returned with equal interest. "The moment I realized someone was determined to kill me—in answer to your question, there have been five attempts of which I am aware—I canceled our plans to visit Gunter's and have been trying to identify the villain ever since."

He added that he had traced the threat back to his work for the Alien Office during the war, and Verity acknowledged the words with an absent nod.

But she was no longer listening.

Not really.

As he explained the reason for their aborted outing to the tea shop, the heat that had suffused her limbs at the touch of his hands slowly drained from her, like a bucket with a small hole, and she felt besieged by a strange sort of coldness. The sentiment he expressed was so familiar, so well trod and prosaic, she actually heard it repeat in her ears as Sebastian Holcroft had said it all those weeks ago in his cheerful breakfast room: *As soon as I realized that I severed the connection with the woman mentioned in the* Courier-Standard Dispatch.

Hardwicke had not used the same words, but they were verbatim nonetheless.

It was particularly mortifying to find herself subject to them because the woman in the Holcroft situation had in the month since been revealed to be the Duchess of Kesgrave's younger cousin, a delightful bit of pampered fluff called Flora Hyde-Clare. To be held to that standard was intolerable to Verity, and yet she was grateful to know the truth. Hardwicke always spoke in such lavish terms—astoundingly competent, highest possible esteem—but his actions revealed a decidedly less complimentary opinion.

Years ago, she had learned to stop listening to the nonsense people blathered: to the governors of Fortescue's Asylum for Pauper Children, who claimed to cherish children; to La Reina, who had left her on the doorstep of the orphanage with a note promising to visit often.

Only actions counted.

It stung, yes, but only because she had allowed herself to be gulled into thinking Hardwicke was in some way extraordinary. With his wartime efforts and his subtle manipulations of public perception and expectations, she had begun to see him as her equal. His infatuation played a part in it, she could see that now. It was easy to be fascinated by a man who professed to find her fascinating in return.

And no doubt Hardwicke subscribed wholly to all the lovely words he spouted. Men were extremely skilled at holding contradictory notions. He could believe she was a remarkable woman and still think she needed to be protected from the world like a silly schoolroom miss. It was to his lordship's credit that he had managed to worm his way so deeply into her affection.

Usually, she was too shrewd to be hoodwinked.

Hardwicke, failing either to notice her withdrawal or realize its significance, identified Kingsley as the source of his troubles. "You remember him, I trust? Sidmouth's asinine under-secretary who hired an immoral conniver to inform on the reform movement? He guzzled three-quarters of a bottle of Courvoisier at a tavern in Petty France and blathered to every man present that I was Grint's secret spy in the Alien Office who toppled the French Empire, seemingly all on my own. Since then, I have been beset by vengeful Bonapartists. I did warn you that many remained in London. It helps nothing, but I am in possession of an apology from Kingsley, which rambles for four pages and manages to be both sniveling and snide, expressing remorse while insinuating it was my fault for engaging in espionage in the first place. The espionage to which he is referring, of course, is with the Yarwellian Society. You must read it for yourself. You will find it diverting and infuriating."

Although firmly in control of her emotions, Verity felt her grip slacken just a tiny bit at the eagerness in his tone, for it revealed the insidiousness of his respect. He could admire her intellect, respect her ingenuity, and sincerely honor her bravery all the while seeing her as an inferior female in need of coddling.

A Flora.

She grinned broadly.

It was excessive for the circumstance, but that was Verity Lark, version 2, all over: amiable to the point of sickening sweetness.

She made the original Verity Lark's teeth ache.

Hardwicke, announcing that he had provided the general substance of his problem, tightened his hands, making her newly aware of the contact. Gently, she extricated her fingers from his grasp and lauded the frank candor with which he had shared his ordeal. She was being satirical, and although she had meant for the words to ring with sincerity, sarcasm seeped in. In a bid to hide her error, she added she was grateful for his honesty. But that only made it worse, for now she sounded bitter.

Pressing her lips together to forestall further comment, she stared blankly at Hardwicke. It was another retreat, which struck her as vaguely cowardly, but she would not undermine the effectiveness of Verity Lark, version 2, by questioning her methods.

If he suspected he had made a misstep in his treatment of her—and that description was, she allowed, a vast understatement—he did not reveal it as he begged her to tell him everything. "How the devil did you wind up at the embassy and who the devil is Dupont and why did someone break into your bedchamber? You have kept me in suspense long enough."

But Verity, from whom Hardwicke had withheld vital information for four days, thought he could stew in his curiosity for at least another hour. Glancing outside the window, she said, "We are so close to Bethel Street now, I think it would be better if we waited 'til we arrived at my home. That way, Delphine and Freddie can provide their perspectives, which will give you as complete a picture as possible. I would not want unintentionally to leave something out."

Was the delay petty?

Yes, absolutely.

But there was nothing she could do.

Verity would Verity.

# Chapter Six

*Friday, June 12*
*4:51 p.m.*

To pass the time as they waited for Freddie and Delphine to return, Verity read excerpts from *Mrs. Meacham's Book of Household Management, Including Sections on Cookery, Cleaning, and Plant Rearing*, specifically the gardening passages that addressed how to thwart common pests such as mice and snails. It only seemed appropriate, as her friend had borrowed the book from the lending library at the urging of his lordship himself.

"I did not 'urge' Miss Drayton to borrow it, per se," Hardwicke corrected as Lucy carried in the tea tray. "I merely suggested she take a look at it if her squirrel problem persisted, as my mother has found it helpful in dealing with rats."

"Ah, so it was at the marchioness's urging," Verity said with a knowing nod. "I stand corrected. Anyway, as Mrs. Meacham was saying before you rudely interrupted: 'Multiple growing seasons have endeared me to the benefits of manure, which are manifold, and covering your garden with a heavy coating of manure in the winter will enrich your soil. When soil is rich, it is resistant to droughts and produces great yields. An abundant harvest is vital because insects are encouraged by feeble vegetation.'"

Raising her eyes from the book, Verity said, "Oh, dear, Delphine will not appreciate the charge of feebleness. She prides herself on robust plants."

"That is the prescription for insects, not squirrels," Hardwicke observed, advising her to continue reading. "I am sure Mrs. Meacham has more wisdom to share than simply to spread cow dung over your crops."

"How right you are!" Verity said with a bemused shake of her head. "Do forgive me for doubting your wisdom—or, rather, the marchioness's."

Hardwicke duly promised to convey her apologies to his mother in a somber tone that revealed no resentment of her treatment. But he knew her aim was to torment him with dizzying mundanities. Arriving at number twenty-six, she had professed herself astonished to find Delphine away from home, remembering only belatedly that her friend had gone to the newspaper office with Freddie.

"For her own protection," she had added darkly.

Hardwicke resisted this tantalizing tidbit, however, owning himself delighted to be in her company regardless of the circumstance. In response, she had reached for the weighty tome on household management, which was sitting on the sideboard.

She would show him delighted.

Despite her efforts, he appeared to be just that, exhorting her to continue with her reading, which made her want to put the book down with a thud. It was so very dull.

She resisted, of course, for that was exactly what he

wanted her to do. As always, he recognized the game she was playing and somehow knew the moves better than she.

Flipping ahead several pages, Verity picked a random paragraph and began reading. "Of the many methods for eliminating the terrestrial pulmonate gastropods that routinely make short work of my cabbage plants, all of which I address here, I find a vinegar-water solution to be the most propitious," she said, the deep frown between her brows lightening as she noticed the drawing at the bottom of the page. She turned the book outward so he too could see. "Ah, she is talking about slugs. Gastropods are slugs! Isn't gardening fascinating?"

Hardwicke, agreeing it was remarkable the things one learned, asked how many parts water to vinegar Mrs. Meacham recommended for her marvelous formulation.

As Verity shared the recipe, which also called for a tincture of salt, she glanced at the clock and thought Delphine and Freddie should return within the half hour. She dearly hoped so because she was bored to flinders.

*Friday, June 12*
*5:49 p.m.*

As Verity did not have the time to write her friends a detailed letter about all that had transpired that afternoon, her message said only that Hardwicke was at the house to discuss recent ominous events at the French embassy. As a consequence, they knew nothing of his lordship's insulting treatment, an oversight she sought to remedy the moment they set foot in the front parlor. Slamming the stultifying compendium on household affairs shut, she clasped the book in her arms as she rose to her feet and announced that she had encountered Hardwicke quite by chance on the pavement outside the embassy. "He was there investigating his own mystery. You see, several attempts have been made on his life in recent days —do not worry, he has come through them swimmingly!—and the trail he was following led him there as well," she explained, looking Delphine and Freddie in the eyes before adding with particular emphasis. "That is why he canceled our outing to Gunter's. He was worried about my safety."

Understanding was instant.

The anxiety both friends immediately felt for Hardwicke's safety was supplanted by impatience at the display of typical male conduct. Freddie drew his brows together in a moue of concern while Delphine darted an irritated glare at Hardwicke, who should have known better than try to protect Verity without informing her of the situation or gaining her consent. What was the point of his saying with unsettling sobriety that he was prepared to commit to anything if he was in fact not prepared to commit to dealing with her honestly? If Verity required one thing in a husband, it was absolute trust.

An impossibly lofty goal for marriage, to be sure, but then Delphine had never imagined her friend would contemplate holy matrimony with any man. She valued her freedom too much to submit to another.

And why should she?

She had spent the first seventeen years of her life under the crushing bootheel of the Wraithe and the next six chained to the scullery. Sloughing off the twin yokes of poverty and servility had required all her ingenuity, and she would never clip her own wings for a fleeting passion or even an enduring regard.

But that was what was so remarkable about Colson Hardwicke. Inconceivably, he was cut from the same cloth as

Verity—as unnervingly astute, as disconcertingly capable, as dauntingly reckless, as wildly practical. Possessing these traits himself, he seemed to have respect for Verity's proficiency and sincere affection for her mad starts.

He would not chastise her for jumping on the footboard of a moving carriage.

Or so Delphine had thought.

It seemed, however, that she had failed to take his full measure, for the man she had believed him to be would never have made such a cork-brained blunder.

Trying to protect Verity from danger!

He might as well have called her "dearie" and sent her to bed early.

Worst of all, he had denied Verity the respect of allowing *her* to worry about *him,* something she did with vigor and sincerity.

Thoroughly annoyed, Delphine shook her head and turned to Verity to offer a consolatory word. As she did, she noticed Mrs. Meacham's hefty tome in her friend's grasp and realized the situation was even more dire than she had suspected if Verity had resorted to seeking domestic advice. "Whatever are you doing with that book, which you described as insipidness in written form?"

Avidly, Verity replied that she and Hardwicke had been learning all about gastropods. "The author has a wondrous concoction that disperses the ghastly creatures with just a light sprinkling."

"The solution causes them to melt," Delphine explained with a hint of disapproval in her tone, for Mrs. Meacham had failed to mention that alarming detail while extolling the virtues of her homemade blend. "If you have a slug problem, I advise you instead to make shelters for them by laying out scraps of burlap. They detest the sunlight and will eagerly seek out the shade for slumber during the day. Then you just gather up the cloths with the slugs attached and toss them away."

Although Verity had been certain her friends would comprehend the depth of the slight, she had not anticipated such an ardent show of support. Fervently, she thanked Delphine for the helpful clarification and asked Freddie if perhaps the *Gazette* should not publish a corrective to Mrs. Meacham's book. "If she is advocating for the wholesale liquification of gastropods without disclosing that information, who knows what else she is hiding from her readers."

Freddie, hailing it an excellent suggestion, proposed Oakenbottom to write it, as he frequently contributed literary reviews to the newspaper, and Verity glanced at Hardwicke out of the corner of her eye to see how he was receiving these trivialities. By all measures, he appeared unbothered and patient, his features smooth as he listened to the exchange. Verity was tempted to try him further by opening to a random page and asking Delphine to offer an opinion on its accuracy, but she was too eager to hear about the murder attempts to prolong his agony.

Delphine proposed an ongoing series, for she had problems with several books devoted to the care and upkeep of the home, such as *Advice on Domestic Supervision* by Mr. Gardner, whose method for cleaning cotton would render any number of chemises unwearable. Although she could spend the next half hour taking issue with the author's various prescriptions, she dipped her head apologetically as she turned to Hardwicke. "But this is all neither here nor there! I am sorry to hear you have been subjected to murder attempts, Lord Colson. How distressing for you! I hope there were not very many?"

Calmly, he replied that there had been five.

Clearly daunted by the number, which was several more than she was expecting, Delphine looked at Verity in concern.

"It is too far-fetched to think these attempts and our late-night intruder are merely a coincidence, isn't it? They must be related."

"Thank you, yes, Miss Drayton," Hardwicke said firmly, as if he had been waiting for precisely this opportunity to take control of the conversation. "Miss Lark did not want to discuss the topic without your and Mr. Somerset Reade's invaluable input and now I see why, for you have a keen understanding. I also believe the two events are related. The men who pursued me without success switched their focus to Miss Lark on the assumption that she would be an easier mark. That she and I have spent a considerable amount of time together in recent days has not gone unnoticed, and I assume they thought they could gain control of my actions by gaining control of hers."

Did it sting for Verity to discover she had been endangered by proxy?

Not even a little bit, no.

If anything, she admired the assailant's pragmatic approach to an intractable problem, for Hardwicke was not an easy man to kill and singling out the woman whom he was courting was a rational decision. She must have looked like an appealing target indeed, with her pretty pink dress and the lovely bonnet with its extravagant plumage that Delphine shoved into her hands as she was striding toward the door. Even her height seemed dainty in comparison to Hardwicke's tall frame. Watching them together, the killers would have no reason to expect a challenge from her, especially if they observed her simpering in Lord Goldhawk's presence. Initially confused by the introduction, she had held herself back at first, unwilling to engage in a situation she did not fully comprehend.

To an outsider, of course, it would have looked like insipidity.

Freddie, concurring with Hardwicke's assessment, nodded and said it explained one of the more puzzling aspects of the incident. "The intruder had said something to that effect, although I do not recall the precise words."

"'We will get him in the end,'" Verity quoted.

"Yes, that was it," he affirmed with a nod. "Get him in the end. We assumed he was talking about Robert, which was a logical conclusion given the information available to us at the time. We even thought it might refer to Twaddle, although that seemed considerably less likely because nobody knows who he is. But then we found out the intruder was a secretary at the French embassy and were thoroughly dumbfounded. Neither Robert nor Twaddle has written anything so incendiary about the French people as to provoke a violent response."

Smiling faintly, Delphine insisted it was true. "I have spent the entire day sifting through old issues of the newspaper to find an offending article and there is nothing. Twaddle's Bonapartisan sketches are more cutting than I remember, especially after Napoleon escaped Elba, but not so vicious as to incite retaliation."

Hardwicke raised his chin as he looked at Verity to confirm the intelligence. "Dupont was a secretary at the embassy?"

Delphine turned to him sharply. "What do you mean he *was* a secretary? Did something happen to Mr. Dupont? Verity, please do not tell me Dupont is dead."

Her friend, unable to comply, broke the news as succinctly as possible. "Dupont is dead."

"For God's sake, Verity!" Delphine cried.

Bristling with defensiveness, Verity insisted there was no reason for her friend to be angry with her about it. "*I* did not kill the man, as Hardwicke can attest."

"It is true," Hardwicke replied mildly. "She was standing

directly beneath Dupont as he hurtled three stories to his death."

Alas, this evidence, although exculpatory, did little to soothe Delphine, who found her friend's placement *in the path* of a falling victim to be somehow worse.

"Here, let us talk about it calmly," Verity said, gesturing to the settee as she crossed the room to return Mrs. Meacham's compendium to the sideboard. "There is nothing to be gained by getting upset. Do let me pour you a cup of tea, Delph. The brew Freddie keeps on hand at the *Gazette*'s office is intolerably weak, for he uses only a few leaves at a time. It is little wonder you are churlish."

Although Delphine took issue with both the description and its attempt to minimize her concerns, she did allow that the tea could stand to be slightly stronger. Freddie, who had withstood this criticism before, most frequently from Verity but occasionally from other journalists on the staff, replied that it was an unavoidable economy. Tea was not without its costs, and being judicious in his portioning was the only way he could afford to provide it at no charge.

Amused, Verity noted that *judicious* was a judicious way to say "miserly." Then she poured tea and handed Delphine the saucer. "There, darling, now do let us be rational about all this. I am sure I have played a role in a whole host of calamities over the years, but in this one I am blameless. Recall, if you will, that I was lying in my bed when Dupont attacked. I know you like to accuse me of Veritying, but there is nothing more Delphinish than sleeping in your own bedchamber."

"Of course the attack was not your fault," Delphine said waspishly. "I am not a ninny to blame you for that! But I can hold you responsible for everything that happened after you disarmed him. Tying him up in the cellar and allowing him to escape so you could follow him was a madcap scheme. I urged you to give him over to Lord Colson to handle."

Solemnly, Hardwicke said, "Thank you."

Delphine regarded him coolly over the edge of her teacup. "Of course, I did not know you were contending with your own difficulties at the time."

Blandly stated, it was nevertheless a cutting rebuke, and Verity had the pleasure of watching a vaguely stunned expression flicker across Hardwicke's features before they assumed their usual impassivity.

Verity, not wishing to appear to share Delphine's outrage, replied that shadowing their intruder to discover more about him was a sensible plan, for if they knew nothing of his intentions, then they could do nothing to guard against them. Then she turned to Hardwicke and gave him a general overview of the attack and the events that followed. "As Dupont was an ineffectual and incompetent kidnapper, I assume it was his first outing. Although he worked for the Ministry of the Police for five years, it was as a clerk. That was during the comte's tenure as minister, and there is some speculation among his colleagues that their prior association is why he was promoted to secretary so quickly. As for who his fellow plotters are, I have yet to figure that out. As I said, he reported directly to his superior, Guillaume Beaufoy, after leaving our cellar, and met compatriots at a tavern after work. Any of them could be part of the plot. Or none of them. Or any of the dozen colleagues he interacted with during the day."

Hardwicke, noting the wide range of suspects, asked what she had learned when she returned to the building after the murder. Delphine pressed her lips together in disapproval of the reckless behavior but otherwise refrained from comment.

Verity launched into a description of the chaotic scene she had encountered in Dupont's office: the various members of the embassy staff all talking at once and staring in horror at Dupont's corpse splayed on the pavement, convinced—or purporting to be convinced—that the secretary had thrown himself out of the window.

Then she related the information she had discovered, noting that Beaufoy must be considered a suspect because he was the person Dupont had run to from the cellar. "But I don't think I can eliminate any of the first half dozen men to enter the room. At the same time, it would be foolhardy to assume the murderer remained behind to gawk or admire his handiwork. Although Farrow did not see anyone else in the hallway, the killer might have darted into another office before anyone caught sight of him or he might have hidden behind the door and slipped out during the hubbub. I could not inspect the hallway because the ambassador was returning to the building and I did not want him to see me. I had interviewed him earlier in the day, so he knew me as a reporter and would not have taken kindly to my interrogating his staff about Dupont's death, even if it was not murder."

Now Freddie was the one who gasped. "John Pennie interviewed the Comte de Morny?"

Preening in delight at the eagerness in his voice, Verity said Pennie had conducted a seventy-five minute interview with his excellency, the comte. "But I must caution you against getting too excited by the prospect because he was not among the most interesting subjects Pennie has ever interviewed. He tended to ramble. That said, I did get enough fodder to cobble together several gossip items. And you must not be alarmed if Twaddle seems unduly focused on macarons. He is merely going where the story led."

Freddie, owning himself untroubled by any of the prattler's fixations—and here he made specific reference to the consuming lighthouse lamp interest of 1809—asked if the *London Daily Gazette* could run the interview under Pennie's headline. "Or must he remain at *The Times*?"

Verity felt strongly that the reporter's sycophancy suited

the other paper too well for him to consider a move at the moment. "But I did not get the sense that Morny cared enough about me to learn my name. I think I can send a gracious note thanking him for his time using a name similar —Jo Penford, for example—and he won't know any differently. I am sure he did not hold on to my card."

"Excellent!" Freddie said with satisfaction, then immediately apologized to Hardwicke for the lengthy digression. "I am sure you could not care less about the minutiae of the *London Daily Gazette*."

"On the contrary, I hang on Mr. Twaddle-Thum's every word like most of London and cannot wait to learn more about his macaron fascination," Hardwicke assured him.

Nevertheless, Freddie urged his lordship to tell them what he was doing while Verity was inside the embassy questioning the staff.

"Presumably, searching Dupont's body," Verity said matter-of-factly. "He would have had several seconds to find evidence before the crowd gathered."

"That is correct," Hardwicke replied.

"And did you find evidence?" Delphine asked.

Before Hardwicke could reply, Freddie interjected to request that his lordship start at the beginning so that all parties present in the room could know the whole story. "I find it disorienting to jump into an account in the middle. Perhaps you could tell us when the first attempt on your life was made."

If Hardwicke registered the second rebuke—stated even more blandly than Delphine's but equally critical—he displayed no awareness of it as he cited Saturday, June seventh, as the date of the initial attack. "But I did not realize it was an attack. The leather strap on my saddle gave way, nearly sending me crashing to the ground, where I would have almost certainly been trampled under the hooves of other horses, as it was a busy morning on the Row. I managed to hold my seat and rein in Titus before I lost control. My groom was beside himself with distress at his oversight, but it was an old saddle that needed replacing, which Barnes himself had been telling me for months, so I did not think two thoughts about it."

Verity allowed it was a reasonable conclusion to draw, as the straps on a saddle tended to wear away slowly over time and then all at once as the leather grew thin enough to snap. The assassin had probably chosen the method because he noticed the buckles were in sufficient disrepair for the tear to appear natural.

Hardwicke continued, explaining that the second attempt was also made to look like a stroke of bad luck: The axel on his gig broke in half, and although this time he did suffer injuries—bruised ribs, a scraped shoulder—none of them were life threatening. "Arranging two accidents in two days, however, was a significant misstep because it alerted me to the threat. I may be an indifferent caretaker, but the men I employ are not. They are meticulous in their duties, and it was simply too difficult to believe that two items under their care would break in rapid succession. Barnes set about proving both were intentional and by the time I returned from my drive in Hyde Park with Miss Lark on Monday after-noon, he had evidence. At that point, however, I no longer required it because the culprit, impatient with subtlety, shot at me in my gig. The bullet pierced the back cushion several inches from my head, precisely where Miss Lark was sitting."

If Hardwicke thought this near miss would be a miti-gating factor in his favor, he was not entirely wrong. Gasping, Delphine reached out to grab Verity's forearm as if the assassin himself had just pounded furiously at the door, and Freddie flinched. Verity appreciated the immediacy of their response, for she herself felt the strange presence of a looming menace. A quiver of alarm shuddered through her even as she called herself a fool for indulging a quiver of alarm.

Nothing had happened.

No attempts on her life had been made.

Hardwicke could speak with all the implacable stoicism he wanted, but it would never alter the fact that she had not been in the carriage. The assailant held his fire.

Later, yes, she was in undeniable peril.

But in that moment, before the attacker decided to change tack, she had been as safe as an infant in its mother's arms, and she would not allow Hardwicke to convince her to fear a phantom. Whatever self-justifying argument about her safety he intended to make, it could not nullify one simple truth: He had put her at greater risk. By withholding the information about her own safety, he had increased the danger to her and the women who resided with her in Bethel Street.

And he only withheld it because she herself was a woman.

Despite her long list of accomplishments, many of which he had claimed to be in awe—fending off a massacre, bounding down the stairs in that rundown house in Mantle Street pretending to be an infantry, enlisting the help of the Duke of Kesgrave—she had been shoved to the margins of the story as resolutely as Flora Hyde-Clare had been consigned by her beau, Holcroft the Holy.

It was so galling she could almost not speak.

Except she could.

Verity Lark always had something to say.

Tilting her head to the side in a pose of underwhelmed curiosity, she asked about the other two attempts. "I believe you said there were five?"

Fury flashed in his eyes, hot and fierce, the baffling,

gorgeous teal almost igniting at her cool appraisal, at her dispassionate response to his chilling revelation.

Had he actually expected anything else?

After all the time he had spent in her company, did he honestly believe she was so lacking in pluck and audacity that she would cry out in terror at a hypothetical threat?

Was that truly the image he held of her?

The anger was gone as quickly as it appeared, and Hardwicke regarded her with the same sort of bland disinterest she had shown. "You are correct, Miss Lark. I said there were five. Someone took another shot at me on Tuesday morning, then they pushed me in front of an oncoming carriage in the evening. There have been no attempts since then, which I attributed to the fact that I had begun to investigate by visiting my old haunts and the would-be killer decided it was wise to remain out of sight while my interest was keen. I assumed he would try again in a few weeks. It was not an outlandish conclusion based on the circumstance," he added stiffly before acknowledging that it appeared now as though the man had instead changed his strategy.

Delphine released her grip on Verity's arm and leaned forward in her seat. "I do not understand. Why would someone seek to hurt you now, so long after the end of the war? Wasn't your work for the Alien Office done out in the open? By all accounts you were a disgraced wastrel happy to gather coins in whatever way possible with no care of whose interests it served, and everyone knew it. So why would someone decide all of a sudden that you had worked against the French cause in a systematic and significant way? It simply does not make any sense."

"But it does!" insisted Freddie, placing his teacup on the table with a loud clatter. "Think about it, Delph. The Alien Office is too astute to go through the bother of placing a man in a valuable position and not making further use of him, which means not *all* of Hardwicke's work was done out in the open. The dissolute son without two pence to rub together was more than just flimflam; it was a purposeful distraction. Like a magician performing a trick, he gave his audience of French émigrés something shiny to watch while he switched the boxes under the table."

Hardwicke confirmed this speculation with an abrupt nod.

"So not just an agent provocateur but a spy as well," Delphine murmured thoughtfully. "Yes, I can see why someone might harbor resentment against you."

Although he darted a glance at Verity, Hardwicke nonetheless kept his attention on Delphine as he acknowledged her comment with a self-conscious shrug. "As you observed, Miss Drayton, I operated in broad daylight as a drunken ne'er-do-well who would do anything for a few coins. To be useful I had to have access to information, and among the various sources I cultivated in my quest to be useful was an operative high up in the English government known by the secret name Typhoeus. It was Typhoeus who provided me with some of the most sensitive information. The dispatches detailing the shabby state of our army that I sold to the French were from Typhoeus, and when the papers proved to be forged, I was not held accountable because I was a jug-bitten flibbertigibbet who did not know his knee from his nose. They blamed Typhoeus."

"And you are Typhoeus," Delphine said.

"I am Typhoeus," Hardwicke replied.

"The father of all monsters," Verity observed softly, unaccountably annoyed at herself for not suspecting that the play was deeper. As soon as she learned the truth about the signet ring, she should have made the same deductive leap as Freddie because the Alien Office *was* too calculating not to wring every ounce of use out of one of its operatives. It was so obvious in retrospect, and yet she had made no attempt to find additional layers of secrecy because a second son deliberately tarnishing his good name in service of his country struck her as sufficiently covert.

That was true, yes, but a more significant factor in her oversight was the indignation she had felt at discovering how effortlessly Hardwicke had exploited Twaddle to achieve his ruination. She had fallen in line with his plan like an obedient little soldier.

Amused by her observation, Hardwicke turned to Verity and explained that he had nothing to do with selecting the nickname. "Grint assigned all of them, and although I was insulted to be compared to a fire-breathing giant with coils of vipers for legs and demon eyes, I knew better than to complain. One fellow grumbled about being called Charybdis, for she was the daughter of Pontus and Gaia, and Grint changed it to Scylla, who was a nymph."

He wanted her to smile in return.

It was there, in the way he looked at her, his strange gaze alight with levity.

Instead, she kept her expression blank as she reviewed what she knew and arrived at the obvious answer. "It was your identity as Typhoeus that Kingsley revealed. That is why you are suddenly a target."

Delphine inhaled sharply. "Why would he do such a horrible thing?"

But Freddie did not find it shocking at all. "You humiliated him, destroyed his credibility, and had him removed from his post. This was his reprisal."

"Hardwicke did not have Kingsley removed from his post," Verity snapped impatiently. "Kingsley did that all on his own by being flagrantly incompetent at his job. Allowing a man with his intellectual limitations to remain in a position of national importance was reckless and irresponsible. Sidmouth knew it and acted accordingly."

A spark of pleasure lit Hardwicke's eyes at her ready defense of him, and although he had misunderstood the source of her irritation, she knew better than to clarify. Any attempt to point to her deep disgust for the former undersecretary would merely sound to him as though she were protesting too much.

Instead, she remained silent as Hardwicke credited Verity with Kingsley's removal. "If she had not secured the Duke of Kesgrave's support, then Kingsley would still be inadequately performing his duties. Sidmouth, however, was mortified to have his subordinate's shortcomings displayed before a man whom he considers his equal, and he had to do something to prove he did not allow fools to run tame in his department. Regardless of how it was managed, Kingsley responded to his lowered status by swigging a bottle of excellent brandy and babbling Typhoeus's identity to half of Petty France."

"It is abominable, and I hope he is thrown into Newgate for what he did," Delphine said fervently, then almost immediately softened her stance, for she would never wish that torment on anybody. "But there must be some consequence for his actions. One cannot be allowed to go around blabbing the country's most vital secrets."

"Except when Twaddle does it," Verity added wryly.

Her friend told her not to be absurd. "The prince regent's spending habits are not state secrets. The very opposite, in fact, for we pay for his excesses with our taxes, and we have the right to know what our money buys."

"Do not tell me, Miss Drayton, that I am in the presence of an anti-royalist," Hardwicke said with an air of feigned dismay.

"The divine right of kings is drivel!" she replied.

"And I thought the Yarwellians were radicals," he said with a regretful shake of his head.

Delphine laughed at this nonsense, then immediately remembered she was peeved at his lordship for ruining everything by daring to coddle Verity. To return the conversation to a more businesslike footing, she asked how he had figured out Dupont was the culprit.

Verity rolled her eyes and swore the secretary had nothing to do with the attempts on Hardwicke's life. "He was as incompetent as Kingsley."

"Well, he did fail five times," Delphine pointed out reasonably. "Six times if you count the attempt against you. That seems in line with his skills and abilities. You can see him growing increasingly frantic as he changed his methodology, from making it look like an accident to getting close enough to Lord Colson to shove him."

Unable to refute the logic, Verity remained convinced the kidnapping was too slapdash to be anything but Dupont's only strike. "Any man who had tried and failed to kill Hardwicke five times before would have learned something from his botched attempts."

"Yes," Delphine said agreeably. "To find an easier victim."

"Fair enough," Verity conceded and turned to Hardwicke in expectation.

With an apologetic glance at Delphine, he admitted that the first he had learned of Dupont was the moment his shoulders tipped out of the window to hurl toward Miss Lark. "Given the little you have told me of your encounter with him, I would hazard he was killed by a confederate who considered him a loose thread to be snipped. You say he escaped from your cellar? If so, then his associates would have been worried that Dupont could be recognized, which would lead the trail back to him. And he would not have been wrong, as he could and it did."

"But Dupont did not know that," Delphine said sadly, relating in detail Verity's elaborate show of female ineptitude. "She all but convinced him he had captured himself."

"Somehow I do not think that is the report he gave to his superior," Verity replied.

"Be that as it may, I do not know why we must be in such a rush to call it murder," Delphine said. "It could be suicide like his colleagues believe. Maybe *he* feared being recognized and decided to end it rather than live in constant terror."

"It won't wash, Delph," Verity said sadly.

"It won't indeed," Hardwicke added. "He was pushed. I saw the hands."

At this stunning revelation, Verity swiveled her head. "You did?"

"Briefly, yes, but it was only a flash. I cannot describe any identifying features," he said before she could ask for a description of the murderer. "And to clarify an earlier point: I was at the French embassy to call on Morny, with whom I met on multiple occasions when he made secret overtures to Sidmouth when he was Lord President of the Council. I found him to be sly and untrustworthy but informative. I did not have a chance to speak to him, however, because as I was nearing the entrance to the embassy, Miss Lark swept by me on her way out. Her shoulder came just short of brushing mine."

It was, Verity thought, a scurrilous charge, for she knew herself to be highly aware of her surroundings at all times. The core principle of Twaddling was astute observation.

Nothing could be known if nothing was seen.

And yet the truth was, she *had* been distracted as she left the building. After detaining her for more than an hour, the comte had arranged for a porter to escort her from the premises, and her mind had been busy trying to figure out another way to approach Beaufoy. If she had indeed come within an inch or two of Hardwicke without noticing, it was a combination of those two factors.

Even so, the oversight was mortifying.

"It was your shoes," Hardwicke said, deepening her embarrassment because he had warned her before about the revealing nature of her footwear. "If you are wondering how I recognized you, Miss Lark, it was your shoes."

Was he gloating?

Almost certainly, yes, she decided.

And with good reason.

She had even recalled his exhortation that morning as she was throwing off her dress and donning Pennie's blue waist-coat. The reminder was the reason she had donned the new pair, which looked exactly like the old except for the lack of scuff marks and tears.

"Seeing Miss Lark, I immediately changed course to follow her," he continued in that same maddening tone, an evenhanded timber that lacked inflection and yet still managed to convey superiority. "She went to the side of the building, her head tilted upward toward the higher floors. I looked up as well, and a movement in one of the windows on the top floor caught my attention. As I was watching, the body pitched backward over the sill, and I saw the danger to Miss Lark at once. I ran over, pushing her out of the path and knocking her to the ground. My treatment was rough because I acted without thinking, and I hope you will accept my apology for the harm I caused you."

To her great dismay, Verity felt on the verge of blushing, for it was a further humiliation: to be thought so fragile that a small shove to the pavement would hurt her.

It was, she supposed, the least she deserved.

After all, she had subjected him to sixty-eight minutes of gastropod management.

Freddie—dear, darling Freddie—scoffed at his lordship's

concern and said Verity had taken worst spills on her own doorstep. "There was the time the flower seller in Covent Garden followed Lucy home because he was sweet on her, and you chased him off with the broom. But then you realized Mr. Loewe was climbing out of a hack and launched yourself into a somersault over the handle of the broom."

"The secret to a successful tumble is tucking in your shoulders and staying limber," Verity said with a placid smile.

"Why?" Hardwicke asked.

"I suppose because stiffening one's body makes it more brittle," she replied, deliberately misunderstanding the question.

"Miss Lark is notoriously clumsy," Delphine explained. "She cannot take two steps without tripping over her own feet. All the neighbors think it is a sad pity that poor Robert will forever be saddled with the girl, who is as shy as she is graceless. The situation is so hopeless, they have stopped inviting us to their houses for tea and all but Mrs. Green have given up on arranging a match for Robert."

The various ways they managed their neighbors was a rich topic that could fuel hours of conversation, and Verity, sensing Hardwicke's interest, preempted further discussion by asking him what his examination of Dupont's body had revealed. "You had more than enough time to do a thorough search."

Hardwicke noted that the horde of onlookers descended with remarkable speed, for there had been a great many people already milling about the area when Dupont had taken his plunge. Despite the crowd, he had been able to make his inspection under the guise of checking the victim for injuries. "His pockets were empty, but I found a scrap of paper in his hand. He must have clutched it during the fall," he said, producing the fragment and handing it to Verity without her asking. "As you can see, it was ripped from a larger page."

Verity placed the crumpled sheet on the table next to the tea tray and ran her hand over it to smooth its wrinkled surface. It was a corner piece, with two rough edges, and the majority of the words were truncated by the tear, leaving less than half of the original information available to her. Even so, she tried to make sense of the remnant, which contained two incomplete words and four sets of numbers. In order, from top to bottom, it read: 41, ghe, smit, 930, 60/a, 4/we.

Presented with an intriguing puzzle, her mind immediately began trying to make sense of it and she noticed at once the familiarity of the three letters: ghe. Just a small number of words in the English language began g-h-e, and of the few she could call to mind, only one matched the name of a street she had passed last night and again that morning en route to the Dupont residence. It would be foolish, of course, to limit herself to the English language, for there were several French surnames that started with those assortment—Ghesquière, Gherardi, Gherbi, Ghenimi—and she could think of foreign words like *ghee* and far-off cities such as Ghent.

Even with these options, she could not stop herself from settling on the most obvious interpretation: Gherkin Lane. From there, it was easy enough to identify the other information, for forty-one must be the number of the house and s-m-i-t the name of the person Dupont was to meet there at nine-thirty, presumably in the morning. The other numbers were slightly harder to decipher, but Verity thought the price of the home—60 guinea per annum—was a logical guess for the first one. The second number was perhaps a salary, with the /we indicating a weekly sum.

Although hardly conclusive, these speculations were pretty good for an initial effort, and confident she had a partial understanding of what she saw, Verity arranged her features in a perplexed expression. Looking up at Hardwicke, she professed herself confounded by the scrap and asked what he thought it could mean.

"I understand as much as you, Miss Lark," he replied.

With her brow deeply furrowed, she handed the rumpled slip to Freddie and lamented the fact that so many words began q-u-e. Then she paused to allow Hardwicke to point out that the descender curved to the left, not right.

Naturally, he did not.

Given his low estimation of her abilities, she was not at all surprised when he accepted her misapprehension without comment and rattled off a list of likely prospects: queen, queue, quest. She considered responding with a catalogue of her own (questionable, quench, queasy) to provide further obfuscation but found herself curiously reluctant to continue the exchange. The fact that he believed her to be such a clunch as to mistake a *g* for a *q* was more disheartening than she had expected, and she thanked him for sharing the intelligence he had gathered before inviting him to leave.

It was on the tip of her tongue to offer a simpering comment about being worthy of his trust, but the words rang bitterly in her ears even before she said them. Consequently, she offered a banality about the weather instead, cautioning him to travel safely in the rain.

Finding nothing strange in this retreat to civil dullness—dear God, would the insults never stop?—Hardwicke took his last swallow of tea, owned himself grateful for the hospitality, and rose to his feet. He promised to apprise her of any further developments in the case and advised her to be careful going forward. "With Dupont's death, I believe the threat against you has increased, not lessened."

Owning herself much gratified by his concern, Verity all but shoved him out of the house.

# Chapter Seven

Saturday, June 13
8:41 a.m.

Delphine was so infuriated by Hardwicke's treatment of Verity, she was still seething about it the next day at breakfast. As she selected a slice of gammon from the plate, she shook her head and murmured, "He Holyed you."

Verity, in the act of raising a cup of steaming tea to her lips, affirmed the statement by repeating it. "He Holyed me."

"I cannot fathom what he was thinking!" Delphine grumbled angrily. "Remember when we were alarmed by his astuteness? He seemed so very clever, figuring out your identity as Twaddle and then discovering where you lived. And now we find he is naught but a great blistering clodpole like all the rest."

"Well, he is a man," Verity replied with an air of tolerant resignation. "We cannot expect them to exceed the limitations of their sex. They see a woman and assume her to be

helpless in the face of danger regardless of how much competence she displays."

Freddie, who had slept again in the parlor out of concern for
his friends, insisted Verity was being a bit harsh. "I agree Hardwicke should not have shunted you to the side as though you
were not fully capable of looking after yourself, especially after
being made aware of the danger, but I think we can allow him a
little latitude for the way fear might have corroded his judgment.
The bullet going precisely where Verity was sitting must have
been unsettling," he said, then startled slightly when Delphine
dropped the serving fork loudly onto the plate and stared at him
with a gimlet eye. Turning briefly to Verity, he observed the same
expression and promptly amended his stance. "He Holyed you!"

Delphine nodded in approval. "You know I do not wish to
speak ill of any person, but it is particularly insulting to our
dear Verity to receive the very same treatment as a girl of
Flora Hyde-Clare's ilk. She is barely twenty years of age and
as flighty as a feather! A day-old kitten deserves more
respect!"

Soberly, Verity thanked her for her support. "I know your
disappointment is markedly worse because of your high
expectations. You actually believed Hardwicke was about to
propose marriage."

"I still believe it," Delphine said with blithe certainty as
she raised a knife to cut the ham. "Even if his brother disap-
proved of the match, which I do not think he did, he would
not allow it to stand in his way. The reason for my marked
disappointment is I know you will never accept him now."

Verity, driving her fork into the gammon like a spear, did
not appreciate the confidence in her friend's tone, for none of
them knew the truth about Hardwicke's intentions and it was
galling to hear Delphine speak of the matter as though it
were settled business. Delphine did not have privileged access

to the man's thoughts, and even if she did, the information was still utterly irrelevant. "I would never have accepted him *then*."

"Why not?" Freddie asked mildly.

Annoyed to be pressed on a hypothetical, Verity placed the knife onto the table, lowered her arms to her side, and said calmly, "As shocking as it might be, I must inform you that Delphine's conviction does not make something true. It was not marriage that Hardwicke had in mind. You must trust me on this, for if there is one thing I learned from La Reina it is the way gentlemen perceive women of a lower order."

But Freddie, who was willing to concede the accuracy of her statement, insisted they proceed for the sake of discussion from the assumption that Delphine was correct. "As an exercise, I mean. Why not accept an offer of marriage from Hardwicke?"

Verity smiled faintly as she glanced around the room. "And give up all this?"

It sounded glib, the way she asked the question, the way her gaze happened to land on the most threadbare items in need of replacing: the settee, the curtains, the rug. Even the sideboard was worn from repeated knocks with the chair.

But she meant it in the sincerest way possible.

*All this* was so much more than she had ever dared to imagine, and it did not encompass just the things that surrounded her or the house that contained them. It was freedom and self-determination and the ability to do whatever she wanted with her time, including doing nothing at all with it. (To be sure, she had never availed herself of that last option, but it was there, it existed.)

That she had anything of her own was a marvel.

That she—the cast-off daughter of a lightskirt raised in

misery and deprivation—had so much was a small, tiny miracle she would never take for granted.

Surrendering it to Hardwicke on the gossamer promise of love?

That would indeed be holding it cheaply.

Freddie knew all that, for there was very little about her heart that he did not fully comprehend, and suggested—just for the sake of argument, you understand—that she would not be giving anything up if Hardwicke proved worthy of her trust.

As the point was moot, she readily granted it. In the highly specific circumstance he described, she might be able to look at marriage as an opportunity to gain something, not lose everything. "But Hardwicke has already fallen short of the ideal. He cut me out at the exact moment he should have sought my assistance. The fact is, he did not trust me to handle myself, and by not trusting me, he put me, Delphine, Lucy, and Cook directly in harm's way. I find both unforgivable but especially the latter."

Seeing no way around this implacable truth, Freddie sighed heavily and turned to Delphine to ask if she planned to spend the day in the *Gazette*'s offices again. "Verity is right about the danger. We do not know enough about the plot to kill Hardwicke to lower our guards just yet."

Delphine, citing the inferior quality of the tea available at the establishment on the Strand, announced that she would rather take her chances at home with potential kidnappers. "Dupont was bumbling. Perhaps his replacement will be as well."

"I know you are teasing me," Freddie said with a slight frown. "But I am willing to make a concession. If you come with me to the Strand, I will add an extra half spoonful of leaves to the pot."

Delphine gasped. "Not a *full* half teaspoon!"

Ignoring the mockery, Freddie increased his offer to a whole teaspoon.

"Heaping, I hope," Delphine replied.

Muttering about profligate spending and the challenges of overseeing a small business concern, Freddie nevertheless agreed to her exorbitant terms. "But when the reporters redouble their complaints about watery tea after this Dupont muddle is resolved, I am directing them to you."

Delphine accepted this threat with equanimity. "I am sure once you see how much more productive the staff are with a decent cup of tea in their bellies, you will permanently change your policy. In the meantime, I shall gratefully enjoy your munificence and accompany you to the *Gazette*'s office. In truth, I had the nugget of an idea yesterday while rereading Twaddle's old Bonapartisan sketches and am eager to explore it further, for they really are clever little stories and deserve to be read by a larger audience. With that in mind, I thought we might collect them in a book. Hire a caricaturist to illustrate each one and publish them all in a charming little volume. What do you think?"

Freddie, of course, thought anything that wrung a few more shillings out of Mr. Twaddle-Thum was a brilliant stroke and enthusiastically endorsed the idea. Verity's response was more measured, for she did not think the pieces were weighty enough for their own book, even one that was charming and little.

And who really cared about Napoleon now that he was exiled to some rocky island off the coast of Africa?

"Everyone," Freddie said flatly. "Literally every man, woman, and child in this country cares about Napoleon and are happy to ridicule him and his supporters at the drop of a hat. It is why someone has made five attempts on Hardwicke's life and one attempt to abduct you. I am surprised, Verity, that you do not see that. Furthermore, the sketches *are* quite clever and stand as fine entertainment on their own."

Delphine clapped at this spirited defense of Twaddle's work and proposed Mr. Twirlybird, whose illustrations the *London Daily Gazette* had published previously, for other projects. "I adore the way he draws the prince regent, with his generous belly spilling over his spindly legs and his head almost a small dot."

"Another excellent suggestion, Delph," Freddie said, noting without irony that weak tea appeared to have an invigorating effect on her mind. "Perhaps you have been dulling your senses with overstimulation."

Delphine rolled her eyes, and Verity swallowed the last of her breakfast before excusing herself to keep Dupont's appointment in Gherkin Lane.

⁂

*Saturday, June 13*
*9:21 a.m.*

Hardwicke complimented Verity on her shoes.

"A dark, rich brown, a gold-colored buckle—excellent!" he said with a nod of approval as he pulled his shoulders away from the tree against which they had been resting. "I know what it is like to have a favorite style. I myself am excessively fond of Marchetti's soldier boot. It is the leather, you see. As soft as butter! I cannot say how Marchetti does it. He is a magician."

That he had been waiting for her to turn the corner there could be no doubt. The way he detached himself from the trunk, with an unhurried grace, indicated that he had been expecting her for some time and was amused at the prospect of surprising her.

Verity revealed no surprise.

Having misunderstood his lack of interest in deciphering the cryptic message yesterday, attributing it to a desire for secrecy, she was not astonished to realize he had already figured it out. Although puzzling, the code was not sophisticated and anyone with a comprehensive knowledge of London roads would have almost immediately recognized g-h-e as Gherkin Lane. If she had failed to anticipate Hardwicke's sweeping familiarity with the street plan of the city, it was only because she had yet to fully reconcile the reality of Typhoeus: a cunning alter ego who possessed skills and talents not available to debauched second sons.

And even if Hardwicke had known nothing of Gherkin Lane, the sparse assortment of words bearing those three letters would have led him to speculate its existence.

His presence there was not astonishing at all.

No, the astonishing thing was that Verity had failed to contemplate the possibility. She had been too offended at being Holyed to consider his next move.

It was, she thought, an egregious oversight she would not make again.

Acknowledging her own shortcomings, however, did little to mitigate the resentment she felt at his superior attitude. Smiling broadly, he radiated satisfaction, regarding her with the smug complacency of an adult finding a small child crouching under the drawing room table during a game of hide-and-seek.

Seeking to knock some of the wind out of his sails by depriving him of the hoped-for reception, she adopted a similar pose and greeted him warmly. Then she congratulated him on arriving on time and dressing with appropriate simplicity for the assignment. "It would never do for my impoverished cousin to outshine me. Now we must not dawdle. I do not want to be late for my meeting to see the house. It would make a poor first impression."

Hardwicke issued no protest at finding himself relegated to poor relation and fell in step next to her. "Why do you believe this is Dupont's first visit to the house?"

Although rudimentary in nature, the query was an attempt to discover what she knew about Dupont's activities and Verity revealed only what she had seen on the scrap of paper, which was an appointment to look at a house with an eye toward leasing it. She did not address any of the other information, which she only partially understood.

Hardwicke agreed with her analysis as they drew closer to number forty-one, and rather than snidely reply that she did not require his endorsement, she reminded him that he was there on her sufferance—and only as a favor to his mother, who begged her to take him under her wing. "The poor woman worries day and night about your lack of common sense. If only you were not such a slowtop!"

Nodding gravely, he said, "I shall just stand next to you and look pretty, shall I?"

Spoken with solemnity, the rejoinder was nevertheless jovial, and although Verity recognized he was teasing, she also believed he was sincere. The plain outfit suited him, its rough tailoring somehow emphasizing the fine proportions of his frame, and he knew it. His teal eyes glimmered with aware-ness, and his well-formed lips twitched as they struggled, and failed, to contain his amusement.

His beauty was a maddening conceit, an immoderation of nature, and it struck her as patently unfair that a man who already had so much to recommend him also possessed the ability to cause her breath to catch in her throat. All excesses were difficult to bear, but there was something particularly intolerable about an excess of good fortune, and the over-whelming irony of his existence was that the one thing that held him back—being second in line for succession—was the very thing that propelled him forward. If Colson Hardwicke had been heir to a marquessate, the beau monde would have coddled him like an egg, rendering him soft and runny and dull.

Verity brushed aside these thoughts and said, "Silence is ideal, thank you."

Hardwicke asked if simpering was permissible just as a man on the pavement several feet away waved at them excitedly and dashed forward.

Extending his arm, he grasped Hardwicke's hand firmly in his own and gave it a hearty shake, "Mr. Dupont! I would know you anywhere, for you are exactly as my clerk described down to the color of your hair. Only he did not mention how strikingly tall you are!" he exclaimed, tilting his head back in a dramatic fashion, as if striving to see the top of a mountain. "I am Mr. Smithson from Cotswold and Co., with whom you have exchanged several letters. I am thrilled to show you the house, as I know it is exactly what you are looking for aside from a few modifications, which I am sure you will find minor. Before I take you inside, let us stand here and note the building's excellent condition, from the clean white facade to the freshly painted gate. The entire terrace is well cared for by its owner, who numbers among the most thoughtful and generous men I have ever known. In the decade I have been leasing this house, I have never heard an unkind word against him. Everyone who meets him is impressed."

Smithson prattled with breathless speed, darting from giddy introduction to gushing admiration of the house, and Verity waited for a pause to correct his misunderstanding. It was all very well for him to claim to have recognized Dupont from his associate's description, but he had clearly made an assumption based on a thin pretext. The color of Hardwicke's hair was neither remarkable nor much darker than her own, and the agent would suffer little embarrassment in discovering he had drawn the wrong conclusion.

Hardwicke, however, jumped in first.

"Your enthusiasm for the property does you credit, Mr. Smithson," he said pleasantly, noting that the building looked sturdy and well-tended. Then he begged the agent's indulgence as he introduced Mr. Gorman, his impoverished cousin with no discernable skills and an increasingly exasperated mama. "He is in London seeking employment. Perhaps there is a position in your office? He is a bit doltish, but he knows his letters and can count all the way to seventy-five."

Smithson displayed no alarm at this blatant angling and allowed that anything was possible. "We can discuss it when we return to the office—after we sign the papers. Now let us cross the road and observe the house from the other side. The building has a certain charm from this perspective as well. As they say, distance makes the heart grow fonder," he added with a buoyant laugh, delighted by his own witticism.

Returning to the other side, Smithson advised them to pay attention to how few carriages passed by. It was, he insisted, an excellent neighborhood for raising a family. Then he pointed to the curb and cautioned Mr. Gorman against tripping. "We do not want to send you home to your mama with bruised knees."

Hardwicke thanked him for his consideration, for his cousin tended to be clumsy as well, and asked if the flowers in the planter to the left of the door were *Primula vulgaris*.

"They are indeed the humble flower we call primrose," Smithson said admiringly. "I must say, for a Frenchman, you have an excellent command of the English language."

"My cousin was speaking Latin," Verity said snidely, her irritation with his fawning heightened by her relegation to the simple-minded relative.

In reply, Smithson looked at Hardwicke with patient

understanding for the burden of thickheaded relations, and she began to suspect that Mr. Gorman would not receive an offer of employment from Cotswold and Co.

"And I can barely detect an accent," the agent continued in the same admiring tone as he withdrew a set of keys from his pocket and applied himself to the lock.

In truth, Smithson could detect no accent at all because Hardwicke had failed to adopt one, either because he had forgotten or lacked the ability.

Regardless of the cause, it was a mortifying development, and she was startled that a man of Hardwicke's experience did not have the appropriate accent at the ready. Surely, Typhoeus had identified the common speaking patterns of all the major languages in Europe and studied them accordingly. She would not expect him to perfect the innumerable regional dialects that dotted the Continent, but knowing how much Gallic insouciance to inject into his speech as an embassy worker living in London for little more than a year struck her as the bare minimum.

He had been employed as a spy during the war with Napoleon, after all.

It would be different if he did not know how to impersonate a Russian émigré, for London was not thick with them.

Crossing the threshold into the house, Verity began to wonder if Typhoeus existed outside Hardwicke's imagination. Was he a fully formed character or just a name Hardwicke had bandied about when it was convenient?

The latter seemed horrifying to her, and she could not believe that English spy craft was in such a ramshackle state. If that was its true condition, then it was a marvel that they won the war at all, let alone routed Boney twice.

Smithson, leading them through the ground floor of the house, praised the generous amount of sunshine that poured in through the windows and pointed out the excellent condition of the furniture. "The owner replaced everything earlier this year. As I said, he is a considerate man who wants only the comfort of his tenants."

On the first floor, he drew their attention to the bedchamber at the back of the house, which was decorated in brightly colored patterns that had begun to fade. "Everything in this room is new as well, including the linens on the bed. I all but guarantee you will have a lovely night of sleep here."

Hardwicke agreed that everything appeared to be well cared for and asked when the previous tenants had moved out. Smithson, mounting the stairs to the second floor, said it had been only a few weeks. "They were desolate to leave before the end of the season, but they had business to attend to in the country. They left in a flurry. That was early May, I believe."

Judging by the coating of dust on the balustrade, Verity thought it was more like late February. Nobody had used the railing in at least three months.

As they reached the landing, Hardwicke asked if the price was negotiable. "Or is it fixed at sixty guineas per annum?"

Smithson tittered awkwardly and said, "Now, now, Mr. Dupont, you know you have already browbeaten me down from seventy guineas. You must allow me to make some money on the transaction. If the price is still too dear, I am happy to show you other houses in other neighborhoods. They are on roads that are not quite as cozy as this leafy one, but they are perfectly adequate. But before you decide this house is above your touch, let us proceed to the nursery. I know it is what any new mother would want for her child, and I am sorry that Mrs. Dupont could not accompany you today to look at it. I hope she continues in good health and her spirits are not affected by her situation. From your reports, I know her confinement is several months off yet."

Hardwicke deftly addressed these remarks, assuring the agent that Mrs. Dupont was in fine spirits and entrusted him with all decisions regarding their living arrangements. "She is in charge of hiring the servants and oversees the marketing. If I dare to pick out one onion bulb, she pins with me a furious glare."

"Wives are wonderful creatures," Smithson said with an appreciative shake of his head. "My own jealously guards the kitchen, as though I would not know the first thing about boiling water. I am delighted to leave her to it."

As the two men continued to discuss the endearing quirks of their spouses, Verity contemplated the two new pieces of information and tried to decide which was more meaningful: that Mrs. Dupont was increasing or that she was staying in London. Assuming the baby was a happy development, she thought the Frenchwoman might consider the latter an unwelcome turn. It was one thing for her to live in a foreign country but another altogether to raise her children there. She would want to be back home, amid family and familiar traditions. Indeed, she had practically admitted as much when she said it was time to return to France.

If Mrs. Dupont was set on that course, then perhaps she had quarreled with her husband over his high-handed decision to remain in England, and the murder, far from being an act of political subterfuge, was naught but a sordid domestic affair. Unwilling to abide by her husband's authority in this matter as well as many others, Mrs. Dupont shoved him out of the window to end the argument once and for all.

Or maybe she discovered her husband's plan to kidnap one English citizen and murder another and decided he was too much of a liability to her and the baby.

Verity knew these theories had little merit.

For one thing, if Mrs. Dupont had visited her husband that afternoon, then someone would have mentioned it. It seemed impossible that she had been in the building without anyone noticing.

Nevertheless, Verity was obligated to add her to the list of suspects now that she had stumbled across a motive, for that was the nature of a murder investigation: Proof was required before an idea could be dismissed.

It was one of the reasons she detested murder investigations.

Their excruciating tedium was the other.

Assuming Mrs. Dupont was innocent—only as an exercise, of course—Verity wondered what the information meant in regards to her husband's complicity. His actions, which had already struck Verity as reckless, seemed more so in light of his increasing obligations. If entering into a secret plot to further a hopeless cause was foolish with only a wife to support, then it was utter madness with a child on the way.

Ah, but was it, she wondered, contemplating the pressures of impending fatherhood. With another mouth to feed, he might have rashly agreed to a dangerous enterprise in the hopes of securing funds for his growing family. He did not appear to be motivated by idealism, and the larger house signaled an improved circumstance. The Duponts' current residence, which measured eighteen feet in front, was probably about thirty guineas per annum. Gherkin Lane cost twice that, and Dupont could not expect to see a commensurate rise in his salary any time soon, as he had been promoted to secretary less than a year ago.

Consequently, he must have been promised a significant reward for abducting Miss Lark.

All things considered, it had doubtlessly seemed like a rational decision. Miss Lark was not a particularly stalwart creature despite her height and was generally thought to be several years older than she was, what with her retiring ways and her reluctance to leave her home more than a few times a week.

By the same token, Dupont's failure to fulfill his assignment would have appeared worse than it was, convincing his employers that he was a liability. Only a henwit would be so inept as to allow an elderly female to thwart him, and eliminating him ensured he did not further endanger the operation.

The fact that the murder had taken place at the embassy argued in favor of one of his colleagues being the killer, which in turn meant that his conspirator—one or many—was among that cohort as well. As Delphine had noted of a related matter, the events were too closely related for a coincidence.

That was true, yes, but the porter was quite inattentive to his duties, which meant that someone could have slipped unnoticed into the building and moved around freely as she had been doing for the past two days. Having yet to receive replies from Twaddle's spies, she was not prepared to assume Dupont's friends from the tavern were uninvolved. Until she had more information about the three men, she could not dismiss them from contention.

No, wait, she thought, picturing the extra glass on the table. There had been a fourth man whom she had not seen, presumably because he had left before Dupont's arrival. Recalling him now, she decided to return to the tavern to learn his name. The secretary and his friends appeared to be regular patrons of the establishment, which meant it was likely the barkeep would know something about the absent drinker, perhaps even his identity. The fact that the man had run off before taking a sip of his ale struck her as meaningful, for it indicated a pressing development that could not wait, and she wondered if the two events could be related. Dupont's failure to kidnap the frail Miss Lark might have required the other man to step in with a solution. If he had been tasked with eliminating the bungling secretary, then he simply might have wished to avoid the hypocrisy of sharing a convivial drink with a man whom he would push from a third-story window the next day.

As Smithson pointed out all the advantages of the nursery, including a corner he described as a "quiet spot for paternal rumination," he peppered Hardwicke with questions about his work at the embassy, trying to ascertain, she decided, whether the other man could actually afford the residence or was wasting his time. Returning them to the ground floor, he suggested they visit Cotswold and Co. in Lilac Street and sign the paper right away. It was best to act quickly before another tenant snatched the house away.

"I have another tour later this afternoon and one tomorrow morning," he added with a sly look in Hardwicke's direction. "I would be sad if one of them let the house instead of you, for I know your family would be happy here."

"I expect so too," Hardwicke said coolly, "but I cannot make a decision without considering all my options. I am sure you understand that I must not allow myself to be swept away by an appealing rumination nook. You will hear from me within the week."

"A two-year lease is available!" Mr. Smithson exclaimed emphatically, his volume rising dramatically. "The owner just informed me this morning that he is willing to agree to two years, just as you requested. You see, he is as kind and considerate as I said. Shall we pay that call to my office now and look over the paperwork? I can show Mr. Gorman around the office, and we can see if he has a facility for real estate."

Verity simpered.

Hardwicke declined, insisting vaguely on all those options to consider. "As it is, I have to get to the embassy. I cannot lease anything if I lose my position. I am grateful for your time and knowledge. This was very informative."

Smithson flinched at the word *informative,* sensing within it a sweeping dismissal, but he smiled bravely and swore it was his pleasure. "Rarely have I met a more discerning lessee."

Verity waited on the doorstep as Hardwicke took his leave. As impatient as she was to interview the barkeep at the Speckled Pig, she could not run off and leave Hardwicke behind. It was not that she was loath to abandon him—the very opposite, in fact, for she was quite eager to be gone from his presence—but rather that she could not abandon a character before the performance was finished. The dull-witted Mr. Gorman could not cease to exist until he was out of Smithson's line of sight, presumably after he turned the corner onto the next street.

Hardwicke promised for a third time to write as soon as a decision had been reached, and Verity imagined he would indeed send a polite missive declining the pleasure by nightfall.

It was the decent thing to do, for Smithson was blameless in the drama and seemingly desperate to find a tenant for the house.

Directing a curt nod at the agent, Verity bid him goodbye and followed Hardwicke as he turned left on the pavement. Walking at a brisk pace, she considered the best way to approach the barkeep to discover the missing drinker's identity. Given that it was almost noon, she did not want to lose valuable time by going home to change. That meant whatever ruse she devised would have to correspond with her current ensemble, which was not outlandish by any means. The brown trousers and navy tailcoat suited any number of characters who—

"You will have to tell me what it means," Hardwicke announced.

Verity came to an abrupt halt. They had yet to reach the corner, but she did not care. The authority in his voice, the insistence that she *had* to do anything, was intolerable. Mr. Smithson was too far away to hear their conversation, and even if he was watching them stride out of his life with a heart heavy with regret, he would not think it strange that Dupont was compelled to chastise his clunkhead cousin.

Raising one brow in a disdainful sneer, she said, "Will I?"

Mildly, he said yes. "I have had less time than you to gather information about our victim and as a result do not understand the significance of his renting a new house."

Although Verity found several things about this statement objectionable, she leveled her attention at the most offensive. "*Our* victim? I was not aware *we* had a victim, Hardwicke. You have the attempts on your life, and I have the attempt on mine. I have made no effort to interfere in your investigation into your potential killers, and I will thank you to do the same to mine," she said, bidding him a brisk good day and continuing toward the next street with long, determined strides.

She did not expect the gambit to prosper.

Obviously, Hardwicke would not allow the conversation to end there, for what he said was true: He knew nothing of Dupont, and if he wanted to figure out why he had been killed, he would have to start by gathering the information she already knew.

The notion appealed to her. The image of him retracing her steps while she broke new ground was pleasing.

Nevertheless, she made it all the way to the corner before Hardwicke caught up to her and said, "Look, I understand you are miffed because—"

Incapable of comprehending the word, she stopped

suddenly, turned on him roundly, and said with a snarl of contempt, "I am ... *what?*"

Hardwicke stood firm, making no attempt to reverse his position or soften his stance. "Miffed, Verity. I said you were miffed."

Yes, that was right, he actually said *miffed.*

The bloody, blathering idiot.

How *dare* he?

But even as the fury pulsed through her, an odd sort of peace suffused her.

It had been a confusing hodgepodge of days.

From the moment Hardwicke had announced in the parlor that he was ready to commit to anything, she had been grappling with a tumult of emotions: many of them new, some of them strange, all of them confounding. The attraction she felt for him was undeniable, for never before in her life had she been struck by an inexplicable compulsion to touch someone.

At the unlikeliest moments—to simply hold out her hand and stroke his.

It was the teal eyes and the strong jaw and the pillowy lips, to be sure, but also the alarming astuteness and the clever mind.

Oh, how she felt that tug of his clever mind.

Even with the breadth of a room between them, she felt as though she were sitting next to him, her shoulder grazing his.

Forcefully, she had held herself back because she knew he was not serious.

And also because she did not know what *serious* meant in this context.

Hardwicke was earnest and intent, his pursuit utterly sincere. He wanted things from her—glorious things, splendid things—and her confusion over how to respond to his desire had little to do with the position he had in mind, for she was no more comfortable with the concept of wife than mistress. As determined as she was never to consent to the latter, it unsettled her far less than the thought of agreeing to the former. All her wrangling over his intentions with Delphine and Freddie was really just her working to convince herself that the matter would not come to a head.

And then he severed the connection.

She had been relieved.

Disappointed and sad and bewildered and annoyed, yes, but also relieved that the onus of making a decision had been taken out of her hands.

Finding out she had been Holyed changed everything again, and even as she struggled to comprehend the depth of the affront, she had felt a whisper of regret. As horrifying as it was to be saved from herself like a helpless infant, it was gratifying to know she was still wanted.

But miffed?

There was no complexity to the term, no bemusing mix of emotion in reply.

Coolly, she said, "Goodbye, Hardwicke."

And walked away.

It was almost like a strut, the way she moved with unhurried grace, the way her footsteps fell with careless ease.

Hardwicke scrambled after her.

Although her pace was measured, he dashed swiftly to run past her and then stand before her to halt her movements, his brows drawn heavily in a frown.

He was alarmed.

Presumably because he saw it—the light fade from her eyes.

Smoothly, she stepped around him.

He reached out to grab her arm but dropped his hand before making contact.

Instead, he walked next to her and said, "Forgive me, Verity, I was out of line. I should not have made light of your anger."

It was a genuine apology sincerely given, and Verity accepted it graciously. "Thank you, Hardwicke."

"It was also wrong of me to withhold the attempts on my life from you," he added in the same matter-of-fact tone. "As soon as I realized what was going on, I should have sent you a note telling you of the danger and explaining my intention to stay away from you while I figured everything out. I knew it was the wrong way to handle the problem the moment I saw you again, and if I could go back and change my behavior, I would in a heartbeat. I am indeed sorry."

Verity could see that he was, and yet his attempt to rectify the mistake only worsened it, for his use of the first-person singular—while I figured it out—revealed how little he understood her. He did not perceive her as an ally in the fight but as a delicate creature to be kept away from it.

"What is done is done," she said.

"Good," he said, smiling faintly.

But he had the wrong end of it yet again, for she did not mean *done* as in the past, but *done* as in over. "I am glad we settled that and you may be assured that I harbor no hard feelings," she said.

And then she bid him good day.

"Devil it, Verity, you are being irrational!" Hardwicke exclaimed, clenching his hands into fists at his sides.

More amused than insulted, she glanced at him sideways and said, "Oh, dear, 'miffed' *and* 'irrational' in the spate of a few minutes. Here, let me call myself 'hysterical' to spare you the trouble and we can consider our account settled. Very good, yes? Thank you. Good day."

But Hardwicke, refusing to rise to the bait, stood his ground and insisted she was not approaching the problem with her usual rigor. "You want to identify Dupont's killer as quickly as possible because you recognize the danger to Delphine and your staff. In that case, you should welcome my assistance. Despite your opinion of me, you know I excel at mysteries and espionage. Failing to take advantage of my expertise just because you are angry with me *is* irrational. And you know it."

It was true.

Verity did know it.

Refusing his assistance out of a reflexive obstinacy was foolish and served no purpose. Previously, she had felt a need to best him as a way to prove she was as capable as he. His recent actions, however, had put an end to that absurdity. There was nothing she could do to convince him to see her as an equal, and rather than resent him for his limitations, she should exploit him for his resources.

With that in mind, she announced that he was correct. "The faster I can put this episode behind me, the better. And two heads are generally thought to be superior to one."

If he thought it was odd that Verity Lark would resort to a platitude, he did not make a comment to that effect. Instead, he nodded and asked again about the significance of the appointment to look at the rental property.

# Chapter Eight

*Saturday, June 13*
*11:47 a.m.*

Hardwicke proved his utility almost immediately.

Discovering that their next stop was the Speckled Pig in Petty France, he owned himself acquainted with the proprietor and swore they could learn the identity of the absent man without donning elaborate disguises or concocting a complicated story. They would ask Benson for the name of the fifth member of the group, and he would supply it. The exchange would be straightforward and transparent.

Verity did not believe it.

In her experience, people withheld information the moment they realized someone else wanted it. Even so, she agreed to follow his lead, for the damage to her investigation would be minimal if he was wrong. In that case, she could easily revert back to her original plan, assuming an elaborate disguise and weaving a complicated story.

All his misapprehension would cost her was time.

Arriving at the tavern a little before noon, they found it sparsely populated, with only a handful of patrons rowdily drinking in the corner. A barmaid in a burgundy-stained apron carried a quartet of tankards to the table, where they were enthusiastically received with a boisterous cheer. One of the men held his glass aloft and cried, "*À votre santé!*"

Hardwicke crossed the floor in several bold strides and called out to the man behind the counter, who was the same one as the night before: medium height, bald pate, red scar across his chin. Benson, looking up from the glass he was drying with a grimy rag, recoiled at the sight of the Marquess of Ware's dissolute son. He rounded his shoulders, tucked in his torso, and muttered a string of scathing expletives. Finishing his tirade, he threw the cloth onto the mottled wood and said with more weariness than rage, "Bloody buggering hell, Wicke, I thought I'd seen the last of yer rotting corpse. What in blazes are ye doing here, you arse-prick?"

Hardwicke sauntered to the counter and rested his forearm comfortably on it, his lips pulled together in an exaggerated pout. "Benny, is that any way to greet the man who saved your life? It has been almost two years, and I thought for sure my absence would make your heart grow fonder. You cannot mean you are unhappy to see me."

Benson glowered and opened the bottle of clear liquid at his elbow. He doled out a generous serving, swallowed it in three gulps, and promptly refilled the glass. He made equally short work of the second pour before holding out the bottle to Hardwicke, who refused on the grounds that he was not there to socialize.

"Ye never are," the tavern owner grumbled. "Always too busy trying to figure out how to help yerself."

Hardwicke introduced Verity as his associate Mr. Gorman, then apologized for the boorish reception. "You see,

Benny here has a nasty habit of emptying his customers' pockets when they're not looking, and one night he made the poor decision to steal five guineas from a man called Robert McVane."

"Trigger McVane," Benson added for her benefit.

"Also known as Hell and Fury Hawes's second in command," Hardwicke further clarified, mentioning the infamous crime lord who ruled over the worst rookery in London. "He had you figured out from the moment he set foot in the tavern, but you were too stupid know it. You did not even wait until he was two sheets to the wind. You relieved him of his money after only the first drink."

"I didn't recognize him, did I?" the tavern keeper mumbled. "Dressed like an urchin and stained like a chimney sweep. But I heard the rattle of coins in his pocket—the most glorious sound on earth."

"Benny had no sooner slipped the guineas in his own coat pocket than McVane turned on him, pistol in hand," Hardwicke said.

"In hand—hell!" Benson spat. "His finger was on the trigger and the cold steel was pressed against my temple in a motion so fast I'm still not sure how it happened. He accused me of stealing his coins and I swore up and down that it wasn't me. I was lying through my teeth, like ye do when yer staring death in the eye, and I knew I had only a few minutes left. He would search my pockets and find the guineas and put a hole in me. But he didn't find anything, not even a farthing! I don't know who was more shocked: me or McVane. He apologized for the misunderstanding and ordered a round of drinks for everyone while I stood there, stunned. Wicke, damn his eyes, had already taken the money from me. Deuced smooth about it too. I never felt a thing."

Having witnessed many of Hardwicke's talents, Verity was not surprised to find out he was an adept pickpocket as well.

That he indulged in common thievery, however, was a startling revelation. "You have the same nasty habit, do you?"

"The bleeding bastard set me up!" Benson seethed furiously, pounding his fist against the counter. "He knocked Trigger on the back to make him suspicious. That's why he pinned me with the gun. He felt Wicke's jab, knew something was havey-cavey, and realized his pocket was lighter."

Hardwicke shrugged off the accusation. "'Twas not I who dipped your hand into McVane's pocket. You did that all on your own, my friend. And I would argue it was no less than you deserved for being so naked in your intention. I would never have been able to set you up if you had not stared at McVane with intense longing."

Benson scowled more darkly and poured himself another glass.

Verity, watching this interplay, realized she had misunderstood Hardwicke's motivation. It was not greed. "What did you need from him?"

"Access to his cellars," Hardwicke replied. "A meeting among several influential Bonapartists was to take place there and I required access to the room, which has a priest hole that is ideally suited for eavesdropping. Benny was curiously unwilling to make use of it, so I had to provide encouragement. I remain grateful to him for making it so easy."

"Curiously!" Benson sputtered angrily. "Those savages would have gouged out my eyes before throwing me into the Thames if they suspected a thing. A bullet to the brain would have been kind in comparison."

Hardwicke smiled faintly and reminded the tavern keeper he had been provided that option and adamantly refused. "And nothing dreadful happened! Nobody knew I was there except for a few voracious rats who enjoyed an unusually hearty meal, and you were well compensated for your troubles. I not only returned the five guineas you stole but also gave you three more as a mark of my gratitude."

"Aye, ye did," Benson growled. "An extra few guineas for my trouble—not exactly fair compensation for the danger ye put me in. And now ye are back again. Whatever it is, I will not do it, not even if ye give me ten guineas."

But the wheedling note in his voice made it plain that he could be persuaded if the proposed amount was offered.

Hardwicke duly placed five coins on the counter and said that they required little to earn. "All we want is a name."

Benson narrowed his eyes, suspecting a trick. "A name?"

"A name," Hardwicke repeated with placid affirmation.

"All right, then, a name," the proprietor agreed, reaching out a hand to slide the guineas toward him.

"Uh-uh," Hardwicke said chidingly. "First, the name."

Indignant, Benson swore he could be trusted, then immediately added that he did not know the name of everyone who drank in his tavern. "Some nights it's so thick with patrons I can't see across to the other wall."

"That is unfortunate for you, as the payment is contingent upon the name," Hardwicke said. "And do bear in mind what will happen if you try to fob me off with a fiction. From what I understand, Trigger McVane has only grown more cantankerous with age."

"A fine way to begin a business negotiation, accusing me of dishonesty," Benson complained under his breath.

Verity assured him it would not be a problem. "The man we seek is almost certainly a regular customer of yours. He was here on Wednesday at around six o'clock. He was in the company of three men who sat over there." She gestured to the square table under a pair of sconces and described the members of the group who had remained.

The proprietor tilted his head to the side and stared at

the table as if trying to imagine the scene. "On Wednesday around six," he repeated softly, as if speaking to himself.

"He was gone by six-thirty," she added helpfully. "He ordered a pint of ale but did not drink it. The other men stayed and finished their drinks."

Still, his expression remained blank.

"After he left, another man joined them at the table," she continued. "He was called Dupont. He took the seat the other man vacated."

Startled, Benson turned to her sharply. "Dupont?"

"Yes, Auguste Dupont," she confirmed. "The unknown man was sitting with the same group Dupont sat with. Do you recall them now?"

But Benson did not answer. He pressed his forehead against his palm and murmured, "The poor bastard, meeting his Maker like that."

Of course he knew of his death. Word of it would have spread quickly to the tavern, where workers from the embassy gathered. "It is indeed a tragedy. So unexpected and inexplicable. I sense that he was a friend of yours. If so, I am sorry for your loss."

"Aye," Benson said with a sigh as he poured himself another glass. "It is a loss. I still cannot believe it happened. But now I do realize which group of men you are talking about, for they are regular customers, as you said. They come once or twice a week, and Dupont always joins them, for they are good friends, all four of them. But it is just the four of them. I know of no fifth."

Hardwicke reached into his pocket and extracted another two coins. Dropping them on top of the others, he said, "For your grief."

Benson stared at the money hungrily, then shook his head with regret. "I swear, it is always just the four of them. They come at the same general time, although at intervals depending on when they leave their jobs. Whoever arrives first buys drinks for the entire table and they typically sit along the back wall, but not always beneath those sconces. Every so often, one of them will come in with another friend but not with a regular and definitely not on Wednesday."

Verity believed him.

She could feel his frustration, all those lovely coins so tantalizingly close and yet just beyond his reach. If there were just some way he could grab them. Alas, he could not lie because he feared Hardwicke's wrath too greatly. That meant the pint of ale on the table had been Dupont's all along. If that was the case, then why did Dupont go up to the counter to secure his own drink from the tavern keeper? Aware of the custom, he knew one of the glasses on the table was his.

His earlier plea receiving no reply, Benson said, "At least allow me to keep the grief fee. My sorrow is genuine. I'd known Dupont for more than a year and we got into scrapes together."

If he had not required a drink, then Dupont had another reason to confer with the barkeep—a man whom he had known for more than a year and gotten into scrapes with.

Struck by the obvious explanation, she contemplated Benson in a new light. He was greedy for coins, not adverse to risk, and an admitted associate of the culprit. His partnering with Dupont on the abduction was not implausible.

Refusing the appeal, Hardwicke began to remove the guineas one by one from the counter, causing the proprietor to whimper softy.

Verity told him to hold off. "I have another way for Mr. Benson to earn the coins."

Blinking avidly, the barkeep leaned forward and said, "Yes, thank you. Tell me! I will do whatever I can to help."

"Tell us about the plot to abduct Verity Lark," she said.

Hardwicke reared back as the owner of the tavern twisted

his lips into an overly bright smile and attempted to chuckle with amused condescension. "Your friend is babbling, Wicke. I have no idea what he is talking about."

It was a feeble denial and Verity considered it beneath her notice. "You do not have to wrack your brain for every minor detail. We are interested in the broad strokes. For example, who came up with the plan? How many people were involved? What was Dupont going to do with Miss Lark after nabbing her? Give us that information and you may have the money. Is that not correct, Hardwicke?"

Curtly, Hardwicke said, "Yes, but he will find it difficult to spend with the many broken bones in his body."

Benson's face grew pale.

Irritated, Verity darted an impatient look at Hardwicke, whose ferocity would make gathering the information only more difficult, and said, "He is teasing! You know old Wicke, always fast with a joke."

The barkeep, who knew nothing of the sort, insisted he had no hand in whatever mischief Dupont had been devising at the time of his death. "I was here the whole time!"

Obviously, he was not.

Nobody who made an unprompted fervent assertion of their location was where they claimed to be. It was one the most basic precepts of Twaddling. That meant Benson was in Bethel Street on the night of the abduction attempt, presumably in the carriage.

Thoughtfully, she noted his participation. "You waited outside while Dupont entered the house. He was supposed to carry Lark out or signal to you if he needed help. But he never did, did he? How long did you wait outside before deciding it was too dangerous to remain?"

Like a feral dog trapped in a corner, Benson bared his teeth and snarled. Before he could launch into a spirited defense, Hardwicke told him to stifle it. His tone was cool, almost indifferent, and the other man shrunk back in response to the commanding apathy.

"They were going to keep her in the cellar here," Hardwicke explained, looking briefly at Verity. "Isn't that right. Benny? You were going to keep Miss Lark locked up in your cellar with the rats and the roaches. Tell me how it is not as bad as it sounds. Tell me how you were going to keep candles burning for her and serve her deliciously prepared meals and share your finest wine. Come, Benny, say something to convince me that you are not a cheap bastard who would keep a woman in a pitch-black cellar because you do not want to waste the tallows."

Now the barkeep's skin lost all trace of color as he stared at Hardwicke with blank terror, his jaw bobbing up and down as he struggled for a reply. Issuing a protest would sound meaningless and hollow, for Hardwicke knew him too well. Any attempt to lessen his lordship's fury would be recognized as the barefaced lie it was.

And agreeing with the statement—well, Benson could not conceive what horror that would unleash.

In the end, he shut his mouth with the clang of his teeth and bowed his head in a facsimile of shame.

Or perhaps it was sincere.

Verity did not care either way.

Of course Hardwicke was in a high dudgeon at the prospect of her being imprisoned in a vermin-infested cellar with neither food nor light. She was a delicate female who had to be shielded from danger and hardship and the awfulness of the world.

Swaddle her in wool and place her on a shelf.

Never mind the fact that she had confined *herself* to pitch-black rooms on more than one occasion. To find out the actual price of the Gold State Coach, she had spent hours in a dark basement biding her time in an even darker trunk. It was not pleasant, to be sure, but the hardest part was the boredom. As locking her charges in the linen closet on the deserted wing on the third floor was among the Wraithe's most beloved punishments, Verity would have long since ceased to exist if she could not withstand imprisonment.

"Very wise," Hardwicke said with quiet approval as Benson pressed his chin against his chest. "Do not waste my time and perhaps I will not break quite so many bones. Now you heard Mr. Gorman. Tell us about the abduction."

"I know nothing! Nothing at all!" the tavern keeper cried. "You must believe me. Dupont did not tell me more than what was required for the job and I did not ask. I didn't even know the identity of the victim other than she was a woman of middle age who would faint with terror. We drove to the house and he told me to be prepared to drive the cart away as fast as possible. He would go into the house and fetch the woman. I asked if we should have a signal in case one of us ran into trouble and he laughed. He said it would be the easiest four guineas I ever made. Then he went into the house. And he never came out."

As this narrative aligned with Verity's understanding of the events, she did not doubt its veracity. Dupont's overconfidence had been his downfall. "How long did you wait?"

Color returned to Benson's cheeks as he admitted he did not linger above fifteen minutes. "Dupont said he would be right back and when he didn't return after ten minutes, I grew anxious. And then I saw light in the windows upstairs and realized something had gone wrong because now the whole house was awake. That is when I drove off."

Verity wondered if he had even stayed that long, for there had been no sign of a carriage by the time she had peered out the window. "Then what happened?"

"Then what happened?" Benson echoed as though the query itself were incomprehensible. "I brought the cart back to the stable, returned to my rooms here above the tavern, and went to sleep. I had no idea what became of Dupont until he strolled into my tavern on Wednesday night. It was a huge relief to see him, I can tell you."

"He still owed you money, didn't he?" Hardwicke asked blandly. "You had failed to collect your fee beforehand."

Indignant, Benson said he had secured half of the money in advance. "But you are correct in that he did owe me the rest. And he refused to pay it! He claimed that *I* had not finished the job. I said I waited as long as I could for him to appear and he never did. And it was the truth! I had to leave or be discovered myself!"

"And what did become of him?" Verity asked.

"He encountered Miss Lark's brother," he said succinctly.

Well, that was not the answer Verity expected to hear. "Miss Lark's brother?"

"A great behemoth of a man," Benson confirmed. "He sneaked up behind Dupont and hit him over the head with a club. He was stunned because he thought the brother was out of town. That was what the neighbors had told him."

Verity, digesting the outlandish tale her would-be abductor told to salvage his pride, was not surprised Dupont had been given that information. Robert was known to be frequently away from home, either in pursuit of a story or visiting one of several elderly relatives in the surrounding villages. "A very unfortunate turn for Dupont. How did he convince the brother to let him go? Why was he not turned over to the authorities for breaking and entering?"

"Convince nothing!" Benson replied heatedly. "Dupont escaped all on his own. The behemoth tied him to a chair in the cellar and Dupont managed to unravel the knots. Then he crept out of the house and went to the embassy. He had no choice. He did not want to draw unwanted attention by doing anything unusual. He was quite ragged by the time he got here. I am sure that is why he argued about the money. To insist that *I* fulfill my end of the bargain before being paid when *he* was the one who failed to uphold his end! I did exactly as I was told. It is not my fault he was waylaid by the large brother."

"How were you to fulfill your end of the bargain?" Verity asked.

With an anxious look at Hardwicke, he explained that Dupont wanted to try again. "But we would do it while she was walking to the market or in the square. He said it would be easy to nab her from the street because she would be alone and nobody in London would bother to intercede in a domestic squabble. I told him in no uncertain terms that I would not help him hurt a defenseless woman."

"Did you?" Hardwicke said, seemingly unconvinced by this fervent and principled stance. "Or did you tell him in no uncertain terms that you would not help hurt a defenseless woman without additional compensation?"

A flush stained Benson's cheeks as he swore it amounted to the same thing, as Dupont was adamant that further funds would not be forthcoming unless he aided him in the second attempt. "That is when I informed him that the price for use of my cellar had doubled to four guineas. He growled that I was not being fair, but he was too tired to argue and said we would discuss it the next day, when I was in a more reasonable mood. I told him to find a new cellar because refusing to work for free *was* reasonable. He took his glass and stomped off. That was the last I spoke to him. His death is shocking. And yet I am not surprised the strain of getting involved with an evil plot to abduct a helpless woman when he was already anxious about supporting a wife *and* child. The exhaustion could not have helped his frame of mind. He must have spent a sleepless night trying to figure out where he could deposit his victim if not here or where to get the blunt to pay me or what to tell the other plotters."

It struck Verity as perverse that a man who was worried about providing for his growing family would consider leasing a house that cost twice as much as his current residence—unless the abduction plot was *how* he could afford the new home.

When she proposed the notion that Dupont would be well compensated for his participation in Miss Lark's kidnapping, thereby getting the funds to compensate the tavern keeper only after the successful completion of the mission, Benson furrowed his brow doubtfully and said that Dupont was a zealot. "He and his Frenchie mates come in here and down a few pints and drink to the glory of Boney, incessantly holding their glasses up high and toasting to the empire. I don't know why he wanted the gel, but I wouldn't be surprised to find out it was more patriotic humbug. That's probably why he was so stingy about paying me—he was saving every farthing for the cause. The dim-witted fool!"

Having established Dupont's lack of interest in restoring Napoleon to the throne, Verity wondered if he had instead been moved by the prospect of revenge. It was possible to enjoy the comforts of peace while nurturing a lethal resentment against Typhoeus for helping to bring it about. Wanting the English spy dead was not the same thing as wanting Napoleon to return to power.

These speculations, however, did not explain how Dupont could have enough money to lease a larger home but not enough to secure Benson's help. Even if he found it personally offensive that his friend would seek to exploit his misfortune by demanding more money, taking a principled stand against exhortation while in the middle of a kidnapping operation was patently stupid.

Whatever his intellectual limitations, Dupont had to

recognize the primacy of carrying out the assignment over proving a point.

Consequently, the secretary did not have the funds—yet.

Something else had to happen first.

But what?

The assassination of Typhoeus was the obvious answer, and if she could not fathom where a large sum could fit into the plan to murder Hardwicke, then she did not have enough information yet.

Somewhere in the plot was a pot of gold. She knew this because there was always a pot of gold. Sometimes it was hidden; sometimes it glittered in plain sight.

If Verity could locate the gold, she would know who killed Dupont.

Unfortunately, she had made little progress in identifying the victim's fellow schemers. Benson claimed to know nothing, and she feared it was true. When pressed on Dupont's friends, he could not say one way or another if they were involved but thought it was unlikely. If they were, he insisted, then Dupont would have borrowed the money to meet his fee. "Whoever Tipsy is, I am certain he is not one of them."

Well, now we are getting somewhere, Verity thought as she asked who Tipsy was.

Curtly, Benson replied that he did not know—as he just stated!

"Yes, yes, Benny, we understand you do not know his identity," Hardwicke snapped impatiently. "That was made clear. What Mr. Gorman is asking is where does Tipsy fit in the abduction plot. Who is he within the group?"

Benson insisted he did not know that either. "Dupont mentioned him only once, and it was in passing. He asked how long he could keep the woman in the cellar and I said until Michaelmas for all I cared. He looked aghast and said

Tipsy wanted the situation resolved well before then. I did not ask who Tipsy was, and he never said the name again."

Admittedly, it was not a lot of information, but Verity still thought some conclusions could be safely drawn from it, such as Tipsy held a higher position in the organization than Dupont. Otherwise, his preference would not be relevant in any discussion. And the name Tipsy—obviously, that was an epithet bestowed in scorn rather than a fond nom de guerre. As it was a rather specific reference, she assumed the other man was either frequently fuddled or unable to hold his drink. Both prospects revealed Dupont's deep contempt for his associate.

'Twas not a huge amount of information on which to create a portrait, no, but it was not nothing, and every little piece of the puzzle contributed to the whole picture.

She assumed Hardwicke felt the same way, as the look he directed at her over Benson's head was pointed and meaningful. But then he turned abruptly away and focused his unusual eyes on the barkeep. "How long were you and Dupont planning on holding Miss Lark as your prisoner? You generously offered your cellar for three months and Dupont insisted such munificence was not necessary. What number did you arrive at between the two of you? How long was Miss Lark to be trapped in the dark?"

He spoke softly, almost gently, but the quiet menace in his voice was chilling, and Benson responded with appropriate apprehension. Flinching, he opened his mouth, then swiftly shut it as he contemplated the correct reply.

The correct reply was zero.

*We were going to hold her zero days, Wicke. I swear.*

But he knew an outright fabrication would never fly and considered how to articulate the truth in a way that would make it sound less egregious. After an uneasy glance at Verity to ascertain whether he had to contend with her ire as well, he said, "Barely a full day, maybe a few hours into a second! As soon as she had served her purpose, she was to be returned to her family, not a hair on her head harmed. Dupont wished her no ill will. She was merely a pawn to be exploited."

Oh, but this was the wrong thing to say. Despite the care he had taken with his words, Benson blundered into the worst possible answer, which he realized almost immediately, taking a step back as Hardwicke leaned forward and ordered him from the premises. "Disappear from my sight before I do something violent."

The other man tittered awkwardly, unable to believe Hardwicke was serious.

Leave his own tavern!

And at that hour—it was just past twelve. The afternoon crowd would soon begin to gather.

The self-conscious laughter slowly trailed off as he realized Hardwicke was disinclined to make jokes in general and specifically opposed to it now. He pressed his lips together and looked at the barmaid, who was taking the order of a patron several feet away. He appeared on the verge of calling out to her, perhaps to explain something of the situation, then reconsidered the wisdom of lingering even that long. Rather, he flung the rag aside, clambered under the counter instead of lifting it at the hinge, scurried across the floor, threw open the door, and disappeared onto the street.

Verity, watching the humiliating display, turned to Hardwicke and observed that his approach to conducting interrogations was ineffectual. "The goal is to encourage the free flow of information, not to chase off the target. I had more questions for him."

Hardwicke, claiming to understand the purpose of an interview, nevertheless asserted that pressing Benson further would have been a waste of their time. "He does not know the identity of Tipsy."

"He may *think* he does not," Verity said churlishly. "But in my experience people do not know what they actually know. If we had learned more about the people with whom Dupont interacted, we might have gotten several interesting prospects."

"Tipsy does not frequent the Speckled Pig," Hardwicke replied with conviction.

Verity begged to disagree, noting it was a drinking establishment—which was to say, a place where people became tipsy.

"That is true, but I think we may reliably conclude based on other evidence that Tipsy works at the embassy, and this tavern is not frequented by men who work at the embassy," Hardwicke explained.

The authority in his voice was maddening. The man truly thought he knew everything. "Dupont was here. Dupont, who worked at the embassy."

"Precisely," Hardwicke affirmed, as if her comment validated his argument. "His is the exception that proves the rule."

"You cannot know that for certain yet," she said.

But he could, for the Speckled Pig was famously the last Bonapartist stronghold in Petty France. "Many of my old sources are still regular patrons, for they remain ardent supporters of Napoleon and his lost empire. No self-respecting embassy worker would show his face here and risk being aligned with an unpopular faction. It would spell ruin for his career."

Verity could not quibble over these conclusions. They were logical, succinct, and based on intelligence he had gathered himself. As she had followed an embassy worker to the tavern in an effort to comprehend why he had tried to kidnap her, her understanding of its clientele was skewed by her introduction to it.

That, of course, she *could* quibble over, for Hardwicke had withheld vital information from her for stupid and condescending reasons, but she knew better than to raise the point. Airing her grievance would only reveal her bitterness. Consequently, she thanked him for saving her the trouble of having to interview dozens of customers and added that she had also wanted to see the room where she was meant to be kept.

Hardwicke allowed that was a reasonable request. "But we do not need Benson for that. Follow me."

Verity did.

# Chapter Nine

S aturday, June 13
  11:56 a.m.
      When Verity observed that the cellar beneath the
Speckled Pig was not entirely inhospitable, she was not trying
to provoke Hardwicke. The ceiling was higher than she had
expected based on the proportions of the building, allowing
her to stand upright and not feel as though the wooden
beams were slowly descending to crush her, a sensation she
knew from her own basement in Bethel Street. The clay floor
had only sporadic puddles of stagnant water, which she could
easily scoot around as she crossed from one end of the room
to the other in pursuit of exercise during an extended incarceration. The activity would also provide necessary heat, for
the air was damp and chilly. Even so, it was not stale. Smelling
the currents, she could tell that it got a fair amount of
ventilation.

Additionally, there were mouse droppings.

A daunting amount, in fact, which was a peculiar thing to
find consolatory, but she knew it meant the rat problem had

been addressed since Hardwicke's stay. There would not be so much evidence of the pesky little rodent if the larger predator were still in residence.

All in all, she could imagine passing several unremarkable hours in its confines, sitting on the casks of wine between bouts of calisthenics and conceiving all the ways she could torment her captors once she was free.

Verity made remarks to this effect as she rapped her knuckles against the wall at regular intervals in an effort to find the aforementioned priest hole. She had started with the wall immediately to the left of the door and then proceeded to the one opposite. "It is always best to have a seating option other than the floor, as the floor is where the dampest, coldest air can be found. The higher you are, the warmer and dryer you will be. On a related note, I would not mind if the cellar had a window to admit daylight and improve the ventilation, but our three candles provide almost enough illumination to see into the corners of the room. A fourth candle would be better and a fifth ideal."

Unable to detect a hollow area behind the plaster, she took a thoughtful step back and swept her eyes around the room. If the priest hole was not in the wall, then it must be beneath the floor. And yet that seemed unlikely, as clay could not be segmented in the way a wood planks could. The break in the floor would be obvious, unless it was hidden beneath one of the casks of wine.

To confirm this supposition, she turned to Hardwicke and met his furious gaze.

Despite the glower of rage, his tone was effortlessly bland as he begged her to kindly stop assessing the cellar as if it were a bedchamber assigned to her at a house party in the Peak District.

Verity laughed, highly amused by the notion of being

asked to any rustic sojourn, let alone one at an old family estate in the country. "If this is the quality of accommodation I should expect at such an event, then I will be sure to refuse all invitations. Having said that, I genuinely take comfort in the lack of rats. Dare I anticipate such luxury in the country? I believe you said your own family seat is riddled with the detestable creatures?"

Hardwicke did not appreciate her attempt at humor, and his strange teal eyes seemed to darken to blue in the gleaming light of the candle as his scowl deepened. "It is dank and dark and fetid, and God knows how many evil diseases lurk in these festering pools of water, and he would have kept you here for three months."

The ferocity of his wrath surprised her, for he clearly took great exception to her actions, a development that struck her as wildly presumptuous and hypocritical. If anyone in the room had just cause be incensed by the other's behavior, it was she—from whom so much had been withheld in an asinine attempt to protect her from danger. This cellar, which had never held her, like the bullet that did not wound her, was a figment of Hardwicke's imagination, and his growing indignant at her for not shrinking in terror from a wisp of smoke was utterly absurd.

That he expected her to feel any trepidation at all reaffirmed that he did not really know her.

Verity felt her own temper snap at how grossly he had misrepresented himself, and she clasped her fingers behind her back to keep a firm hold on her anger. To succumb to emotion would be to give him the advantage.

Calmly, then, she replied, "Nobody keeps me anywhere."

As before, the words were said without malice, without purpose, without any intent of inciting him further. She was merely making an observation that was no more or no less than the truth. If it offended him, it was only because he had no idea who she was.

In the same cool tone, she continued. "As I am highly adept at picking locks, I'm fully capable of freeing myself from any situation I find displeasing for any reason. As you may recall, Dupont chose to abduct me in the middle of the night. That means I would have had several hairpins at my disposal to arrange a swift exit from this room. From there, it would be an easy thing to creep up the stairs, slip through the tavern, and step onto the street. I would have been home in time for Delphine to grumble about my being late for breakfast. Now please, if you do not mind, I would like for you to show me where the priest hole is. I am curious to see it."

Hardwicke did not move. The candlelight flickered around him, creating the illusion of movement, but he remained firmly in place as he glared at her. "You are not nearly as remarkable as you think you are, Verity."

Somehow it was startling to hear it said aloud.

There was nothing novel about the sentiment—he had long ago made his opinion known—and yet it still felt like a punch to her stomach. She tensed her shoulders to absorb the blow and marveled at how naïve she had been to think he was different.

Well, that was something to behold, she supposed: Verity Lark gullible and green.

No, she was not as remarkable as she thought.

She clenched her hands more tightly and assured him with admirable indifference that she was well aware of the low esteem with which he regarded her skills and abilities. "There is no reason for us to have a candid conversation because you have been quite blatant in your beliefs. Let us return to more interesting matters. With respect to the priest hole: Is it hidden in the floor under one of the casks of wine?"

His jaw clenching, he snarled furiously at her to stop

asking about the bloody priest hole. "To hell with the infernal priest hole! You are being deliberately obtuse and you bloody well know it. You think nothing is beyond your abilities. You think you can overcome any challenge, master any difficulty, solve any problem, find any buggering priest hole in any buggering cellar! You admit no frailties, allow no weaknesses, and are seemingly incapable of asking for help. And your confidence—it is astounding. I am sorry, Verity, but no, you are not as remarkable as you believe you are. Nobody is, for your conceit is beyond anything the human world can contain. Why the hell did you assume Dupont targeted you for something you did? How did it not occur to you to wonder if it had something to do with me? You were in the meeting with Kingsley. You saw for yourself what a preening ass he is."

Hardwicke was striking in his wrath, all simmering outrage and searing illogic, his gorgeous eyes seething, his shadow a giant black beast on the wall behind him. Caught in its frenzy, he had no idea how ridiculous he sounded— accusing her of vanity while making flagrant display of his own, decrying her proficiency while crediting her with omni- science.

Addressing each point would be madness.

Any attempt to undercut his assertions would have the paradoxical effect of bolstering them. The argument itself would legitimatize them.

Furthermore, she owed him nothing.

Colson Hardwicke had no claim to her person, no right to her past or present. Her thoughts and feelings were entirely her own, and she would not stand before him and attempt to justify her existence. She would not list the hardships that had formed the foundation of the confidence he found so abhorrent. She would not detail the indignities that had coerced a dogged determination from deep within her.

Every trait to which he objected was the spoil of a hard-won war against reality, and if anything, *that* was her conceit: that Verity Lark had earned her place in the world.

That was it—the extent of her hubris.

All she ever had was daring and pluck.

Take them away and you were left with one more lonely little child weeping under a thin cotton blanket in an orphan asylum.

Having resolved to say little, she found it impossible to say nothing. A great many charges had been leveled against her and she felt compelled to make some small defense. She could not simply point to a cask and ask if the priest hole was hidden beneath that one.

Well, she could.

And quite easily.

The remark would enrage him further, a prospect she did not find unappealing.

Even so, she resisted the impulse because she already had the upper hand. He had lost his temper while she had held on to her own. Goading him further for her own amusement was childish and indulgent.

Instead, she reminded him of their initial meeting, in Mrs. Norton's bedchamber, a prompt that was not without its taunting edge. "Mitchell was there to kill me. He made a muck of it by identifying the wrong Twaddle, but that does not detract from his intention, which was—again—to kill me. And Miss Copley drove a knife into my shoulder just a few inches to the left of my heart. Those examples are from the past two weeks alone. Who knows what other fuss Mrs. Norton kicked up in my name or if there are other Twaddle-Shams out in the world, giving fresh offense. Or if someone from the Society of Yarwellian Philosophers took issue with Robert's reporting on their movement or another reform-minded organization. Or if Blasingame sought revenge against Twaddle for ruining his plan to sabotage his competitor. You see, I am perfectly capable of inciting others to violence all on my own and can just as ably extricate myself from the danger. I had the matter with Mitchell well in hand before you interceded. You are just miffed because I did not ask for your help."

His top lip flared at the use of *miffed,* but he did not deny it. He took a step back, causing the shadow on the wall to loom larger, and pressed a palm against his forehead. He held the position for several seconds before lowering his hand and asking if that was strange. "Given all that has transpired between us, is it truly so strange that I would hope you would tell me when someone tries to harm you?"

"You mean, the way you told me when someone tried to harm you?" she asked, her tone neutral. She did not have to imbue it with any inflection at all to convey the bitterness she felt at the inadequacy of his regard.

Irritated by the question, he snapped, "It is not the same—"

But he broke off, unwilling to finish the thought.

Verity assumed it was because he realized how terrible it would sound. "No, my lord, it is never the same. Across space and time there is always something that makes it different when it applies to women. The *it* varies, the hypocrisy does not," she said agreeably, as she noted the belligerence on his face. He still believed his situation was unique. She twisted her lips into a mocking smile. "Come, now, did you really think you were the first man to offer me carte blanche and then tell me my place? The two usually come together as a matched set, like a teacup and saucer."

His expression altered at once, suddenly growing blank, and Verity wondered at its cause. Was it a prick to his ego to realize he was not the first man to take an interest in her? Her habit of donning multiple disguises a day made her difficult to know, and it was not unreasonable to suppose nobody before him had ever made the effort. Or perhaps he was annoyed by the lack of awe she displayed in grouping him with other men.

To be considered one among many was an intolerable insult.

Or maybe he objected on decorous grounds, finding her willingness to discuss an intimate matter with such unabashed frankness a shocking breach of propriety. He might prefer to conduct his affairs by oblique reference, making coy overtures without lowering himself to state the thing plainly. Perhaps even as he was slipping the silk dressing gown off her bare shoulders he would still never say the words.

Imagining England's greatest spy—Typhoeus himself, father of monsters—as a blushing maiden improved her spirits and she almost smiled with sincere amusement.

Since it was simply too absurd to consider, she cast about for another explanation for Hardwicke's sudden impassivity, which was, she admitted, disconcerting. As she did, he stepped around the largest puddle in the room, pointed toward the corner, and drew her attention to a faint line about eighteen inches from the floor.

"The priest hole is here," he said matter-of-factly. "It is hard to see because someone painted over the panel. But it is right here."

Verity watched as he ran his fingers over the outline and removed the board that concealed the space. It was narrow and deep, and although she wondered how long he had been trapped within its confines, she found herself curiously reluctant to ask.

*Saturday, June 13*
*2:40 p.m.*

Verity believed Hardwicke's transgression was the greater one because it came first. Although averse to trusting anyone other than Delphine and Freddie, she could not rule out the possibility that she would have mentioned the abduction attempt to Hardwicke had they still been in contact.

In fact, she rather thought it was likely.

She could not know for certain, of course, because he had severed the connection a few days before the event without explanation and only a pathetic creature with no respect for herself would run to an indifferent suitor to request his help.

If Hardwicke supposed for one moment she would approach him under those unfavorable conditions, then his mental acuity was far less sharp than she had conceived.

As she had endured the larger insult, she naturally possessed the greater impetus to bear a grudge, and if she had wanted to subject Hardwicke to her caustic indifference to make him feel the devastating absence of her warmth, then she would be well within her rights to do so.

But she did not.

For the sake of the investigation, she treated him with the same cordiality as always, displaying respect for his intelligence and admiration for his abilities. When he arrived at a deduction that struck her as accurate, she offered a compliment.

It was, as far as she was concerned, the only way to conduct a partnership, and if they had any hope of figuring out who killed Dupont and threatened them, then they would have to work together.

Hardwicke, apparently, did not consider an amiable rapport to be necessary to the apprehension of a murderous villain, for he refused to be anything but stiff and polite.

Hardwicke, whose grievance was the lesser!

It was yet another thing to be angry about.

"Let's see," Verity said, glancing at the notes John Pennie had taken during his interviews with the inhabitants of the victim's office in the minutes following his deadly plunge. Hastily written, they were barely legible even to her, who was well familiar with the shorthand the reporter regularly employed. "Next is Perreault. He was the seventh person to arrive in the room. He entered after Ardisson. He said he did not hear the scream and only came to look because of the fuss in the hallway."

Hardwicke, who was seated next to her at the table in the Bethel Street parlor, a cooling cup of tea at his elbow, leaned forward and squinted his eyes as he pointed to a scribble next to the clerk's name. "What does this say?"

Although they had begun the compilation exercise with a good two feet between them, he had slowly scooted his chair closer to hers to get a better look at her notebook. Now he was barely inches away, his shoulder occasionally brushing against hers as he struggled to make sense of her writing.

Verity pursed her lips thoughtfully for a moment as she examined the looping scrawl, then replied, "Brandy. That is right. I smelled brandy on his breath, which makes him a contender for Tipsy. Plus, he was a little pugnacious."

She drew an asterisk text to his name, indicating that he was a first-tier suspect along with Farrow, Ardisson, and Beaufoy. Although the other occupants of the room could not be removed from consideration, she and Hardwicke had to begin their investigation somewhere and these four men were the most promising: Farrow because he was outside Dupont's office in the seconds after the murder, Ardisson because he was unaccountably distraught as perhaps only someone who had ruthlessly shoved a colleague out of a window could be, and Beaufoy because he was the person to whom Dupont rushed to report after fleeing her cellar.

Hardwicke agreed with her assessment.

As was consistent with his new orneriness, he did not add anything constructive to the conversation and it fell to Verity to propose how they would proceed. "Let us divide the list. I will take Farrow and Beaufoy, and you may have Perreault and Ardisson."

The proposal was an act of aggression, as the two men she had assigned to herself were the more interesting prospects by far, and she expected Hardwicke to object. In a display of condescension, she intended to swap Farrow for another without comment.

Instead, Hardwicke slid his chair back several inches and rose to his feet. "That sounds reasonable, thank you. I will send a message informing you of my progress later today and trust you will do the same."

Verity almost protested the lack of protest, for she could not believe he was satisfied with the second tier of the first-tier suspects.

Obviously, he was not.

But Hardwicke was too clever to cede a point by falling in line with her expectations. Thwarting them was far more gratifying.

As she stood to escort him out, Verity wondered if he planned simply to ignore the distribution of suspects. It was what she would do in the same situation: Assign Perreault and Ardisson to Twaddle's network, then pursue Farrow and Beaufoy.

Perhaps she would send a message to Mags and a few of the other fellows as a precaution. It would also not hurt her efforts to have the additional information at her disposal, for the truth was, she never knew which seemingly minor detail would turn out to be hugely significant.

Settling on the course of action, she promised to keep him apprised of her own investigation in return and paused to see if he would propose they discuss strategies for discovering the truth. Given that Dupont had had a scrap of paper in his grasp when he fell, she thought finding the larger sheet would be sufficiently incriminating—that was, if the murderer had not already disposed of it.

Even if he had, she was certain there would be other evidence.

People always left a trail—that was what made Twaddling so rewarding.

It was a fairly obvious approach, which is why she would have no problem sharing it with Hardwicke, but he had no interest in lingering. He thanked her for the cup of tea, which he had not touched, and bid her good day. When she followed him into the hallway to accompany him to the front door, he insisted it was not necessary.

"I know the way," he assured her in that same frosty tone in which he had said everything for the past two hours.

Verity duly hung back, hovering in the doorway as he strode down the corridor, incalculably annoyed by his stand-offish behavior.

Petulant child!

*Saturday, June 13*
*8:11 p.m.*

André Farrow was a lumbering drunk.

Swaying to the left, then veering to the right, he struggled to hold himself upright by clutching Verity's shoulder with slippery fingers. Every time he lost his grip, he laughed with baffled astonishment and held his other hand to his mouth as if to contain his mirth.

One time he pressed so hard, he bit his palm and yowled in pain.

Then he snorted and chortled again.

"All right then, step up," Verity said firmly as Farrow's body threatened to pull them both down. At the bottom of the high staircase, they had to overcome the steep climb to reach the clerk's rooms, which lay at the tippy top. Getting him to the first landing had been something of a small ordeal, and she was vexed to have to repeat the exercise.

There were far easier ways to gain information about a subject.

She had been engaged in precisely that activity earlier in the evening, when she arrived at the pub and settled on a bench near Farrow. Originally, there had been half a dozen patrons between them at the long table, but one by one they had all stood up and moved to get away from the gregarious soak who chattered relentlessly in incomprehensible French. They did not know what he was saying, but his prattle had a Gallic pomposity to it that they recognized as inherently distasteful.

As the crowd at the table thinned, Verity found herself drawing closer to her quarry, and by the time the last man scurried away, she was too entertained by Farrow's nonsense to leave as well.

He was now rambling about dirt under his fingernails.

Wait, no, not *his* fingernails.

Mademoiselle Vachon, with whom he had eaten dinner the night before. She claimed to have passed the day embroidering quietly in the drawing room, but there was soil under her nails.

He would not fall for *that* ploy again!

Intrigued, Verity wondered about the first occasion, and when she found herself suddenly sitting next to Farrow, she decided to engage him in conversation rather than change seats herself. She had no concern of being recognized as John Pennie. Even if his brain had not been pickled by alcohol, he would never see past the awkwardly disheveled Turnip to the impeccably dressed reporter.

The two men simply had nothing in common.

In response to her suggestion that perhaps the mademoiselle enjoyed gardening, Farrow began to sing "Chanson de l'Oignon" in a surprisingly robust tenor. He rebuffed all attempts at conversation—ah, yes, so now he did not want to chatter—and only responded when Verity asked him to teach her the words to the marching song. Happily, he complied, eager to translate the lyrics into English, although none of them sounded quite right to him.

For ten minutes, he vacillated on the meaning of *au pas,* swearing up and down that "at walk" was the best approximation, only to decide "to the charge" was closer. When he finally settled on "to the beat," he dropped his tankard on the table with an air of intense satisfaction and called for another one. He ordered an ale for Verity as well, insisting it was his treat. She demurred, as she was a stranger with no claim to his generosity, a notion with which he took immediate issue, for were they not friends?

Verity submitted to this persuasive argument.

Accepting their drinks from the barmaid, Farrow raised his glass high and toasted to onions. Then he took a large gulp, burped loudly, and giggled with delight.

Noting his high spirits, Verity thought it was unlikely he was lumbering under the weight of a guilty conscience. Even so, she managed to turn the subject of the conversation to the recent tragedy at the embassy and although some of his giddiness left him at once, he did not seem particularly shifty or furtive. Plainly, Farrow relayed the story as he remembered it, repeating some of the details three or four times. He seemed to get stuck on the angle of Dupont's left arm as it lay on the pavement and closed his eyes to recall it.

A few seconds later he snored.

Listening to the wheezy grumble, Verity took a sip of ale and wondered if Farrow was out for the night or taking a brief nap. It really did not matter, of course, for she had no patience for either and knocked her shoulder against his to rouse him.

"Yer gonna have to do better than that," a voice said behind her.

Verity turned to find the barmaid regarding her with humor. "Ye gotta give Andy a proper thwack to wake him," the woman explained, transferring the bulk of a serving tray to one hand so she could demonstrate with the other. Walloping him on the back, she said, "Time for bed-bed, Andy darling."

Sputtering, Farrow jerked his head forward and back.

"Ye gotta go home. Here, yer new friend will help ye," she added, then looked at Verity and explained that he lived nearby. "Just two doors to the left, the brick building with the flower boxes under the windows. He rents rooms there. Ye don't have to get him up the steps. Just drop him inside the front door. The tenants are used to stepping over him."

"Are they?" Verity murmured, aware that the tendency to pass out drunk in the entryway of his rooming house made him an excellent candidate for Tipsy.

The barmaid nodded and said he imbibed too freely two or three nights a week. "Sometimes it's all we can do to get him out the door. I've rolled him out a few times."

It took several tries, but Verity eventually tugged a bewildered Farrow to his feet, and as she half-dragged him out of the pub, she wondered if his habit was too roundly formed to warrant the epithet. Swill Tub or Sot would be more on the mark, and it was difficult to imagine his sodden wits concocting a diabolical scheme.

Of course, appearing unable to concoct a diabolical scheme was in fact the best way to concoct a diabolical scheme, as Hardwicke himself had discovered. Jug-bitten flibbertigibbets were never looked at in askance.

With this thought in mind, Verity not only heaved Farrow over the threshold of his boarding house but also up the two flights to his room. Opening the door, she lugged him into the room and pulled him across the floor to his bed. She dropped him on top of the tangled heap of blankets and shoved him back onto the mattress when he immediately slid off. He snorted loudly, mumbled something about rémoulade (how mortifyingly French!), and rolled over onto his side.

Confident Farrow would sleep until morning, she made a thorough inspection of his living quarters, beginning with the box underneath his bed, which contained three poorly carved flutes, a crushed ostrich plume, and the worn sole of a shoe. Next, she searched the clothespress and the cabinet. In a trunk near the window, she found a tangle of clothes in need of mending, a miniature of a dark-haired woman wearing a pearl necklace, and a Bible with roses pressed between its pages. In the second room she found another cabinet, this one containing several novels by Jacques Cazotte, Farrow's correspondence, and a journal with a detailed account of his daily activities.

Feeling no urgency to leave, Verity sat down at the table near the hearth and read all the documents, starting with the letters, which were from his family. His parents, proud and grateful to have a son in such a respectable position, took every opportunity to contrast him with his brother, who oversaw the operation of a gambling establishment on the outskirts of Rouen. His sibling, keenly aware of their parents' disapproval, which they made no attempt to hide, wrote long letters bemoaning their endless complaints.

It was all fairly mundane family business.

The journal likewise contained nothing to connect Farrow to either Dupont's death or the scheme to murder Hardwicke. In recording his private thoughts on the matter of the secretary's plunge, he expressed only horror and drew a coarse sketch of the body as it had appeared to him on the pavement below. The dozens of lines around the dead man's left arm were indicative of his inability to properly describe its position earlier in the pub.

Apparently, Farrow had been puzzling over it for some time.

Verity turned to earlier pages, reading about events of the previous week, then the previous month, and ultimately the previous year. He was a surprisingly faithful chronicler for a drunkard who had to be hauled out of the pub on a thrice weekly basis, with neat handwriting and a nimble turn of phrase. His description of the ambassador as an attention vortex was apt, and his courtship of a dancer in Covent Garden who was secretly married to a gardener explained his wariness of dirty fingernails.

Having no reason to hurry, she flipped through the pages of the journal, perusing a paragraph or two, skimming ahead when she found nothing of interest. When she was finished, she returned it to the cabinet along with the letters. Then she shook the Cazotte books, opened the tins next to the fireplace, and ran her fingers over the floorboards in search of hidden notes or a torn scrap of paper with half of a Gherkin Lane address on it.

None of these endeavors yielded anything of interest. Aside from an overly enthusiastic rendition of a marching song beloved by Napoleon himself, André Farrow revealed no undue attachment to the French Empire, and Verity could not believe a man of his excesses would earn a sobriquet as mild as Tipsy. Eliminating him from her list of suspects, she straightened the tins on the shelf, covered him with one of the blankets, and slipped silently out of his rooms.

# Chapter Ten

*Sunday, June 14*
*10:36 a.m.*

The Beaufoy family—Beaufoy, his wife, and their three children—attended church at St. Mary's in Cadogan Street. They reached the building well after ten o'clock despite leaving in plenty of time to arrive before the service began. Michel, the young child for whom the birthday recommendations Verity had found in the rubbish were intended, was easily distracted and stopped frequently on their walk to admire the curve of an iron gate or the shape of a pretty flower or a puddle in the street. Impatiently, his father would try to hurry him along, grabbing him by the elbow and tugging, which produced the opposite of the desired effect. Twice the little dear sat down on the pavement and obstinately crossed his legs. On both occasions it fell to Mrs. Beaufoy to cajole the surly boy back on to his feet and nudge him gently forward.

By the time they entered St. Mary's, the best pews were taken and Beaufoy squeezed all five of them into a single bench toward the rear, ruthlessly wedging the worshipper at the far end against the seat's arm.

Confident the family was settled for the next hour or so, Verity returned to the house to search for incriminating evidence among Beaufoy's belonging. From her observation earlier that morning, she knew the envoy extraordinary employed eight servants in total, and several had already left for the day to spend time with their families. All that remained in the house were the cook and two footmen, none of whom worried her unduly. The former would most likely be engrossed in preparing the roast for dinner, with the latter hovering nearby as he enjoyed a rich cup of coffee or tea at his employer's expense.

These assumptions proved accurate as Verity entered the residence via the front door, which she unlocked with ease. Wasting no time, she darted into the first room she passed, a drawing room decorated in gracious blues and plaster moldings. The furniture was sturdy and neat, with few pricks or stains, and the only piece of interest was the escritoire. All it contained, however, was Mrs. Beaufoy's correspondence with her sister, whose morning sickness with her second child was somewhat worse than with her first. The physician had advised a tincture of ginger but as of yet it had not yielded satisfactory results. She begged her sister to send advice and suggestions.

Coming to the dining room next, Verity paused on the threshold and noted the table in the center was large and could accommodate up to ten people. Above it hung an elaborate chandelier. The couple either enjoyed entertaining or felt the maintenance of Beaufoy's position required it. As envoy extraordinary, he probably had to host colleagues or visiting dignitaries from time to time. The house, which was of a comfortable size, on par with the one Dupont had been scheduled to look at the day before, was well suited to guests, she thought, as she inspected the sideboard for secret missives or hidden compartments containing secret missives.

She found neither and proceeded to the first floor. At the top of the staircase, she located the parlor, an elegant room also swathed in shades of blue. On a pedestal table near to the window lay three issues of *Ackermann's Repository*, and a pair of porcelain figurines rested on a display cabinet whose drawers held playing cards and jars of snuff.

The Beaufoys' bedchambers were down a short corridor, and although she readily identified her target's room by the simplicity of its furnishings and lack of hair ribbons, she examined both spaces to be thorough. Mrs. Beaufoy was in the middle of composing a letter to her mother. Only three paragraphs in, she had so far expressed concern over her sister's health, recounted her children's recent exploits, and aired her frustration at the ever-changing menu for the upcoming reception for the Spanish ambassador, for his excellency kept switching dishes, from pigeon to capon to squab. Beaufoy's room likewise contained a narrow table he used for writing, as the scribbled drafts of his new-spirit-of-cooperation speech attested. He continued to struggle over its wording, and in the margin of the version dated that morning he had added notes reminding himself not to hesitate between sentences and to avoid awkward interjections such as "um" and "er."

"Remember, do not undermine the dignity of France with uncertainty!" he had written.

Nevertheless, he appeared to be making progress, having composed a full page of remarks.

Discouraged to find nothing incriminating, Verity climbed to the second floor. Although she had little expectation of stumbling across a concealed trove of evidence hidden among the children's playthings, she was obligated to check.

There was no point in conducting only a mostly comprehensive search.

Peering across the street into the embassy, Verity spied two porters, one standing near the entry way, just on the other side of the door, and the other passing by the entrance at regular intervals, an indication that he was patrolling the corridors.

Clearly, both men were guarding against intruders, and although she could see only two from her vantage, she assumed there were others. With this in mind, she decided to enter the building through one of the windows in the back. It was a risk because sometimes the method required breaking glass and the shattering sound could draw attention. But she had grown adept at imitating a robin to mask the noise.

Such a maneuver was not required, however, because the window opened easily, and she slid effortlessly over the windowsill. She landed on the floor with a soft thump and examined her surroundings. It was an unremarkable office.

Very good.

She walked to the door and pressed her ear against it to listen for footsteps. Hearing none, she opened it slowly.

As expected, the corridor was empty.

Verity darted to the left and ran to the staircase.

Breaking into the embassy was a risk, to be sure, but no greater than Twaddle's usual antics and several times less hazardous than infiltrating Carlton House to find out the menu for the prince regent's birthday fete in advance of the celebration. Even if the guards were plentiful, which she thought likely they were not, they would be accustomed to a certain rhythm and pace. Every Sunday they walked the floor, their heels landing with jarring clarity on the marble, the sound echoing in the empty hallways.

Repetition had a lulling effect.

Verity knew this from years of experience.

She had slipped unnoticed into dozens of buildings and frequently observed bored guards examining their own finger-nails or reading the newspaper or fiddling with the wick on a candlestick. Sometimes they fell asleep or gathered in a group at one end of the hallway to chat. Every so often one of them would notice something amiss and investigate it further. On those occasions it was best to duck into a dark corner or behind a door or in a display of giraffes if that was the only option available. (Why, yes, she *had* almost been caught sneaking around Montague House several hours after it closed to examine the Rosetta Stone to confirm that an industrious librarian had filled in the inscription with white chalk to make it easier to read.)

As she climbed the stairs now, she darted her eyes from the left to the right, constantly evaluating her environment for a place to hide. She heard footfalls as she approached the landing and held back until they receded. Confirming the area was clear, she rounded the bend and darted up the next flight to the second floor. Beaufoy's office was to the left, and although she pinched her shoulder cramming herself behind a large urn, she had evaded notice. The bruise was minor, but she would have gracefully suffered any number of minor injuries to gather information regarding the envoy's participation in the scheme to abduct her. Uncertainty irritated her. The absence of proof proved nothing—a truism she always found irksome but was espe-cially vexing now because she knew that by the time she returned to Bethel Street Hardwicke would have sent around a polite missive announcing the conclusion of his own investigation.

She could not have Hardwicke making firm determinations while she floundered.

Leaving the safety of the urn, Verity ran the final few yards to Beaufoy's office, entered it silently, and launched into a quick but methodical search. Obviously, the best piece of evidence would be the torn half of the scrap Dupont had been holding when he died, but anything indicating either a passionate love of Napoleon or a devious mind bent on mischief would do—at least as a place to start.

Reading his papers, she realized the envoy extraordinary was organized and ambitious. He kept a copy of Morny's schedule in an effort to anticipate his employer's requirements as well as a journal in which he recorded the tasks he needed to do that day. Next to each entry was a note detailing how the task was performed and its degree of success.

Alas, there was no item mentioning the abduction of Miss Lark or the assassination of Lord Colson.

There were, however, screeds against Boney written in the margins, long-winded tirades about the encompassing egoism that allowed a man to think he can subvert the will of God and crown himself emperor. And then to wage war with other nations in a bid for further gratification—the conceit was unimaginable!

Verily, Beaufoy was no admirer of Napoleon.

If not for the man's warmongering his knee would not ache every time the weather turned damp, an occurrence that happened with alarming regularity in the chilly clime of this dreary city.

The diplomat was glad Boney had been banished to St. Helena.

Good riddance!

It was, Verity thought, returning the schedule to its position on the desk, the first piece of evidence that argued against Beaufoy's guilt. If in his private thoughts he espoused naught but hatred and disgust for the deposed leader, then she could not believe he would work to support him with his public actions, especially when those actions could have dire consequences. Beaufoy had a lovely family, and it would be foolhardy to risk their safety and welfare for something he actively despised.

If he subscribed to the cause, it would be different.

Or if the cause benefited him.

But a scheme to exact revenge on a former spy for events long since passed—that required a fanatic. As Beaufoy did not fit that description, Verity looked for further evidence to support his innocence, which was difficult. She did not find the torn scrap despite searching every nook and cranny of the office, including the ash in the fireplace and in the hollow of the desk legs, but the absence of proof remained inconclusive.

It was vexing indeed!

Having gleaned all she could from the office, Verity made sure everything was in its place, cautiously opened the door, and strode to the steps. She ran down two flights of stairs until she arrived at the ground floor and turned to the right, all but knocking into the guard, who was resting one elbow on the balustrade.

She pulled up sharply, her shoulders wrenching from the hard backward wrench as she scampered up the stairs backward, her movements so swift and abrupt papers would flutter in her wake.

Fortunately, the guard was not holding a newspaper and registered the slight breeze as only the quiver of a fly, which he absently brushed away from his neck. Roused by the insect or possibly the thought of more, the guard lowered his arm and resumed his rounds, allowing Verity the opportunity to dart into an office on the ground floor ... no, wait, it was a storage closet ... and climb out the window.

It was time to establish contact with her quarry.

*Sunday, June 14*
*3:17 p.m.*

Verity, identifying herself as Mr. Smithson from Cotswold and Co., apologized for arriving late for their appointment. It was Sunday, you see, which was a highly unusual day for conducting business, but as Mr. Jacoby's most successful leasing agent—she had secured three new rentals the previous week alone—she went where she was told and never bothered her employer with needless questions.

"Mr. Jacoby said you were eager to list your home with us," she continued, adopting many of the same mannerisms of the leasing agent she had met the morning before, including his habit of biting his bottom lip between sentences. "I assure you, we are just as eager to list your home. I must say, from what I have seen already, the property is lovely. I stood across the street, as is my custom, and noted the house has what I call pavement appeal—that is, the sense of warmth and comfort you get from an edifice when you examine it from the pavement."

If Beaufoy was surprised to find himself face-to-face with the very person whose name was on the torn sheet clutched two days ago in a dead man's grip, his expression gave no indication. Instead, he explained in pristine English that the caller had made a mistake. "We do not have an appointment with you or anyone today. I am sorry you wasted your time. Please enjoy the rest of the day."

Although he moved to close the door, Verity did what

Verity always did: remained firmly in the way. Biting her lip, she pulled a slip of paper from her pocket and held it up for Beaufoy's inspection. "Are you sure? I have the information right here in Mr. Jacoby's own handwriting. It says 33 Gore Lane and that I am to call at three o'clock. Again, I am sorry for my tardiness. I received this message only forty-five minutes ago and had to change before paying the call. I could not represent Cotswold and Co. in my gardening smock."

Beaufoy replied again that they did not have an appointment. "You have interrupted your day for nothing, which is a pity. But please enjoy what remains of it."

Gravely, Verity cautioned him against working with Slattery and Sons, who, unlike Cotswold, did not offer a happy-tenant guarantee.

"I am not working with Slattery and Sons," Beaufoy said with the first hint of impatience. "Or any other firm for that matter. We are not looking to lease a new home. We are more than comfortable here."

"Ah, but are you happy?" Verity asked leadingly and paused to allow the diplomat to answer. When he did not respond, she continued. "If you are not happy, then I urge you to consider moving to a home more suited to your needs. I am certain you have heard of Cotswold and the fine work we do. Perhaps a friend recommended us? Or a colleague?"

Despite this pointed reference, his face remained impassive, and Verity wondered if he truly did not recognize the name or if he had simply learned how to control all reactions during his tenure as a diplomat.

Both seemed conceivable.

If it was the former, then the argument that precipitated Dupont's fall probably had nothing to do with the notice itself. It was merely the thing he happened to have in his hand when the shove came. If it was the latter, then Beaufoy was a diabolical opponent.

"We are happy, thank you," Beaufoy said, making another attempt to shut the door.

Verity, her foot still firmly in the way, noted movement in the hallway and called out to Mrs. Beaufoy, who had strode toward the door with curiosity. She was holding their youngest child, the one who was fascinated by iron gates and blossoming flowers, and he squirmed in her grasp. Lowering him to the floor, she greeted Mr. Smithson warmly.

Before his wife could embroil them further, Beaufoy rushed to explain that the leasing agent was just leaving. But *leasing agent* was the wrong thing to say, for Mrs. Beaufoy's face lit up with excitement as she owned herself eager to find a new situation. "Do not misunderstand me: This home is *charmante*," she said in an accent more pronounced than her husband's. "But there are five of us now and it is a little *petite*. And it would be *merveilleuse* to have more room for all of us and the servants. And I would like to hire more staff. There is so much work to do and so few of them."

Beaufoy opened his mouth to object just as Verity praised this goal. Having a home large enough to accommodate one's entire staff was vital for one's happiness.

"*Précisément!*" Mrs. Beaufoy said eagerly, noting that she had been dreaming of a larger home for several months. "This house was *adéquate* when we first came to London and did not know how long we would stay. Guillaume did not know if he would like the assignment. His superior has a reputation for being *mauvais caractère*. But now we are settled, and Guillaume is *prospère* at the embassy, and the lack of space has become *cofiner*. I am so pleased to meet you, Mr. Smithson. Please come in and join us for tea. Nanny was just about to serve the children some cakes. I know! We shall have brandy to mark the occasion. Guillaume will fetch a *joli millésime* from the cellars, won't you, *mon amour*? We so rarely indulge, either of us."

Beaufoy blushed, mortified by his wife's assumptions, and although he tried several times to interrupt, it was not until she had ended her speech on this celebratory note that he managed to explain that it was all a misunderstanding. "We are not moving houses. I did not invite Mr. Smithson here. He was sent here in error and was just about to leave."

But Verity, who was not so easily deterred, stated that she had been clearly sent to 33 Gore Lane by a higher force to rectify a great unhappiness. "The offer of brandy is extremely unusual in my line of business, and I am not sure Mr. Jacoby would approve. But, yes, Mrs. Beaufoy, I should be delighted to have a glass, as it appears the hand of fate has brought me here to rescue you from these cramped quarters."

Firmly, her husband rescinded the invitation.

Verity, continuing as if he had not spoken, asked Mrs. Beaufoy what she saw when she closed her eyes. "I find it most helpful to begin with a picture of your ideal home, and then together we can discuss what is vital to your happiness and what is expendable. Cotswold and Co. represents some of the finest residences in all of London, and since you are staying here for the foreseeable future, you should find a residence that matches your vision as closely as possible. You are French, aren't you, Mrs. Beaufoy? And as a Frenchwoman, you have had a difficult time of it recently, with the detestable war. You want comfort now and peace. I believe we can find you both."

"This home is peaceful!" Beaufoy said with indignation.

"But is it?" Verity asked, tilting her head toward the doorway and cupping her ear. "I am certain I hear screaming."

"Those are my children," he replied stiffly.

"Exactly," Verity said. "And if your home were larger, you would not be able to hear them right now. Peace, as I said, and well deserved after the long war."

The color in the envoy's cheeks darkened as Mrs. Beaufoy noted that their nanny frequently said the same thing.

Verity lauded her wisdom and suggested a large garden so that the children could play outside. "Cotswold and Co. have several listings for houses with generous outdoor spaces. We should discuss that requirement and others over that glass of brandy. You say you rarely indulge? Isn't that unusual for the French?"

Mrs. Beaufoy allowed that it was and said that her husband could not abide by most vintages, for they were harsh and inferior, with a bitter aftertaste that lingered. "He is cursed with a refined palate and can only enjoy *le meilleur*, which is difficult to find and costs so much when we do, especially in England. We can afford to buy only a few bottles at a time."

"That is correct!" Beaufoy said, seizing the opportunity to interject. "Our resources are limited, and we must restrict ourselves to what we can afford. To live within one's means *is* ideal, and that is why this house suits us. We can pay the rent and settle our bill with the grocer in a timely fashion. Anything less is unacceptable to a man of honor. Thank you, Mr. Smithson, for generously giving us your time. But it is Sunday, and it is not Christianly to allow you to work on the Lord's day in open defiance of His strictures. It goes against my conscience."

He issued the statement with convincing earnestness, seemingly more concerned about the leasing agent's soul than his own, and Verity was annoyed by how difficult it was to discern his true opinion from his words. That was a product of his profession, of course, for feigning sincerity was the bread-and-butter of diplomacy. It was with that in mind that she had decided to introduce herself as the name on the sheet of paper: She had hoped to unnerve Beaufoy into revealing honest emotion. The sudden appearance of Dupont's leasing agent on his doorstep defied sense, and a guilty man would immediately fear that his secret was known.

Finding his lack of response irritatingly inconclusive, she nevertheless believed the visit to his home had been fruitful. Mrs. Beaufoy's revelation regarding her husband's drinking habits made it unlikely that Dupont had taken to calling him Tipsy as a sly taunt behind his back. It was possible the diplomat behaved differently at the embassy, either imbibing any old swill liberally or hoarding expensive wine secretly, but she had not seen evidence of that in his office. There were no bottles of brandy in the cabinet or desk.

He seemed duly sober.

In addition to his sobriety was the notable lack of motive. Despising Napoleon, he had no cause to risk his life and position to strike back against one of England's greatest spies. Even if he resented the reparations his country was forced to pay in the wake of its defeat, he was sensible enough to know that was Boney's fault: Countries that did not conquer foreign lands were not required to offer restitution.

Taken together, these developments argued for his innocence.

Beaufoy urged Mr. Smithson to return to his gardening. "It is a worthy pursuit, and you should take advantage of the good weather while it lasts."

His wife, seconding this observation, added that it had been an appalling spring so far and that the children were behind in their riding lessons. At the mention of horses, the little boy on the floor leaped up and asked if they could visit the stable. He repeated the request several times, his whine growing more insistent with each mention, and Beaufoy darted an impatient look at his wife, silently imploring her to calm the child. Calmly, Mrs. Beaufoy lifted the boy into her arms, her grip firm despite his attempts to writhe free, and told him he could play with the horses in the nursery. Then, as she turned to walk away, she noted how lovely it would be to live in an area that had mews.

Verity, in Mr. Smithson's most officious tone, advised the departing figure to make a list of features her ideal residence would have so that when her current situation became intolerable, she and her husband would be able to find a new one as quickly as possible. "Include how many servants you want to hire and which neighborhoods please you the most. Here, I will leave my card with your husband."

But before she could reach into her pocket, Beaufoy closed the door with an emphatic clap.

*Sunday, June 14*
*4:44 p.m.*

Hardwicke was in the parlor when Verity returned.

Delphine, settled comfortably on the settee, sat across from his lordship, nibbling delicately on a slice of cheddar cheese as she discussed the challenges of cultivating onions. Although *Mrs. Meacham's Book of Household Management, Including Sections on Cookery, Cleaning, and Plant Rearing* was not on hand for convenient reference, several of its most helpful suggestions were discussed with knowledgeable familiarity.

Whereas Verity had to read paragraphs directly from the compendium to bore her visitor, Delphine could do it from memory.

To his credit, Hardwicke did not look bored.

If anything, he appeared engrossed.

"Keep the topsoil loose, you say," he murmured.

"To improve drainage and increase root activity," Delphine intoned wisely. "It is a mistake to assume topsoil does not need to be tilled. Compact soil is dry and poorly aerated. Generally, if it is hard for you to dig, then it is hard for roots to grow."

"Fascinating," he said with a gentle shake of his head. "And what do you recommend for cabbage?"

"Lots of room between plants and fish emulsion," Delphine replied.

As delighted as Verity was at the image of Hardwicke patiently listening to a detailed recipe for emulsifying the fluid remains of fish, she decided her time was better spent discovering what he had learned about his pair of suspects and then sending him on his way. Although he had said he would provide a report on his progress via messenger, she was not altogether surprised he had decided to make it in person.

Presumably, he had found out something interesting and wanted to see her expression when he revealed it.

"Oh, good, you are here, Hardwicke," she said, striding into the room as she removed Mr. Smithson's hat. "That saves me the trouble of writing."

Hardwicke rose to his feet and sketched a bow as he bid her good afternoon. "In fact, I was saving my own self the trouble. I have removed Ardisson and Perrault from the list and added the ambassador himself."

Well, that was indeed something interesting, Verity thought, sitting down, her eyes hardly flickering at the disclosure. Nothing had steered her in the direction of Morny, and she was deeply curious to know what had pointed him. Pouring herself a cup of tea, she encouraged him to explain.

Hardwicke, owning himself happy to comply, began by detailing how he had eliminated his first two suspects. "To start: Perrault injured his wrist on Monday, when he tripped on a slippery curb, an accident that was witnessed by three people, and could not muster the force to push Dupont with the sprained joint. Ardisson was talking to Karembeu in the hallway when Dupont fell, which I confirmed with two sources, one of whom mentioned that Morny had been briefly part of the conversation before continuing along the corridor toward Dupont's office. That puts him in reasonable proximity to the crime. He would also have the good sense not to remain in the vicinity. Immediately going outside to take control of the tragedy is precisely what the head of the mission would do."

Verity, recalling the lavish assortment of decanters half filled with richly colored liquids in Morny's office, noted the ambassador's apparent fondness for alcohol.

"Cognac is a particular weakness," Hardwicke agreed. "And he knew Dupont from the Ministry of Police well enough to send him to Paris to keep an eye on his rivals in the Ministry of Foreign Affairs. It is not implausible that if the comte was looking for someone to carry out a perilous and illicit assignment, he would ask him. That said, I cannot see Morny engaging in machinations that are so heavy-handed. He has a light touch, and if he wanted Typhoeus dead, I would already be in the grave."

Verity, agreeing with his understanding of the ambassador's character, added that it was difficult to imagine him risking his own security now, after the many deft manipulations to land on the right side of the conflict in France had come to fruition. If murdering one of his own underlings was impudent, then killing an English war hero was utter madness.

Naturally, Hardwicke felt compelled to demur, for *war hero* was an exaggeration, but the gist of her observation was accurate. "Revenge is a fool's mission, and the comte is cunning and practical. It does not make sense to me. And yet there is no accounting for the logic of small resentments."

"You only know what you know," Verity murmured thoughtfully. "There could be entire dramas involving Typhoeus of which you are unaware. Or what you thought of as a cordial relationship might have been something else altogether to him."

Hardwicke allowed that the explanation was possible, noting that he had been recently reminded of how easily one could be misunderstood despite the clarity with which one communicated—although, he added, sometimes the misconstruction was deliberate.

He spoke coolly, dispassionately, as though describing a scientific phenomenon he had once observed with uninterest, and yet he stared at Verity with fierce concentration.

Startled, she realized it was an accusation against her.

More than twenty-four hours later, and Hardwicke was still smarting over her refusal to melt into a puddle of terror and panic at the prospect of being imprisoned in a damp tavern cellar for a few hours.

Verity wanted to be astonished by it, for the inability to calmly accept a truth and move on to the next concern seemed to run counter to his work as a spy, which required him to be nimble in his actions and opinions. And yet it was all of a piece with his perception of her as a helpless female who must be protected.

All women were weak.

Delphine, also taking note of the criticism implied by the look, glanced at her friend inquisitively, and Verity, no more able to comprehend the small-mind limitations of male thinking, lifted her shoulders in a light shrug. Then she asked Hardwicke if there was anything else he wanted to add before she reported on her two suspects.

"Thank you, no," he replied politely. "I have nothing more. You may proceed."

Verity launched into an account of her interaction with Farrow. "The evidence is not as conclusive as Ardisson's injured wrist, but I believe it is persuasive. Farrow harbors no love for Boney and as such has no motive. Furthermore, he is too much of a drunkard to conceive a plan as elaborate as the one in which Dupont was engaged, and I cannot fathom anyone seeing Farrow in the state of advance inebriation to which he frequently succumbs and thinking to describe him with as mild a term as Tipsy."

Finding this assessment reasonable, Hardwicke agreed to remove Farrow from contention. "And what of Beaufoy?"

"Like Farrow, he has no obvious motive," she said. "He also hates Napoleon and blames him for his damaged knee, which was wounded in the war. He has much to lose. He has a wife and three children, and although they do not live extravagantly, they have a comfortable home in Gore Lane. Beaufoy is ambitious. I believe he has his eye on the ambassadorship after Morny leaves the position. Finally, he does not appear to drink to excess or much at all. According to his wife, he limits himself to only the finest brandy, which is rare and expensive, and I could find no proof to the contrary when I searched his home and office at the embassy."

"You do not think he did it," Hardwicke observed pensively.

Verity exhaled heavily and admitted it seemed unlikely. "The only evidence I can cite to support his guilt is circumstantial: He was in the office very soon after the murder was committed, and he was the first person Dupont went to see when he escaped our cellar. Both events have alternate explanations that are equally reasonable, which makes me think we should eliminate him as well."

Freddie, entering the parlor in time to hear this statement, asked who they were eliminating now and who had they eliminated before.

"Farrow then, Beaufoy now," Verity said.

As her friend crossed the floor, Delphine held out the plate of cheese and meat for his inspection. "We are reviewing suspects for the Dupont murder. Verity was just saying that she does not think Mr. Beaufoy is the culprit."

Gratefully, Freddie accepted a piece of cheddar and sat down in an armchair. "Well, I should certainly hope not! Can you imagine the frenzy it would create if a high-ranking member of the French mission to the Court of St. James's killed an English war hero on English soil? It would be nothing less than an international incident on a grand scale and would most likely spark a resumption of hostilities between the countries. At the very least, the renewed spirit of international cooperation would be dealt a deadly blow."

Delphine advised him against describing Hardwicke as a *war hero,* for their unfettered admiration embarrassed him, and Verity gawped in dumbfounded astonishment as Freddie's statement echoed in her head: *resumption of hostilities between the countries.*

Hearing it stated so plainly made everything clear, and raising her gaze in profound understanding, she found herself staring into Hardwicke's strange teal eyes.

They, too, were bright with comprehension.

# Chapter Eleven

*Sunday, June 14*
*5:28 p.m.*

Freddie acknowledged Delphine's remark with an absent nod, his attention focused on the idea he had just proposed. As the editor of the *London Daily Gazette,* he could not help evaluating the possibility with dispassionate interest, as though already seeing the story on the front page of his own newspaper. "I suppose if you wanted maximum impact from the assassination, you would do it in the embassy building because that would make it appear as though the French government had sanctioned it. From that perspective, shooting him in Hyde Park or on the street seems like a wasted opportunity. And arranging the deed so that it looked like an accident?" he murmured with a disapproving press of his lips. "Why even bother? If your goal is to create chaos or undermine the fragile peace between our countries, then killing Typhoeus as publicly as possible is the only logical way to go about it. I mean, just picture the headlines!"

Appalled, Delphine called him a heartless wretch for discussing their friend Lord Colson's demise so callously, and a blush rose in his cheeks as he muttered that it was a hazard of his occupation. Defensively, he added that Verity understood, then he sought out her gaze in a bid for solidarity.

But she was still staring at Hardwicke.

Stunned by the revelation sparked by Freddie's original comment, she realized now how much she had failed to understand.

Decisively, she said, "Two events."

Hardwicke, nodding in agreement, replied, "Separate attempts."

Verity put down her teacup as she marveled at the complexity of the plot.

But no, it was not complex.

It was simply crowded.

So many cooks fussing over the same broth.

Confused, Delphine asked what they meant by their statements just as Freddie said, "No, really? No! But I suppose ... "

Delphine begged them all to clarify at once. "I do not appreciate these oblique references to something quite dire or shocking!"

Verity darted a look at Hardwicke, as if to gain his consent, before explaining that they had been operating under a misapprehension. "We assumed the plotters' decision to abduct me was the direct result of their failure to murder Hardwicke. We decided they had switched tactics when he proved too difficult to kill: gain control of me to gain control of him. But the attacks are unrelated. The attempts against Hardwicke have nothing to do with the attempt against me."

Although Delphine narrowed her eyes dubiously, she did not argue. "And you think this now because of what Freddie said about an assassination subverting the peace between our countries? I do not understand. It still seems like a great leap to me."

"Well, yes," Verity allowed graciously. "But not really because there were so many discrepancies in the way the various attacks were carried out, and abducting me to manipulate Hardwicke is a difficult way to go about something fairly simple. The killer has the advantage. It is just a matter of time until Hardwicke is dead. Attempt after attempt—sooner or later, one would succeed because a murderer has to be lucky only once, but the victim has to be lucky every time. Why, then, incite Hardwicke's fury by abducting the woman you believe he is courting?"

"You do not," Delphine said, perceiving at once the distinction her friend was endeavoring to make. "You provoke Typhoeus's rage only if it is useful to you—in this case, arranging for his surrender in exchange for your life. That is the first step to creating the newspaper headlines that have people like Freddie salivating."

"Well, I say, Delph, *salivating* is an awfully strong word," Freddie protested. "Do I have an innate appreciation for the more sensational aspects of certain timely events? I do, yes. I am only human *and* I operate a newspaper."

But Delphine paid little attention to his self-justifying reply because she was still sifting through Verity's explanation. "And by *discrepancies,* you mean the variations in the attempts of which we are aware: Some were made to appear as accidents and others were blatant and in one the would-be assassin drew close enough to Hardwicke to push him. The implication is that these attempts are unrelated to each other. Rather than there being one large plot to murder Typhoeus, there are many small plots. Is that correct? Dozens of people are trying to kill Hardwicke?"

Hardwicke, who revealed no alarm at this revelation,

insisted that *dozens* was perhaps a bit hyperbolic. "Let us say only half a dozen."

"Yes, *only* six," Delphine murmured, regarding him with the same exasperation with which she often looked at Verity. "Fending off only *six* murderers is much easier than fending off twelve or twenty-four."

Soberly, Hardwicke replied that in fact it was. "Obviously, fending off three murderers is easier still, but I am grateful it is not nine."

Delphine, who would have responded churlishly if Verity had issued this sensible reply, agreed that it was wise to keep the threat in perspective. "Nevertheless, I think it behooves us all to be a little more worried by the fact that we are contending with several nefarious entities, not just one. Whatever solution we devise to address the abduction threat will not help us fix the assassin problem, and I am not certain which concern should take priority."

Hardwicke said the abduction threat.

Verity, whose mind was already racing with the challenge of how to discourage a pack of killers all at once, for that was the only way to handle the problem—with a single stroke, or else be forever plugging holes in the dike as new ones emerged—gave the opposite answer. "Without question, we must dispense with the assassins first, for they are the more pressing threat. We cannot rely on good luck, and with every attempt the risk of success grows. Furthermore, as individuals, they have the advantage because they can move with greater speed and efficiency than an elaborate cabal. The men behind the abduction plot are clearly in disarray, as demonstrated by their killing one of their own. It will probably take Tipsy at least another week to find someone to replace Dupont. I am safe until then."

What Verity did not add—although she thought it, of course, for it was nothing less than the truth—was that she was always safe. The fact that she had swiftly disarmed her intruder, turning the tables on him by taking him prisoner and confining him to her own cellar, underscored just how capable she was at defending herself. She held her tongue because it would only provoke Hardwicke and distract from the topic at hand.

Even with her restraint, he turned to her with a vaguely thunderous glare, a deep groove lodged between his brows, and said that the abduction scheme was more urgent because it was more recent. "There has not been an attempt on my life since Tuesday."

"Has there not?" Verity asked coolly. "Or is that what you want us to believe?"

Devil it! She had not intended to allude to his condescending treatment of her. The damn words had slipped out unbidden.

Responding with the same aloofness, he said he wanted nothing from her. "I am merely suggesting that we take the logical course by continuing to identify Tipsy. If you would prefer to be illogical, Miss Lark, then by all means let us be illogical. What do you propose, then, as a solution for the problem of multiple assassins?"

His tone was doubting.

He could not conceive that she already had a half-formed notion percolating in her head. And he should have because it was a variation on the gambit he had used on her to set himself up as a spy in the first place. Twaddle could find evidence that pointed to someone else as the heroic Typhoeus. Whoever it was could not still be alive, for then their life would immediately be in danger, but she imagined it would be possible to find a dead soldier whose reputation could withstand burnishing.

She felt confident her network would be able to supply her with a few names.

But the question was, how would the infamous gossip "stumble" across the truth?

The tale would have to be plausible or else potential assassins would recognize it for the ruse it was.

Before Verity could finish these thoughts, Freddie said, "There is no contest between the two. Of course we will devote our energies to figuring out who is behind the attempted abduction because it is a matter of national importance. Whoever is behind the scheme wants to spark discord between England and France and possibly reignite hostilities. We cannot stand by and allow malignant forces to disrupt our hard-earned peace. And with Morny's speech to the Tip-Tapp Club on Friday extolling a new era of international cooperation, we do not have much time. I am convinced they will strike before then in order to create as much chaos as possible. As you can imagine, the display of contempt would be intolerable for Liverpool, who will be in attendance, and England would have no choice but to strike back twice as hard out of humiliation."

Here, Delphine tepidly informed him that the comte had just been added to their list of suspects. "Hardwicke himself gathered the evidence against him."

Taken aback by the development, Freddie turned to the other man with a doubtful expression. "Are you sure, sir? The head of the envoy seeking to destroy his own mission? Isn't that just a little too diabolical? It would mean Morny has no loyalty at all to Louis XVIII or the constitutional monarchy or anything else he has sworn to defend."

But Verity, who had an aesthetic appreciation of all schemes regardless of their immorality or cunning, thought it was the perfect amount of diabolical, as his post put him above suspicion. "In any plot or ploy, you want to be the last person anyone would suspect. That is the best situation if you can arrange it. And Freddie is right. The political repercussions of Tipsy's machinations do make that problem the more pressing one, and I think it is reasonable to take Morny's speech on international cooper—"

Verity broke off.

*Morny*'s speech?

But Beaufoy had been preparing remarks on that exact topic all week.

She asked Freddie if he was certain the comte was the one making the speech.

"I am, yes," Freddie said firmly. "Who else would make it?"

"Beaufoy," she replied.

The editor wrinkled his brow in confusion. "Why would the ambassador have his deputy deliver an important speech to the Tip-Tapp Club when he is capable of doing it himself? I suppose if he fell ill or had an urgent family matter to which to attend, then Beaufoy would step in, although I think it is more likely that Morny would ask them to reschedule the event to a later date."

"Attention vortex," Verity murmured as several ideas occurred to her at once. "In his journal, Farrow described the comte as an attention vortex, which rings true because he waylaid John Pennie when he was en route to interview Beaufoy. He assumed I was only interested in his second in command as a conduit to him and assured me such efforts were not necessary. And yet Beaufoy is writing the speech on international cooperation. I have seen several drafts as he struggles to refine the language. He was even working on it this morning because I read a draft dated today and he has written notes to himself on how to deliver it. Why would Beaufoy write a speech he has no hope of delivering?"

Astounded by the implication, Freddie stared blankly as Hardwicke complimented Verity on the astute deduction. Delphine, who had also followed the line of reasoning, refused to accept the level of depravity that would induce a man to murder simply to seize the opportunity to make an important address.

"It's not about the address," Verity explained patiently. "The speech is merely one of a myriad of responsibilities he would assume as the new ambassador after he discredited the old one. That is the plan: He needed to capture Hardwicke alive so that he could deposit his fresh corpse on Morny's doorstep to make it appear as though he murdered a famous English spy in revenge, effectively ending his career. Given the comte's history of switching sides to convenience himself, the turn would not be impossible to believe. But Morny is wily. He has excellent instincts, and he might be able to convince the authorities that he was the victim of a nefarious plot. Even so, the best he could hope for is banishment to one of his country estates. Liverpool could not allow him to remain on English soil, and the French king would be horribly embarrassed. Better all-around to bury reminders and pretend nothing happened."

But the ruthlessness of the scheme continued to defy Delphine's understanding, for the distinction between the speech and the post seemed too minor to justify homicide. "And furthermore, why would Dupont call him Tipsy when you yourself discovered that Beaufoy rarely imbibes?"

Confident her theory was correct, Verity realized their understanding of Tipsy must be wrong. Perhaps Benson had misheard the term or maybe it was a reference to something other than alcohol.

What else made one tipsy?

His injury!

Yes, of course.

"He suffered a wound to his knee during the war," Verity said, noting that the damp English weather did his frail joint no favors. "It gives way from time to time—that is what Morny said."

"Causing him to wobble unsteadily," Freddie added, then addressed Delphine's second point, urging her not to discount the vast difference in status between an ambassador and an envoy extraordinary. The former lived lavishly at the expense of his home country, with a retinue of servants, while the latter enjoyed a more ordinary existence. "Morny's chief responsibility is making and maintaining social connections and providing entertainment and hospitality. That demands luxury and splendor. Although Beaufoy does not possess the grand lineage of Morny, the Foreign Ministry would put him in charge of the embassy immediately to ensure a smooth transition and to patch up the riff in international relations as quickly as possible."

Verity, recalling her conversation with Mrs. Beaufoy, noted that the envoy extraordinary's wife would appreciate the gracious proportions of Morny's Grosvenor Square home. "She would like a larger house with more room for the children and servants."

"A larger house," Hardwicke repeated pensively, rising to his feet and strolling to the window to gaze out onto the road. "A larger house such as the one in Gherkin Lane? It seems as though Dupont took Beaufoy's scheme for discrediting Morny and decided to use it to discredit Beaufoy instead. It would explain why he had fallen with the scrap of paper in his grasp. He knew how revealing it was and did not want Beaufoy to see it."

Verity allowed this conclusion made a particular kind of sense but could not fathom why Dupont would go to such lengths when Beaufoy's promotion would benefit his career, especially if remaining in London was a priority. "Morny was sending him back to Paris to work in the Ministry of Foreign Affairs. Beaufoy would have let him stay. He had to have promised Dupont something he wanted in order to secure his help."

"His old position?" Delphine wondered. "With Beaufoy taking over for the disgraced Morny, the embassy would need a new envoy extraordinary."

Freddie shook his head, unconvinced that a lowly secretary could rise so quickly even with the endorsement of the ambassador. "Whatever Beaufoy had pledged, it could not have been as prestigious or important as envoy extraordinary. Dupont must have realized he would go farther with Morny's support."

"And perhaps Dupont did not quite trust Beaufoy, who came up with such a devious scheme to betray his superior," Delphine suggested.

Verity, agreeing with both these assessments, further speculated that Dupont must have planned to have Hardwicke in hand before revealing the truth to the comte. "He needed proof so that the claim did not just sound like an outlandish story. He was confident Morny would be generous in his gratitude. That is why he was looking at larger houses, and he had no reason to worry about Beaufoy spotting it because Beaufoy rarely visited him in his office. But then Varon could not find the ledger and Beaufoy grew impatient and bounded up to the third, calling on his secretary and seeing the sheet with an appointment with a London leasing agent for a house twice as much as his current establishment.

In a flash, he had perceived everything.

Perhaps they quarreled.

Or maybe Beaufoy did not even bother to ask a single question and simply shoved Dupont out the open window as the other man tried to snatch the paper from his grasp.

Problem solved.

Except another one was immediately presented, for

Beaufoy now required another new minion to abduct the frail
Miss Lark.

Verity had no sooner made this observation than
Delphine said, "No, Verity, you are not going to apply for the
position."

Verity laughed, for the idea had not occurred to her.

Although now that her friend mentioned it. ...

Familiar with how the other woman's mind worked,
Delphine said no again, then darted her eyes at Hardwicke to
see how he was receiving the prospect of Verity hurling
herself into danger. He appeared unbothered, which she
found quite aggravating indeed. He had lied and obfuscated
when a nebulous threat loomed in the distance, and now that
an actual one hovered directly overhead, he was indifferent.

'Twas just like a man, she thought irritably.

"You cannot believe Beaufoy still means to go through
with it," Freddie said, shocked at the possibility of making a
second attempt after such abject failure. "His plan fell so
spectacularly short of his goal, he was driven to murder to
protect himself. Hiring another minion would expose him to
more danger."

"But you just said it yourself, Freddie," Verity replied.
"Beaufoy has already killed for his plan. He is too committed
to its success to abandon it now. I know this to be true
because he is still working on his speech. He intends to
capture me, manipulate and murder Hardwicke, and incrimi-
nate Morny by Friday. It is a daunting list of things to do. I
am confident he will seek assistance, although I trust he has
learned from his mistake and will not recruit from inside the
embassy."

"You shrugged it off as though it were a great joke, but I
know that thoughtful tone," Delphine said darkly. "You are
thinking about how you can insert yourself. But I am serious,
Verity, you will not don Jeremiah Stubb's green jacket and

introduce yourself as a sharpshooter with the 95th Rifles. I still have a hole in my favorite pelisse from the last time you dug out the Baker."

"To start, do give Lucy the garment so that she may sew up the tear," Verity said smoothly. "I do not know why you have these strange scruples about giving her work, especially when you have knitted blankets for her two nieces. Next, I am in fact contemplating the very opposite: how to convince Beaufoy that he must abduct Miss Lark himself. The best way to prove his guilt is to catch him in the act of committing the crime. Ideally, we would apprehend him as he is about to execute Hardwicke, but that is too fraught a proposition. It is my hope that once we have him red-handed, we will be able to maneuver him into confessing to Dupont's murder. I am not sure yet how we will do that, but first things first: persuading Beaufoy that he is the only one who can kidnap me. I shall have to make myself an appealing target."

Delphine, who did not appear to like this idea any more than the previous one, tightened her lips, while Freddie suggested she might develop the limp she had long been threatening to adopt on the grounds that an infirmity would make her more pathetic.

"A splendid notion," Verity said with sincere admiration, for she had indeed been contemplating the very thing for several months. As a rule of thumb, she believed that the more wretched a woman was, the less she was noticed by other people: the more pitiable, the more invisible.

Delphine deepened her frown.

Hardwicke said, "Obviously, the tack to take is for Miss Lark to introduce herself to Beaufoy as Benson from the Speckled Pig. We can assume Beaufoy knows he exists because Dupont planned to use his cellar to detain Miss Lark, but it is unlikely the two have ever met. Beaufoy would never set foot in Benson's tavern because it is infested with Bonapartists—it is too risky for his career—and Benson would have no cause to visit the embassy."

It was, Verity thought, an eminently practical solution, for the tavern keeper would be fairly simple to impersonate, thanks to the distinctive scar on his chin. "Benson shall approach him tomorrow."

"Very good," Hardwicke replied, turning his back fully to the window as he looked at her. "You must present the plan to him as something too complicated for him to attempt on his own and then give him enough details for him to realize it's not difficult at all."

"And then I will name an exorbitant price so that he is sure to refuse my help," Verity snapped impatiently. "Thank you, yes, Hardwicke, I do know how to gull a target. I have done it once or twice."

Hardwicke sketched a bow and apologized. "Naturally, you have the matter well in hand, and since that is the case, I shall bid you good night. It has been a most illuminating evening, and I leave here much better informed than when I arrived. For that, I am grateful to you all."

Flummoxed by his response, Delphine stared at him with her mouth ajar before saying with disgust, "That is it? You are just going to leave without discussing the next steps in the plan? You're going to propose that Verity dangle herself before Beaufoy like a worm on a hook and then saunter away? We're not going to talk about how we will know if Beaufoy takes the bait or who will make sure he goes after Verity on our schedule, not his own? You are truly going to leave without sorting out *any* of the details? I fetched *biscuits* for you, Lord Colson, and this is how you choose to respond—by treating the opportunity as though it were nothing, by *squandering* it? You are a sad disappointment to me, my lord. A very sad disappointment."

Hardwicke was stunned, the teal of his eyes seeming to

consume the whole of his face as he gaped at her. The color rose in his cheeks, a violently bright pink, and Verity wondered if anyone had ever reprimanded him before. Devoted followers of Twaddle knew the Marquess of Ware had lambasted his wastrel son harshly for stealing a valuable family heirloom before formally disinheriting him, but as subsequent reporting revealed that the theft was merely for show, Verity assumed no stinging set-down had actually been issued.

As the flush spread across his face, his expression sharpened into confusion. He narrowed his eyes, trying, she supposed, to make sense of the allegation.

Presumably, "I fetched *biscuits* for you" was not the sort of charge commonly lodged against him, even by his most ardent critics, and he would not have recognized the significance of the gesture when Delphine had made it the week before. She had thought she was bestowing her imprimatur on a grand romance between equals when she had left the couple alone in the parlor for five minutes but instead all she had done was expose her friend to further indignity.

It was clear to all three of them now that Hardwicke was deeply unworthy of her.

Mortified by the prospect of Hardwicke figuring out the source of Delphine's outrage, Verity nevertheless kept her tone cool and unconcerned as she replied, "There is no need for us to discuss particulars because they are readily apparent. Hardwicke will of course keep watch over Beaufoy so that we are not surprised by his behavior and will enlist either Grint's help in the surveillance or another ally. There is no reason to be concerned, my dear."

"Does Grint know?" Freddie asked. "About the attempts on Typhoeus's life and their cause? Is he aware of his former colleague's despicable behavior? Is Sidmouth?"

Generally churlish now, Delphine insisted that the home

secretary must know about his own former underling's treachery. "And if he does not know, then let the *London Daily Gazette* be the first newspaper to demand his resignation. We cannot stand idly by and allow our government to be run by a pack of incompetent ministers. It was bad enough when the Home Office allowed itself to be convinced that a milling crowd was about to launch a revolution."

The unnatural color faded from Hardwicke's cheeks as the conversation turned to less personal topics and he replied that Lord Sidmouth knew all about Kingsley's perfidy.

"And what consequences is he considering?" Delphine asked archly.

"At the risk of disappointing you further, Miss Drayton, I must confess that I have no reply. The home secretary does not share his thoughts with me," Hardwicke said.

Although it sounded like a rebuke, his tone was both gentle and sincere.

Then Hardwicke added that she was right to chastise his conduct because he should have reviewed the details of their scheme before taking his leave. "I was precipitous, and your concern for your friend is appropriate. I hope it will put your mind at ease to know that Miss Lark is correct. I will keep watch over Beaufoy with Grint's assistance. He will have no opportunity to take us unawares. We will sort out the remaining details after Miss Lark establishes contact with Beaufoy."

Delphine nodded. "Thank you."

Hardwicke paused for a moment, almost as though he expected her to say something more, but when no additional comment was forthcoming, he asked if there were any other issues he should address before departing. Receiving none, he bid them good evening. "As I observed previously, it has been enlightening."

Delphine, murmuring in agreement, offered to show him

out. He assured her it was not necessary and swept from the room.

🐚

*Sunday, June 14*
*6:58 p.m.*

As soon as she shut the parlor door behind Hardwicke, Delphine pivoted on her heels and pinned Verity with a meaningful look. "What did you do?"

Taken aback by the accusation, Verity said. "Excuse me?"

"To Hardwicke," Delphine added with a bite of impatience as she leaned her shoulders against the door. "What did you do to Hardwicke to make him furious with you?"

Glancing briefly at Freddie, then back to her friend, Verity expressed befuddlement at the question. "Was he furious?"

Delphine expelled air with comical exasperation as Freddie posited that his lordship might have seemed a trifle annoyed.

"That was fury," Delphine insisted. "What did you do to him?"

"Nothing, I promise," Verity replied. "When would I even have had the opportunity to give offense? I haven't seen him since yesterday morning, when we inspected Benson's cellar together, and there was nothing remarkable about the encounter. Truly! In fact, we had the same deary old quarrel about my not running to him the second I realized someone wanted to abduct me, and as usual, he took the high ground despite the fact that he did not run to me the second *he* realized someone wanted to murder *him*. I told him I was accustomed to the hypocrisy, for he was not the first man to offer me carte blanche, then immediately seek to curtail my freedom."

Delphine gasped. "You did not!"

"Of course I did," Verity insisted calmly, further confounded by her friend's reaction. "I encounter hypocrisy almost everywhere I turn, and I know you do as well. Just yesterday you complained about Marcus at the newspaper office expecting you to clean up the tea he spilled because you looked the most like his wife of any person in the room."

"Not that, you infuriating nodcock," Delphine screeched. "The other!"

Somewhat chastened by the extremity of the response, Verity looked at Freddie and swore she was not trying to be provoking. "But I do not understand why Delphine is so incensed. What does she think I did?"

"Impugn Hardwicke's honor," Freddie said.

"By demanding equal treatment?" Verity asked doubtfully. "Have I not been doing that very thing for weeks now? Why would he suddenly decide to take a pet over it?"

"The carte blanche," he said softly.

Verity, finding this answer no more helpful than the others, pointed out with curt frustration that if Hardwicke could not stand to have his offer discussed in frank terms, then he should not have made it.

"He did not!" Delphine snapped. "*That* is why he is so angry."

Recognizing the ground beneath her feet, for it was so well trod, Verity pressed the palm of her hand against her forehead, uncertain how to reply—or even if she should make the effort. As her dealings with Hardwicke had taught her, it was demoralizing to have the same argument over and over.

"I imagine it is quite lowering to discover the woman you are courting with your whole heart thinks you are merely toying with her affections," Freddie said kindly.

Not toying, Verity thought.

Never toying.

But that was still not the same thing as marriage—which, to be clear, she neither wanted nor sought.

Delphine crossed the floor to where Verity was standing next to the table and took her hand to lead her to the settee. Drawing her to the cushion beside her, she said, "You must know how heartily I resent you for making me sympathetic to Hardwicke's plight, for I am still incensed with him for Holying you. And yet you have managed to turn this whole thing on its head, and my heart aches for the poor man. Obviously, courting you was never going to be a simple endeavor, but you have somehow made it a Gordian knot."

Despite the air of heaviness in the room, Verity was amused by Delphine's tone—the way she sounded so genuinely disgruntled by her inability to duly hold a grudge. "I wish you would believe me when I tell you there is nothing to twist yourself up over. It was never going to happen. I promise you, my dear, it was never going to happen."

Wearily, Delphine said, "It is not, no, because he introduced you to his brother and still you believed the worst and now he knows you have no faith in him. I do believe this time the damage is irreversible, and I cannot say why that makes me sad, but it does. I mean, I knew there was no chance after he Holyed you, and yet I am sad."

Unnerved by the earnestness on display, Verity resisted the urge to make her case once more because her friend already knew. In her heart, she knew that the Marquess of Ware's cherished son would never wed La Reina's unwanted by-blow. Delphine had allowed her deep and abiding affection for Verity to cloud her judgment, which was in actuality very sweet.

Verity did not mind being loved that much.

"He is making amends," Freddie said, eliciting a fierce

scowl from Delphine, who squeaked in protest. Ignoring her chirp, he continued. "Proposing you lure the villain who he believes called for your abduction and killed Dupont is Hardwicke attempting to get back in your good graces. He is demonstrating his willingness to allow you to fling yourself into harm's way. And he did not tell you how to go about the thing with Beaufoy. He suggested some broad strokes, yes, but you and I both know that a plan comes down to its details and he left all of those up to you. It is a show of trust. He is making amends."

During the course of this speech, the pugnacity left Delphine's face, and watching her friend's expression soften, Verity wondered if she was genuinely persuaded by the argument or merely wanted to believe it.

Verity was not convinced.

Her stubborn practicality would not permit flights of fancy, however lovely, however appealing, however much they made a part of her ache—a part she could not even begin to name—but she did not want to be the dark cloud that hung over their brilliant day and excused herself to figure out how she would approach Beaufoy in the morning.

# Chapter Twelve

*Monday, June 15*
*7:35 a.m.*

Having promised Delphine she would not wear Jeremiah Stubbs's rifle jacket, Verity assumed it was perfectly acceptable for her to don his dark green pantaloons with black linen gators as well as his leather half boots that had trudged miles in thick, sludgy mud. She paired them with the dark blue coat of the Royal Engineers, deciding that a hodgepodge of military styles would give the appearance of scruffy indifference, and added a scar to her chin with a mixture of paste and dark red dye.

Then she stood back and examined her handiwork in the mirror. The resemblance to Benson was good—not exact but close enough to fool someone who had only the slightest acquaintance with the original and no lingering sense of his height. It was possible that Beaufoy had been introduced to the tavern keeper, but she rather thought Hardwicke's conclusion was accurate and the diplomat avoided the Speckled Pig to escape the taint of its politics.

Now to put it to the test, she thought, slipping several coins into her pockets before dashing down the staircase and leaving the house. As she walked to the Beaufoy residence to wait for him to emerge, she reviewed the approach she had settled on the night before: an air of excessive confidence undermined by displays of incompetence. To that end, she positioned herself across the street, several doors down, her shoulder pressed against a tree as though she sought shelter behind the trunk.

Obviously, he could see her.

That was, if he looked.

If Beaufoy was like the majority of targets she pursued, it would not occur to him to wonder if someone was tracing his steps, and she made a point of darting out in front of him a few times to alert him to her presence.

As he turned onto Trevor Place, he still seemed oblivious, and she bumped into a newspaper seller to make a small hubbub that she immediately pretended was not *her* hubbub. Her hands loosely grasped behind her back, she lifted her nose in the air and blithely crossed the street. Beaufoy's eyes followed her as she stepped onto the pavement.

She had him now.

To give him the opportunity to get in front of her again, Verity paused to buy a newspaper and then made a great show of flipping through the first few pages. Then she folded it in half, tucked it under her arm, and continued in the wake of the envoy extraordinary.

Beaufoy turned on her three blocks later, stopping suddenly, pivoting swiftly, and grabbing her lapels with his fists. "Aha!"

Verity affected surprise: eyes open wide, jaw lowered, forehead raised. Then she sputtered uselessly for a few seconds before saying, "Monsieur Beaufoy, it is a pleasure!"

Her accent was atrocious, and she clomped on the words,

throwing all her weight behind the first syllable of each so that they sounded like MOAN-sir and BUH-foy.

Beaufoy winced at either the abuse of his mother tongue or the whiff of bad breath that assaulted his nose. "Who are you? Why are you following me?"

"Apologies, moan-sir, for giving ye that impression," Verity said with a self-conscious titter. "But I wasn't following ye. I was choosing my moment."

The envoy's eyes narrowed with suspicion. "What does that mean—choosing your moment? Choosing it for what?"

"We need to talk about. . ."

Trailing off, Verity nodded her head with a meaningful tilt, as if to allow the gesture to stand in for the word she could not say.

Impatiently, Beaufoy shook her again. "Talk about what?"

Verity looked him in the eyes and said pointedly, "You know."

Beaufoy swore he did not. "If you are a thief trying to pick my pockets, then you have made a grave mistake. I am trained in the art of hand-to-hand combat and will disarm you in seconds."

"I ain't no thief," Verity replied with a hint of indignation. "We have unfinished business, you and I. It was begun by a mutual friend who recently *fell* into trouble."

Taken aback by the meaning, which he could not fail to comprehend, Beaufoy loosened his grip and growled, "Who are you?"

Verity stepped back and smoothed the front of her jacket. "An ally in the struggle against tyranny—that ye may believe! I am eager to say more but wonder if the street is the right place for it. May I invite ye to my tavern, the Speckled Pig?"

Appalled, Beaufoy said he would sooner set foot in a cesspit. But he agreed their current location was not ideal for a conversation about a delicate subject and suggested an alley off a neighboring street. Leading them there, he kept his eyes trained on Verity, as though he still doubted her intentions and would run off with his wallet at any moment.

Stopping uncomfortably close to a heap of manure, Beaufoy demanded to know what business he could have with a miscreant like him.

"I told ye, I ain't no thief!" Verity growled. "I'm an upstanding member of the community. I own property and employ people! And I had an arrangement with our mutual friend, and I don't think we should allow his *end* to be the end of our business. I assume yer goals remain the same. Mine do."

If Beaufoy had not known Dupont was working with a confederate, then this moment would reveal it and Verity tried to gain some insight by reading the expression on his face.

To his credit, the diplomat revealed none of his thoughts. "What are your goals?"

"To provide satisfactory service in exchange for reasonable compensation," Verity replied.

"And what is this service?" Beaufoy asked.

"I think ye know."

"Do I?" he wondered.

Verity, who appreciated his caution, decided she had been sufficiently evasive and answered more candidly than the tavern keeper ever could. "Ye do know, but for the sake of clarity I will be frank: The service our friend hired me to perform was helping him kidnap an elderly female and stash her away in my cellar for a few days until ye could use her to lure the English spy."

"*Sacré dieu!* You do not need to scream it from the rooftops," Beaufoy said, anxiously peering around them as if to suddenly find a hovering crowd. "I know well enough what our mutual friend was doing. It was at my behest!"

Verity did not need the confirmation, and yet she was grateful to have it. Everything was mere speculation until it was corroborated by a source. "And that is why I have sought this meeting. Ye are in need of a new confederate to finish the job our friend began and who better to hire than the person who already knows the details. I will carry out the plot exactly as we intended. And it will cost you only thirty guineas."

Momentarily stunned by the sum, Beaufoy smiled in cynical amusement. "And you said you weren't a thief!"

Graciously, Verity acknowledged it was a trifle high.

"Trifle?" he repeated in disgust. "It is *astronomique!*"

"Ye say that because ye don't know the plan," she insisted. "It's difficult and exposes me to huge risks. That is why the price is so high. Our mutual friend understood that."

Beaufoy rolled his eyes in disbelief. "Dupont agreed to pay you thirty guineas? No, it is not possible. He would never have agreed to that sum because he did not have it. Do you think I am an *imbécile*? Is that what you think?"

Verity, shrugging with apathetic scorn, announced it was no business of hers how Dupont fulfilled his financial obligations as long as he did. "He *said* he would come into more money soon. He had found the golden goose and all he had to do was cook it. It sounded like nonsense to me, but sometimes that's how ye Frenchies are. Things get lost in the translation."

Here, she paused to allow the envoy to absorb Dupont's smug gloating and watched with satisfaction as anger sparked in his eye. But he held his temper in check and calmly replied, "Be that as it may, our mutual friend is not here, and you are dealing with me now. I am not a fool."

"Ye wouldn't complain if ye knew the plan!" Verity exclaimed. "It's complex and dangerous. Very few men would have the courage to even try it."

Having all but begged him to ask for the details, she was not surprised when he demanded to know the specifics. Nevertheless, she owned herself hesitant, for he would find it too complicated to follow and then get angry at her for confusing him.

"Nonsense," Beaufoy scoffed. "Tell me now!"

Verity complied, beginning with a disjointed account of Dupont's first attempt to abduct Miss Lark, which was foiled by her blasted brother.

How dare he show his face after announcing his plan to be out of town!

"So ye see the first difficulty: Ye can't snatch the old gel from her house because the brother is always around, even when he isn't supposed to be," she added and was gratified by the impatience on Beaufoy's face. That meant she was telling him things he already knew, which was a relief. There was always the possibility that Dupont had made up a different story for his superior. "And ye see the second problem too: The brother is alerted to the danger. They all are! The entire household! They've changed their behavior, and the old gel is allowed out of the house only once a day to take a walk in the nearby square. But the square is actually three blocks away, and that is the third challenge."

Already annoyed, which Verity took as an excellent sign, he snapped, "How are the three blocks to the square a challenge?"

"It is all the squirrels and birds on the walk," she said. "The dog wants to chase them, but he can't because he is on a lead so he just gets more and more riled up. Ye don't know that because I haven't mentioned the dog, but there is a dog. After the kidnapping attempt that the brother thwarted, he got a ferocious dog to warn the house of intruders, and Miss Lark goes on a walk every day in the company of the dog. It has highly developed instincts for the hunt, which makes the

238

abduction complicated and dangerous because it is very protective of the gel *and* has large teeth. I've seen it snap a tree branch in half with a single clap of its jaw. Ye can't snatch Miss Lark while the dog is near. Ye have to wait for it to run off after a squirrel or a bird, which it only does when she lets it off the lead in the square, and by now it is chomping at the bit to maul a small creature because it has been denied the pleasure for the duration of the three-block walk."

"So you distract the dog and then take the girl," Beaufoy said, still unimpressed. "And I give you three guineas for your trouble, four if the woman is unharmed."

"Ye are forgetting the limp," Verity said.

Mystified, Beaufoy repeated it. "The limp?"

"The limp that causes her to walk sluggishly, which is why the dog is so frantic by the time he finally gets to the square. Three blocks would not be worth mentioning if she moved at a normal pace, but she is as slow as a snail. I am sure I mentioned the limp because it is the next hurdle," she added. "If ye are to have any hope of getting her out of the square before the dog returns from fetching the ball you threw as a distraction, then you have to make sure she is close enough to the entrance. Ye have to coordinate it exactly and remember the shrubs."

She paused meaningfully.

Beaufoy did not immediately take the hint, but after a dozen seconds of silence he dismissively noted that most squares had shrubbery.

"But this square doesn't! It only has trees, stone paths, benches, a hermitage, a statue of Alfred the Great, and a fountain. So ye can't throw the ball into the underbrush and hope that the hound will take extra long to find it while ye half drag the partially lame old gel out of the square. But ye can't use a ball because the dog is too excited by the all the lively creatures to pay any attention to it. You have to throw a squirrel or a rat—all the while making sure you do not attract the notice of the other visitors enjoying a turn around the square. That is the ultimate difficulty and perhaps the one that carries the greatest risk because potassium nitrate, charcoal, and sulfur are unreliable and could explode in yer grasp if not handled carefully enough, and any task that could end with my losing a limb is worth thirty guineas."

For a moment Beaufoy stared at her aghast, then his expression cleared and he chuckled. "I understand now you are teasing me. You think you are being *drôle* because you are English and have a terrible sense of humor."

Stiffly, Verity replied that she would never make light of a subject as grave as a dismemberment. "I am deadly serious. I *could* lose my arm! But there is nothing for it because something has to be done to distract the bystanders so they don't rush to Miss Lark's rescue, and a minor explosion is the only way to do it without hiring someone to help me, which I wanted to do but Dupont said I must not mention the kidnapping to anyone. Trust me, it's the best plan. And if ye can think of something better then propose it yerself."

"If *I* can think something better?" jibed the diplomat sneeringly. "A child tied to his mother's apron strings could think of something better. Your plan is preposterous. To start, I would abduct her on the *way* to the square. I would stop my carriage next to the curb where she exits her house, conk the dog on the head, grab her by the shoulders, and shove her inside my conveyance. Dead squirrels and explosives—you are mad, monsieur. I would not pay you a single guinea to enact that plan, never mind twenty of them. I do not know what Dupont was thinking to agree to it, but it proves that I was right to question his judgment. He was as daft as you. Dead squirrels and explosives! *Mon dieu!*"

"But the neighbors!" Verity protested. "They might see you take her. And what if she calls out for help? Or the dog—

it is a rackety little thing! The neighbors complain about its bark all the time! If that basset hound starts barking, everyone will come outside to yell at the mongrel. And then they'll see you stealing the old gel!"

Beaufoy chortled as he exclaimed, "A basset hound! *That* is the ferocious dog?"

"Its teeth are huge!" Verity insisted. "It could bite my hand right off!"

With a contemptuous snigger, Beaufoy dismissed these concerns, insisting he was fast and nimble enough to heave one lame middle-aged woman into a carriage without kicking up dust. And even if someone happened to catch sight of him, they would not know who he was, for he would be dressed as a coachman.

It was not as though someone would run after a carriage.

Gamely, Verity countered his argument, pointing out the many flaws in his plan, although all of these were actually advantages. She noted, for example, that the street rarely got traffic, which meant that his carriage would stand out as an unfamiliar oddity.

Everyone on the street would notice it!

And Beaufoy would have to act quickly because Miss Lark was supposed to leave on Wednesday morning to visit a cousin in the country. "That leaves ye with only twenty-four hours! That is not enough time to come up with a plan let alone gather all the things ye will need for it. I already have the dead stuffed squirrel and the gunpowder. All I need is yer approval to proceed and twenty guineas, then I am ready to go. And I will remind ye: There is no danger to ye! I assume all the risk. I should think yer safety and security are worth a few coins. Let me put my life on the line for ye, moan-sir, it would be an honor."

"The 'everything' consists of a coachman's costume, which I will borrow from my own groom," he said with confidence.

To bolster it, she rattled off a series of questions that she knew he could carelessly brush aside. "Will your driver's clothes fit? Are you the same size as he? If the coat requires tailoring, who can you trust to do it? The last thing you want is for a seamstress to hear the story of Miss Lark's kidnapping and recall the work she did for you."

As this threat was virtually nonexistent, Beaufoy rightly ignored it and asked what time Miss Lark took her afternoon walk.

Grumbling with resentment, Verity said it was around two o'clock. Then she reminded him of the cellar at Speckled Pig, which Dupont was going to use to hold the girl. Would he need to rent it as well or could he keep a prisoner in his own house? "I do not want to make assumptions about yer domestic situation, but it would be very awkward if yer wife found a strange woman in yer basement, even one with a limp."

Having endured so much nonsense from her that morning, Beaufoy opened his mouth to reject this notion almost out of habit. But then he paused and considered the query, his expression turning thoughtful as he allowed that other members of his household could present a problem. "I accept your offer, thank you."

Delighted to be getting something from the transaction, Verity said the price was three guineas per day, which he accepted with equanimity. Then, ascertaining that he would need her help carting his captive down the steep flight of stairs, she added a surcharge for each individual step, varying the amount depending on its condition. Naturally, the wobbly tread in the middle cost twice as much as the termite-ridden one at the bottom, which was fifty percent more than the sturdy step at the top.

The rapacious Mrs. Buglehorn could not have done better.

Annoyed by these supplements, Beaufoy refused to pay them and held the line at three guineas *for the duration*. "You will not get a single pence more. Take it or leave it!"

Backed into a corner, Verity bitterly agreed to his conditions, which further increased his sense of competence. Then he arranged to call at the tavern at approximately three in the afternoon the next day with what he was now calling "the package," bid her adieu, and sauntered out of the alley with an air of accomplishment.

*Monday, June 15*
*11:11 a.m.*

Securing the appropriate dog took a little longer than Verity expected because she had not planned on Lottie Banks's suspicion. Wrapping her narrow arms around the hound's scruffy neck, the little girl looked up at Verity, who was dressed in the ink-stained wool of Robert Lark's everyday attire, and narrowed her blue eyes. Then she announced that Pinkie did not perform favors. "Isn't that true, Mama?"

With a wry smile, her mother confirmed it was correct. "No matter how many times I beg the little scoundrel to please leave off chewing the chair legs in the dining room as a personal favor to me, she refuses to comply."

"There!" Lottie said with a triumphant look. "Pinkie cannot help you. She is a scoundrel, so it's against her nature."

Verity, lowering to her knees next to the six-year-old child, gently petted the soft fur on the basset's head. "Pinkie is lucky to have a friend who understands her so well."

"She understands me, too," Lottie said. "When I wake up in the middle of the night because I heard a noise and am scared something is hiding under my bed, Lottie licks me on the ear and it makes me laugh and then I'm not afraid."

"Golly, then you are *both* lucky," Verity replied.

Lottie tightened her grip on Pinkie's neck, and although it must have been uncomfortable for the animal, she did not make a whimper of protest. "Yes."

"I can see you and Pinkie have a strong bond. Nothing can break that," Verity said. "She would not forget you if she came and stayed with me for one night. And it would only be the one night, I promise."

The girl appeared willing to consider the notion of a single night. "What would Lottie have to do? She isn't good with tricks. She doesn't sit or stay when you ask her to. Mama says she is a disobedient rascal and belongs in a barn. But we do not have a barn, so she stays with me."

Verity swore Pinkie would not have to do anything at all but be Pinkie.

"She could probably do that," Lottie allowed. "But she can't be too Pinkie for too long because then she will get tired."

"If you tell me how long Pinkie can be Pinkie, then I will abide by that. The rest of the time Pinkie will do nothing at all," Verity said. "Do you think Pinkie can handle that?"

Soberly, Lottie said that she did. "Pinkie does nothing very well."

Verity pressed her lips together, determined not to grin at the solemnity in the small child's voice. "Do you think we can give it a try, then? Just for one night? Pinkie will be back by five tomorrow afternoon. That is a sacred vow from me to you. I will allow nothing on earth to interfere with my keeping it."

Still, the girl looked doubtful.

"You can trust Mr. Lark," Lottie's mother said. "He works with your father at the *London Daily Gazette,* and like your father, he writes articles that help people. He wrote one article about an awful woman who was mean to a group of children, and his story made her go away. Now the children are treated kindly. And I'll tell you what: I will sleep in your bed with you tonight and lick you on the ear if you get afraid."

Her daughter laughed and said, "Eww, Mama, you're not a dog!"

"I'm not?" Mrs. Banks asked as if surprised.

Lottie giggled harder.

Now Verity smiled and darted a grateful look at the other woman, whom she had met only a handful of times. It was generous of her to agree to the loan of the family pet, and Robert had offered his colleague compensation. Banks refused to hear a word of it. He had toiled alongside Lark at the newspaper for almost five years and respected the work he did. If Pinkie in some way helped him write another important piece for the *Gazette,* then he was delighted to lend him the pup.

Her expression grave once again, Verity held out her hand to the little girl and said, "Do we have a deal?"

The young child regarded the hand cautiously, then took it with a nod and said it was all right if Mr. Lark brought Pinkie back at five oh five if necessary.

"Arrive here a whole five minutes late?" Verity asked with a theatrical shudder. "Thank you but no!"

Lottie laughed harder and kissed Pinkie on the top of her head.

*Monday, June 15*
*2:11 p.m.*

Pinkie did not appreciate the lead.

Unaccustomed to the restraint, she pulled against it, tugging Verity behind her on the pavement with fitful and erratic movements. The dog darted suddenly to the left, then to the right, seeking, it seemed to her human companion, to confuse the leash. Sometimes, Pinkie stopped in her tracks, changed directions, and encircled Verity's legs with the line. When that happened, Verity stepped gingerly around the leather strap, mindful of her limp, which was supposed to be pronounced. Once, Verity tripped as her toe hitched on a bend in the lead, and she smiled picturing how feeble she looked to curious spectators following her in secret.

Here I am, she thought, amused wryly. An easy target. Come and get me.

Alas, Verity did not have any curious spectators following her in secret.

She tried to find one, her eyes sweeping her surroundings while she struggled to keep up with the enthusiastic dog. She saw a few neighbors staring at her quizzically out of their windows and inspected half a dozen passersby for signs of Beaufoy.

There were none.

The lack of effort bewildered Verity.

At the very least, Beaufoy should make some attempt to confirm the accuracy of the intelligence Benson had given him.

Was there really a dog?

Did the woman truly have a limp?

These details were easy enough to corroborate—they did not, for example, require breaking into the target's residence

—and knowing what exactly to expect, even if that just meant the width of the pavement, ensured a smooth operation.

Leaving the particulars up to chance struck Verity as madness.

It was always possible that Beaufoy sent an emissary in his stead to verify the information. He was, after all, a man with an important position and could not disappear in the afternoon two days in a row without anyone noticing. Even so, Verity thought it was unlikely. If Beaufoy had another minion on whom he could rely to perform odd and possibly nefarious tasks, then he would have told the barkeep immediately that his services were not required.

Rather, the envoy extraordinary had not bothered to conduct the required surveillance because it was not necessary. He was already in possession of all the pertinent details.

His misplaced confidence was to Verity's advantage, of course, and she appreciated slapdash work in an opponent. Nevertheless, it offended her sense of order and professionalism. Preparation was the backbone of any successful undertaking. Even when she had no doubt about a thing, she always had some doubt about the thing.

Certainty was for fools.

Consequently, she continued on her walk to the square with the dog dragging her the entire way and remained for a full half hour, enjoying the damp air and the hound's antics.

Determined to give Pinkie the highest marks in her report to Lottie despite the rascally creature's behavior, Verity was pleased to see how well her conduct matched the description given to Beaufoy. As reported, the dog dashed about the square, trying to catch squirrels and birds, and when it was time to reattach the leash, Verity, whose limp would not allow her to run, had to seek the assistance of a fellow visitor.

An excellent outing all in all.

# Chapter Thirteen

*Monday, June 15*
*4:11 p.m.*

After returning from her unduly long walk, an exhausted Pinkie splayed out on the rug in the parlor and promptly fell asleep to Delphine's delight. As her friend cooed over the pup, Verity retired to Robert's study to focus on the projects that had been allowed to languish in the days since the failed abduction. Without a fresh item from Mr. Twaddle-Thum on Friday, Freddie had been forced to print one of the many stories the gossip kept on hand for times when she was unable to produce an article for one reason or another. In general, the cache contained reports about the mainstays of society—Lady Jersey, Mrs. Fitzherbert, the prince regent—and made wry observations about traits and scandals already widely known. In this case, it was a tally of Brummel's debts with comments from nearly a dozen of his creditors.

It went without saying that Verity could not allow the

*Gazette* to publish two articles in a row from the pile of perennial favorites. It was acceptable only as a last resort.

Fortunately, she had two dozen notes from Twaddle's network and quickly settled on Lord Larkwell's drunken fisticuffs with his own valet, whom he accused of wrinkling his silk breeches on purpose. Nobody was hurt, lots of money changed hands in the form of wagers, and the servant in question was immediately hired by Lord Bedford, who admired his spine—and by "spine" he meant the one the valet invented for Larkwell.

Having appeased the demands of the Twaddleship, Verity consulted Robert's list of article ideas and contemplated which one would require the least amount of research. Although the hour was not so late as to preclude going abroad, the thought of changing out of her walking dress held little appeal, for it was the third outfit she had worn that day. Her time would better be spent composing a story than assuming yet another disguise.

Robert Johnson showed promise. An ambitious Whig with lofty aspirations, he had recently been caught soliciting bribes from shipowners who sought changes in the Navigation Acts. He defended the action by insisting he did not have the political clout to bring about the desired alterations, rendering the existence of the payments moot. Decidedly weak, the argument had been well received by several fellow members of Parliament, who, presumably, sought to reserve the right of degeneracy for themselves, and as Verity had written a profile of Johnson in May, she already had quotes from him and his colleagues. She could cobble them together to compose an article on the corruptive influence of success.

Yes, she thought, tidying up the papers on her desk. That would do very well.

As she was dipping her quill into the ink, the door to the

study opened, and she lifted her head to ask Lucy for more hot water, as her tea had grown cold.

Instead of the maid, however, she found Hardwicke crossing the threshold. Dressed neatly, he wore fawn-colored buckskin breeches with well-polished Hessians and a tailcoat in a deep blue shade that complemented his eyes.

Struck by the handsome figure he cut, Verity felt her breath catch in her throat and she scowled as he approached the desk. She could not conceive why he was there, as the message she had sent him over an hour ago had assured him everything was in place for the abduction tomorrow. Beaufoy had been convinced to nab her himself in front of the house on Bethel Street, and she had secured the necessary accoutrement, including a mild-tempered basset hound and a lead.

Either ignoring her frown or not noticing it, Hardwicke bid her good day and said he was there to take her for a drive in Hyde Park.

Considering the current state of affairs, Verity thought it was a most inopportune time for the invitation and tried to imagine what his game was. "You want to take a drive in Hyde Park now, when we are in the middle of a delicate operation to stave off an international incident and apprehend a killer?"

"I do, yes," he said.

Pensively, Verity twirled the quill between her fingers. "Why?"

"You are far too secure here—behind your desk in the confines of your study in the safety of your home," he explained calmly, the bite of his words curiously at odds with the bland voice. "If you are truly going to be a target for the men who wish to assassinate me, then you need to be more visible. The first shooting attempt was made after I returned you to your home, but if we are lucky an assassin will take aim at me while you are still in the gig. The odds for it are a bit long, but we can always hope."

Verity rose from her chair, fascinated by the spectacle of his anger, for it was exactly as Delphine said: Hardwicke was furious. Outwardly projecting aloofness—relaxed shoulders, detached tone—he nevertheless pulsed with rage. Verity could feel it vibrating off him in waves. As if studying a rare beast in a menagerie, she stepped around the desk to draw closer, almost as if to press her nose against the bars of his enclosure, and watched for a reaction.

Hardwicke did not move a muscle.

Curiously, she said, "You are mad."

Smiling faintly, he insisted he was in possession of all his faculties. "I am simply giving a lady the opportunity she ardently desires to be slaughtered in my stead."

"I misspoke," Verity said evenly. "I meant livid. Irate. You are incensed."

"Am I?" he asked blandly.

The slightly satirical edge to the query only confirmed what it was supposed to refute, and Verity marveled at the perverseness of his fury. Hardwicke seemed morally offended by the ignominies *he* had been made to suffer.

It was remarkable.

Seeking to comprehend how he had arrived at that position when there was no evidence to support it, she said, "I am riveted by this air of righteous indignation you have chosen to assume. Clearly, you feel as though you have been wronged, and you have come here proposing the opposite of what you believe is right to make me seem ridiculous. But I cannot fathom what insult you think you've endured. You were not the one who was Holyed."

Although the term was new and not yet established in the lexicon, he readily intuited its meaning and replied that the two situations were not comparable. "Sebastian did not want Miss Hyde-Clare to be exposed *further* to the danger that she herself kicked up. Whereas the danger you were exposed to was entirely of my own making. You cannot resent me for seeking to protect you from my own folly. It is unreasonable."

As brief as the reply was, it contained almost too much information, and Verity struggled to focus on the detail she considered most pertinent. It troubled her to hear him describe the work he had done during the war as "folly," for it was heroic and important and part of the reason more of their countrymen did not die fending off an egomaniacal bully. And the way he blithely denounced the legitimacy of her feelings—it roiled her blood. She could not imagine anything more infuriating.

And yet the tidbit about Miss Hyde-Clare inciting the original threat...

"What do you mean by 'the danger she herself kicked up'?" she asked, trying to recall exactly what Holcroft had said about the discovery of the master of the roll's venality. "Was she the source of Grimston's downfall? What led her to suspect him?"

Hardwicke laughed.

His teal eyes seethed hotly, he laughed with seemingly sincere amusement as he shook his head and said, "Christ, Verity, you are amazing. By all means, yes, let's discuss the Altick affair in great depth so that your voracious inquisitiveness may be appeased. That is the only thing that matters, isn't it? God knows why I thought I could come here and have a rational conversation with you. I must have been mad, precisely as you said."

Accustomed to this accusation, for Delphine frequently lodged it against her, usually at three in the morning while anxiously pacing the parlor in expectation of her friend's overdue return, Verity accepted it with equanimity. There was no point in bristling at the obvious, especially when she did not think the charge was negative. Uncovering lies was an objective good, and his inability to comprehend her need for the truth made it plain to her yet again that he did not know with whom he was dealing.

If she was going to accept the criticism without caviling, however, then she must insist he do the same. To that end, she noted that he had not called on her with the intention of having a rational conversation. "You came here to argue and even began the quarrel before you set foot in the room. Tell me, how did the Verity in your head respond to your contemptuous invitation? Did she apologize for causing you undue worry? Did she thank you for protecting her?"

Hardwicke smiled faintly, his lips tilting up, but he was not diverted, not at all, and there was something unnerving about the way he looked at her—as if a ship had left dock before he had a chance to climb on board and now he was watching it sail away.

"You are amazing," he murmured again with a shake of his head. "Somehow you manage to twist everything around. Night is always day with you, Verity, and I do not know how to get you to see the stars when you are blinded by the sun. But you are correct in that I did arrive thirsting for a fight because I have spent twenty-eight hours fuming over your steadfast determination to misunderstand everything I say. I perceive now the futility of my actions. I cannot earn your trust when you have no trust to give."

Verity felt something lodge in her throat.

Anger, fear, sadness, relief—truly, she could not begin to identify it.

Even so, she resented the press of its weight.

More than that, she resented Hardwicke for making her feel it.

It was so easy for him to stand there and blame her for everything.

He lied to her and yet somehow it was her fault.

What kind of broken male logic was that?

Refusing to allow it, she said, "You cannot earn my trust by giving me none in return. You lied to me about the attempts on your life and then took exception when I dared to complain about it."

Verity expected him to grow more irritated still by the observation, but he received it with calm agreement. "That is true, yes, but for the record, let me state unequivocally that I did not Holy you. *Holying*—by God, that is an awful term, surely, the estimable Twaddle can do better—means breaking off contact to save a woman from a perceived threat on her life resulting from her own actions. I broke off contact to save me—*me*, Verity, not you. I did it to save myself from having to live the rest of my life without you. I did it to save myself from having to live the rest of my life with your death on my conscience."

It was shocking how matter-of-factly he spoke, how the lack of emotion seemed to create its own reality by removing all meaning from the words. It was as though the swaths of bright red in Raphael's *Cardinal* were suddenly washed away and the viewer could no longer discern the subject's standing in the Church by his garments.

"I know you regularly expose yourself to danger," he continued in that same deadened tone. "It is a point of pride for you, putting yourself in perilous situations and then smoothly extricating yourself. You are everything: brave and reckless and indomitable and undaunted. You are magic, Verity. I concede it! But your being exposed to a bullet in the head simply for sitting next to me—how can you expect me to bear that?"

There was just enough inflection in the question to make her appear sullen or childish for thinking to propose he withstand such mental tortures, and she recognized it for what it was: another manipulation. He was inventing a situation that did not exist simply to argue against it. She had never asked him to bear anything, and it was sullen and childish of *him* to imply that she had.

"Alas, you are quarreling with the Verity in your head again because all *I* required was the truth," she said over the lump in her throat. "All I wanted was for you to deal honestly with me. In this case, that meant telling me that several attempts had been made on your life and that you would prefer if we did not appear together publicly because concern for my safety would affect your judgment, thereby imperiling you further. Instead, you sent note after note fobbing me off with vague excuses."

Taken aback by the reply, Hardwicke furrowed his brow as he narrowed his eyes. "'Note after note'? Verity, it was just two messages over four days. You make it sound as though I were Lady Mary Montagu reporting on my travels to the Ottoman Empire. There was no great trove of letters."

Color rose in her cheeks as she realized she had unintentionally revealed something horrifyingly personal about the way time seemed to move for her when she was waiting for word from him.

Stiffening her shoulders despite the prickly heat suffusing them, she said curtly, "Regardless, my point stands. The situation called for more communication, not less, and rather than seek my help in neutralizing the threat against you, you chose to shield me from all knowledge of it. But that never occurred to you, did it? All your fine words, all your physician's canes, all your avowals of respect and admiration, and yet you do not see an astoundingly competent female when you look at me."

He agreed.

In that voice of horrifying detachment, he conceded the

accuracy of the statement, saying with a firm nod, "Oh, yes, that is right. I see a lightskirt."

Did it cut to hear it said aloud?

Of course it did not cut.

Her whole life had been a variation of this exchange in one way or another.

It was good to have the truth spoken.

Finally, he was dealing honestly with her.

Grateful for it, she said, "Thank you."

And then it was back, the furious teal, the shuddering rage, and his hands, darting out as though to seize her shoulders, hovered in the air between them for a heart-pounding second before clenching into fists as he took a step back. With a rumble that seemed to shake his whole body, he growled, "This! It is this, this, *this*, Verity! I respond impetuously to a threat out of fear, and you act as though I have betrayed some sacred tenet of trust. But *you* have never trusted *me*. I declared my intentions as plainly as any man could, and still you thought I meant to set you up as my mistress. Your dignity is everything to me, Verity. I would never try to undermine it or seek to demean you. That you could think I would is inarguably the greater betrayal."

Verity's limbs trembled.

Just ever so slightly, like a shiver, as though she were cold, and she pressed her arms tightly against her body to still them.

It was all so persuasive—his outrage, his pose of injured indignation.

She knew it was not real, and yet this thing inside her thundered toward it like a horse across a moor. He was everything she would want if she was foolish enough to want anything, and her mind was riven with cozy little scenes, she and Hardwicke conspiring to infiltrate the Bank of England as they sipped tea before the hearth, she and Hardwicke hiding behind Lord Melville's settee to prove accounting malfeasance. She loved his mind, its diabolical shrewdness, and even as her heart withered at the cruelty, she admired the deftness with which he claimed the higher ground—all while slithering in the mud.

Naturally, he had deployed an attack.

It was the only reliable defense.

Wanting it to be over, for it was almost too painful to endure, especially the trembling, which felt vaguely like panic, she said, "You may make all the eloquent assertions you want to appease your ego, my lord, but we both know you would never have married me, not with my mother."

His eyes seething, he reared forward to make another spirited defense of his decency when he suddenly stilled his movements and stared at her with dumbfounded amazement. "Who the devil is your mother?"

She scoffed.

Incapable of believing he was ignorant of this one particularly salient fact, she dismissed the query as the meager ploy it was. Hardwicke was irritatingly astute, in possession of lavish resources, and an adept investigator. There was no way he had not delved into her past and discovered everything. All he had to do was ...

But here she paused because the answer was not readily apparent.

Of the assortment of dots that speckled her past, she could not identify the two he would have to connect to find La Reina. The line that stretched from Lorraine Price to Verity Lark felt thick and distinct to her, like the leather lead that attached to Pinkie's collar, but in fact time and distance had worn it thin.

He could find the strand, yes, but he had to know where to look for it.

Moreover, he had to know there was a strand to look for.

Seeing the bewilderment on his face, she realized he had not.

Hardwicke had no clue how her mother had entered the conversation.

Verity grappled with how to respond.

Keep the secret or let it out?

Neither option seemed tolerable.

Telling him the truth now, she would watch the fight fade from his stance and have the curious pleasure of knowing she had been right all along. It would be the end she had desired. But the words stuck in her throat, and she thought it was better to simply issue a crushing reply about how her mother was none of his business.

The temerity of your even asking, sir!

She would look like the veriest ninny, to be sure, but that was not the issue.

The issue was Hardwicke knew about the strand and would immediately start looking.

Regardless of the path they took, they would wind up in the same place and she ordered herself to say the words now.

*Get it over with.*

These calculations whirled in her head for only a few seconds, but still it was too long, for the moment she opened her mouth to reply, Delphine stepped into the room. On her heels was Grint, who greeted her with familiarity.

"Mr. Gorman, it is a pleasure to see you again," he said.

It was perplexing and strange to be addressed with such confidence, and knowing it could be attributed to only one thing, she looked at Hardwicke, astonished to discover the depth of his anger at her.

Talk about betraying sacred tenets!

Grint stepped forward, one hand raised in caution, and he said, "Please, Miss Lark, do not glare at Wicke. He did not reveal your secret. I figured it out on my own."

Smoothing her features to a bland smile, Verity turned to the under-secretary and apologized for her puzzlement, for she did not know who he was or what he had figured out. "But I am sure you will explain. A mystery—how thrilling! Let us adjourn to the parlor. I will join you in a moment. I was just straightening up my brother's study. He can be so slovenly in his habits. Do give me just a moment to finish. Delphine, please ring for tea. Lord Colson, you are welcome to stay, but if you have somewhere else to be, do not let us keep you from it."

Nobody protested, although Verity saw a ferocious light spark in Hardwicke's eyes, and Delphine herded the two men from the room, asking Grint what he planned to do about the Kingsley matter. The under-secretary coughed awkwardly.

After they left, Verity closed the door, stood in the middle of the study, and gave herself a minute to feel her emotions, to permit fear, sadness, confusion, and joy—oh, yes, there had been a sliver of pure joy when she realized the sincerity of his affection—to roil her mind in an unsettling swirl.

Hardwicke was correct: She had never allowed herself to trust him.

And the truth was, she distrusted him still.

As soon as he had all the data to make an informed decision, he would withdraw his offer. Amending it slightly to align with his new understanding would demean them both and continuing as if impervious would bring shame to his family.

He had no options.

It was for the best, of course, as she had no wish to upend her comfortable existence by saddling herself with a husband, who would only impose rules and seek to modify her behavior.

And yet regret was there, too—a sense that it would all be different with Hardwicke.

But it would not be anything.

So be it.

The sixty seconds up, Verity took a deep breath and joined the others in the parlor.

*Monday, June 15*
*5:29 p.m.*

Grint was determined to be charming.

Despite being peppered by Delphine with impertinent queries regarding the way the Home Office conducted its affairs, all of which strongly implied her disapproval without stating it openly, the under-secretary remained unfailingly polite. Returning each criticism with a compliment, he had praised the design of the room ("elegant and warm"), the biscuits ("delicious and nutty"), and the atmosphere ("welcoming and comfortable").

He rose when Verity entered and made a great show of introducing himself properly, which he had not had the opportunity to do when they last met, in Kingsley's office. He bowed over her hand, as though they were in a ballroom, and waited for her to take a seat before regaining his own.

Regarding her curiously over his prominent chin, he said, "I cannot properly convey, Miss Lark, what a pleasure it is to meet you. Wicke has not told me much about your exploits, but from what I have managed to glean from the few things he has revealed, I know you are a singularly impressive female. I would like to thank you again for your help with the Fitch debacle. I cannot imagine what would have happened if you had not intervened."

Annoyed by the meaningless pleasantries, Verity plainly

stated the inevitable outcome. "The army would have precipi-tated a massacre in St. Dunstan's Field."

"You are correct!" Grint said approvingly. "Let us not mince words. A great tragedy would have ensued, and the Home Office would have been directly responsible—as we are ultimately responsible for the attempts on Wicke's life and your aborted abduction. Miss Drayton is right to question how we handle sensitive matters."

"All matters, sir," Delphine interjected as she held up the plate of biscuits and offered him another. "I question how your office handles *all* matters, not just the sensitive ones. I have noted several instances of incompetence in the past few months. Would you like me to list them? I have them written down in my daybook."

Graciously, the under-secretary thanked her for her thoughtful offer but insisted he was quite conversant with his own department's shortcomings. "I expect our record to improve now that we have rooted out Kingsley. Thank you again, Miss Lark, for your help."

"Why are you here?" Hardwicke asked.

It was the first time he had spoken since Verity had entered the room ten minutes before, and although his coun-tenance was impassive, she could feel his irritation.

If Grint sensed it as well, he gave no indication as he said, "I wanted to apologize to Miss Lark personally for the danger the Home Office has put her in. It is insupportable."

Hardwicke stared at him for several long seconds, then turned to Verity and explained that the under-secretary was there to evaluate her with an eye toward recruitment. "If he deems you acceptable, then he will begin to offer you assignments."

"It is true, Miss Lark," Grint said, displaying no resent-ment at the revelation of his motives. "I would love to work with you on a delicate situation that is currently bedeviling me. But that is not why I called. I want to assure you that I have one of my best men keeping an eye on Beaufoy. He will have no opportunity to attack you a moment before you are ready. The other reason I am here is to gawk."

A provoking comment, to be sure.

Verity refused to rise to it.

Delphine, however, duly complied with the under-secretary's expectation by repeating, "Gawk?"

"At a woman so remarkable she almost defies belief," Grint replied.

Hardwicke murmured his name warningly, and the under-secretary looked at him with wide-eyed amazement. "No, it's true, Wicke, Miss Lark is an impossible creature."

Well, yes, *that* was accurate, Hardwicke agreed.

Delphine asked how Grint figured it out.

"I knew something was afoot the moment Wicke began courting Miss Lark because she is not in the first blush of youth," he said with an apologetic glance at Verity as he added that it was quite a strange development. "Wicke is not generally in the petticoat line, but I have never known him to keep such mature company. Again, I do not mean to give offense to Miss Lark."

"You have not," Delphine assured him.

Grint smiled, as though genuinely relieved. "Good. Then it will also not bother you to know that I found it so strange, I poked around a little and discovered from your neighbors Miss Lark has a reputation for being shy and reticent. That made Wicke's interest even more inexplicable."

Snidely, Delphine noted that she began to perceive the problem with the quality of the work the Home Office was producing. "Its staff members are too easily distracted from the government's business."

"Oh, but you see, Wicke's showing interest in an unsuitable woman *is* the government's business," he replied smoothly. "It was possible he was pursuing a mission for another organization or looking into something for a friend as he did for his friend Mr. Holcroft. As a representative of the home secretary, I have a vested interest in either possibility and was thus obligated to find out. I must add here, Miss Lark, that while investigating you, I read several of your brother's articles. Very impressive reporting. I hope to meet him one day soon, perhaps after he returns from his trip."

Uncertain if he was toying with her, Verity gave a noncommittal answer and he continued to explain how he had deduced the truth.

"Having learned through my research that Miss Lark was a retiring spinster, I was surprised to discover she had agreed to act as bait to entrap Beaufoy. It seemed like slightly more excitement than the old girl could handle. But even more surprising was the fact that Wicke had no issue with the plan. If Miss Lark was all that she appeared to be, then there was no way he would consent to let her risk herself. It would not only offend his gallantry but also endanger the plan's success. And that is when I began to piece together the puzzle," he said, leaning back in his chair with a satisfied air. "It was actually quite difficult to connect you to Mr. Gorman. You are to be commended, Miss Lark."

Although tempted to ask how he had made the leap, Verity had no wish to gratify his ego further. Already, he seemed quite proud of himself for making the deduction. Instead, she asked what the Home Office knew about Beaufoy or the threats against Hardwicke. "Miss Drayton asked how you planned to deal with Kingsley, but I did not hear the answer."

Again, he laughed awkwardly, asserting that the matter had to be handled delicately. "We cannot simply string him up as a traitor."

"Why not?" Verity asked.

"That is what I said!" Delphine exclaimed. "And he gave some nibbling answer about pride and reputation."

"Of the Home Office," Grint added meaningfully. "I do not care if I am a laughingstock or even Sidmouth, but we cannot expose the entire department to ridicule. It would undermine the country's confidence in the institution itself, which would have intolerable consequences. We cannot have that!"

"So Kingsley divulges the name of England's greatest spy and suffers no harm or penalty at all?" Verity asked.

"Well, he did lose a highly influential position within the government," Grint noted.

"That happened before he drunkenly revealed Typhoeus's true identity," Verity reminded him in disgust. "In fact, it was because he lost his position that he blabbed about Hardwicke."

The under-secretary admitted the solution was not ideal but was at a loss to propose a better one. "And as you were present at his downfall—indeed, were responsible for his downfall—I know you know that I harbor no affection for him myself. It is just one of those things that we have to endure for the sake of our country."

*He* may endure it along with the spineless Sidmouth, but Verity would not. If the Home Office could not bother itself to devise a punishment appropriate for treason, then she would. Grint spoke of hanging, but there was no reason why the retribution had to be so public or final. All she required was that Kingsley suffer in some material way. To make that happen, she would have to identify what was important to him and then ensure it was taken away. During their encounter, he made it quite plain that he valued prestige, but he had already lost that with the removal from his position.

Very well, then, she would find something else.

Suspecting Grint would not be helpful in that process, she

asked instead what was being done to ensure Hardwicke's safety, as he could not live the rest of his life as a target for random assassins, and the under-secretary again regretted the lack of a good answer.

"Given the fragile peace between our two countries, the Home Office cannot be seen harassing French citizens who are simply going about their day-to-day business. For now, at least, we must rely on Wicke's ingenuity. I fear that might sound harsh to you, Miss Lark, but such are the demands of politics. Wicke understands. He is a patriot!" he said, adding that he had no doubt his operative would prevail. "He is smart and capable, and I am certain he will come through this with his usual savoir faire."

Far from being not a good answer, it was a terrible one, and Verity found herself more in sympathy with Hardwicke than she had believed possible. Despite the many services he had performed for England during the war and the sacrifices he had made, his country perceived him as a lone agent. It was only natural, then, that he would default to handling the threat against his life on his own—that was how he had always handled threats against this life. He did not have a Freddie or a Delphine peering over his shoulder, offering advice and gently nudging him in the correct direction. He had even said something to that effect during the Fitch debacle when he handed her the list of Yarwellian members to investigate: *The challenge is for me not to interfere.*

Although grateful for the new understanding of him, she was also irritated by it, for it no longer mattered. Even an hour ago, it might have made a difference.

Struck by an inexplicable wave of sorrow that washed over her at this thought, she shook herself mentally and turned to Delphine. "I see now why you were so snippy with him when I entered the room. Does he ever give a satisfying answer?"

"No, he does not," her friend replied firmly.

"The nature of the beast," Grint said with a resigned sigh as he rose to his feet. "It is the nature of the beast, I'm afraid. Government business is never satisfying, even when it works out in one's favor. That being the case, I must confess that I am quite satisfied by this meeting. It is a pleasure to see you and to speak candidly about the current predicament we find ourselves in. Once again, your country appreciates your assistance."

"Verity is a patriot," Delphine said blandly.

If he noticed the satirical edge to the remark, Grint gave no indication, saying only that their country needed more women like Miss Lark. Then he apologized for presenting himself unceremoniously on her doorstep. "I thought it was important that we meet before your encounter with Beaufoy tomorrow, so that I may have a better sense of you. Now I shall get out of your way and allow you to do what you must to prepare for your meeting with the envoy extraordinary. Wicke, I would appreciate it if you escorted me out. We still have business to discuss, and I know you want to grumble about my impertinence in coming here. We might as well do both over a glass of port."

Hardwicke agreed to this proposal without hesitation, and Verity wondered if he intended to press Grint for everything he had discovered about her. Although the under-secretary had not impressed her as being particularly cunning or clever, he had risen to prominence as head of the Alien Office during the war and had outmaneuvered the enemy on multiple occasions.

Clearly, there was more to him than met the eye.

It was possible he had discovered Verity Lark's parentage.

If not, Hardwicke would likely figure it out soon. She had put him onto the trail and now he just had to figure out where it led.

Grint continued to take his leave, thanking Miss Drayton for her hospitality and owning himself delighted to meet her. Then he strode out of the room. Hardwicke followed, sparing only an absent glance at Verity before turning right into the corridor.

# Chapter Fourteen

*Tuesday, June 16*
*8:11 a.m.*

Arriving at the bottom of the staircase the next morning, Verity found Delphine and Lucy arguing over who would accompany Pinkie on her morning walk.

"It is not your responsibility, and it is unfair of us to add to your responsibilities," Delphine pointed out reasonably. "It is only right that I should take her."

Lucy swore she did not mind. "The weather is fine, and I like to stretch my legs."

"In fact, it is a little chilly outside, and I would feel wretched if you caught a cold tending to something that is outside your duties," Delphine countered.

"Oh, but, miss, I would feel just as bad if you did!" Lucy said.

Amused, Verity proposed ending the impasse by taking Pinkie herself.

Delphine insisted it was the worst possible solution.

"With your limp, you will be gone for ages, and it is better if the neighbors do not see you."

Lucy did not blink at the revelation of her employer's new infirmity, of which there was currently no evidence. Having dusted Robert Lark's bedchamber on a weekly basis for six years, she was accustomed to the residence's peculiarities, and ever since Verity returned from an unknown outing bearing a knife wound in her shoulder, the maid had come to understand that the household situation was more complicated than just one fictional brother.

Consequently, she seconded Delphine's argument. "Yes, miss, you have your limp to think about, and we do not want to bother the neighbors. I will take Pinkie after I bring up the muffins and tea. It won't take more than a minute."

Accepting defeat graciously, Delphine looped her arm through her friend's and led her into the parlor. As they crossed the threshold, she announced that now would be a good time to tell her about Hardwicke. "You have had all night to brood about it."

Verity smiled and said she did not brood. "I ruminate."

"Yes, but with a frown," Delphine noted. "That is the definition of brooding."

Allowing the distinction, Verity nevertheless said there was nothing to tell.

"Nonsense!" her friend disclaimed spiritedly. "I did not walk in on nothing yesterday afternoon. It was incontestably something. Hardwicke looked as though he could not tell his own thumb from forefinger. What did you say to the poor man?"

An evasive reply rose to Verity's lips, and she would have responded glibly had Lucy not entered at that moment with the tray. It took the maid just long enough to deliver it to the table for Verity to reconsider the utility of affecting an indifference she did not feel.

As she poured the tea, she said, "Hardwicke does not know who my mother is."

Delphine, unimpressed with this revelation, tore the muffin in half and contemplated the spreads: berry jam or butter. "Of course not, dear. Why would he?"

Verity did not have an answer.

Bearing an analytical mind that plotted complex schemes in great detail, she had never stopped to wonder how he would have attained the information. She had merely assumed it existed in his head like divine knowledge.

"Even so, I cannot see what it would matter if he did," Delphine continued, firmly rejecting the jam in favor of the butter, which would be lovely and melty on the still warm pastry. "As he is a notorious wastrel, he cannot stand on his consequence—nor would he if he could. I do not know Hardwicke well, but I do know that about him."

Ah, yes, *this* was reason she should have held her tongue. "He ruined his reputation to aid his country. Heroism is not comparable to harlotry, as I am sure his family would be the first to tell him."

"Hardwicke does not care what his family thinks," Delphine asserted confidently.

Although not hungry, Verity recognized she needed sustenance for the day ahead and selected a muffin. "Then why did he introduce me to his brother?"

Delphine exclaimed triumphantly.

More amused than surprised by her friend's outburst, Verity tore off a piece of muffin and popped it into her mouth. She chewed without enthusiasm, noting that she did not really have an appetite for the pastry, which tasted like paste in her mouth. "You have a point you wish to make?"

"I do not, no, because you just made it for me," Delphine replied. "You concede now that Hardwicke means marriage."

Verity broke off another small chunk and held it between

her fingers for a second, then dropped it onto her plate. "I concede now that Hardwicke *meant* marriage. Realizing the extent of his folly, he changed his mind."

"Because of La Reina," Delphine said.

"Because of me," Verity replied flatly as she removed another bit of muffin before deciding it too was unappetizing. "He does not yet know about La Reina."

Bewildered, Delphine ceased slathering on butter and asked what had convinced him of his error if not the identity of her mother.

Tossing the muffin lump onto her plate, Verity snapped, "It is for the best. Let us talk of something else. Tell me, how do the potato plants fare?"

Before Delphine could render her judgment, which was mostly favorable, Freddie strode into the room and grinned at the sight of muffins. Proclaiming them delightful, he sat down at the table next to Verity and announced that he could not stay as he had intended. He had meetings with advertisers that it would be unwise to reschedule. That said, he wanted to know what had been discussed regarding the plan for later. "Is Hardwicke arriving soon to review it?"

"We are not talking about Hardwicke," Delphine said sweetly.

A furrow formed in the middle of Freddie's brows as he looked from one woman to the other. "Why are we not talking about Hardwicke? What did he do?"

Verity called Delphine a beast.

"*I* am a beast?" her friend asked coolly. "Look what you did to your muffin."

Duly complying, Verity glanced down at her plate, which was covered in crumbs.

Oh, dear.

She seemed to have mauled her muffin.

Mortified, Verity asked again about the potatoes.

Hardwicke identified himself as the bud vase.

"I will be tucked in here," he said, placing the slim vessel on the table next to the sugar bowl, which denoted the wagon of coal that would be stationed in front of number twenty Bethel Street. Across the road two doors to the west would be Grint disguised as a fruit seller. With his back toward Verity, he would be pushing his cart toward the eastern end of the street. "And because we do not want the street to appear too crowded, we will stick the comte behind your neighbor's voluminous shrub."

Delphine, examining the layout of Bethel Street as represented by sundry household items, pointed to the jar of ink and said, "None of the neighbors have a voluminous shrub. Mrs. Paisley has a sickly ficus that will not make it to next week, let alone the summer, if the weather does not improve."

Hardwicke begged to differ. "Mrs. Paisley's third cousin twice removed died last week and left her a lively arborvitae that takes up half her doorway. It would pose a problem except she hopes it will discourage her son-in-law from calling. Mr. Muir is a pompous man bursting with opinions, and she thinks it will be beneath his dignity to squeeze past a hedge to enter her house."

Delphine, who had been compelled to answer for the condition of her own home's entryway arch—pristine, of course, but good luck getting Mr. Muir to agree to any judgment that was not his own—thought the tactic had little luck of prospering. "I would have advised Mrs. Paisley to move and leave no forwarding address."

A fleeting smile passed over Verity's lips as she examined the scene as described by Hardwicke, for she was familiar with her friend's encounter with the officious busybody and grateful for the moment of levity in an otherwise sober meeting. After their heated argument, she was determined to hold her emotions in check, treating him with measured respect. She kept her tone calm and her eyes focused on the matter at hand.

Consequently, she questioned the wisdom of allowing Morny to take part in the operation. Given his willingness to chat with a reporter of whom he had never heard for more than an hour, she did not think he could be trusted to keep the secret. "He will march upstairs to confront Beaufoy at once or call the clerks into his office one by one to tell them or invite a reporter to hide behind the arborvitae with him and record his every movement."

"You are underestimating him, which many people do and is one reason why he has managed to survive for so long with his changing allegiances. He is wily," Hardwicke replied, meeting her gaze briefly before returning his focus to the bottle of ink, which he moved slightly to the left. "In my dealings with him, I have found him to be calculating and sly, and if he could figure out how to use the Beaufoy information to his advantage in a way that runs counter to our plan, he would do it in a heartbeat. That is why Grint has summoned him to the Home Office for a meeting this morning. He will tell the ambassador everything he needs to know and then deliver him to the shrub."

"I see Mr. Grint has *some* sense after all," Delphine observed wryly.

Hardwicke conceded that the under-secretary was not at his best the day before. "This business with Kingsley has unsettled him. He detests the man but knows he cannot strike back too harshly or it will look like retaliation for minor slights and stings. And Sidmouth's only concern is preserving his own reputation, which means avoiding a scandal. Grint is boxed in in every direction."

Curling her lips in disgust at the mention of the repellent home secretary, Verity looked up from the assortment of items on the table to the street outside and tried to picture the scene as described by Hardwicke. The abduction was premised on the assumption that nobody cared if a decrepit spinster was snatched from the pavement, and the coal wagon and fruit cart would not serve as deterrents. London was large and impersonal, and the vast majority of its residents would prefer to keep their heads down than get involved in a tussle on the street. Beaufoy could be anyone: an irate husband asserting his legal authority over his wife, an angry brother bringing his recalcitrant sister home, a concerned physician regaining control of a senile patient.

It was better to turn away and trust that the matter would work out for the best.

Regardless, Beaufoy would not have to worry about either man interfering because the collier would be inside the house making a delivery and the fruit seller would be pushing his wares in the opposite direction.

The path to Verity would be clear.

Contemplating her own position—embodied in the silver cream pitcher—she turned to Delphine and warned her against hovering by the window. "Presumably, Beaufoy will be watching the house as he waits for me to emerge, and we do not want him to see you. It is one thing to count on the indifference of strangers, but the indifference of intimates is a little less reliable."

"Well, naturally, no," Delphine scoffed, slightly offended. "I am not a greenhorn from the provinces pressing my nose against Ackerman's window. I will look down from the attic through the white cotton curtain. Freddie and I already confirmed that you cannot see me from the pavement."

"Have you?" Verity asked, at once amused and impressed by the degree of thoroughness her friend had displayed. "We shall make a proper Twaddler out of you yet."

"As long as Twaddling includes piles of garbage and dirty linens, no, you shall not," Delphine replied definitively.

Hardwicke moved the pitcher from the center of the table to the edge and suggested they review the plan one more time now that they had all the pieces on the board. "It is all very simple and I cannot imagine anything going awry, but that is usually when things go awry. We begin with Miss Lark: At two o'clock she leaves her home in the company of Pinkie for their daily walk."

Lying on the rug in the middle of the floor, the canine coconspirator lazily wagged her tail at the mention of her name.

Delphine cooed softly at the dog's antics as Hardwicke placed the pitcher on the edge of the serviette, which represented the pavement. Next, he slid the saltcellar three inches forward so that it was aligned with the Verity pitcher. "We do not know what type of vehicle Beaufoy will use, but it is safe to assume it will be nondescript and easy to maneuver, such as a pony cart or a hack. If he had any sense at all, he would arrive well in advance of the appointed time to familiarize himself with how the street is laid out. According to Castleheart, he has yet to visit the scene."

"Castleheart?" Verity asked.

"The man Grint has keeping an eye on Beaufoy," Hardwicke explained. "I have worked with him before. He is sharp and reliable."

Contemplating the saltcellar with a thoughtful frown, Delphine wondered if they had overlooked something in regards to Beaufoy's scheme, for it did not make sense to her that the envoy had done no reconnaissance at all. "Are we sure he intends to abduct Verity himself? What if he hired someone to do it and we have no idea of the plan?"

"It seems inconceivable to you, Delph, because you had the sense to check the opacity of the cotton curtains in the attics," Verity explained with a hint of admiration. "But it did not occur to Beaufoy to worry about what he does not know because he believes he already knows everything."

"Surely, nobody can be quite so confident. It is a kidnapping, not a visit to Hyde Park," she said with asperity. "Due diligence is required."

"Imagine Mr. Muir planning an abduction," Verity said. "Would he measure the space between the arborvitae and the doorframe? No, he would just knock over the plant if it got in his way. A mystifying number of men have an overly developed sense of their own competence. Twaddle has built an entire career on it."

Hardwicke confirmed this observation, noting that the ineptitudes of arrogant men had sustained his career as well, most famously Napoleon himself in the hours before Waterloo, when he was unaccountably convinced he would win despite several factors not being in his favor, starting with the weather. "In the unlikely event, however, that we have underestimated Beaufoy, I am sure Miss Lark will ably handle any threat that arises. She not only neatly thwarted the first abduction attempt but also tricked her would-be abductor into revealing his identity."

The compliment was strange.

Hearing Hardwicke profess so much faith in her abilities after everything that had transpired between them was disconcerting, and although she knew better than to take him at his word, she could not help but feel that this time he meant it with a sincerity that translated into action.

Or, rather, inaction.

He would trust her to handle it on her own.

It was at once gratifying and bittersweet.

"For now, let us proceed on the assumption that everything will go as planned," Hardwicke continued. "In that case, Beaufoy will grab Miss Lark soon after she steps out of her home. He will either press his palm against her mouth so she cannot cry out or jam a cloth into it. Then he will shove an unresisting—"

"A lightly resisting," Verity interjected. "We do not want to make it too easy."

He duly amended his statement to incorporate the new language. "Beaufoy will shove a lightly resisting Miss Lark into the conveyance. As soon as he closes the door behind her, Grint and I will run over to apprehend him."

Delphine took issue with this aspect of the plot as well. "*Must* he shove her into the conveyance? Are we positive that grabbing and jamming are not sufficiently incriminating? They sound sufficiently incriminating to me."

Verity said there was no point in leaving anything to chance. "Having arranged for the kidnapping, we should allow Beaufoy to actually do the kidnapping. If he puts me in the conveyance, he will not be able to claim an innocent explanation, such as he grabbed me because he thought I was about to fall down or he was overzealous in lending me a handkerchief. Shoving me into his carriage is unambiguous."

"I suppose that makes sense," Delphine said, begrudgingly swayed by the logic. "But perhaps in your light resistance, you might drive your elbow into Beaufoy's side."

Laughing, Verity said she would see what she could do.

Delphine nodded with approval and returned her attention to Hardwicke. "You and Mr. Grint apprehend Beaufoy. Then what?"

"I imagine the Comte de Morny darts out from his hiding place to saunter about the street as though he had singlehandedly captured his deputy in the middle of a horrendously violent attack," Verity said with sour disapproval. But then she heard the words repeat in her head and her expression lightened. "Oh, I see, then Comte de Morny darts out from his hiding place to saunter about the street as if he singlehandedly captured his deputy in the middle of a horrendously violent attack!"

"Any inclination to handle the matter quietly for the sake of the embassy or the dignity of France will be swept away in his desire for acclaim," Hardwicke added, his teal eyes bright with amusement.

"An attention vortex," Verity murmured.

Hardwicke nodded and said Mr. Twaddle-Thum should request an interview. "I am reasonably certain Morny would be delighted to have his exploits recounted by England's most intrepid gossip. No doubt he will translate it to French and have handbills printed."

"What about Dupont?" Delphine asked. "How do we get Beaufoy to confess to pushing a man out of a third-story window or are we meant to overlook the murder of his secretary? Although Dupont does not appear to have been particularly admirable, he is as deserving of justice as the next person."

"Grint will take care of it," Hardwicke said,

But Delphine, whose unfavorable opinion of the undersecretary had been made known, expressed doubt over the outcome. And even if Grint managed to wrap up *this* murder scheme competently, there was still the small matter of the untold number of other murder schemes for which he had no plan at all. "And let's not forget Kingsley, who let slip the dogs of war. Apparently, under Grint's aegis, it is perfectly fine for bitter functionaries to cry havoc. If I were you, Lord Colson, I would reconsider my employment."

Hardwicke, allowing that her criticisms were fair, reiterated that she had not seen Grint at his best. "He is in an untenable position. Now I suggest we review the plan one more time. Miss Drayton, please reset the silver cream pitcher, and I shall return the saltcellar to its starting position. Miss Lark, if you could place the comte behind the inkwell?"

Verity duly picked up the candlestick that stood in for the ambassador and placed it behind the ink-jar shrub.

*Tuesday, June 16*
*1:56 p.m.*

Pinkie knew something momentous was happening at twenty-six Bethel Street.

Her tail wagging furiously, she looped in circles in the narrow hallway, yipping with excitement, and Delphine watched apprehensively as Verity stepped around the dog to fetch the leash from the hook next to console.

"Do be careful," Delphine said, twisting her hands together. "It would be wretched if you tripped now and actually had to limp."

"It would be fitting *and* hilarious," Verity said as she picked up the lead and dropped to her knees to secure it to the dog's collar. "Perhaps you should go upstairs now, Delphine. Pinkie is an astute creature, and she is reacting to your anxiety."

Rather than scurry up to the attic, her friend tilted her head to the left and wondered if the mobcap was a bit too much. "You are meant to be old but not senile. Maybe you should put on a bonnet. What about the one you wore to Fortescue's last week? It is scuffed but not shabby."

Lucy said she liked the mobcap. "It makes the miss look forgetful, not senile."

Delphine's expression remained doubtful as she began to worry Verity looked too hale for an abduction. "Maybe you should have added a few wrinkles."

Verity laughed and pointed to the staircase. "Go!"

Grumbling about a judicious application of face powder to make Verity's face paler, Delphine left to take her position in the attic.

Verity turned her attention to Pinkie. "Now it is your turn, you unruly darling. Please come here so that I may attach your lead."

Pinkie barked, dashed around in another circle, and ran over, knocking her head into Verity's knee. Tipping back, Verity steadied herself with one hand, fastened the leash, and rose to her full height. Then she slipped on her pelisse, which, being too heavy for June, added to her slightly addled air.

"There," she murmured, smoothing the wrinkles of her walking dress with one hand as she turned to face Lucy. "How do I look?"

Although Lucy had only a glimmer of understanding of what was happening, she gamely told her employer that she made a fetching kidnapping victim. "I would be happy to abduct you myself, miss."

Verity duly thanked the maid, straightened the wool on her shoulders, tightened her grip on the lead, and grabbed the door's handle. "I do not expect this to take very long, so do please make sure tea is set out in the parlor for Delphine and me and possibly Lord Colson. I am not certain if he will stay."

"Yes, miss," Lucy murmured, revealing no surprise at the presumed swiftness of the abduction either.

"And a treat for Pinkie!" Verity added. "She is the true hero of the piece."

Cook, she was assured, was baking liver biscuits as they spoke.

The dog barked as though in endorsement of this plan and tugged on the leash to go outside.

"Very well, then, you eager beast, let us go do our business quickly and efficiently," Verity said sternly as Lucy disappeared downstairs, then added with a light chuckle that by "business" she did not mean that Pinkie should relieve herself. "Any Twaddler worth her salt knows to empty her bladder before embarking on an escapade."

Opening the door, Verity was met with the same scene she had spied from the attic window only ten minutes before, and if it did not match Hardwicke's tabletop description precisely, it was remarkably close. Three doors down to the left, in front of number twenty, stood a wagon piled high with coal, its collier nowhere to be seen. She trusted Hardwicke's form was huddled behind the bulky peaks. Across the road, Grint heaved the fruit cart along the pavement, his progress slow as he pushed against the weight. Next door, prominently displayed in the middle of the entranceway, as though to block Mrs. Paisley's son-in-law entirely, was the flourishing arborvitae behind which the ambassador to the Court of St. James hid.

And there, off to the left about six feet away, was Beaufoy's conveyance. It was a hackney coach, presumably unlicensed, with a mud-splattered black door and chipped yellow paint on the side. The envoy sat on the bench, his slim frame hidden by an overly large brown coat with folds. His appearance was further obscured by a wide-brimmed hat, which would hide most of his face. He held a whip in his right hand and appeared to be talking to his horses.

Pinkie wagged her tail furiously and pulled on the lead until her breathing became labored. Then she let out two fierce yaps, and Verity congratulated her on delivering her lines with the proper amount of feeling. Closing the door to the house, Verity took one leaden step forward and straightened her arms with an almost farcical jerk to make it appear as though the dog was walking her, not the other way around. She stumbled slightly on the second step, and as she regained her balance, she scanned her surroundings from left to right to make sure everything was still in place.

Coal wagon: check.

Fruit seller: check.

Oversize shrub: check.

Murderous diplomat: check.

Elegant carriage drawn by matched chestnuts: check.

Wait, no, she thought, the elegant carriage was not part of her tally.

And yet there it was, stopped in front of number twenty-eight to the right.

It was not a welcome sight, to be sure, but she had included the possibility of unknown factors in her calculation and knew that it did not necessarily present a problem. The whole scheme was based on the theory of indifference, which Beaufoy had posited himself, and given the condition of the horses—their wildly gleaning brown coats—Verity knew the owner of the carriage was a personage of some wealth who could have no interest in the exploits of the lower-order residents who called Bethel Street home.

The groom had most likely paused to get his bearings.

Categorizing the risk from the carriage as low, Verity turned to the left. The hack was about five feet from her now, and she saw Beaufoy switch positions. He inched closer to the edge of the bench, his movements steady and careful.

Clearly, he did not want to startle the infirm woman walking the dog.

To allow him to climb down unnoticed, Verity glared at Pinkie and begged her to slow down. "Please, darling, there is no rush. The park isn't going anywhere."

As though taking cues from an unseen director, the dog snapped at a squirrel.

Under the guise of tugging on the lead as hard as she could, she glanced at Beaufoy out of the corner of her eyes.

One leg was over the side.

Now two.

Both feet hit the ground just as Verity limped sluggishly past him, and although she did not allow her entire body to grow tense in anticipation, she could not stop her shoulders from stiffening. The most important thing was not to struggle too much or too competently. She had to fight her instinct to protect herself and affect helplessness.

Imagine you are the Wraithe finding a corpulent rat in your bed, she thought, recalling the sickening scream the vicious headmistress let out before she began flailing madly in every direction, her fear so sharp she wound up tripping over her own feet and falling into the bed right on top of the rodent.

Yes, precisely that level of terror.

Pinkie barked again—truly, an excellent performer—and Verity heard the faint crunch of Beaufoy's shoes on the pavement. He was close now.

So close.

He would strike at any—

Verity gagged, struggling for air as Beaufoy's wrist hooked around her throat and tightened against her trachea. He jerked his arm back, increasing the pressure, while his other hand shoved her right hip forward. The movement forced her head to drop onto his shoulder, and he stepped back, back, back as he pulled her to the ground, his own footing steady and sure. Still choking her with one arm, he clasped both her arms together, constricting his grip and further restricting her breath, and Verity, having barely registered the shock, had only enough time to think, Holy bloody hell, before Beaufoy wailed in pain, releasing her, and a peeved voice said above her head, "You have caused me no end of trouble, child!"

Gasping for air, heart pounding, every muscle in her body rigid and ready to attack, Verity looked up from the pavement and saw the Dowager Duchess of Kesgrave.

# Chapter Fifteen

*Tuesday, June 16*
*2:03 p.m.*

Verity laughed.

Not a gurgle, not a chortle, not a chuckle—a full-throated, hysterical laugh as though someone were tickling her with relentless ferocity and she was without defenses.

It hurt.

Oh, yes, it did, the spiky pain stabbing her ribs as she struggled to breathe.

But who could blame her?

And how could she stop?

It was so astoundingly funny—this family of rich nobles, their confounding ability to appear suddenly at the most astounding times.

First Kesgrave, knocking politely on her door while she was nursing a knife wound and running to Whitehall to stop a massacre.

*We have important work to do, brother mine. Do hurry up!*

And now his grandmother, here, just as Beaufoy wrestled her to the ground, bashing him on the head with ... with ...

Frantically, Verity swiveled her head and spotted the cane.

Of course it was a cane.

The woman was well over seventy!

Baffling and more baffling, she thought, incapable of comprehending how they both had such exquisite timing.

Was it simply a matter of money?

Were they so affluent they could bribe Providence?

Or did they subscribe to a service that allowed affluent dukes and duchesses to bend reality to their will? Did the company advertise in the back pages of Debrett's?

Clutching her stomach to ease the brutal ache, Verity heard the pounding of footsteps and saw Hardwicke take hold of Beaufoy, who was still too stunned to react. He stared over her head at the dowager, who raised her cane higher, as if prepared to take on the disheveled newcomer in his coal-stained clothes.

Verity laughed harder.

Grint called out as he crossed the road, but she could not hear the words over her own hysteria, just their cadence, and then Morny was there, issuing invectives and commands in French. Beaufoy, his senses returning, cried that he was being abused by a pack of women and ordered their arrest.

"Seize them now!" he exclaimed.

Hardwicke handed Beaufoy to Grint, then hunched down in front of Verity, his teal eyes dark with concern, just as Delphine came flying out of the house at breakneck speed. Her nerves quivering as she wrapped her arms around her friend, she glared at Hardwicke and seethed, "You said 'grabbing,' my lord. Where was the grabbing? What he did was ... was ... was..."

She had no word for it!

"Jujitsu, Miss Drayton," Grint said.

Delphine scowled at him. "What?"

"The maneuver Beaufoy used to overpower Miss Lark is from a style of fighting known as jujitsu," he explained. "It is practiced in the East and is not widely known in England or on the Continent."

Tartly, Delphine thanked him for the geography lesson.

Struggling to constrain her amusement, Verity took several deep breaths and insisted between chortles that she was fine.

No, really.

Now Delphine rounded on her. "Don't you dare start taking that attitude with—"

Verity grasped her friend's hand, squeezed, and gestured to the gray-haired woman still gripping her walking stick like a club. "You do not understand: This is the Dowager Duchess of Kesgrave."

Furiously, Delphine waved her other hand in the air, as if to swat away the information, and swore she would not allow herself to be distracted by trivialities. "It is what you always do and I will not—"

Then she broke off her tirade and stared blankly. "Wait. What did you say?"

"This august personage who rushed to my rescue"—Verity pointed openly at the other woman now, eschewing all propriety—"is the Dowager Duchess of Kesgrave."

Delphine's expression cleared at once as she digested the information, then it immediately clouded again as she realized the information did not make sense. She managed to form the word *what* but could not produce sound.

"Yes, my feeling precisely," Verity said with a chuckle.

And only a chuckle!

She was in control of herself now and would not fall prey to another fit.

But it was all still so hilarious to her!

Freddie would never believe it, not for a minute.

Considering what had to be done in order of importance, she knew the dowager must be addressed first but could not bring herself to do so. In an act of pure cowardice, she turned to Delphine and asked her to bring Pinkie inside. "The darling girl looks terrified."

Delphine, contemplating the dog, who lay silently on the pavement, her head resting on her paws, noted that she seemed more abashed than afraid, as if she feared the whole contretemps had been her doing. Brushing her hand over the mortified creature's head, she purred, "You poor dear. You are not to blame. It was all the fault of the bad man. You see him—the bad man who is struggling to break free of Mr. Grint's grasp. Come, we will get you some liver-flavored biscuits. You like liver biscuits, don't you? Yes, you do!"

Pinkie managed a feeble yelp-bark and wagged her tail half-heartedly, which pleased Delphine, who continued to murmur soothingly as she led the dog inside.

Well, that only delayed the inevitable for thirty seconds, Verity thought petulantly, pulling her shoulders back as she raised her chin to confront the dowager. Obviously, her sudden appearance had something to do with the duke. He had shared with his grandmother the details of his bizarre meeting with La Reina's by-blow and she had come to ogle her.

No, not ogle.

Warn her away.

The prospect of her family being embroiled with a woman of Verity's ilk, however slightly, must horrify her to her toes, and she wanted to ensure it did not happen.

Despite her discomfort, Verity smiled at the notion, for the horror went very much in both directions, and it was not she who had established contact. It was the duke who had come knocking on her door, and the dowager would do better to aim her flinty stare at him.

Oh, but that was naïve, expecting the frail old lady to put her foot down with a grown man of three and thirty of whom she nurtured a particular fondness and who wielded considerable power in his own right. It was far easier to come to Bethel Street to issue an edict, and as the duke had no doubt shared all the grisly details of their encounter, she probably assumed she had the means by which to ensure compliance. Verity would agree never to contact Kesgrave again, and in exchange the dowager would not say a word about Mr. Gorman.

Naturally, Verity would accept the proposal. It made no difference to her and would allow the dowager to feel as though she had successfully exerted her authority. Satisfied, she would promptly take her leave.

And that was her goal: to keep her interaction with the Dowager Duchess of Kesgrave as brief as possible. Alas, the business they had to conduct could not be done on the pavement. Verity would have to invite her inside.

Decorum was the very devil!

Mindful of her duty, Verity rose to her feet with as much dignity as she could muster and thanked the septuagenarian for coming to her rescue.

"Is that what I did?" her grace replied dubiously as her gaze swept past Verity to where Beaufoy struggled against Grint. "It does not appear to be that simple. I rather suspect I interrupted an unfolding drama."

As any attempt to refute the claim would be an insult to the old woman's intelligence, Verity conceded that they had been in the process of apprehending a villain. "You could not have known that. Regardless, you bravely rushed to rescue a stranger without any consideration for your own safety, and I am grateful for it. I knew the attack was coming and yet somehow, he still surprised me. I was genuinely at the disadvantage."

The dowager made a noise that sounded like *harumph*.

The comte stepped forward and introduced himself with a lavish flourish, sweeping one hand across his body as he bowed low, his courtly manners on full display. "I can only echo Miss Lark's praise, for you are indeed courageous to intercede. This man is a murderer and could have done grievous harm to you as well, but you spared no thought for yourself. I shall send a dispatch to my king at once proposing that France bestow on you a medal of honor for your unparalleled courage. It would be my privilege to present it to you at a ceremony that is sure to be attended by the prince regent himself."

Although the dowager had the good sense to demur, Morny insisted that he must do something to reward her heroism and she demanded an explanation. "It has been several minutes since I walloped that man with my cane, and I still have no understanding of what is happening."

Grint, securing Beaufoy's arms behind his back with twine, supplied his name and position, identifying himself as Lord Sidmouth's representative. "I trust you know Lord Sidmouth? He is well acquainted with your grandson the duke, whom I had the pleasure of meeting myself recently. As you have rightly surmised, there is more going on here than meets the eye. This man is Guillaume Beaufoy, formerly of the French embassy. Now he is a prisoner of the crown charged with murder."

Beaufoy insisted that it was all a terrible mistake. He had not meant any harm! Identifying the dowager as the only person present whom he had any chance of persuading, he pleaded for her understanding. "I saw this ... this ... this"—he foundered for the words to properly describe the leaden-footed Miss Lark—"*ravishing* creature and momentarily lost my head. I thought only of making her my own and acted with heedless zeal. I am sure a woman of your years knows what it is like to be ruled by the heart."

The dowager did him the courtesy of listening to his appeal, then said, "Mr. Beaufoy, I am certain that is not true. Regardless, I am not your judge or jury."

Beaufoy appeared taken aback by the announcement, as if he had not considered the matter of justice in practical terms. Thinking about it now, he proclaimed confidently, "No jury would convict me. There is no evidence of a crime. As I said, I was overeager to express my admiration for this ravishing creature, but expressions of love are not illegal, not even in England. You say I am a murderer, but I have harmed nobody and have myself suffered a painful thump on my head with her grace's cane. You cannot do anything to me."

Hardwicke, speaking for the first time, said they had all the evidence they needed to guarantee a trip up the gibbet. "You thought Dupont was your dupe, but he outsmarted you. After you told him your plan to remove his excellency, he came to me and offered to sell the information to the British. He knew the English government would pay to keep one of its greatest war heroes safe. That is when he proposed capturing you in your own net."

Beaufoy stopped chafing at the tether binding his wrists to stare blankly. "Rubbish!"

"Is it?" Hardwicke murmured curiously. "Did it not occur to you to wonder why he was so quick to agree to abduct Miss Lark or aid and abet a murder for his employer? Nothing you could offer him would be enough to compensate him for the danger to himself. He had a wife to take care of and a child on the way. Why would he imperil all that to satisfy your ambition when he could satisfy his own without risking the noose?"

Although Beaufoy's expression remained impassive, Verity

thought she detected a slight stiffening of the shoulders at the revelation of Mrs. Dupont's condition and decided it was a well-placed detail. Hardwicke was doing an excellent job of mingling fact and fiction, and even she, who knew the whole truth, found herself marveling at the complexity of Dupont's scheme.

Hardwicke, continuing in this same vein, his tone a mix of curiosity and conceit, asked Beaufoy what Dupont had told him about his so-called first attempt to abduct Miss Lark. "Did he claim that her brother was in residence and suddenly came upon him? That was to stall because the home secretary insisted we tell the ambassador what was going on under his very nose and he needed time to arrange a meeting. Miss Lark's brother is still away. Ask any of the neighbors if they have seen him in a sennight."

Beaufoy, his eyes darting from the left to the right, from ambassador to under-secretary, swore it was all nonsense. "I have no idea what you are talking about."

But beads of sweat had begun to form at his temples because Hardwicke's narrative sounded plausible.

"Yes," Hardwicke said with relish. "Your plan was clever but with one minor oversight: You assumed Dupont's loyalty without doing anything to secure it. So he took your plan and improved upon it, and the worst that would have happened was you would have been sent home to France in disgrace. But when you realized what Dupont was going to do, you panicked and pushed him out of the window."

Beseechingly, Beaufoy returned his attention to the dowager, as if she held the keys to his salvation. "Please believe me, your grace, he does not know what he is saying. It makes no sense."

Hardwicke smiled without humor and said it was perfectly logical. "You realized the truth when you saw the information about the house on Gherkin Lane in his office.

Dupont could not afford sixty guineas a year, not on a secretary's salary. But on an envoy extraordinary's ... well, that was entirely possible. You knew he planned to betray you. That is why you pushed him out the window and then hid behind the door as others rushed into the room."

Beaufoy's face turned gray at the accusation, which proved its accuracy, and he brushed away the drops of perspiration as they dripped down the sides of his face. Initially fluid, his movements became rushed and fitful, as if swatting flies that encircled his head.

Mercilessly, Hardwicke mocked him for not destroying the evidence. "Only one thing connected you to the crime: that piece of paper with the appointment, the other half of the torn slip that was in Dupont's hand when he fell. If you had not stored it in your writing desk under endless drafts of your speech at the Tip-Tapp Club, then we would have no proof. But like a fool you kept it. So much for your clever schemes!"

Laughing riotously, Beaufoy cackled and said, "Ha! You fool! You think you have me but I'm smarter. I *did* destroy it! I burned it in the hearth the second I returned to my office. You have nothing! You can prove nothing! Remove these ropes from my hands at once!"

Nobody moved.

Beaufoy issued the order again, swiveling his head back and forth, his frustration growing more and more frantic as the men failed to respond.

Hardwicke, his tone neutral again, asked Grint if he had everything he needed.

Smoothly, the under-secretary said he thought so.

Morny concurred.

Their composure incensed Beaufoy.

How were they not seething with infuriation at being thwarted?

He had outwitted them!

The proof was gone! He had burned it!

He repeated the claim wildly, fiercely, with a sneer of triumph that slowly gave way to confusion at their resolute refusal to admit defeat and gradually he began to perceive the problem with his assertion.

Did Grint have everything he needed?

Yes, a confession to three men of high standing in their respective governments was sufficient to ensure conviction.

Stupefied, Beaufoy trailed off.

Seeing the recognition slowly flare in the other man's eyes, the comte said, "You were too clever for your own good. You should have just killed Typhoeus and been done with it."

Beaufoy jeered at the notion that he cared about the English spy. "All I wanted was for you to be gone. You are a monster of selfishness and greed, bearing no loyalty to anyone but yourself, and you prance across the stage and preen as if ennobled by your inconstancy. You are the rot at the heart of France, and it must be rooted out for the sake of the country. If I received a promotion in the process, then it was merely a reward for making a difficult decision."

Morny, who had kneeled before Napoleon and renounced the king as many times as he had kneeled before the king and renounced Napoleon, revealed no dismay at this appraisal. His opinion of himself was either fixed or impervious to the criticisms of a murderer. Coolly, he observed how very fortunate it was for Beaufoy that he would be in Newgate soon and spared the ordeal of seeing him.

And that was all the attention he gave his former deputy, calmly pivoting to the right to present the other man with his back and addressing Verity. "My nation owes you a debt of gratitude, as do I. We would never have apprehended Beaufoy if not for your willingness to put yourself in harm's way. I also understand from Mr. Grint that you were crucial in discovering his scheme. You are an impressive woman, Miss Lark, with a talent for subterfuge. Your feigned limp is a thing of beauty."

Gratified by the compliment and only slightly embarrassed to receive it in front of the dowager, Verity said, "Thank you, your excellency."

Next, he addressed Hardwicke, whom he called Wicke like his lordship's other wartime associates, and owned himself deeply troubled by the Typhoeus quagmire. "Although I would not call myself an accomplished tactician, I do have some experience with mitigating the consequences of decisions that no longer serve my purpose and would like to help. Let us arrange a meeting to discuss it. I shall be busy the next few days cleaning up this calamity with Beaufoy and then I have my speech at the Tip-Tapp Club—you should come to it, by the bye. I have several insightful things to say about the way forward for both our countries. After that, however, I am available to meet at your convenience."

Hardwicke was noncommittal on both points, which the ambassador either did not observe or was too diplomatic to note, and turned to Grint. "Let us depart. I have half a dozen dispatches to compose and send before I may have my supper."

As the two men took their leave of the dowager, Verity amused herself by imagining the ideas the ambassador would suggest to extricate Typhoeus from the quagmire. Given his fondness for attention, she assumed the solution would somehow entail placing himself at the center of the drama, perhaps by taking out an ad in *The Times* announcing himself as the great English spy.

No, not an ad. He would arrange an interview with the newspaper so he could expound on his exploits to great lengths over tea and macarons.

A facetious thought, it nevertheless sparked a practical

one, and she stiffened as she realized whom Twaddle could unveil as the true Typhoeus: Kingsley.

Grint said that the disgraced under-secretary would suffer no punishment because his malevolence and incompetence reflected badly on the Home Office.

But what if the revelation bathed the Home Office in glory?

Surely, it would redound to Sidmouth's benefit if he counted a master spy among the minions in his department. It would remove the target from Hardwicke's back and place it squarely on Kingsley's, where it belonged. And since the Home Office could not allow its own hero to be shot in Oxford Street or drowned in the Serpentine or whatever cruel and inventive death with which the lucky assassin happened to succeed, it would have to ensure Kingsley's safety, perhaps by sending him to a tiny village in Scotland where nobody would recognize him.

Banishment to the Highlands struck her as a fitting retribution for his actions.

Arranging it would be easy enough.

All it required was a notice from Twaddle praising the under-secretary's brave exploits to the skies. Nobody would doubt it then.

Would Hardwicke allow it?

Possibly, yes.

It might offend his sense of honor to place another man in harm's way.

But it was not harm's way exactly, not if the Home Office responded as it should, and the scoundrel deserved it for babbling secrets while in his cups.

Ultimately, Hardwicke would agree.

Verity was confident she could convince him and liked the symmetry of their relationship ending the way it had begun: with a manipulation of Mr. Twaddle-Thum.

Eager to gain Hardwicke's approval for the plan, she first had to dispense with the Dowager Duchess of Kesgrave, who had yet to reveal her reason for visiting. Although she wanted to invite her to leave along with Grint and Morny, she yielded to the dictates of civility and asked Hardwicke to escort her grace to the parlor.

The dowager consented to this proposal, laying her left hand lightly on Hardwicke's forearm while the majority of her weight rested on the sturdy cane. As she walked toward the house, she said, "I hope, Miss Lark, that you have refreshments other than liver-flavored biscuits."

Was that a sally, Verity wondered, taken aback by the remark.

Was the Dowager Duchess of Kesgrave teasing La Reina's daughter?

It was unfathomable.

Hardwicke assured her that Verity did. "I have been served filbert biscuits and rolled wafers, both of which are of excellent quality."

"Visit here often, do you, Lord Colson?" the dowager asked archly.

"Not as much as I would like," he admitted, darting a pensive look at Verity as he helped the septuagenarian over the threshold.

He has already figured it out or, at the very least, is halfway there, Verity thought as she entered the house to find Delphine sitting at the bottom of the staircase. She was rubbing Pinkie's belly while Lucy alternately gushed over the hound's adorableness and tried to ascertain how many people would be staying for tea.

"We shall need service for four," Verity said, adding that the Dowager Duchess of Kesgrave would like to sample the filbert biscuits and rolled wafers. "So please add those to the tray as well."

Unprepared to welcome an august member of the peer-age, Lucy gasped and began to neaten her clothes, tugging self-consciously on the hem of her dress as she lowered into a deep curtsy. She wobbled unsteadily, leaning too far forward, but managed to regain her balance as she rose. Then she backed away slowly, as if afraid to remove her eyes from the noble visitor.

Verity, who was in no danger of succumbing to another fit of laughter, found Lucy's antics highly entertaining, especially when the girl decided she was far enough away to turn around and run. It was understandable, of course, for there was no reason the maid should be prepared to interact with such consequential visitors.

She had no idea the quality of Verity's relations—and even if she did, it would not signify. Verity herself was in full possession of the information and was still stunned by the dowager's presence. Delphine was equally dumbfounded as she stared up at the dowager from her spot on the bottom step, neither rising to greet the woman properly nor glancing away to hide her interest. She recalled her manners when Verity coughed pointedly and stood for an introduction.

Clearly unsettled by the peeress, Delphine returned her attention immediately to the dog and said, "And this scoundrel is Pinkie."

With an air of dignity that was as disconcerting as it was unanticipated, the dowager bid Pinkie a warm good day, which was received with an enthusiastic bark.

An awkward silence followed this unexpectedly convivial exchange as Verity marveled at the dowager's amiability. Presumably, her demeanor would change to strict and fore-boding when the subject switched to future contact with her grandson.

Hardwicke suggested they adjourn to the parlor, where they could all sit down, although by "all" he clearly meant the elderly peeress who had recently swung her cane with remarkable force.

If the dowager felt singled out by the remark, she did not reveal it as she acquiesced to the suggestion and allowed Hardwicke to lead her to the room. He escorted her to the settee, where she sat down and he took the cushion next to her. Verity and Delphine sat in the bergères opposite, and Lucy, arriving with the tray just as they had settled, placed it on the table between them. She adjusted the location of the plate of biscuits, sliding it a few inches closer to their important guest, then turned and left the room as quickly as possible.

To forestall another discomfiting pause, Verity asked Delphine to pour the tea and then thanked the dowager again for interceding on her behalf. "As I noted previously, you had no way of knowing the attack was part of a plot to apprehend a murderer, and the speed and skill of his assault were surprising. I am truly grateful for your help."

"I should have realized all was not as it appeared, as Damien did not mention a limp, and it was too pronounced to be overlooked," the dowager said, bringing the tea to her mouth and taking a delicate slip. Then she returned it to the saucer with a gentle clatter. "I am relieved that my interference did not muck up the works. And you, Lord Colson, that was deftly handled. I assume your father is aware of your work on behalf of our government and is not genuinely angered by your exploits?"

"We have an understanding," he replied mildly.

The dowager pronounced herself relieved to hear it, then added peevishly that in her day clandestine machinations were carried out in privacy. "Arranging a kidnapping in the bright light of day on a public thoroughfare is both ill-considered and uncouth. These things should be done under the cover of darkness in the middle of the night."

Solemnly, Verity offered her agreement.

"Well, I am sure it is not *all* your fault," the peeress allowed graciously. "Criminals in general are abhorrent creatures and will behave despicably no matter how strongly you point them toward decency. We can only do what we can to fend them off. And in fact that is why I am here, Miss Lark, to discuss despicable behavior. To that end, I would ask if you and I could please have the room so that I may speak freely."

Accustomed to the moral judgment of others, Verity nevertheless felt a chill pass through her at how matter-of-factly the Dowager Duchess of Kesgrave rendered it. She had no right to expect sympathy or consideration from the woman who had been forced to endure La Reina as her daughter-in-law, and yet she had allowed herself to be lulled by her guest's displays of geniality.

It was a derisible mistake.

The warmth with which one treated an adorable basset hound did not naturally extend to the cast-off by-blow of your despised adversary.

If anything, it was the opposite.

The dowager's kindness toward animals was another expression of her innate decency—a quality a bastard daughter like Verity could never possess.

Like earlier, when she braced for Beaufoy's attack, her shoulders tightened in expectation, and annoyed that a few cutting words could have the same effect on her as a physical assault, Verity said no.

She would not send Delphine away.

It was a small thing, a minor rebellion, but it was the only act of defiance available to her at the moment. Staunchly, she said, "Miss Drayton is my dearest friend. I have no secrets from her."

What the dowager thought of this reply was impossible to discern. Her expression remained aloof as she looked to her left and asked archly, "And Lord Colson? Do you have no secrets from him as well?"

Startled by the query, Verity realized she had forgotten Hardwicke.

Well, not forgotten, per se, but rather failed to consider him as an entity separate and distinct from Delphine. Somehow she had lumped him into the same group as her dearest friend, and although she knew he did not belong in the category, she recognized the expediency in allowing him to remain in it. The dowager would be unstinting in her disdain for Verity, which would tell him everything he needed to know without her having to say a word.

That was, everything he did not already know, which she suspected was very little. Given the preponderance of evidence, it did not require a particularly keen intelligence to figure out the identity of her mother. Even if Hardwicke could not identify where exactly Verity fell on La Reina's family tree, he had to know she dangled from one of its branches. It was the only explanation that accounted for the strange way members of the Matlock family kept appearing in her life.

Vaguely amazed by the calm she felt, Verity said, "No, I do not, your grace. None at all. You may proceed."

The dowager did not.

Granted permission to speak, she now appeared oddly reluctant to begin and pressed her back against the settee. She raised the tea again to her lips, lingering over the sip, and grasped the cup in both hands. She kept her silence for another few seconds, four or five, maybe six at the most, and said, "I understand from Damien that your childhood was less than pleasant."

That was all she said, just the one brief sentence, and Verity, sitting across from her, wondered if it was her turn to speak.

Well, she would not, for she had nothing to add.

A distasteful expression swept across the dowager's features.

It was, Verity thought in puzzled astonishment, a stab of ice in her heart. How was it possible that all these years later, she could still feel ashamed of the so-called unpleasantness that had been visited upon her as a small child?

A small, helpless child—and yet somehow she felt complicit.

It was madness.

Furious at the Dowager Duchess of Kesgrave for creating these sensations—for coming into her home to create them— she opened her mouth to ask her to leave,

But her grace spoke first.

"No, that is wrong," she said tartly, the fingers grasping the teacup growing white. "I understand from Damien that your childhood was brutal."

Again, she stopped at the end of the brief statement, this time leaving the word *brutal* to hang in the air, and Verity realized the distaste was not for her. The dowager felt it for herself, for the way she was treading lightly around the subject because it pained her to talk about it.

"I gave her money," the dowager announced. "That wretched headmistress at Fortescue's—I gave her money to see to your care and she responded with brutality."

Verity was flabbergasted.

She could not have been more astounded if her visitor had taken off her shoes and started doing backward somersaults over the settee.

The dowager, either unaware of the impact of her words or indifferent to it, continued. "I discovered your existence while searching for information about your mother that I could use to dissuade her from marrying my son. I threatened her with exposure if she went through with the wedding, but it had no effect. She dared me to share the information. She knew the shame of the scandal would cause me more pain than her. She delighted in tarnishing the Matlock name. She was a vile creature," she said, sighing heavily and placing the teacup on the table. "I am sorry if it hurts for you to hear me say that, but it is true. She was vile."

It did not hurt Verity, no, not at all.

What cut her to the quick was hearing herself used as a pawn—an ineffective one, which somehow made it worse. If one was going to be moved around a board at the whim of others, then the effort should at least produce the desired effect. She had hated the thought of being someone else's puppet for so long, she could not recall a moment of her life when the notion did not repulse her. Every action she had taken from the day she had left the scullery in Mount Street had been in service of her own agency.

Did it help to remind herself she had been a small child?

A babe in arms scarcely a little older than one.

Alas, it did not.

Smothering this roil of emotion, Verity met the other woman's eyes and said it did not hurt her.

The dowager held her own gaze steady, her lashes blinking at irregular intervals, and announced she was actually pleased she had arrived when she did. "The shocking scene and its revelations about your place in it have allowed me to form an impression of you that is distinct from your mother. I find that helpful because I am unsettled by how much you look like her. You could be her twin."

Verity, who had known about the resemblance for only eleven days, had no reply to this observation as well.

None was required, however, for the dowager explained that she could not in all conscience leave the child—La Reina's baby daughter—in the condition in which she had found her without doing something to improve her situation.

"That is when my representative contacted the woman in charge of the asylum and arranged an annual stipend to provide the child—you—with basic amenities and a luxury or two. Since Kesgrave told me of your upbringing, I have been trying to find out what went wrong and have learned that the wretched headmistress kept the money for herself and treated you abominably as a result. I cannot fathom the sort of viciousness that would steal money from an infant and then resent the baby for her meager good fortune. Regardless, that is what happened, and it is my fault. The brutality you suffered as a child was my fault, Miss Lark, and I am sorry."

Verity felt the impulse to laugh again tickle at her throat, for it was such a wealthy aristocrat's way of understanding the world: assuming she could buy decency and perceiving it as a direct violation of her will when it was not delivered on schedule like a frock.

Delphine noted it too, for she said, "It was brutal for all of us, ma'am. It had nothing to do with your money. The Wraithe was cruel. That is the extent of the story, so you do not need to tease yourself over making the situation worse. That was impossible."

Far from taking comfort in Delphine's exoneration, the dowager appeared angered by it. "That might be the case, Miss Drayton, but it has no bearing on the fact that my actions caused unintended harm. I am here to right the wrong I did Miss Lark and will not leave until I have discharged the debt."

The color rose in Delphine's cheeks as she put her tea down with so much force the liquid sloshed over the side of the cup. "The wrong you did was leaving a helpless child in the care of Fortescue's Asylum for Pauper Children when you had the resources to see her settled elsewhere. It would no doubt have been cheaper in the long run. A savvier horse trader would have spotted the better bargain."

If her grace took offense at being compared with the cutthroat dealers who examined the stock at Tattersall's, she gave no indication. Instead, she calmly agreed with Delphine. "But I cannot undo the mistakes of the past. All I can do is make amends for them now. That is why I have instructed my bank to advance you money in the amount of four hundred and seventy-five pounds, Miss Lark. I arrived at the figure by calculating how much I gave Miss Wraithe over the course of fifteen years and multiplying it by a reasonable interest rate and a compensatory sum for the abuse you were forced to endure. You will find all the information you need to access the funds here."

She held out a note card.

A soft cream color with a thick edge, it looked benign, but Verity almost recoiled at the sight of it. The folly of nobility —believing every problem could be solved with money.

Well, to be fair, most problems could, Verity allowed cynically.

Nevertheless, this one could not.

Folding her hands in her lap to make it clear that she would not be accepting any slips of paper, she said, "I appreciate the effort you made on my behalf. You were under no obligation to me, and that you considered my welfare to be your responsibility is a credit to you. There is no debt to discharge. You may inform your bank that I will not be drawing on the funds."

As if she had anticipated this precise reply, the dowager placed the note card on the table and said she understood Verity's reluctance to accept the offer. "You are disconcerted by my visit, especially at this time, and do not believe the money is owed to you. Trust me, it is. I am sure your friend Miss Drayton would agree it is only what I deserve for not being savvier at horse-trading. As soon as I am gone, she will waste no time in explaining that to you. I will leave the information here for when you change your mind."

"No, ma'am, I won't," Delphine said firmly. "I am sorry you are troubled by something that happened over three decades ago, but it is not my responsibility to help you ease your conscience. We are all encumbered by burdens that weigh us down, however much we wish it were otherwise, and the only recourse is to bear them with as much grace and fortitude as we are capable."

Scowling, the dowager snapped, "I have lived more than twice as long as you, Miss Drayton, so I will thank you not to lecture me about burdens."

Delphine apologized at once.

And rightly so, Verity thought, for she knew well the burdens the dowager shouldered: two sons, both cruel, one homicidal. It was little wonder she had shown up at Bethel Street bearing the direction of Coutts. In Verity Lark she had seen one weight she could lift.

Gently, Verity said she would not change her mind. "I will not accept the money under any circumstance, your grace. But I will accept what you came here today to do. It means something to me to know that you tried to help me. It is a small gift to me, and I thank you for it. I hope that is enough for you to consider amends to have been made."

The dowager did not.

Verity saw the pugnacity on the other woman's face and knew she wanted to argue over the insignificance of the gift compared with the generosity of the offer. But she restrained herself, seeming to realize she did not get to dictate the terms of her absolution. She had only two options—accept the proposal on offer or reject it—and the fierceness left her face as she arrived at a decision.

With a brisk nod, she tore the note card in half.

There was a finality about the action, a sense that their business had been concluded, and Verity grappled over what to do next. It felt churlish to eject the woman from her house and yet she could not bear the prospect of sitting in the parlor making polite conversation around cups of cooling tea.

What would they even talk about?

The weather or the duke or Mr. Twaddle-Thum's latest report.

Verity inwardly winced at the thought of the Dowager Duchess of Kesgrave reading the gossip's overly fawning accounts of Her Outrageousness's investigations.

Surely, the other woman recognized it was time to depart.

*She must be as uncomfortable as I am.*

Alas, the very opposite appeared to be the case, for the septuagenarian's rigid pose loosened and she selected a rolled wafer from the plate. Finishing it in three easy bites, she agreed with Hardwicke's assessment, noting that the biscuit was very fine.

Delphine, as if seeking to temper her earlier ferocity, offered to have Cook send over the recipe, and although she could not have expected the dowager, with her full kitchen staff and French chef, to accept the proposal, she nodded with sanguinity when that was precisely what happened. "Ordinarily, we give out recipes only as a swap. The rolled wafer recipe, for example, is from Mrs. Newsome next door, which we traded for our suet pudding."

Hardwicke mentioned that his own cook had bartered an impeccable baked custard for the orange biscuits.

"Of course we are happy to make an exception for you," Delphine added.

The dowager, however, would hear none of it and insisted on supplying a recipe in return, per the custom. "I trust you like meat pies? Poulin makes an excellent meat pie with lamb. The secret is in the seasonings. The rosemary, I believe."

Clapping in delight, Delphine swore that she adored a well-prepared meat pie. "And I am excessively fond of rosemary. I grow it in my garden."

Hardwicke owned himself enamored of the herb as well and asked if he may also have the recipe, to which the dowager replied that her answer must depend on what he had to offer. He paused to think, and Verity, listening to the exchange, could make neither heads nor tails of it, a confusion Pinkie seemed to share, for she rose to her feet and let out a series of sharp, severe barks before settling down again.

# Chapter Sixteen

*Tuesday, June 16*
*3:51 p.m.*

Although neither Twaddle nor the duke was introduced into the conversation, Delphine did in fact mention the weather while expressing sympathy for the dowager's rheumatic complaint, which was well-known by society. Even Sidmouth had asked Kesgrave about his grandmother's troublesome joints as they waited for information at the Home Office.

Nevertheless, she refused to linger on them now, only acknowledging that the cold, damp spring had done little to improve her situation as she accepted Hardwicke's assistance in standing. When she reached her full height, she turned her flinty gaze on Verity and thanked her for an enlightening interlude. "I must confess, I anticipated a very different type of encounter during the drive to your home and am sincerely pleased to know how wrong my expectations were. It is a salutary lesson to me in judging a child by her antecedents, for you are nothing like your parents."

The dowager continued in the same vein for several more sentences, lauding her hostess's open-mindedness and willingness to forgive, but Verity listened only vaguely, too distracted by the new piece of information to give it her full attention.

Her grace had said *your parents,* employing the plural.

*She knows who my father is.*

Of course she does, Verity thought irritably. The dowager had found her at Fortescue's as an infant. She could have done that only by following a trail that led to the asylum and began in La Raina's bedchamber.

Even so, it was a disconcerting discovery, more so because it indicated that her father was no better than her mother.

Apparently, she came from two despicable people.

Verity could not conceive why it mattered.

She was over thirty and fully grown. Whatever influence they might have exerted over her had long since waned.

And yet!

Distracted by thoughts of her father, she belatedly realized that Hardwicke had no intention of leaving until he had had a private word with her. Although she had no desire to discuss the events of the afternoon, neither her mother's illustrious connections nor Beaufoy's shockingly effective maneuver, she did want to mention her solution to the Typhoeus problem and suggested they have a brief talk in the parlor. He consented as Delphine excused herself to see about something in the kitchen and followed her into the room. Sitting across from him on the settee, Verity contemplated the best way to propose the Twaddle scheme, and, as she raised her eyes to regard him thoughtfully, she was startled to see a look of pronounced sympathy on his face.

Dear lord, he pitied her!

Having heard the details of her miserable childhood at the orphan asylum, Colson Hardwicke perceived her now as a desperate creature in need of his compassion.

A victim!

Humiliated to the core of her being, Verity could not imagine anything worse, not a single, solitary thing, and she felt something inside her break as the desire to run overwhelmed her. Like the small child he pitied, she wanted to race as fast as she could in the opposite direction until she was nothing but a tiny dot on the horizon, and the impulse itself, the fact that she was capable of feeling it, further mortified her.

Verity Lark often felt terror, yes, but never panic.

Fear was acceptable; flight was inconceivable.

But now panic settled on her chest, thrusting against her lungs, thundering in her veins, and she stiffened her back to hold the line in open defiance of every instinct she possessed. She would stay there, fixed to the cushion, while he said his piece, while he mewled sympathetically over the brutality of her youth, while he pressed his lips in woeful despondence for the tragic plight of the unloved child.

And she would remain in place after he finished because it would never do to scurry away the moment he was done. Smoothly, without revealing an iota of discomfort at his maudlin cooing over long-healed wounds, she would explain her idea to make Kingsley the hero of the Typhoeus myth. Her ability to coolly propose the scheme would demonstrate more convincingly than any protest that she did not care about his pity.

If she had any inkling that she was exposing herself to it, she would have asked him to leave the room before the dowager made her mea culpa. But she had been so certain the scene would play the other way, and in allowing him to stay for it, she had thought to expose him to the unvarnished truth of her existence via the ruthless condemnation of the dowager. She could think of no better way to convey the reality of her situation than provide a demonstration of how his own family would respond if he made the shocking decision to court her.

There was no escaping the *ton*'s narrow-minded provincialism—Twaddle relied on its deep-seated intractability—and it was that petty insularity of which she had been happy to make herself a victim.

But only that.

Even with her composure, Hardwicke found something about her to pity and the lines of concern on his face deepened. "You still do not trust me, do you, Verity?" he murmured, his voice soft with both disappointment and wonder. "Even after all this, you cannot bring yourself to trust me. You trust Delphine and Freddie because they endured the brutality of the Wraithe with you, but you cannot bring yourself to allow anyone else into the circle. It is a tight and closed sphere with no spare inch of space."

There was an air of finality about him, and as he rose from the chair, she realized he was leaving. He had reached his limit of ... of ...

In truth, she did not know.

Perhaps it was simply that she refused to follow the rules of the game as prescribed by him.

Having deigned to bestow his romantic attentions on her, the least she could do was display a proper amount of gratitude if not return his regard without quibbling.

He had, she conceded, made a reasonable effort to pierce her shell, and his frustration at what he perceived as his lack of progress struck her as fair. He was too clever to keep pushing on a locked door, and his assessment was accurate: She did not trust him. How could she trust him when she allowed him to see the ugliest part of her and his reply was to walk out?

And, truly, she was relieved to see him go.

He was far too astute for her piece of mind.

And those eyes—that unfathomable shade suspended between blue and green: bluish green, then greenish blue.

They fascinated her.

Everything about him fascinated her.

And that was the problem.

She had never been intrigued by a man, not even slightly, and now she was riveted by a teal-eyed scoundrel who understood as much of the world as she. In every way that mattered, she regarded him as an equal and he saw her as a wounded child.

Truly, she was fortunate he was leaving.

And yet the icy twist of dread in her stomach.

The cold knot of fear in her belly.

It grew, from pea to plum to peach, with every step he took toward the door, and in her head, she heard the words *do not go* reverberate with increasing fury. Like the bell in a high church tower tolling the hour, they clanged with discordant ferocity, and although the sound unsettled her nerves, she could do nothing to stop it.

She could not move.

She could not speak.

Frozen in place, all she could do was watch him walk away, and the regret she felt was mixed with relief because what he said was true: She could not allow him in.

Simply, simply, it was beyond her capability.

The circle was fixed.

If only Hardwicke could hear the ruckus in my head, she thought with bitter amusement. Then he really would have a reason to pity me.

The cold spread to her limbs, causing her whole body to shiver, and she pressed her arms against her sides, unwilling to fold them across her chest because even that small gesture would reveal too much.

She could wait until he was gone.

It would not be long now.

The room was of average size and the doorway was only——

But Hardwicke did not go toward the entrance. He angled to the right, walked over to the sideboard, and picked up a leatherbound book.

A diary.

Verity's diary.

Puzzled, she watched as he opened it, flipped through the pages, and located a date he deemed satisfactory. Grasping the quill that lay on the table, he announced that he was entering an appointment to visit Gunter's with her the next day. "I have written it for three o'clock, but if you would prefer another time, then we will change it. And now I am scheduling a drive in Hyde Park for Thursday at five. Again, the day and date and time are contingent upon your approval."

He spoke affably, unhurriedly, his hand darting across the page as he made another notation. "Everything, Verity, is contingent upon your approval," he said, then asked how she felt about antiquities. "For Friday I have suggested an outing to the British Museum to look at the Elgin Marbles, as Quartermaine in the foreign office suspects trouble in that quarter and I have been asked to investigate Knight's motives for swearing they are Roman copies. Going forward, I will inform you of all assignments as they are presented to me."

The riot in her head quieted as Verity struggled to make sense of what he was saying. She took several steps forward, her arm stretched out as though to snatch the quill from his hand, and then stopped, too curious to intercede.

If Hardwicke, looking up from the diary, noticed her restraint, he gave no indication as he continued with the same cool dispassion. "Knowing your history with Delphine and Freddie is helpful because now I understand why you are so wary of me. Despite the intense connection I feel with you, you do not know me, not in the way I want you to know me, not in the way I *think* I know you. When you refused to help me with Fitch, you said you could not enter into a situation of which you were not cognizant of all the details. I understand that. Information is a balm for me too. That is another thing we have in common. We have so much in common, Verity, sometimes it makes my heart stop."

As if flummoxed himself, Hardwicke shook his head, then he turned the page of the book even though his gaze was focused entirely on her. "If you need details to trust me, then I will give you every detail I have, including how I feel right now, which is hopeful. Thank you for allowing me to remain for your conversation with the dowager. When you are ready, I hope you will discuss it with me. But for now, let us turn to Saturday."

He proposed a visit to the ponds at Hampstead Heath—how did she feel about fishing—and then noted that the undertaking would require Delphine's escort, which was a development he welcomed, as he knew he had some ground to make up there. "The contempt with which she renounced fetching biscuits for me was soul crushing. And that is another important detail about me, Verity. My soul is easily crushed."

Hardwicke continued in this fashion, rattling off nonsense about himself ("It is more that the *frog* attacked *me*") while proposing excursions (hot-air balloon launch on Sunday), and Verity felt an odd sort of lightheadedness as she tried to figure out what his new game was. He had the advantage—a calm mind while hers churned with confusion—and was exploiting it to strengthen his hand.

What did he hope to gain?

That was the question.

It was always the question, and posing it now, Verity felt a weariness overtake her.

Distrusting him was habit.

Looking for the trick was habit.

Ascribing sinister motives to his every action was habit.

Weeks had passed since they had pointed pistols at each other in Mrs. Norton's bedchamber, and yet that remained the singular image she had in her head of Colson Hardwicke: a dark figure with a gun. Despite everything that had happened since then, she still held on to it and marveled at her obstinacy.

Surely, at some point, he had earned a reappraisal.

Well, yes, perhaps so, but how to account for the fizz of awareness she felt in his presence, the draw of attraction for which she had no precedent. Naturally, she had responded to the unfamiliar sensations in the same way she responded to all new things—with her fists raised—and contemplating it now, she realized that if he had fascinated her less, she would have trusted him more.

Spurred by the revelation, she allowed that some small quarter could be given, and although she did not subscribe to the immensity of Hardwicke's project, she found herself trusting this one narrow sliver of the venture.

As he vaulted from his love of beets to his dislike of court jesters, she crossed to the sideboard to inspect the week's proposed activities. She was intrigued by the marbles but doubtful of fishing, for it struck her as horribly inefficient to spend an afternoon by a pond when she could secure mackerel at the shop in a matter of minutes. Additionally, she could not conceive of Delphine consenting to impale an innocent worm on a spiked hook.

Employing a nonchalance that matched his own, she began to explain Delphine's aversion to the slaughter of random creatures who had not attacked her garden, but he chose that precise moment to look up and suddenly she was staring into the gorgeous blue of his eyes, the baffling green of his gaze. Her mind emptied of thought as the breath swooshed from her lungs, and the fizz of awareness—oh, dear, that fizz—coursed through with an intensity that made her knees feel like jelly.

Another new thing.

A host of them, in fact.

But rather than curl her hands into fists, Verity laid them on Hardwicke's shoulders, her head tilting forward as she pressed her lips against his. He started with surprise, a sweet *oh* of exhalation, before he opened his mouth and gently deepened the kiss. Verity's mind clouded with desire as her blood pounded with need, and through the haze of sensation she realized he kept his arms at his side.

He did not want to alarm her.

At any moment she could step away.

The gesture, more than anything, demonstrated how well he understood her, and she tightened her own grip, wrapping her arms around his neck. As she pulled him closer, he purred softly in her ear, and a delightful shiver slithered through her as his lips teased the side of her neck. He murmured another sweet nothing, and she felt intoxicated.

"I believe he is saying: Delphine, biscuits, doorway," an amused voice observed.

Startled, Verity darted her head up, knocking Hardwicke on the chin, and spun around to see Delphine hovering at the entrance with a plate of rolled wafers.

Freddie stood beside her, beaming from ear to ear. "It appears as though you have had an eventful day, Verity. Routing a murderer, meeting the dowager, and settling your differences with Lord Colson. All we need to do now is figure out how to convince half a dozen Bonapartists not to kill Typhoeus."

Verity, who was shocked to discover she did not feel one iota of embarrassment being caught in a compromising position by her dearest friends, told Freddie not to worry himself on that score. "I have come up with a plan that will sort it all out handily," she said with confidence as she strode to the door to relieve Delphine of the plate. Suddenly she was ravenous. Biting into a biscuit, she pulled the bell cord to summon Lucy for a fresh pot of tea. "I would have told you earlier, but Hardwicke distracted me."

Amused, the accused insisted he had done nothing of the sort. Instead, he had been performing yeoman's duty as secretary recording outings for the week. "I am hoping, Miss Drayton, that you can be persuaded to lend your presence to our angling expedition to Hampstead Heath on Saturday."

Delphine scoffed at the absurdity of Verity casting a line. "She would never waste a day fishing for her dinner when she could buy it at the shop. It is not only a better use of her time but also allows her to gather information on the owner, whom she suspects is operating an opium den in the back. He stuffs the poppies into turbots, is it?"

"Sardines," Verity corrected as Lucy appeared at the door to collect the old tray and receive the request for a new one. "They are better containers because of their small size. And, yes, my aversion to the inefficiency of fishing is precisely what I was explaining to Hardwicke when he distracted me."

"Again, I must note that I was merely standing here making entries in a diary," he said, holding up the quill as proof.

"As I said, *distracting* me," Verity replied with pointed emphasis. "He is handsome, isn't he, Delphine?"

Her friend concurred, observing that Lord Colson's eyes were quite appealing.

Freddie, owning himself eager to hear Verity's scheme to save Typhoeus, asked if he also agreed that Hardwicke was attractive, could they then turn their attention to the more important subject?

Hardwicke, however, wanted to discuss the fish seller with the thriving opium trade. "Is it the shop in Maple Lane?"

Verity, settling on the settee as Freddie took the adjacent bergère, regarded him with a gimlet eye and said she was not such a flat as to fall for the blatant ploy. "Everyone knows there is not a fishmonger on Maple Lane. It is home to a bookshop, a tavern, and a locksmith. If you hope to get the story before Robert, you will have to do much better than that."

Despite his call to focus on the Typhoeus problem, Freddie found himself intrigued by the prospect of Lord Colson submitting reports to the *Gazette* and asked him if it was something he would ever consider.

Delphine rolled her eyes and said, "Who is wasting time on trifles now?"

But the advantages of having a resourceful former spy and dissolute lord writing for his newspaper had begun to occur to Freddie and he reminded him that he could adopt a pseudonym to protect his identity. "Not Typhoeus, of course, as that name is taken, but perhaps something from Norse mythology."

Verity, who considered selecting noms de guerre among her particular talents, suggested Jormungand. "He is a serpent so massive he encircled the world."

"Tempting but no," Hardwicke said mildly, joining her on the settee.

Undaunted, she nodded, pressed her lips together thoughtfully, and tried again. "What about Fenrir, the mighty wolf who slays Odin? There could be some nice symbolism in that choice if your work focuses on toppling giants."

"Or the Kraken," Delphine said, taking a seat.

Pensively, Freddie wondered if a gigantic squid so large it could drag down entire ships with its tentacles set the right tone for a newspaper. "Perhaps it is just a little too grim?

Ratatoskr, who carried messages from the eagles at the top of the world tree to the serpent at the bottom, is more in line with the *Gazette*'s mission."

Horrified, Delphine said absolutely not. "Squirrels are our mortal enemy."

Hardwicke, expressing amazement at their breadth of knowledge, asked how they were all so conversant with Norse mythology.

Delphine explained that there was a book of Norse myths in the library at Fortescue's. "And by 'library' I mean one sad, dusty shelf in the drawing room. It was the only book that was not the Bible."

"And the Bibles were in French, all six of them," Freddie added wryly.

"That is how Verity taught herself French, reading those Bibles," Delphine said.

Verity nodded. "I fashioned a workbook out of scraps from old cookery books in the kitchens to record vocabulary terms. I kept a running list of insults on the last page."

"Yes, and then you called the Wraithe *un tas de fumier fumant* and she took away the Bibles," Freddie replied with a smile.

Delphine laughed and marveled at how much the malignant headmistress despised being insulted in a foreign language. "She did not even know Verity had called her a steaming pile of manure.

"What she despised were displays of knowledge," Freddie corrected. "Any show of erudition infuriated her. Verity could have complimented her new bonnet in French and the Wraithe still would have banished her to the dunce cabinet and removed the Bibles."

Abruptly, Delphine stopped laughing, and her expression turned stormy. "That horrible wardrobe with the leak and the rats. Verity spent so many hours standing there we started calling it *la garde-robe des cancres*. But then Verity got smart."

Verity, selecting another rolled wafer, insisted she had always been smart.

"Wily, then," her friend conceded. "She realized she was doing herself no favors by constantly drawing the Wraithe's attention. She could get away with more mischief if she passed unnoticed."

"That is when she became docile Verity," Freddie said. "Docile Verity said, 'As you wish, ma'am,' to every word out of the Wraithe's mouth. Docile Verity ate all her gruel. Docile Verity offered to clean the privies."

Slouching on the sofa, her head resting against its back, Verity turned slightly to the left to look at Hardwicke out of the corner of her eye and explained that Docile Verity was not particularly subtle. "The privies, for example, were a bit much, and if the Wraithe had been just a little keener, she would have realized something nefarious was afoot."

A wide grin spread across Hardwicke's face as he slid his hand along the cushion and pressed his pinkie against hers, a small gesture, hesitant and sweet. "Your first disguise."

Verity felt a tingle slither up her arm at the contact, and it, too, was hesitant and sweet. Swiveling her head so she could see him better, she said, "Obviously, the ruse needed to be set up in a logical and plausible way. I could not simply become Docile Verity overnight. Even the Wraithe would suspect that."

Relishing the prospect of a tale, the blue in his teal eyes glittering, he shifted his position so that he was facing her fully. "You had to let her catch you doing something truly awful, didn't you, in order to then be thoroughly cowed by her threats? She had to believe she had broken your spirit like a horse."

He knew her, Verity thought. Barely at all and yet already so well.

It was true, what he had said: They had so much in common, sometimes it made your heart stop.

"Let me guess," he pleaded before she had even issued a confirmation. "It had to be something more outlandish than the traditional torments. Not a frog in her boot or cockroaches in her bed. A persistent annoyance? A low but constant knocking sound while she was trying to fall asleep? Or did things suddenly break? Every chair she sat on for two days inexplicably collapsed under her weight?"

Verity giggled.

*Verity,* not Miss Gorman or Mrs. Delacour or the Turnip or one of her dozen other characters who frequently succumbed to lighthearted mirth.

"I stole strawberries from the kitchens and crushed them into her dress," she said.

"Ah, thievery *and* the destruction of property," he replied with an admiring dip of his head. "A heady combination. I trust you were caught red-handed?"

An inane sally, to be sure, and yet it somehow unleashed a bubble of giddiness in Verity, who looped her fingers through his.

Just loosely.

She did not suddenly grasp his hand.

But it was something new, wholly unprecedented, and as she launched into an explanation of how she had contrived to be caught with an incriminating splash of strawberry juice across her nose, she realized that despite all their dire predictions the circle had already expanded.

*From the* London Daily Gazette

*Wednesday, June 17*

## Twaddle Tales
## by Mr. Twaddle-Thum

You poor darlings! You have given your trust to an inveterate gossip who made one pledge to you at the beginning of this great enterprise—to never knowingly repeat a falsehood—and now I come to you with the express purpose of sharing a wildly inaccurate rumor.

Is it unnerving?

Are you troubled?

Do not fret.

I shall wait for you to compose yourself.

Better now?

Very good, then let us proceed.

Among a particular sect of society there is an alarming project afoot to rehabilitate the reputation of a certain gentleman of disquieting moral turpitude. I know you know to whom I refer because you have been reading these on-dits for years, and the reports of his depravity have the ring—ahem!—of truth. Not content with slipping precious family heirlooms into his pockets to settle gambling debts, the Coal Son further mortified his sire with drunken displays and public brawls.

You must not ask me to recount his furious confrontation with the melancholy man in Holland Park, for describing how a grown man could come to fisticuffs with limestone statuary is beyond even my considerable talents.

Suffice to say, the immovable object won.

Despite these mortifying exhibitions, whispers of an alternate history have begun to wend their way out of the dark alleyways of Petty France, and they murmur of valor and glory and brave acts of derring-do, insinuating that the lowest among us has performed the highest service.

They would place a medal of honor upon the ne'er-do-well's chest.

It is an appealing story.

Of course it is.

We all hope for the prodigal son's return.

I do as well.

But having pledged only honesty in these pages, I cannot allow a grave injustice to stand.

Courageous deeds *have* been performed but by a man of such humility and grace my quill has ne'er mentioned his name. He is Mark Kingsley, lately of the Home Office and Lord Sidmouth's second in command, and his modesty is so great he sought to elude your praise by placing his achievements on the shoulders of a lesser man—an act of redemption *and* an attempt at evasion. Caring nothing for the danger to himself, Mr. Kingsley, known to his enemies as Typhoeus, deftly manipulated Napoleon and his generals by providing false information about the state of the British Army's readiness during the height of the war. In this endeavor, the Coal Son proved useful, but as an oblivious fool deployed by Mr. Kingsley, not a wily spy.

If Mr. Kingsley had been a little less noble in his renunciation, I would have turned a blind eye to his deception. If he had extended the credit to one of our downtrodden friends, such as poor Mr. Fawcett, whose wrongful imprisonment in Newgate lasted almost a fortnight, I might never have composed these paragraphs.

But to make a hero of the Coal Son—no, I cannot stay silent!

And yet you must, my darlings.

Mr. Kingsley has made his desire for obscurity known, and it is incumbent upon us to honor it. So if you see him sipping claret at White's or dancing the quadrille at Almack's or perusing the windows in Bond Street, pass him silently and permit him this small dignity.

The least a grateful nation can do is not offer its thanks.

**VERITY LARK RETURNS WITH ANOTHER ADVENTURE SOON!**
In the meantime, look for the
Duchess of Kesgrave's latest investigation:
*A Vicious Machination.*
Available for preorder now.

# About the Author

Mistress Lynn Messina is the author of 14 novels of questionable morality, including the *Beatrice Hyde-Clare Mysteries* series and the *Love Takes Root* series of lurid romances.

Aside from writing scandalous fiction to corrupt well-behaved young ladies, Mistress Messina hosts a Socials page where a certain dubious gentleman by the name of Mr. Twaddle-Thum regularly shares scurrilous and certainly false gossip.

Mr. Twaddle-Thum is likewise the author of a worthless little news sheet known as *The Beakeeper.* It prides itself on being filled with nothing but utter tripe and nonsense. It can, however, serve as a remedy for a spot of Sunday afternoon ennui.

Mistress Messina resides in the uppity colonial city of New York with her sons.

# Also by Lynn Messina

The Bolingbroke Chit

The Impertinent Miss Templeton

## Stand Alones

Prejudice and Pride

The Girls' Guide to Dating Zombies

Savvy Girl

Winner Takes All

Little Vampire Women

Never on a Sundae

Troublemaker

Fashionista (Spanish Edition)

Violet Venom's Rules for Life

Henry and the Incredibly Incorrigible, Inconveniently Smart Human

# Welcome to the Bea Hive

## FUN STUFF FOR BEATRICE HYDE-CLARE FANS

## The Bea Tee

Beatrice's favorite three warships not only in the wrong order but also from the wrong time period. (Take that, maritime tradition *and* historical accuracy!)

## The Kesgrave Shirt

A tee bearing the Duke of Kesgrave's favorite warships in the order in which they appeared in the Battle of the Nile

**Available in mugs too!**

*See all the options in Lynn's Store.*

Made in the USA
Las Vegas, NV
15 April 2024

88723308R00198